# HARD-WIRED

# HARD-WIRED

## a novel by
## Joseph Dobrian

REX IMPERATOR, New York, N.Y.

BOOKS BY JOSEPH DOBRIAN

FICTION

Willie Wilden (2011)
Ambitions (2014)
Hard-Wired (2016)

NON-FICTION

Seldom Right But Never In Doubt (2012)

TRANSLATION

The Butcher Of Paris, by Jean-François Dominique (2015)

A story always involves, in a dramatic way, the mystery of personality. I lent some stories to a country lady who lives down the road from me, and when she returned them, she said, "Well, them stories done gone and shown you how some folks *would* do."

—Flannery O'Connor

To Grace.

# HARD-WIRED
## by Joseph Dobrian

### BOOK I

### BOOK II

### BOOK III

## BOOK IV

## L'ENVOI

# HARD-WIRED

## BOOK I

## 1 MY WIRING

This is a story about my dick and balls. I could say that this is my memoir about *getting through*. But maybe it's also about *getting to*. "A quest," I say, self-importantly, "for personal redemption." Imagine a self-satisfied chin-lift there. But in the final analysis, this is a story about my dick and balls.

Let's begin with a nightmare I had, many years before I wrote all of this down.

My family was still living in Waukoshowoc, Wisconsin. This would have been 1959, three years before we moved to Iowa. I was eleven years old, in the sixth grade. Old enough that the boys and the girls no longer took phys. ed. together, but not old enough that we had to change into gym clothes. The girls were over at the other end of the school gym, doing whatever their instructor had them doing. We boys were sitting cross-legged on the floor of our side of the gym, with our instructor, Mr. Marzetti, facing us. He was big, slightly flabby, with a dark complexion, a black crew cut, and a heavy five o'clock shadow even though it was morning. Someone had brought a big wooden block, maybe thirty inches high, into the gym. Mr. Marzetti was standing next to it. He addressed us.

His words were indistinct. I couldn't hear all of it, because it was a dream, but the sense of it was clear. Because of a new school rule, each of us boys was to have his dick and balls cut off. Mr. Marzetti instructed us to line up next to the wooden block, and be prepared to drop our pants when our turn came. We saw now that he had a meat axe in his hand.

The boys, incredibly, fell into line. Nobody protested. Nobody even hesitated to comply. I can't remember who was first, but it was a classmate of mine in real life, a kid I knew. He stepped up to the block and laid his dick and balls on the surface. Mr. Marzetti took one sharp downward swing with the meat ax, severed them, then swept them onto the floor with the edge of the blade. The boy staggered away, clutching at his crotch, and the next boy stood up to the block and placed his junk there, with the same result.

I was lagging behind, not quite getting into line. I think nobody noticed me. People generally didn't notice me much in gym class because they all knew I was the fat, slow kid who cried and couldn't do even the easiest stuff. It was the third kid's turn when I decided I had better get out of there. A door, over on the girls' side of the gym, led outside to the school playground.

Out of the corner of my eye, as I started to dash for the door (or rather, as I waddled to the door at the best speed I could manage, which wasn't much), I saw the fourth boy, a kid I had always been pretty friendly with, stepping up to the block. He was the shortest boy in the class, so he had to stand up on his tiptoes to get his junk up onto the block—but he was doing his best to comply, and down came the meat axe again.

Mr. Marzetti was focused on his task and didn't notice me leaving. None of the girls (who seemed oblivious to what was happening to the boys) tried to stop me. None of the boys called attention to my departure. I glanced back for an instant as I went through the door. Four of the boys, now, were lying on the floor, moaning and clutching at themselves. I could see the back of boy five as he stood up to the block and Mr. Marzetti swung the cleaver down. The rest waited their turn. The floor around the chopping block was slick with blood and scraps.

I was outside. The playground was deserted. I ran, inasmuch as a fat little boy with deformed feet could run. Through the playground, to the street, running: I wasn't sure where to.

The next thing I recall, I had gone several miles, running all the way—an incredible accomplishment considering my age and condition. I was utterly winded, utterly exhausted, but I had to keep running.

I was in a neighborhood of Waukoshowoc that consisted mostly of older, bigger, fancier homes. Somehow, I knew that I was near a house where a lawyer lived, and I knew that the lawyer would be at home. I staggered up the front walk, and up the front steps, of a big white Colonial house. I pounded on the front door—then I let myself in.

The lawyer was a white-haired man in his sixties. I didn't know him. I had never seen him before. I just knew that he would be in that house and that he was a lawyer. He was fairly tall and heavy; he had thick hair and a big white moustache, and a red face. He wore a dark three-piece suit with a watch-chain across his waistcoat.

Again, I don't usually remember dialogue in dreams, or if I do it's only a little of it, but I remember telling the lawyer why I was there, what was happening at my school, and how I had managed to escape and had run all the way to his house.

The lawyer listened to me, sitting stock-still in a big over-stuffed swivel chair at his desk—this was his home office we were in, and I don't recall how I got into that room once I had barged into his house—and he was nodding, looking thoughtful, not saying anything while I babbled out my account.

Then, finally, when I ran down, he said something; I didn't catch it all, but I heard the word "injunction." It's surprising that I knew what an injunction was, at that age, but I did. He said "injunction." He picked up the phone on his desk and dialed a number and said something—by this time I was half-sitting, half-lying on the floor of his office; it had a thick, soft, olive-green carpeting—and when he hung up the phone he turned to me, looking kindly at me. He said, "It'll be okay. We'll get an injunction. You won't have to have it done to you." I remember hearing that, clearly.

I felt such relief, and such gratitude to that old man, and—God forgive me—such glee that I was going to be the only boy in the school who had gotten to keep his junk. Then I woke up. Gasping, terrified. I lay there in my bed, only slowly realizing that it had been a dream. Even after I had convinced myself of that, it was a while before I could fall back to sleep.

§

Here I am in my old age, or getting near to it anyway—I turned sixty-nine in this spring of 2017—and I still torture myself with memories of what a rotten child I was. I even remember—and condemn myself for—evil thoughts that I never voiced, never acted upon.

A person sometimes has the urge to do something truly horrid. Probably most of us have private thoughts that the Devil and all his imps would be ashamed of. But if you have those thoughts, those evil impulses, you usually fight back the urge to act on them. You don't do whatever you were thinking about doing, because you're not crazy enough or wicked enough to do it, right? Most people have those moments, I suppose. But I have had an awful lot of them. I can still remember times when I was a little boy, when I only *thought* to do something unkind, or downright horrible, and I didn't do it, but I'll still recollect even those impulses that I never acted upon, brood about them, and remind myself that they are proof of what a bad person I am.

It's a pathological thing, I guess: my obsessing about what a louse I have been, all my life. I'm no expert in human psychology, so I can't know this for sure, but I can't imagine that normal people constantly remind themselves of all the bad things they have ever done—all of their words or deeds that were mean, or inconsiderate, or tactless, or just plain crazy. Sure, I'm willing to believe that we all sometimes look back and think something like, "I was a bit of a bully as a kid," or "I wish I had been more considerate of my family," or "I wish I had worked harder." I'm sure nobody has gone through life without regrets. But maybe I take it to an extreme.

Almost invariably, almost every day of my life, my first thought on awakening—I mean literally my first thought, when I open my eyes and roll over in bed—is a memory of one shameful thing or another that I did way long ago, usually in my childhood. I'm not kidding, not exaggerating. I'll remember a time when I accidentally insulted someone, or was intentionally cruel, or petty, or vindictive. Or I might merely remember a petty or vindictive *thought*, that I had never acted upon. That will be my wake-up message to myself. And almost every morning, as I sit up in bed, I'll say out loud, "I hate you."

I have a daily ritual that I can't force myself to not go through. I'll look myself in the eye, in the mirror as I shave (I shave my whole head, every day, because I'm bald now except at the fringes), and I'll say, "You suck, Andrew Palinkas. You *suck*. God, you... you make me *ill*, you worthless piece of garbage."

Or words to that effect.

Whatever I am now, whatever I have made of myself, whatever place I have put myself in—whether it's good or bad, whether it's enviable or not—I put myself there. It might be easier if I could blame my disappointments or regrets on other people. Like my parents, or my teachers, or the kids I had to deal with when I was growing up, or society in general. The conventional wisdom is that your parents screw you up as they bring you up. Whatever neuroses you have, were instilled in you by your parents. But I believe that that is only partly true.

You're not a blank slate at birth. Other people do to you whatever they do to you, and in some cases, I suppose, if a person ends up unhappy, it might not be his fault. I'm sure there are innocent victims, people who got totally messed up by other people, or by circumstances beyond their control.

I'm not one of those. That's all I'm saying.

If I had to point to the one time in my life when I felt best about myself—that is, proud of having done something right for a change—I would have to point to a sequence of events that took place in my last year of high school, 1965-66, when I was seventeen to eighteen. But one thing I did, during that time, was something that my parents—my mother anyway—might say was the *worst* offense I ever committed.

If my life has had a crowning achievement, that might have been it. When I was a teenager, I used to roll my eyes when an older person would tell me, "These are the best years of your life!" But as it turned out, in some ways, they were. Not in the sense that they were the happiest years of my life (they certainly weren't) but they were perhaps the years in which my career as a bad person reached its zenith.

I'll tell you, later on, all about that one awful, awful thing that I did back then—after I've told you about all the other awful, awful things I did prior to that.

Oh, I'm kidding. In a sense. Ever since high school, I've only been moderately awful. No criminal record. I've had a career; I have no debts; I have a nice house and a nice car; I'm a Rotarian; I'm getting ready to retire, and pretty well off at that. You could say I'm living the dream. Even if it's a solitary dream. I never got married, never started a family. That, too, has been my choice, no matter how hard I might try to pretend otherwise.

My parents died, both of them, in 2005, within a few months of each other. They were both in their eighties, still living in that same house in State City, Iowa, that we had moved into when I was fourteen, in 1962. Mom contracted a form of Alzheimer's that progressed quickly, and killed her in about two years. Shortly after she died, Dad basically stopped trying to live. He hardly ate, hardly left that house, and he caught a case of bronchial pneumonia at the start of one of those brutal Iowa winters, at the end of that year, which took him off.

Some weeks after Dad died, as I was going through the boxes and boxes of papers and pictures in my parents' basement, I found an evaluation that Mom and Dad had kept: of me, when I was four years old, written by Winifred Winkie, the supervisor of Waukoshowoc Montessori Preschool.

I have a phenomenal memory. My brother, Mark, who is certainly brighter and more successful than I am, will sometimes call or email me to see if I remember the details of some bit of family history that he has forgotten. I bet I can recall the substance, if not every single word, of every conversation I have ever had with anyone. Sure, you might say that's impossible. Maybe it is. Maybe I'm exaggerating. But if I am, it's not by much. If I want to recall it to mind, I can. Any conversation, any interaction.

I have too good of a memory. My life might have been so much more pleasant, if I had been able to forget more of it.

I have to admit, I had put out of my mind most of the behavior and the incidents to which Mrs. Winkie referred in this evaluation—but as I read it, it all came back to me, and way too clearly, at that. Which made me wonder: I say that I remember everything, but how much might I have forgotten?

Could there be more? Could there be some unbelievably, unspeakably horrible stuff that I did, long ago, that I have somehow managed to forget?

Anyway, here is what Mrs. Winkie wrote about me, almost sixty-five years ago:

> Andy had a stiff tense manner when he first came to school. He talked, with adult mannerisms, to teachers or visiting parents rather than to any of the children, usually beginning, "I am the foreman of this ranch," or "I am a fireman," or whatever part he happened to be playing that day. He refused to be called Andy or Andrew Palinkas (bursting into a sort of tantrum of protest if anyone called him by his name) but insisted on being called "Mr. Nobody."
>
> He spent much time walking about soliloquizing about the part he was playing, occasionally volunteering information like, "I swim with my head out of the water so I can keep my hat on." He nearly always wore a hat; sometimes one from home, sometimes one he borrowed from another child at school. His parts in the fall were nearly always cowboy parts, and he often rode one of the wooden horses while Bill C., who liked cowboy play, rode the other.

Beyond this rather accidental relationship with Bill, his relationships with
the children were mostly advances towards girls smaller than himself--El-
sie, Mary, or Debby--and at first he
would be friendly, following her
around, but then he would strike out.
When a teacher interfered, he would be
coldly angry and threatening. He would
sometimes start hitting at one of the
girls, saying as he hit, "I know how it
feels." He did not hit hard enough to
hurt much, but at first he made many
children afraid.

He did not want to fit into his group's
routine, especially at first, but went
in and out mostly as it suited his imaginary world. He usually listened to
stories, and nearly always liked music,
taking eager part in rhythm. In playing
Little Sally Waters we had to take special care to call him "Big," not "Little," but he would sometimes tolerate
being called Andy, by November. If one
of the children said, "You're not a
real cowboy," or some such thing, he
went into a frantic fury. Much teacher
attention went into protecting him from
these verbal expressions that seemed to
him real attacks on his personal security. All sorts of frustrations made
him cry.

(Nov. 22, during music) Andy had been
going around with his hands joined in
front of him, as in playing elephant.
When the group wanted to join hands and
play Monkey in the Chair, he refused to
unclasp his hands and so could not join
hands in the circle; but he wanted to
be in the circle and be chosen. Unable
to resolve the dilemma, or let anyone

help him, he simply cried and jumped up and down.

In the first months of school, he not only protested, "I'm not Andy" but also, "I don't have a mother. I'm a young cowboy who doesn't need anyone." He also worked things over, talking to himself at rest, as "Yah, yah, yah, Andy can't catch me." Mrs. Boye asked "Why not?" and Andy replied, "Andy's little and bad. He tries to catch me to kill me."

At the same time, busy as he was playing his various roles, he was keen and alert about the grown-up world. He always went to talk to new adults (who were always much impressed with him, and so often asked him his name--but got no response, or else the answer, "I'm Mr. Nobody").

The first time Mrs. Lyons came to sing French songs, she first explained in English what the song was going to be about. Before she had said a word of French, Andy came up to her saying firmly, "Are you an American? You don't sound like one."

(Note taken Feb. 14) Andy walks round and round with a valentine he had made earlier, in his hand, saying, "I have a valentine" at intervals. He adds, "I want 'Palinkas' written on this valentine!" This was the first time I heard him ask specifically for his own name, though by February he had become willing to let himself be called Andy or Andrew Palinkas in the usual course of daily business.

This note also gives a good example of
how much more he was able to take part
in the other children's play, and how
much more he had begun to be accepted
instead of being avoided. Ricky N. had
brought just three valentines to school
that day: one for his teacher, one for
his best friend, and one for Andy
Palinkas.

(Note March 30) Mrs. E came to help at
school, and Andy ran up to tell her
about his costume. After he and she had
talked a little while, she said,
"What's your name?" and he answered
firmly without hesitation, "My name is
Andy."

About the "adult mannerisms," first. It's true. All my life, I have
had a stick up my butt, you might say. All through my childhood
and adolescence, adults would comment on how grown-up I
acted for my age. I had a much bigger vocabulary than most kids,
and maybe I was a little more perceptive than the average, so I
could talk about most subjects on a higher level than I might
have been expected to. If I did act older than my age, the reason
is clear to me: It's because all I ever wanted to be, was grown-up.

I hated being a kid. I hated every second of it.

All I ever wanted out of childhood, was out of childhood.

A lot of people will wax sentimental about their childhood,
and talk about how wonderful it would be to stay a child forever.
A whole industry evolved around that play by J.M. Barrie about
a little boy who wouldn't grow up. So when some people talk
about how wonderful childhood was, I have to believe that it
was—for them. Not for me.

Even today, in my late sixties, I sometimes notice myself tingling at the idea that I'm an adult. It's fun to be an adult! Not fun
all the time, but there's more fun to being an adult than to being

a kid. You can eat pizza whenever you want, or ice cream, or cheeseburgers, for three meals a day if you feel like it. You can stay up as late as you want. You can watch anything on TV that you want to watch. You don't have to make your bed. You can get drunk if you want to.

On the other hand, consider the various indignities of childhood. The everyday humiliations. The feeling of personal powerlessness. Never being taken seriously in your opinions. Never having much privacy. Having to ask permission to do most things—unless you *have* to do them because you're told to. Is it any wonder that I took such strong exception to being called "little"? The only mystery to me was why no other kid had a problem with it!

That might have been why I always insisted on wearing a hat. Nowadays, I have to wear a hat—to keep from getting sunburn on my bald head in summer, and to keep warm in winter—but as a child, I wore a hat because adults wore hats. At least, they did, back when I was a kid. Having a hat on my head made me feel more like one of them. Did you know, by the way, that if you're ever taken prisoner in a combat situation, you should keep your hat on—or if you don't have a hat, you should improvise one out of a rag or a dirty shirt? Prisoners with hats are less likely to be abused by their captors, because a hat is a symbol of power and authority. It's funny how I sensed that, even at the age of three or four.

"I don't have a mother; I don't need anyone." Well, that was what I hoped and prayed for! That was my fantasy, because the reality—my dependence on adults—was offensive to me. Offensive and oppressive.

As for disliking my own name: Palinkas sounded funny. Sounded goofy. More like a sound effect than a name. Like piss hitting the toilet. Besides, it sounded foreign. It's remarkable that at age four I knew what a sound effect was, and that I knew the concept of "sounding foreign."

I didn't object to my surname, though, nearly as much as I hated my given name. Andy was a little boy's name, as I perceived it, and I hated being a little boy. The full name, Andrew, I didn't mind so much—except for the fact that the name identified *me*. It identified the person I was trying to get away from. The person I was trying not to be. The person I was trying to pretend I wasn't.

Andy, you'll recall, was little and bad and trying to kill me.

The "me" he was trying to kill was whatever pleasant fantasy I may have been engaging in at the moment. I don't mean to say that there was an alter ego named Andy who was trying to get me to stop the fantasies or the role-playing or whatever you want to call it. No, what was killing me was the knowledge that I was, after all, just *Andy*—a stinky four-year-old who was little and bad. That was the Andy who was getting in the way of my fantasy of being a cowboy, a soldier, a fireman, an *adult*.

"Me" was what I wanted to be. "Andy" was the horrible reality of what I was: little and bad.

That's why I would go into a frenzy if someone suggested that I wasn't really whatever I was claiming to be. Because to deny the reality of my fantasy was to remind me that it *was* a fantasy—and that the reality was that I was little and bad.

Mrs. Winkie remarked that I acted as though these suggestions constituted a threat to my personal security. Yes! That's exactly it!

The girls? I wanted to show affection. Even at that age, I was susceptible to pretty girls. The only way I knew how to express my attraction was to walk up to them, talk to them, touch them, follow them around—and demand that they pay attention to me. I resented it when they rebuffed me. I took it as a rejection of me as a human being, rather than discomfort with my behavior. It made me furious.

Of course I frightened the girls. I understood, at the time, that I frightened them. I hated it. That was the last thing I wanted to do. But at the same time, I recall, I felt a perverse satisfaction—knowing that if the girls didn't like me, at least they were afraid of me.

I wasn't angry at the girls, though. Maybe it looked that way, but it seems to me that if I had actually been angry at *them*, I would have hit them harder, tried to do some damage. I'm not so sure that I was angry at myself, either, for a situation that I didn't believe I could help. Angry at my creator, maybe, whoever that was? At the forces of nature? At Fate?

The best explanation I can come up with is that I was angry at whichever agencies had acted, or conspired, to make me so unappealing. Lord knows I didn't blame the girls. I knew how disgusting I was.

The crying. That was my standard reaction to practically anything I didn't like. I would cry in reaction to actual threats on my personal security, but also in reaction to frustration, to any feeling of injustice or disappointment. I was disappointed easily, and felt injustice keenly.

Once—this must have been a year later, when I was in kindergarten—a bunch of kids got to picking on another kid, not me, on the school playground. Nothing violent. We were playing a game—tag or something. Everett—I can't forget his name—wanted to play, and some of the other kids didn't want to include him. He was this fat, dumpy kid, seldom very clean, never in nice clothes. The other kids were shouting unkind words at him, chasing him away from them, making him run and cry.

I was there, and I started to participate. Not because I had anything at all against this kid—I actually kind of liked him—but

**14**

because everyone else was doing it and this was my opportunity to be one of them.

Moreover, I had never before been on that end of such a transaction. I was curious to see what it would be like. I'll admit it: For a moment, it felt good. That sense of belonging. That sense of being one of the gang. The realization that at least for that moment, I wasn't the lowest kid in the pecking order.

For a second, it felt good. Maybe for two seconds. Then I caught the look in Everett's eyes: the fear, the perplexity. The amazement at this sudden, capricious, unreasoned cruelty. This utterly unjustified cruelty.

I can't forget that look. More than sixty years later, I still can't think of the look on Everett's face without feeling physically sick—and wishing that I could go back in time, to comfort and befriend him.

That's another thing I hate myself for. I didn't have the courage to tell those other kids to ease up. Probably I couldn't have made it stick—or could I have? Might it have been as simple as planting myself in front of Everett and saying, "Okay, enough!"? Too late to know, now. But at least I resolved never again to join in that kind of behavior. I'm racking my brain, as I write this, to be certain that I can't think of another instance in which I partook of group bullying. I find it hard to believe that I never did it again, but I'm pretty sure it's true that that was the first and last time.

Up to age six, children can be cruel, but they're usually not vicious enough to take advantage of one kid and make him a perennial scapegoat. By age seven or so, they are. When you were a kid, did you notice how, usually starting in the second grade, one kid will become the butt of the whole class? And it's usually mostly his fault. It's not necessarily his fault that he's unattractive, or fat, or has poor eyesight, or whatever, but you need to know this; you need to believe and understand this:

That kid is never blameless.

There's always a reason why the butt of the class (usually a boy, but not always) gets picked on, and it's always something he could work on, at least, if not eliminate. He might have a disagreeable personality. He might have an uncontrollable temper. He might have poor personal hygiene. He might be weak and ineffectual to the point where the other kids just plain lose patience with him. Whatever the reason, if he's the picked-on kid, it's going to be his fault to some extent. That's a fact we have to face, if we're going to consider the matter rationally. It's maybe not his fault that he has some defect or other that makes him a target. But it *is* his fault if it's something he could at least try to change, and he doesn't. It *is* his fault if he can't or won't come up with an effective way to resist or cope with other kids' behavior toward him.

Almost every child, at that age, gets picked on a little by other children. It's part of growing up. Most kids learn how to handle it. But the kids I grew up with learned quickly enough that if I got picked on, I would cry. This was partly because I feared I might be in physical danger, but mostly I cried at the *injustice* of it: being attacked by kids whom (so far as I could reason) I had never offended. By crying, I gave them more reason to pick on me. Making me cry was, apparently, fun. Thus, my chief memory of second through sixth grades is of walking to or from school, four times a day, with a squad of other children walking backwards in front of me: chanting, pointing, laughing.

You know what I think is the reason why I couldn't rid myself of that habit of crying? Because it was my coping mechanism. Cry, and get an adult to intervene. Cry, and maybe people would try to appease me. Cry, and use the tears to isolate myself from the rest of the group. This is all hypothesis.

My habit of crying at the least provocation persisted, and it made my life Hell. It was something I told myself I couldn't control, although there must have been a way I could have done it. Any time I felt insulted or slighted, or felt that I was being treated unfairly, my eyes would smart and the tears would come, however I tried to stop them. I knew it was unmanly. I knew that if I wanted to consider myself a grown-up, I would have to stop with the crying, somehow. But it wasn't till adolescence that I was able to get the tears under some control.

Oh, gosh. I remember once, it must have been 1967, when I would have been about nineteen, I got into a discussion with a woman about Jayne Mansfield, of all people. It was right after Jayne had been killed in that car wreck. I was at a Fourth of July garden party at my employer's house, where I fell into conversation with a woman who was a few years older than I was, maybe twenty-five, and we got onto the subject of Jayne Mansfield. I recall saying it was sad, and squalid, the way she had died. This woman replied something to the effect of, "That bimbo got what she deserved." Our disagreement became a little heated, till she ended the discussion by saying, "Maybe when you're a little older you'll feel differently." That did it. That disrespect—on the score of my alleged immaturity—was enough to get the machinery going. Although I held my eyes wide open, dilating my eyelids wider and wider and wider to keep the tears from coming, come they would. I had to physically get away from that woman, get out of her sight, as fast as I could, to avoid letting her see that she'd been correct about my immaturity!

Okay, I was lachrymose. That wasn't all that was wrong with me. I have always been a little heavy. Not grossly fat, but always slightly to moderately chubby. In my teen years, I wasn't all that fat, because I had gotten my height, and I have done my best to stay in not-too-bad shape now that I'm old, but as a pre-adolescent kid, I was fat. There's no getting around it. A fat kid is candy to other kids.

For another thing, I had (and have) defective feet that made it impossible for me to run fast or jump high. I was born with severely flat feet, and with ankle joints so loose that my feet actually flop around at the ends of my legs—there's no tension in my ankles at all—so that I have never been able to run with any speed. If I had to run to save my life, I would be out of luck. I can't do more than waddle—which as you might imagine made me a bit of a liability on the baseball field or the basketball court. To this day, simply walking is a conscious process for me. That is, I appear to walk normally, but because of my condition, I have to think to do it. I have to pay attention, as I place one foot in front of the other, or I'll kick myself. That's why, as an adult, I often wear cowboy boots instead of shoes, even when I'm dressed for business. The high shaft of the boot acts as an exoskeleton, a brace, that keeps my foot on the straight and narrow.

(I wasn't allowed cowboy boots as a kid. I had to wear those clunky orthopedic shoes that didn't help my condition in the least, and made me look like an old woman.)

As for jumping, forget about it. I couldn't get myself more than a few inches off the ground. I was such a hopeless athlete that when the neighborhood kids chose up sides for a game, I wasn't merely picked last. No, it was worse than that. It was, "If we have to take Palinkas, you have to give us..."

Finally, I was a coward. Even when I was playing with other kids without being picked on and made to cry, I would invariably hang back when they engaged in any activity that looked at all dangerous. Which made me even less a part of the gang than I already was.

About the time when it was coming clear to me that I was weak, cowardly, and a crybaby, it came equally clear that my mother didn't like me. Maybe she did like me, when I was very little, but after a few years, I had made myself so disagreeable that I don't blame her if she didn't.

As Mrs. Winkie suggested, in that evaluation she wrote, I did like to put myself forward (as long as I wasn't placing myself in any physical danger): to make people notice me, to show off. That probably embarrassed Mom. Maybe that's what she meant when she told me I was selfish. That was the most awful word that Mom could think of to call anyone—selfish—and I got a lot of "selfish" when I was growing up.

I wasn't selfish in the sense of "greedy." But I certainly was always at the front of my own mind, so maybe I was selfish in that way. What I wanted, in putting myself forward, was the respect and deference I believe that I would have gotten if I had been grown up. I resented the whole idea that I was a child. You could say that the story of my childhood was my long succession of efforts, and failures, to deny my childhood, and be an adult.

# 2 MY FAMILY

It surprised me when Dad—a few days after Mom died and just a few months before he followed her—told me that I would be the executor of his will. I had expected him to appoint Mark. Traditionally, it's the eldest son's duty to execute his deceased father's will, but I figured that in our case, an exception would probably be made. Mark is two years younger than I am, and he's well known internationally as a physicist. I'm pretty sure that if Dad had died first, Mom would have made Mark her executor.

My dad, Steve Palinkas—Istvan was his baptismal name, but he was always Steve—grew up in Pittsburgh in the 1920s and

30s. It must have been a hard scrabble for him, but he was a bright and popular kid—the way he told it to me—and he did whatever work he could find, when he wasn't in school. He was a go-getter, although not excessive about it. He was President of his senior class in high school. He told me once, "I was never a big student government type. I just got elected because I was well liked. If I say so myself."

That must have been true, because if Dad was anything, he was likable. When I was in high school, he was in charge of the Farmers Midwest Mutual office in State City. When you're in the insurance business you have to put in a lot of face-time with your clients, so you had better be likable. Dad was good at remembering names. He was friendly and cheerful. Even when I was a little boy, Dad impressed me, because it seemed that other people invariably liked him.

Dad looked like Jerry Stiller, the comedian, with the marcelled Hungarian hair, sharp features, and the little moustache. (I don't know where my balditude comes from, because Dad kept his hair all his life. I didn't.) His eyes were hazel-brown, and one of them was glass. His right eye had been virtually sightless from birth, and prone to infections, so when he was a teenager the eye had been removed, surgically. Dad had a way of cocking his head, when he was interacting with people, so that he could look at them out of his good eye, and this head-tilt made people think that he was being particularly courteous and attentive, which was probably one reason why he was liked. It also made him look stern and authoritative, when he wanted to.

His having one eye was just a characteristic; I never gave it any thought—except in connection with the fact that on account of that eye, Dad hadn't had to serve in the armed forces. When I was a kid, World War II was a recent memory, and most of the other kids I grew up with had fathers who had served. A lot of those men had stories, which I loved listening to whenever I got the chance.

Dad didn't have any of those stories, which diminished the esteem in which I held him, just the least bit. Not in a big way. I expect most kids are ashamed of their parents for one thing or another, or embarrassed by them, but in general I was rather proud of my parents, and this was just a tiny point against Dad, made even smaller by the fact that it couldn't have been helped. I knew he wasn't to blame, but I just wished, growing up, that Dad had had some war stories of his own, to compete with those that the other fathers in the neighborhood could tell. But he'd stayed in college during the war—University of Wisconsin—and when he graduated he went right into business, even though the war would still go on for another year and a half. He got married, too, to his college sweetheart.

Mom looked like Mrs. Olson, the Folger's Coffee lady. Scandinavian, nearly six feet tall, blonde, with very light green eyes. She was good-looking, but aside from her height she didn't stand out, because she didn't want to.

Paivi Dahlgren Palinkas. Probably if anyone remembers her at all, they remember her for being so quiet and soft-spoken around other people. She had a bit of an inferiority complex. No, check that. She had a lot of one. People would remark that she had an extremely pretty smile, and she did. Those same people would almost always add that she was so modest and unassuming. While she was alive and after she died, both, people would tell me so often what a wonderful, sweet person my mother was, so gentle and kind.

I was always glad to see my grandparents, both sets. They rarely came to see us, when I was growing up, but we would usually travel to visit one family or the other, in the summer or at Christmas or Thanksgiving.

The Palinkas grandparents in Pittsburgh, and the Dahlgren grandparents in suburban Minneapolis, were culturally very different from each other. Both families had come over to America at about the same time—the 1850s—but Mom's folks made better choices. At any rate, the first Palinkas on these shores became a Civil War substitute. You know, in the Civil War, if you were drafted, if you could afford it, you could hire someone to go in your place, and somebody hired Gabor Palinkas. Apparently he saw a lot of action, and then he came out of the Army poor, and with no more job skills than he had gone in with, which meant he was still only a workingman. Somehow he got married and fathered eight children, most of whom didn't do much better than he had done. The last of those was Grandpa Palinkas, born in 1882.

Grandpa Palinkas did a little of this and a little of that—most of it legal, some of it not. He sold insurance and real estate; he was a small-time loan shark, bail bondsman, and bookmaker. Dad grew up without a lot of money but not truly poor. Dad was the second generation born in the States, so the Palinkases were completely American, but they still used a lot of Hungarian expressions. When we visited Pittsburgh, the dinner table was crowded and loud and exuberant. (Dad was the sixth of eight kids, the youngest son of a youngest son.) The cuisine was rich, and heavy on the paprika. Grandpa Palinkas used to drink this awful Hungarian liqueur called Unicum, which tasted like that stuff that burns your throat when you throw up. He said it kept him from going bald. I should have drunk more of it myself.

Mom had ancestors in the Civil War, too, on both sides of her family. Both immigrants, both officers: one Swedish-born from Minnesota; the other Finnish-born from Wisconsin. The Palinkas family had mainly been hustlers who lived by their wits. The Dahlgrens from Minnesota and the Linnas from Wisconsin were a complete contrast to that. They started out as good stolid Lutheran farmers, and became "pillar of the community" types.

Grandpa Dahlgren ran several businesses, too, but they were considerably more profitable than those of the Palinkases. Mom was Grandma and Grandpa Dahlgren's only child, and the Dahlgrens weren't "big rich," but they were well off.

It was because of Grandma and Grandpa Dahlgren that I knew I would never have to worry about money, as long as I lived. They—as I understood from a very early age—would have nobody to leave their fortune to but my mother, and in turn my parents would have nobody to leave it to but me and Mark. Moreover, Dad always made a pretty good living. I knew—from the time that I first realized that some people have more money than others—that our family was considerably better off than most of our neighbors. Especially since Mom would so often warn us not to say or do anything that might allow others to suspect that this was the case. Wealth—even our fairly modest wealth—embarrassed my mother.

The Dahlgrens' household was more prosperous than that of my dad's parents: neater, with fewer people in it, and so very, very quiet. The only time it got noisy at the Dahlgren house was when Grandma and Grandpa Dahlgren decided to have one of their little bickering matches—which they habitually had, a couple of times a day whenever I was visiting there. It was never anything big; it wouldn't last but a minute or so—but I got the impression that Grandma and Grandpa Dahlgren actually enjoyed pushing each other's buttons, pissing each other off. They also loved to put each other down—usually by trying to one-up each other on how knowledgeable or sophisticated they were. For example, if Grandpa Dahlgren used a word or expression that Grandma Dahlgren didn't know, he would explain it to her with a clearly implied, "Gosh, you didn't know *that*?" Which would inspire Grandma Dahlgren to retaliate.

Or Grandpa Dahlgren would make some remark about Grandma's weight. She might suggest that he was losing his marbles. Always something.

Once when I was little, after I had witnessed one of these sessions, I asked Mom (when we were in private), "Why do Grandma and Grandpa still live together if they don't like each other?"

Mom laughed, and in that soft, almost whispery voice of hers she said, "Oh, that's what they do. They have their little arguments, but they have a lot of fun together too. Did you really think they don't like each other?"

"Did they always do like that?" I asked.

"Every day," said Mom. "Every day. For as long as I can remember."

Maybe that's where Mom got it from.

Mom was by no means consistently disparaging or critical or cruel to me. I can think of a lot of times when she was okay: kind and pleasant and gracious to me the way you would expect a mother to be—kind and pleasant and gracious the way Mom invariably was, to everyone outside our family. But the times I remember most vividly are the times when she was angry at me, disappointed in me, disgusted by me, exasperated with me. Sure, I can remember a few times in my life when she praised me without condition, one or two times when she said, "I'm proud of you, Andy." But not many. If you feel personally insecure to begin with, the criticisms and the put-downs will stay with you forever. The praise, you mostly forget.

Well, no, that's not completely true. There was one thing that Mom would truly seem to appreciate about me. When I was a teenager, she did praise me for my theatrical performances, in school plays. She enjoyed those, and she told me so. Which makes what happened later all the harder to explain.

I'm pretty certain it was not generally known—Mom came across as perfectly nice and normal to outsiders, I'm sure—but Mom was not a happy person. It must have been plain old clinical depression, the kind that gets controlled with medication nowadays. I'm assuming that was what she had. Sometimes she seemed fine, like any other woman her age, but quite often— more days when it was than when it wasn't, I'd say—her general manner was sad, gloomy, as though she were contemplating some deep, unnamed sorrow that was always at least in the background of her mind. Every now and then—maybe every couple of years—she would go through a period of a week or two where she would be only barely functional. In bed all day, for days at a time, able to get out of bed and get dressed only if she absolutely had to, but not much more than that.

Most of the time, Mom was pretty regular, quiet, and controlled—but sometimes she would snap, and turn on me. Verbally. With some quick remark that made me feel like I didn't deserve to live—and which, I swear, was calculated to have that effect. Almost always, I had the feeling that whatever I did, I was going to let Mom down somehow, sadden her, piss her off, remind her of what a louse I was—and earn myself another of her put-downs.

"Andy, I'm... concerned... about how much you eat." I heard that all the time, from about age eight onwards. I didn't eat that awful much. I was overweight mostly from inactivity. But like most boys of that age, I was hungry almost all the time, and if I took a pickle or a bit of cheese from the refrigerator between meals, I would often get a "tsk" from Mom. If I helped myself to seconds at dinner, I would get a look.

One morning—I'm pretty sure it was a Saturday, a rainy morning, when I was nine or ten years old (this was when we were living in Wisconsin, still), I announced after breakfast that I was going to start exercising more, to lose weight. Mom said,

"That's fine, Andy." Then and there, in the middle of the living room, I started doing windmills—touching the fingers of one hand to the opposite foot—to loosen myself up.

"You've got to put more into it," Mom said, after I had touched each toe once or twice. Apparently I wasn't doing the windmills fast enough, or with sufficient *élan*, or whatever. Well, for God's sake, they were just stretches, and I was just starting out—and windmills aren't the easiest exercise for a fat kid to do. I stopped what I was doing, straightened up, and, I'll admit, I gave Mom a rather pained look.

"Mom... "

"Oh, I don't care!" she cried. "Go ahead! Be fat!" She flounced out of the living room, down the hall to her and Dad's bedroom, where she slammed the door behind her. Mom could do the dramatic flounce like nobody else I ever met. I sometimes imagined hearing an orchestral "sting," like in a movie sound-track, when she did it.

I couldn't help it: I wailed. I didn't cry, that time; it was a primal yell. I didn't know how to let Mom know I was displeased, except to make her hear it through her bedroom door.

About ten minutes later, Mom came out of the bedroom and apologized: "I'm sorry, I didn't mean to say that; I shouldn't have said it." Okay, fine, but she had said it—and that was the end of the exercising, for a long time, because I had now found out what would happen if I tried it where Mom could see me trying it.

I remember another incident from roughly that same time. I was maybe in the fifth grade. It was the end of a quarter, at school. I had brought home my report card; so had Mark. Mark also had brought a couple of friends over to play. (I rarely had friends over after school; Mark frequently did.) And right there—with Mark and his friends in the living room having milk and cookies—Mom looked at my grades and exclaimed aloud, "Andy! This is a *poor* report card!"

Mark kept his face expressionless, but his friends all smiled at each other, and then sidelong at me. And I didn't have the courage, then or later, to ask Mom how she dared to do that. I don't know. She might have apologized.

Or she might have said something like, "If I had brought home a report card like that, I would expect my parents to say something about it too, and not care who heard it!"

Dad, I got along with, almost all the time. He just wasn't there as much as Mom, when I was a kid. He worked hard, he was at the office a lot. On weekends he did yard work or tinkered with his car. This was a traditional post-war home where the father went out to make a living and the mother stayed home and brought up the kids.

From Dad, I occasionally got praise for this or that. Sometimes he would be a bit too kind. Like, if I bemoaned my lack of athletic skill, he might say, "Don't be so hard on yourself. You're not a star, but you're average." Uh... no, Dad, I wasn't average. I was bottom of the barrel.

Or—and this would make me cringe—sometimes Dad would come home from work and greet me with, "How's my handsome boy?" I knew he was trying to make me feel better because how could he not know I was ugly? He had one good eye in his head.

To have a younger brother who is better than you in every way, who can beat you at anything: That has got to be the worst thing in the world.

I knew, as soon as Mark started to toddle, that he was more what my parents had in mind. What Mom had in mind, anyway. I could see why. He was certainly cuter than I ever was, with bright black eyes and a big grin. I tended to scowl, and my eyes were a sort of sickly olive-green.

(As I got older, my eyes gradually changed color. They're more of a true dark green, now, which I like because that eye-color on a human being is quite unusual. Back then, my eyes were two more points against me, in my assessment.)

Mark gave my parents less trouble than I did, I'm sure. I must have been a source of annoyance to my parents, and maybe embarrassment. Because of my temper, my crying, my contrariness. And I suppose it was perfectly natural that when I started going off to school, leaving Mark and Mom alone, she would bond with Mark more closely than she ever did with me. I understand that; I don't hold it against her.

As we got older, it became apparent that Mark was the better specimen. By the time he was five and I was seven, he was beating me at simple card games like concentration. Even before that, he had learned the trick to pulling a wishbone—which is to hold still and let the other person pull, so that he'll snap off the short end. I suppose it's possible that someone taught him that trick to give him a boost, to keep me from beating him because he was younger and smaller. Or maybe he figured it out himself. He was brighter than I was.

Mark had friends. I didn't. Sure, I had playmates now and then, and I was on civil terms with a few kids in the classroom— but even these kids, with only a very few exceptions, would be unable to resist having a little fun with me. You know, when that one ineffectual, unattractive, easily provoked kid loses his cool, it's almost impossible not to bait him a bit more, to see how far he'll take it. Thus, I went through my elementary and high school years regarding practically everybody with suspicion—and usually, one way or another, my suspicion was justified. Even if, in the final analysis, I brought my woes upon myself.

I wish I had learned to fight. I wish I had learned to throw a punch and make it hurt. I wish I had learned to seriously damage another kid using just my hands and feet, if I wanted to. I was no good at sports, and I wasn't strong for my size, but I could have built up my strength. I could have learned the techniques for breaking a kid's nose or even his kneecap.

I don't mean I necessarily would have done it, but if I had just known that I could do it—could, with one swift blow, put a kid in the hospital or give him an injury that he'd carry for the rest of his life—it might have given me the confidence to stand up to those little shits.

Who can say why I wouldn't stand my ground, why I couldn't turn myself into a terrifying person whom the other kids would have been afraid to fuck with? Another kid, in my place, might have done that. I didn't have the courage.

On my way to and from school, practically every day, I would be taunted and harassed by a group of anywhere from three or four to seven or eight kids. It was usually just verbal, but sometimes I would be hit, or shoved, or kicked in the ass, or have my toes stepped on. I got spat on a couple times. At least once a week, usually much oftener, I would arrive at home or school in tears. Finally, my parents—I can't recall which one—suggested that if Mark and I walked together, the other kids might lay off me, since they didn't have anything against Mark.

We tried it, and it usually worked. Not because Mark was any physical threat—he was little and skinny—but for some reason the kids were reticent about attacking me when Mark was along. So here I was taking my little brother with me—for protection. If you don't have any clue what that can do to a kid's self-esteem, you can thank God for it.

By the time Mark was six and I was eight, when we played with the neighbor kids, "Little Palinkas" was getting chosen before "Big Palinkas" for games. Also, starting at that age, Mark could beat me consistently at chess. I maybe could have been as good a player as he was, but one thing Mark had that I didn't have, at all, was patience. To get good at chess requires study, and deep thought. Above all, it requires enough self-control to not make the first move that looks good to you. Patience and self-control: I never had those qualities. Mark never lacked them.

When I was eleven and Mark was nine, Dad taught us to play golf—which Dad himself wasn't very good at because he had such poor depth perception on account of having just the one eye—and Mark would invariably beat me by a few strokes, even though I was stronger than he was and consistently out-drove him. Again: patience and self-control. Mark had them; I didn't.

In addition to excelling at chess, Mark learned to play the accordion quite well.

§

Our house in Waukoshowoc, where I spent the first fourteen years of my life, was way too small for us. It was a two-bedroom "starter house," and for some reason, Mom wouldn't move out of it. We could have afforded to, by the time I was a few years old—Dad was doing well, financially—but Mom had a phobia: a dread that something awful would happen if we moved out of that house. She knew not what, but it would be something unspeakable. A ghastly misfortune. Or maybe someone in the family—maybe herself—would go mad and murder the rest of us.

I didn't find this out till only a few years ago. Dad explained it to me in his last months, after Mom had died. I had always had the idea that Mom was keeping us in that little house just out of general cussedness. Or maybe she wanted to keep us humble, not let anyone know that we were better off than we looked. That would have been like her. But according to my father, many years after the fact, the real reason why we stayed in that cramped little house long after our family had outgrown it was so that nobody would get killed.

It was a plain one-story tract house with a living room, an eat-in kitchen, bath, and two bedrooms, much like all the other houses in the neighborhood. A residential neighborhood where nothing much ever happened, this was. We had a few nice pieces of furniture, which I gathered had been handed down mainly by the Dahlgren grandparents, but it was all at pretty tight quarters.

We had an upright piano in our living room. Mom knew how to play it, a little, but for the first several years of my life I don't clearly remember her ever playing it in my presence. I certainly don't remember hearing her play after Mark was born, and I have only the vaguest memories of her playing during my babyhood: so vague that they might even be manufactured memories. At any rate, that piano stood in our living room as a sort of icon of what had once been. A piece of statuary rather than a musical instrument.

I didn't show any interest in learning to play that piano. Sometimes as a toddler I would idly hit a few keys, for the sake of making a sound, and I understood that some keys made loud, dark notes and some made light, high notes, but that was all I knew about the piano, and all I cared to know. Mom must have told me, at one time or another, that she used to play it—that could account for my possibly manufactured memory of having heard her play when I was a baby—but she never offered to teach me to play, and I never asked her to.

Mark, when he was about five, did start getting interested in the piano. As soon as his hands were barely big enough to stretch comfortably across five keys, Mom gave him his first lessons. She taught him to play "Mary Had a Little Lamb," and "Chop-sticks"—the first time I can be certain that I heard her play—and pretty soon Mark was good enough to need a professional teacher.

I remember Mom asking me, when Mark started taking lessons, whether I would like them too. I recall it was late in the summer—right before I was to start second grade and Mark was to start kindergarten. It was over the dinner table one evening

**31**

when she told Mark about the arrangements she had made. Then she turned to me and said, "Andy, Daddy and I don't want you to feel that Mark is getting special attention. If you want music lessons too, or if you can think of anything else you'd like to pursue, just say so."

But when Mom made the offer, I told her, "No, thanks. I wouldn't keep it up; you know how I am." Which, looking back, was a strange thing for a seven-year-old to say. I guess it showed more insight than most seven-year-olds would have had, right?

Mom said, "That's what I thought, but I hope you know that we're not trying to favor Mark at all. If you change your mind, let us know."

Okay, fine: I know—knew at the time—that Mom meant it. But I wouldn't take her up on it because I knew that whatever interest I decided to pursue, I would never be as proficient at it as Mark was, at whatever he had decided to get good at.

Even at that young age, I understood—if perhaps imperfectly—that to excel at a musical instrument would require a great deal of practice. Boring, frustrating, maddening practice that would keep me from doing other things (like doing nothing).

Mark, at first, seemed indifferent to his piano lessons. He didn't show any promise of becoming proficient, not for a good year or so. Then, shortly after he had turned six, this happened:

It was a summer evening, and we were visiting Grandma and Grandpa Palinkas in Pittsburgh. I always used to enjoy visiting there because usually one or another of Dad's brothers or sisters would be visiting with their families too, and the house would be pretty crowded, so Mark and I would get to sleep out on the screen porch, sometimes with several of our cousins. I didn't much mind the close quarters, under those circumstances, because the cousins would invariably know some jokes or stories that I hadn't heard yet.

Grandma and Grandpa Palinkas lived in a working-class residential neighborhood: a little more urbanized than the neighborhood we lived in, in Waukoshowoc, but not much more so, at that. It consisted of older frame houses, mostly built around 1900, I should guess. That evening, it was after dinner but not yet dark; Mark and the cousins and I were in the grandparents' front yard—playing freeze-tag, as I recall—when from the front door of the house across the street emerged a young man, maybe twenty years old or so, a clean-cut Joe College type. He was carrying an accordion. He sat down on the steps of the front porch of that house, and started playing.

After a few seconds of hearing that instrument, Mark dropped out of the game and ran across the street—I remember I shouted at him, real quick, "Look both ways!" even though there was no traffic. Mark stopped himself, and did; then he crossed. He ran over to this guy and stood in the yard of that house, next to the front porch, listening. I stayed in the game for another minute or so, but then I went across the street to listen, too. The other kids all trailed behind me.

The young man smiled at us; he was obviously flattered. He played another song or two, then he stopped playing and asked us if we wanted to know more about his instrument. He gave us a quick explanation of what it was and how it worked, then he let us each try to play a few notes—and Mark was hooked.

For the next few months, when Mom would take us to the public library in Waukoshowoc, he would check out records of accordion music. He would listen to them over and over, on the hi-fi in our living room, sitting there perfectly still with this hypnotized, almost rapturous expression on his face. He was only just entering first grade, then, still learning to read, but I'm sure he would have checked out books on the accordion if he could have read them. He began pestering Mom and Dad about whether he might have an accordion for Christmas.

He got one. A light-weight one that he could manage. (A full-size accordion is a heavy instrument; it takes some upper-body strength to play.) I was given the latest edition of *The World Book Encyclopedia* (on the understanding that it was for family use, of course, but officially mine), which I regarded as an even more splendid present. I wasn't as focused as Mark, but I was interested in knowledge for its own sake. I wore out those encyclopedias, over the next few years, the way Mark wore out that accordion before he graduated to a full-size model.

Knowledge for its own sake. At that age, that was a thing for me. It always has been, to this day. My happiest memories of those third and fourth grades were the times when I would be curled up on my bed, poring over one volume or another of those encyclopedias. I read them over, and over, and over again. It was a way of getting lost. I bet I could still recite a lot of the *World Book* from memory.

When I was reading those books, I was escaping. I wasn't Andy Palinkas anymore. I wasn't a stinky little kid, living in a too-small house. I'm not sure what else I was, but I was no longer a boy. I was a wise and learned man, seeing the world—even if only from the vantage point of my bed.

I read a lot. Like, tons. If I went outside, I usually had a book with me. I can hardly remember a time when I couldn't read. By the time I was five years old I could read more fluently than some of my adult baby-sitters—and I know, because I sometimes had to correct them when they read aloud to me.

I have to say, that's one thing my parents did right. They encouraged me to read; they gave me good books. I read all the standard boy-stuff—*Treasure Island; Tom Sawyer;* the *Freddy* series about a talking pig who was also a detective—and by the time I was in fourth grade I was reading Greek and Norse mythology. By the sixth grade I was reading Dickens, and various histories. I was certainly the best-read kid in my neighborhood.

You know what's the trouble with being a well-read kid, though? The mispronunciations. I guess I should have realized that I tended to misproßnounce words because I knew so much, not because I knew so little. I would rhyme *"protégé"* with *"cortège,"* "avenger" with "scavenger," "Damocles" with "fried cockles," and so on. I'd pronounce "misled" as "myzled." I'm still trying to forget the first time I tried to say "Goethe." Childhood is one prolonged mortification.

The fact that we didn't have a television set certainly had something to do with my reading so much. It's a funny thing, because Mom and Dad liked movies, and they would take Mark and me to the movies sometimes—usually Disney, or a light-hearted adult comedy—but there was no TV in our house.

One might think that in retrospect, I would be glad I was deprived of TV, growing up, because it forced me to read—but, no. That was one thing my parents did wrong. My parents, uniquely among all the parents in our neighborhood, refused to buy a TV set. It would have poisoned my mind, and Mark's. That's how Dad explained it to us. There were so many other better ways to spend our time. He and Mom didn't want us filling up our minds with a lot of foolishness.

It's bad enough that I was hopeless at sports. Bad enough that I had an uncontrollable temper, and cried all the time. Bad enough that I was a fat slob. On top of all that, because we didn't have a TV, I was limited in what I could talk to other kids about. Their conversation usually revolved around what they had been watching on TV lately. All I could do was listen, and think about how wonderfully fun it must be to watch TV in the evenings, or on Saturday mornings, and talk about it with friends afterwards.

I was so clueless about TV that I assumed *The Red Skelton Show* was a horror show. You know, the Red Skeleton.

One of the reasons I especially loved to visit either set of grandparents was that when we were there, *I got to watch TV!* I used to wish that I had more friends, as a kid, not so much because I liked other kids—I didn't—but because if I had had more friends I would have been able to spend more time in their houses, watching TV!

Oh, God. That reminds me of one of the most shameful things I have ever done in my life. In my opinion. Anybody else might not judge me too harshly for it, or think that it was that big of a deal, but I have never forgotten it. I have never forgiven myself. I never will, because it was unforgivable.

It was Christmas Day when I was—I'm thinking—maybe eight years old. We had driven that morning from Waukoshowoc to the Dahlgren grandparents' home in Minnesota and we were about to do the present-opening.

And I—with my lack of both common sense and impulse control—with all of us gathered in the Dahlgrens' living room, noted aloud that it was four o'clock and *The Mickey Mouse Club* was about to start, and couldn't we put off the present-opening for a while?

Mom stood up and beckoned me to come with her into the front hall. She gave me one of the most terrible looks I have ever seen from her, and hissed at me, "Andy. When you said that... Grandpa's. Face. Just. *Fell*. I am so disappointed in you." Then we went back into the living room.

Mom was right! She was right to be so angry. I don't dispute that for an instant.

I have done a lot to be ashamed of, over the years. But that incident sticks in my mind as probably the most ashamed of myself I have ever been.

My parents meant it for the best. It would be ridiculous to assert that they had agreed, "Let's keep Andy and Mark away from TV so that they'll be handicapped in their interactions with other children." I don't make that accusation. Look, I'm perfectly aware that Mark and I had it way better than a lot of other kids. If nothing worse ever happened to me than being deprived of countless hours of TV-watching when I was a kid, I should consider myself extremely lucky. I know, I know.

But as ashamed of myself as I was, and am, for that incident, the fundamental grievance was there. The grievance remains. Okay, I guess that makes me a bad person.

§

Mark studied and practiced real hard, on that accordion. I suppose it's proof that he was good, that I didn't mind listening to him practice—him sitting on his bed, while I lounged on mine, reading my encyclopedias. If he had been lousy, I wouldn't have been able to stand the sound of it.

That was the end of any thoughts I might have had about learning a musical instrument. If I had tried, probably Mark would have taken an interest in the same instrument, and excelled at it. I was barely bright enough to be able to envision that scenario, so as much as I have always loved listening to music— all kinds—I still don't know the first thing about how to play any instrument.

It's not quite accurate to say that I was interested in "doing nothing." But pretty close. My interest in make-believe—which, as Mrs. Winkie had reported years before, could be downright fierce—persisted, as I grew older. If anything, *The World Book Encyclopedia* intensified that interest, because the more I learned about how life works, and about history, from reading the encyclopedia, the more I was able to add detail and embellishment to my fantasies, and paint them more accurately.

Now that I consider it, it's amazing to me how much of my time I have spent living in one fantasy or another—not only in childhood, but all my life long—like Snoopy with his "Here's The World War One Flying Ace" persona. I do it less as I get older—after all, a man in his sixties can't easily fantasize about being young and athletic—but still, even now, I'll sometimes fall asleep at night with the sound of artillery roaring in my ears as Union gunners try in vain to knock down my fortifications, and the brave Confederates under my command prepare to launch a surprise counterattack. Or some such nonsense.

When I was in elementary school, I read everything I could get my hands on about the Wild West, so that I could be not merely "foreman of this ranch," but a real person, like Doc Holliday or Bat Masterson. Sometimes I would be a "Gary Stu" character who was buddies with Doc or Bat. I read European history, too, and I might become Louis XIV (I admired his elaborate robes and immense wig) or Charles I (I was drawn to the spectacular manner of his death). This was in some ways more gratifying than playing with other kids, since in my fantasies there was no risk of getting picked on, laughed at, shoved around.

I would occasionally fool around with fantasies of myself as a star athlete, but only rarely, because with my physical defects I knew I had less chance of being an NFL fullback or a Major League pitcher than I had of reincarnating as Louis XIV. Thus my athletic fantasies were incomplete, and less plausible than my dreams of political power.

My favorite fantasy incarnation at that time was King Andrew XVIII. I don't know how I came to choose the Eighteenth as the magic number, but I did, and I was never able to determine what country I was king of, but that wasn't important.

The point of being King Andrew XVIII was that Andrew was an evil despot—an utterly amoral despot. He was, of course, an adult in this fantasy. He had about him an entourage that would do whatever he ordered—much like Hitler, except that Andrew XVIII could be even less circumspect than Hitler had had to be. If Andrew XVIII wanted someone dead, his hired thugs would simply go to wherever that person was to be found, and kill him then and there—although more usually, the person would be arrested, thrown into prison, and subsequently hanged or beheaded following a lightning-swift trial.

(The backstory on Andrew XVIII was that he had been Lord High Executioner for the previous King—I adopted the title myself after I had heard a recording of *The Mikado*—and had seized the throne in a *coup d'état* following the old King's death.)

The people executed by Andrew XVIII's minions were usually my tormentors from school, grown to adulthood, or teachers I disliked. Many nights, I would drift off to sleep while fantasizing blissfully in this way. Several of my schoolmates were killed over and over again, night after night, till I had perfected the story of how each of them had met a horrible end: the guillotine, usually, or hanging. Something quick. I'm a little surprised that I wasn't much interested in torturing them, but I wasn't. All I wanted, in terms of causing them any great distress, was to ensure that they would experience a moment of horror at the very end, when they realized that it was really going to happen to them, that they were going to die at my hands.

§

When I was nine, I fell in love. That is, I developed a passion that has lasted the rest of my life, just as Mark had suddenly developed a passion for the accordion, the year before.

It happened when I saw an ad in *Sport* magazine for a board game called APBA Major League Baseball. This was a game that employed boards, cards, and dice to simulate a major league baseball game. Nowadays, such games are made for your computer and/or your TV, but that technology didn't exist back then. APBA Major League Baseball worked like this:

Say for example you wanted to create a game between the Milwaukee Braves and the Brooklyn Dodgers. Each player was represented by a small card—the size and shape of a standard playing card—that bore a series of numbers. If Don Newcombe were pitching to Hank Aaron, you would roll a set of differently colored dice, one red and one white. The result of that dice-roll would refer you to a number on the card representing Aaron. That number, in turn, would refer you to one of several large printed sheets of heavy cardboard (representing various situations and scenarios) on which you would find the result of the play—sometimes influenced by certain notations on the pitcher's (Newcombe's) card. In this way, you could play out a virtual major league baseball game, making managerial decisions such as substitutions, bunts, and intentional walks. Each player would perform, statistically, very close to the way he performed in real life. That is, if Aaron hit .322 with forty-four home runs in 1957, then in the following year's edition of APBA Baseball you could expect him to achieve approximately that batting average, and hit about that many home runs, if he played almost every day in a 154-game season.

I had had no idea, before I saw that ad, that such a game existed—but once I knew it existed, it was all I wanted. I desired it like a grown man might desire a beautiful woman, only more so. I had always relied on fantasy to get me through, to make life bearable for me. Here was an actual vehicle that would allow me to live a fantasy—and take it to a level I had never imagined.

# 3 I DISGRACE MYSELF

I showed my parents the ad, and made it clear that for my tenth birthday, APBA Major League Baseball would be exactly what I wanted. I tried my best not to pester them about it—but I couldn't help bringing it up now and then. I spent time almost every day sprawled on my bed, mooning over that ad. About a month before my birthday, the magazine (and the ad) mysteriously vanished from my bedside table. I allowed myself to hope that my parents had filled out the order coupon and mailed it in. I also had to allow for the possibility that they had hidden the ad in hopes that I would stop obsessing about a present that I wasn't going to get.

But I got it. On the evening of my birthday—we had spareribs with sauerkraut for dinner that night, which was my favorite—Mom bade me hide my eyes while she brought the cake out and lit the candles. When she and Dad and Mark started singing "Happy Birthday," I opened my eyes, and the cake was placed before me; I wished silently for the APBA baseball game and got all the candles on one puff (thank goodness). Mom went back into her and Dad's bedroom and returned with a huge flat box, prettily wrapped, which turned out to contain the play boards, envelopes full of player cards, red and white dice, yellow dice shakers. And I noticed that as Mom set the box down in front of me she was absolutely glowing, turning the full force of her big smile on me, as though she were truly happy to be giving me something that pleased me—and I suppose she was.

I cut and served the cake at top speed, and ate my portion so fast that the rest of the family had barely got halfway through theirs. Without even thinking of taking seconds, I asked to be excused so that I could go play with my new toy. Mom shot me a grave look, a look of the deepest hurt.

She whispered, "It seems to me you could stay here at the table with us for a little while, Andy—on your birthday." She cast her glance down to her plate, and swallowed hard.

I didn't know how to respond. I didn't respond. I just sat there, frozen, because I had been hit, in effect, and it was a fair blow. I was selfish, selfish, selfish.

So I did stay at the table for another fifteen minutes, thinking that if I had to stay there I could at least have seconds on the cake, but I didn't dare take it. I tried to talk across the table to Mark—making conversation for its own sake—while Dad joined in here and there and Mom looked sorrowful. I finally got up quietly (as though if I moved slowly and made no noise, I would not be noticed), carried my plate into the kitchen, and placed it in the sink with the other dirty dishes. Then I returned, with similar furtiveness, to the dining room. Not looking at anyone, I took the game box out to the living room to open it up and get acquainted with the contents. Mom said, "Tsk."

At lunch the next day—Dad was at work; Mark and I were back from the morning session at school—my selfishness was still on Mom's mind. "You need to learn to control yourself," she told me. She rattled the plate a bit more than usual as she set it in front of me. "You could have sat at the table for those few minutes without acting all antsy. That was very rude."

I hadn't been aware that I had acted noticeably antsy during that quarter-hour. In fact, I had made a special effort not to. But apparently I hadn't tried hard enough. I wondered what Mom would think of me if I started to eat. I felt like I was insulting her every time I took a bite of my bologna sandwich—which, under the circumstances, tasted like sawdust.

"What if there'd been company last night?" Mom demanded. "What would people have thought?"

I kept quiet, hoping she would take that as a sign of surrender. Apparently she did, because all I got beyond that was one more "tsk."

Mom was already sorry, apparently, that she had gotten me something I liked so well—and believe me, she would have far more reason to regret that present, for many years to come.

The version of the game that I got for my birthday, in that late spring of 1958, covered the previous season. That is, the players were all expected to perform statistically as they had done in 1957. Once I had the hang of it, I could get through one game in twenty minutes. I intended to re-play the entire 1957 season—with all sixteen teams (as there were then), 154 games per team—keeping complete statistics. Batting, pitching, even fielding.

However, in a day or so, I realized that I wasn't going to be able to play eight games of APBA baseball every day—which is what I would have had to do, plus updating the statistics. So, on further consideration, I resolved to re-play the 1957 season only as it involved the Milwaukee Braves. One game a day, 154 games, for one team, placing myself on my honor to make the best decisions for both sides. That, I could do, I figured, and I would still have time to play random games between other teams.

Here was where you could find ten-year-old me, at some point practically every day: sitting cross-legged on the linoleum floor of Mark's and my bedroom, with the boards and the cards spread out in front of me, shaking the tiny dice in the little yellow cup that came with the game; rolling them out; matching the result of the dice to the reference number on the card; matching that number to the result listed on the board. Whatever the result, I would record it in a tiny, neat hand on a pad of graph paper. When the game was over, I would update the statistics for each of my players, recording at-bats, hits, stolen bases, and so on—as well as putouts, assists, and errors.

This whole process—game and stats—took about an hour every day, or ninety minutes if I played two games, which I frequently did, that summer, to catch up to the season that was going on in real life, so that both the fantasy and the reality would end in October.

Mom and Dad would urge me to spend more time outside—since after all it was summer vacation—instead of "sitting around in your room pitching dice." But why would I want to go outside? There was nothing I wanted to do out there. I wasn't any good at real baseball. What's more, I was *not* a kid sitting on his bedroom floor pitching dice.

I was Andrew Palinkas, the sensational manager of the Milwaukee Braves. I wasn't ten years old. I was extraordinarily young for a Major League Baseball manager, maybe twenty-three or twenty-four, but I wasn't a kid.

I was heartbreakingly handsome, with thick, wavy hair and deep dimples. I was tall and broad-shouldered, with big arms and no fat on me. I dated Brigitte Bardot. (I hadn't seen any of her movies, but I had seen her picture in magazines and been utterly smitten. I had immediately forgotten Ava Gardner, probably my first love, who in my fantasy had left Frank Sinatra for me.) Mind you, I was still only ten in real life, and not sexual yet, but I already had an appreciation of Beauty.

The Braves won the 1957 pennant in my replay—as they had done in real life. They won ninety-six games, under my guidance, compared with the only ninety-five they had won under Fred Haney. Then, in October, we faced Casey Stengel's New York Yankees in the World Series.

I hadn't ever been to New York City in real life, let alone ever been in Yankee Stadium, but Dad had taken me and Mark down to Milwaukee County Stadium the previous summer, to see the Braves play the Cardinals, so I knew what the inside of a Major League ballpark was like. I could imagine Yankee Stadium. I won't go into all the details, but that series went seven exciting games—as it had done in real life.

Oh, that seventh game. We were the visiting team, at Yankee Stadium, and my Braves were ahead 3-1 going into the bottom of the ninth inning. Lew Burdette was on the mound. He had pitched terrific ball for me, for eight innings. He had given up two hits—a home run to Yogi Berra to lead off the second inning, and a single to Tony Kubek in the eighth—and no walks. A brilliant performance. I was as pumped, going to the Yankee half of the ninth, as if I had physically been there, managing the real live 1957 Milwaukee Braves. A two-run lead, with half an inning to play. Only three outs, and this ten-year-old sensation— I mean, this twenty-three-year-old sensation—will have led his team to a World Championship.

I am there.

I hear the crowd. I hear the "pop" of each of Burdette's warm-up pitches into Del Crandall's mitt. I smell the beer and the hot dogs. I wave to a couple of pretty girls in the stands. One of them (obviously a Yankees fan) sticks out her tongue at me, but then she smiles after all.

The dice roll: 52. Play result: 27. "Ground ball out, A-3B PO-1B (X-Strikeout, PO-C)." That is, if Burdette has the letter "X" on his card, indicating that he's a high-strikeout pitcher, the play result is changed to a strikeout. But Burdette has no X. I can tell from the sound of the bat contacting the ball that Jerry Lumpe, pinch-hitting for the Yankees' pitcher, didn't get good wood on it. A feeble ground ball to third, where Eddie Mathews fields it and fires it over to Frank Torre at first base. One out. We're back up to the top of the Yankee order: Hank Bauer, their leadoff hitter, who has done nothing so far this day.

Dice roll: 36. Play result: 33. "Pop fly out, PO-2B (Y-Strikeout, PO-C)." Burdette doesn't have a "Y," either. Felix Mantilla, at second base, fields the weak popup easily.

Two down, nobody on. The Braves are one out away from the World Championship. Enos "Country" Slaughter steps up to the plate. Burdette, looking confident, takes the sign from Crandall and gives the catcher a quick nod.

Dice roll: 13. Play result: 14. A base on balls, the first one Burdette has given up today. The wily Slaughter worked the count to three-and-two; he fouled off two pitches; he waited, waited... and it pays off. Still: two out, man on first. The tying run now strides to the plate: Mickey Mantle, batting lefty against the right-handed Burdette.

I have our ace closer, Don McMahon, in the bullpen, but I don't think of bringing him in. One more out to go, and Burdette, I feel, has earned this. Let him pitch to Mantle.

Dice roll: 25. Play result: 8. A single to short left. Wes Covington takes it on the hop; Bauer doesn't even think about trying for third base. He stops at second; Mantle, the tying run, takes only a short lead off first.

To the plate strides Yogi Berra.

Forgive me for explaining the obvious, but with nobody out, in that situation, the choice would be clear: Get Burdette out of there. Bring in not McMahon, the right-hander, but the star lefty, Warren Spahn, to pitch to the left-hand-hitting Berra! It's true that Spahn had pitched for me the day before—he had gone eight tough innings in a losing effort—but this was the last game of the season no matter what happened. Spahn could surely have come in to pitch to one batter. Then, if necessary, I could bring in McMahon to pitch to the right-handed Gil McDougald. But with two out, the situation was less clear.

Maybe I'm getting too technical, but I'm trying to make this story make sense: At that time, APBA had not yet developed a way to make a lefty hitter have a tougher time against lefty pitching, and hit better against a right-handed pitcher, or vice versa for a right-handed batter, as is often the case in real life. The manufacturers did figure out how to add that feature, in the early 1970s—APBA was constantly tinkering with the game, making improvements—but in the late 1950s it didn't matter: A left-hander like Berra would perform equally well, in APBA, against lefty or righty pitching.

Also, at that time, APBA had not yet figured out how to work pitcher fatigue into the equation. Burdette would be as strong, in the bottom of the ninth inning, as he would have been in the first. If he were fatigued, it would only be because common sense and my imagination dictated that he would be.

So, consider that. Consider also that Burdette had pitched great ball for eight and two-thirds innings. He would have something to prove against Berra, the guy who had touched him for the one run he'd given up so far, that home run in the second. To take him out, at that point, would have been an admission of no confidence: an insult.

Burdette will pitch, I decide. I have a commitment to his heart.

Berra digs into the batter's box. Burdette peers down at Crandall, takes a full windup, and lets fly.

Dice roll: 66. Play result 1. A gut-wrenchingly loud crack of the bat. An almighty roar—first of anticipation, then of ecstatic triumph—from nearly 70,000 fans.

All of a sudden I was no longer Andrew Palinkas, sensational and handsome twenty-three-year-old manager.

I was Andy Palinkas, boy on the linoleum floor of his bedroom, thinking, "Would I have done that, really now?"

Would the manager of the Milwaukee Braves—whether he was ten-year-old Andy (or twenty-three-year-old Andrew) Palinkas, or sixty-one-year-old Fred Haney—really have left Burdette in, to pitch to Berra?

Never mind the commitment to his heart. Never mind protocol. Never mind that APBA made no provision for the batter's or the pitcher's left- or right-handedness. This was a decision so obvious that eight-year-old Mark Palinkas would probably have made it—but ten-year-old Andy Palinkas had not.

The twenty-three-year-old Andrew Palinkas, I decided, would *not* have left Burdette in. Even if I had just done so. It wouldn't have happened. Not in real life. Not if I had been actually standing in the Braves' dugout, in uniform, in all of my amazingly handsome, virile, twenty-three-year-old glory.

I looked over at Mark. He was lying propped-up on his bed, reading the latest issue of *Chess Life*, re-playing some game or other on a pocket-sized chess set. He was paying me no attention. He had seen nothing. He had no idea what was going on.

Instead of recording the game-ending three-run homer for Yogi Berra, on the tablet of graph paper, I recorded the removal of Lew Burdette.

Handsome and unflappable, twenty-three-year-old Andrew Palinkas strides from the dugout to the pitcher's mound, takes the ball from Burdette, slaps him on the ass in appreciation of a job well done, and waves his left arm in the direction of the bullpen. The partisan Yankee crowd gives Burdette a respectful hand as he walks to the dugout. Spahnie, carrying his warmup jacket, begins his long stroll across the vast outfield of Yankee Stadium. He arrives at the mound; I hand him the ball. I say, "Get this fucker," and stride back to the dugout, feeling certain that Spahn will, indeed, get this fucker: get us the one big out.

He does. Dice roll 64: play result 13. Strikeout. Game over. Series over. The Milwaukee Braves, guided by their youngest-ever manager, are Champions of the World.

I have done cruel deeds in my life. I have perpetrated inconsiderate deeds, immoral deeds. I have previously described one of the most *shameful* acts I have ever committed. This was nothing. This was a kid behaving like a kid. Making a dumb decision and giving himself a do-over. Yet it was somehow important enough to me, psychologically, that I keep beating myself up about it to this day. Almost sixty years later. Go figure.

§

I have played APBA Baseball, on and off, all my life. I play it still. But after that first year, I never re-played a full season with the Braves. Instead, I started to figure out the numerical formulæ that APBA employed to create the statistical realism for which their game was famous. For next year's season, I got some oak tag paper from an art supplies store, and made cards that represented imaginary players, who played on my imaginary team— the Washington Presidents.

With an imaginary team, the fun lay in developing characters for each of the players, giving them each a physical appearance and a personality, even sometimes creating dialogues among them in my mind. Designing the uniforms was fun, too. You would think that the Washington Presidents' colors would have been red, white, and blue, but that would have been way too easy. I decided I had to come up with something unusual, but still tasteful.

Presidents of the United States are expected to dress conservatively, right? So I decided that the Presidents' colors should be black and grey.

Their home uniforms would consist of a white blouse and plus-fours with black piping and numbers; light-grey stirrup socks and black undershirt; light-grey cap with a black-and-white yin-yang insignia. The only hint of color on the uniform would be a silkscreened cherry blossom across the front of the blouse, in light pink, with a couple of green leaves on a black branch. In honor of the cherry trees for which Washington, D.C. is famous. The whole effect was rather Japanese-looking. I'm afraid I didn't draw the cherry blossom well, when I put the uniform on paper, and since I was working with a box of sixty-four Crayolas I couldn't get the colors precisely right, but it wasn't a bad job for a boy who was not quite eleven years old.

Then I got out compass, ruler, protractor, and so on, and went about building a stadium. I remember sitting on our living room sofa in Waukoshowoc, with a clipboard on my lap, working on this stadium, neatly penciling in the names of the seating areas: bleachers, general admission, loge, field boxes, etc. Dad, at one point, glanced at what I was doing and said, "Let me show Mommy this." He took the clipboard and walked it into the kitchen. "Paivi, look at this. Look how meticulous our boy can be when he sets his mind to it. If only he'd be that way about his schoolwork!"

That bugged me a little. That last remark. Okay, if you'd wanted to know why I wasn't so meticulous about my schoolwork, if you'd asked me back then, I probably wouldn't have had the gumption to tell you. I would have looked away, sulked, acted insulted at the question, and not answered it. But I suppose I knew the answer then as well as I know it now: I didn't give a crap about schoolwork. It was something I was being made to do, for no reason that I could understand, and under no incentive of gain. I saw no point in it—it didn't earn me anything— and in any case I have always resented being told what to do. Building a ballpark in the air, so to speak, and designing uniforms for the phantoms who would play in it, well, that was pointless too—but it was fun, and nobody was making me do it.

I'm grateful that Mark never took a notion to design a baseball stadium. His would have been nicer. I have no doubt whatever about that.

Real baseball, for me, continued to be another matter. My first two years of playing Little League, I could barely hit the ball out of the infield. On the rare occasions when I did—since the closest I could come to running was a sort of waddle—I nearly got thrown out at first base from the outfield. I remember one time I accidentally knocked the ball between the left and center fielders and got a double—how I managed to run that far before they got the ball to the infield, I still don't know—but that was the zenith of my Little League career.

Dad tried to buck me up by admitting that he hadn't been good at baseball either, but I knew that that was because of his eye. Dad hadn't been much of an athlete as a kid, but I knew he had run track and been on the swim team at least. I couldn't even imagine doing either of those activities competitively.

In the summer of 1960, when I had turned twelve and Mark was ten, it was Mark's first year of Little League and my last—and we were on the same team. The coach thought Mark was pretty talented.

Mark was made a starting pitcher. When he wasn't pitching, he played shortstop. I played a few innings per game, almost always in right field where I wasn't likely ever to have to field the ball. If a left-handed hitter happened to come to the plate, while I was playing right field, the coach would have me switch places with the left-fielder. (And if a ball ever did come into my territory, it had better come on the ground, so I could chase it down. If it came on the fly, I would drop it.)

Mark hit three home runs in fifteen games that summer. That would have been equivalent to hitting thirty in a season, for a major leaguer. I hit no home runs. Only a few times did I hit the ball out of the infield. By mid-season—when it was clear that I was never going to play any position other than right field, nor bat any higher than eighth, while the coach was making Mark one of his stars—I was so demoralized that I don't believe I got another hit in any of our remaining games.

I blame myself. I should have passed on that last season of Little League. I should have told my parents I wasn't interested in playing that year, and wished Mark good luck, because I should have known right from the start that I would be buying myself nothing but heartache, playing on the same team with Mark. How could I not have known that that was how it would turn out? Well, it's not a matter of "should have known." I did know. I went through with it anyway.

That fall, when I started seventh grade, I was at a different school. I was hoping that maybe I could make a new start, reinvent myself. But in the first hour of my first day of junior high school, the boy sitting right in front of me turned around in his seat and smirked at me. This was a kid I had never seen before; didn't know his name, anything. He said to me, "Hey, Palinkas, I hear your little brother's quite a baseball player. Got to pitch while you played right field. How about that?" And he laughed at me, not quite loud enough for the teacher to hear it. Evidently he had been told—no doubt by the same people who had told him about my baseball exploits—that you could do or say anything you wanted to, to this Palinkas kid, and the worst he could do by way of retaliation was to cry.

I didn't cry, that time, but I had occasion to, several times that year. Seventh and eighth grades are the times when kids are at their most vicious. I don't know why that's so, but it is. It became clear, over just the next few days, that some of my comrades from elementary school had cast the word pretty broadly: Andy Palinkas was someone you could have a lot of fun with, and anyone who wanted a piece of him should feel welcome.

# 4 STATE CITY

Mark and I never deliberately worked against each other. We were uncongenial in some ways but we tried to get along. We got on each other's nerves a lot. We shared a bedroom from the day he came home from the hospital till the day I moved out of my parents' house, and we were at cramped quarters, with no neutral corners for us to go to. I don't know how Mark felt about me at the time—and we have never discussed that situation since—but to me, having to share a bedroom was a particular annoyance, because every night, I would have to see Mark diligently doing his homework, or hear him practicing his accordion, while I either read, or played APBA Baseball. I wasn't interested in doing any more schoolwork than I had to. Just enough, every semester, to pull myself up to a C average.

The situation at school—getting constantly picked on, assaulted sometimes, by the other kids, and nothing I could do to fight back—was out of control, as it had been for years, only worse. I won't bore you with the details; suffice to say that as boys get bigger they can hit harder. And at ages eleven, twelve, thirteen, their viciousness—viciousness for its own sake—reaches peak intensity.

Not to mention that from seventh grade onward, you don't go home for lunch. You eat in the school cafeteria. So on the one hand, I was spared two of the four gauntlets that I'd had to waddle through in previous years. On the other hand, at home, nobody blew a hocker into my food. Yeah, that happened.

I'm convinced, looking back, that if we had stayed in Waukoshowoc for another year, I would have gone over the edge. I would, indeed, have killed myself, or maybe killed someone else: someone who deserved it.

By then, I truly was having detailed fantasies about killing my tormentors. You bet I was. Not mere fantasies about an imaginary King Andrew XVIII having people killed by imaginary hirelings. By this time, it was me, personally, killing people.

The most common scenario was one where I got hold of a good long knife, and without warning I would walk up to one of the little bastards—probably in school, or maybe in the street—and real quickly jam the knife in, in the shoulder, right behind the collarbone, stabbing straight down. Then I would yank the knife out, and the kid would have just enough time to gasp "Why?" before the blood gushed from his nose and mouth and he collapsed to the ground and bled to death in a few seconds. I probably could have taken out at least three of them, maybe more, before I was stopped.

In the spring of 1962, Mom and Dad started having some pretty tense discussions. Apparently most of them took place when Mark and I were out of the house, but sometimes we would hear them arguing in their bedroom, with the door shut. Mark and I would try to listen, and we tried to piece together the stray words or syllables we heard or thought we heard, but Mom and Dad kept their voices down, so we didn't get a lot of it. Between the two of us, Mark and I figured out that they were talking about some sort of disruption. We thought it was most likely a matter of the whole family relocating—to where, we couldn't guess—in which case the move would almost certainly be the result of a career change of some kind for Dad.

But there was also a possibility that we couldn't discount: that maybe they were talking about only one of them relocating—which would mean a separation or divorce. Mom and Dad very rarely had big fights. Minor skirmishes were pretty frequent, but that's all they were. Maybe once a year, they would have a major blow-up that would have them shouting at each other for an hour or more: usually about something trivial that got blown out of proportion because they were both having a bad day.

This time, though, it was clear that something pretty serious was going on. Only once did Dad raise his voice to the point where Mark and I, sitting each on our beds, could hear him clearly through the wall—when he shouted, "Do you expect me to let you sabotage our family?" Then we could hear Mom wailing, but in a few seconds their voices quietened.

Mark and I just looked at each other, and we shook our heads. It's funny how we didn't talk about it, aside from those vague speculations as to what was being argued about. I never asked Mark, then or later, what was in his head when this was going on.

The next day, when I got home from school and before Dad got home, I went into the kitchen and asked Mom straight-out what the situation was. She said, "It's something Daddy and I have to figure out. It might not be anything."

"Mark and I are worried," I told her.

"It's nothing bad," Mom said, in a pretty firm tone of voice. It was clear that she wasn't going to say any more about it, so I went outside and waited for Dad's car to pull into the driveway. When he got out of his car I waylaid him before he could go into the house, and put it to him straight.

"Something's going on," I said. "Mark and I need to know what it is."

Dad told me. He had an opportunity to take over the Farmers Midwest Mutual office in State City, Iowa—about 350 miles southwest of Waukoshowoc.

"Mommy is afraid she wouldn't be happy there," he said. "She's got all these cockamamie reasons. Like State City isn't near a lake, and it's farther from both sets of grandparents. And that it would be a change. You know, Mommy doesn't like change. We'll just have to wait and see what happens."

That very night, after dinner, Dad called up Grandpa and Grandma Dahlgren long-distance (which was expensive in those days), and asked them to please talk to Mom about it. I only overheard one side of the conversation, and Mom didn't say much to her parents, at that, but she was crying throughout. Like, really bawling. The only thing I clearly remember is Mom sitting in the kitchen, or actually almost curled up in a fœtal position, in one of the wooden chairs from the dining table, and sobbing out, "But I don't *want* to!"

When that conversation ended—Mom handed the phone's receiver back to Dad without looking at him; Dad thanked the Dahlgrens and promised to keep them posted, and hung up—I went and stood by Mom's chair. She was still sobbing, shaking, but maybe quieting down a little. I knew I was chiming in at the wrong moment, but I said this to her:

"Mom, listen: I don't want you to think I'm being selfish, but please let's do it. It's good for Dad and it's good for the rest of us too. If we have a chance to get out of here... Seriously, I can't take it anymore. The other kids. I have to get away from here. I don't know if I could stand another year here."

Then I had an inspired notion: to up the ante a bit.

"Mom, I'd rather die than spend another year with those kids. I'd rather kill myself."

I won't swear that I was exaggerating, when I said that. Yeah, I had suicidal thoughts; I have them still. I have had them since I was quite little. But this was the first time I had talked seriously about killing myself, and as I said it, it occurred to me that I wouldn't put it past myself: committing suicide if I had to spend another year at that school, with those kids.

Here had come this all-of-a-sudden opportunity to get out of Waukoshowoc. Let me tell you, when I saw it staring me in the face—barely within the possibility of realization—I was thrilled. When it looked as though Mom might derail it, I almost lost my shit, for fear that she would succeed.

Anyway, when I said, "I'd rather kill myself," Mom keened, *"All right!"* from behind her hands.

"I guess I'm out-voted." (Mark was outside, playing. I don't know how he would have voted.) "Maybe I'm crazy. Maybe I should check myself into the loony bin."

"Nobody's saying that," Dad said. He was obviously trying to sound conciliatory. "But our boy does make a good point. It'll benefit the whole family. In different ways."

Mom sniffled.

Whatever else got said, Mom gave in. For the following week, she was throwing up constantly. Couldn't keep food down. But she finally accepted the situation (I knew she'd accepted it when she gave the piano away, to one of our neighbors), and we moved, in the late summer of 1962, to State City.

This, I told myself, would be relief. That is, I couldn't actually feel relief till we had made the move, but I could look forward to it. State City—because it wasn't Waukoshowoc—sounded like Oz, or Eldorado, or Paradise. It would be an opportunity to start with a clean slate in a new place, where nobody knew me and nobody knew that I sucked.

Combined with that anticipation was terror: that somehow or other, Mom would prevent us from moving after all.

The few nights before we left Waukoshowoc, I had nightmares that I would be left behind there, to finish up my schooling. On the night before we moved, I was seized with a panic attack: this awful clutching feeling in my chest. I almost got out of bed and begged my parents to stay—the way a long-term prisoner, I have been told, will panic on the eve of his release, and beg to be kept confined. But in the morning I was ready to go—and I was afraid that for some reason we wouldn't.

Mom seemed okay. The movers showed up early that morning, and got our stuff out of that house real fast. At nine o'clock or so, the four of us piled into Dad's Ford Customline. When he started the engine, Mom said, "Steve, that doesn't sound right. Do you think we ought to have somebody look at it?" The car sounded the same as always, to me, and evidently it did to Dad, too, because that's what he said.

Mom said, "What if something were to go wrong while we're on the road? Steve, please let's get it looked at."

Dad said, "It'll be fine," just a bit sharply, and we took off. It wasn't till about half an hour later, when we were definitely on the highway and headed south, that I finally breathed easy. I almost said aloud, "We've escaped."

That night, we were in State City, Iowa. We spent that night in a motel; our stuff arrived the following day.

State City itself, I liked, as soon as we arrived there. It was cosmopolitan, for a town of something like 35,000 people. (That was then; it's about 80,000 now.) State City is a university town—and in the early 1960s, State University's School of Music was starting to establish itself as one of the best in the country. Its School of Art was pretty strong, too. State University had plenty of sports, and creative arts, and a lot of oddball academic types. The university made State City the kind of town it was.

But while I liked State City, at first sight, the house we moved into was another matter. I had hoped that we would have a bigger house in State City: one where Mark and I could each have our own room. As it turned out, though, we moved into what Mom and Dad told us would be a temporary residence, a stopgap till we could find something that was "just right."

It turned out to be another starter home, only slightly bigger than the one we had left: one of those three-bedroom-one-bath tract houses with a one-car garage and a small yard, in an all-residential neighborhood, where the nearest grocery store or gas station was a good mile off. Dad needed the tiny third bedroom for a home office, and the basement was unfinished, so Mark and I ended up sharing a bedroom again.

Once we were established in that house, Mom refused ever to move. She would talk about it; she would read the ads in *The State City Examiner*; she would even talk to realtors about this or that possibility. But it was all a sham. My parents stayed in that house till they died.

I offered to let Mark have the bedroom. I would sleep in the basement, and be glad of it. But Mom wouldn't allow that. The basement, she said, was cold and damp and too far from the house's one bathroom.

Still, from the beginning, for as long as I lived in that house, I spent a lot of time in the basement. It consisted of a bare concrete floor and walls, wooden support beams, furnace, boiler,

washer, and dryer, plus whatever junk we stored down there—
but it was bigger than the basement in Waukoshowoc. It had a
spacious floor where I could lay out my APBA Baseball game or
whatever other projects I was working on. It was cool and dark,
in the summer, and I didn't have to see anyone unless Mom came
down to do the laundry. The basement floor became my office.

I know, I know, it's like not having a TV: If nothing worse
ever happened to me than sharing a bedroom with my brother,
I don't have a lot to complain about. But I also know that Mark
and I should not have had to share a bedroom. We wouldn't have
had to, if Mom hadn't been crazy. I know: I'm selfish, and a bad
person, for even having such thoughts.

Mom and Dad seemed to settle into State City just fine. Dad
would come home at night looking and sounding pretty happy
with his new situation, and he'd tell us funny stories about the
people he worked with. Mom got a car of her own, a 1962 Ford
Fairlane, although she mentioned more than once that she felt a
little embarrassed about driving a spanking new car.

"All cars were new once," I told her.

"That's true," Mom said. "Maybe I could kick it a few times,
put some dents in it." I swear it took me a few seconds to understand that she was kidding.

I was going to start the ninth grade, that fall, at Southside
Junior High. I resolved that whenever I was interacting with
other kids, whether at school or elsewhere, I would blend into
the walls as much as possible. I told myself that in Waukoshowoc, I had made a big mistake—starting from when I was a
little kid—by standing out; making myself noticeable through my
quirkiness; revealing my defects. This time, my orders to myself
were clear: make no waves; make no impression on anyone;
speak to others as little as possible; hope that nobody ever gave
me a moment's thought—then move on to State City High
School the following year with no extra baggage.

I was getting my growth. I was at that phase that a boy goes through when he shoots up in height, when his bones are lengthening and he feels exhausted all the time—but I noticed that as I was getting taller, my weight was staying pretty much the same, so while I was still a heavy kid, I was no longer actually fat. I was almost normal-looking, except that now, I was tall for my age. I got to six-foot-three when I finally stopped growing, when I was eighteen or so. Already at age fourteen I was over six feet—and thus noticeable, which worried me a little.

Another concern was that since I was in ninth grade, and Mark was in seventh, we would be attending the same school for the first time since I had got out of elementary school. So my objective was not only to stay out of everyone else's way, as a general thing, but to stay out of Mark's way, specifically. For his sake as well as for mine. I didn't want to put myself in a position where Mark could show me up—because he was so obviously a better specimen than I was—but I also didn't want to handicap Mark, by tainting him with any association with me. I was sure that I would put Mark at a disadvantage if he had to account to the other kids for being my brother.

So, with no spoken agreement—indeed, we never mentioned it to each other—Mark and I went our separate ways that year. I avoided Mark at school, and I don't believe we even walked to and from school together that year, except for the first day. I would have to ask Mark, and I'm not going to, but I'm guessing he was just as glad.

It seemed to work well enough. I was less miserable, our first year in State City, than I had been in Waukoshowoc. I didn't make many friends—but at the same time I don't think I revealed myself as a total freak.

# 5 SOUTHSIDE JUNIOR HIGH

I still hated the way I looked. I still hated being photographed. Above all, I hated being photographed alongside Mark, who was skinny and wiry and nowhere near as repulsive-looking as I was. But our parents insisted on taking a photo of the two of us together, on the first day of school, every year.

So there I was on the day after Labor Day, 1962, dressed a little more neatly than on any other day of the school year, holding an unsullied three-ring notebook, standing next to Mark on the front lawn of our new home in State City, forcing myself to smile while Dad snapped two pictures of us (an extra, in case the first didn't turn out).

As this was happening, I looked across the street at the larger split-level grey house directly facing us, from which two girls—or a girl and a woman; I couldn't immediately tell which it was—were emerging through the front door. One of them looked to be about my age. From a distance I could tell that she was thin, with long, straight dark brown hair and bangs in front, and a sallow complexion. She wore a plain dark blue skirt with a white blouse sloppily tucked into it, bobby sox, and mary janes.

The other one appeared definitely older—even if she was a little shorter than the dark girl. She had a young face; she was slender like a teenager; but she was wearing a maroon dress that looked much too grown-up and business for school. She had her hair waved, and she carried a black patent leather purse, like a grown woman. She was of entirely different coloration from the other girl: reddish-blonde hair, pink cheeks. She appeared the more animated of the two. In that first glance, I could see that she was remarkably light on her feet. Even in the ordinary act of stepping off her front porch, she appeared almost to be dancing rather than walking.

As the two girls reached the sidewalk, the not-quite-blonde-not-quite-redhead embraced the younger girl and kissed her on the cheek. Then this girl/woman turned to her left, and the dark girl turned to her right, and they walked off in opposite directions.

The dark one was walking in the same direction that Mark and I were, and before we were more than a few steps away from our house I noticed her glancing across at us. She had exceptionally large eyes, with dark circles under them and heavy lids above them, which made her look like a lizard. I don't mean to be cruel in describing her. I'm just trying to be honest, because if you're not honest, you shouldn't write memoir.

When we had reached the corner of our street, the girl waved to us to stop, and crossed over to us.

When she'd reached us, she said, "We live across the street from each other, apparently." She slightly over-enunciated. "My name's Charity Childress."

"I'm Andrew Palinkas," I said, and I emphasized "Andrew" the least bit so that she wouldn't assume "Andy"—not that most people took that little hint—and I added, "This is my brother Mark," which I suppose anybody else would consider a perfectly normal way for an elder brother to introduce his sibling, but I felt almost presumptuous introducing Mark, as though I were asserting a primogeniture to which I had no right.

Southside Junior High was only about a half-mile, or maybe a little more, from where we lived. It was a pretty neighborhood we were walking through, with these nicely kept lawns and little flower gardens up next to the houses: all quiet and respectable and middle-American.

Charity and I exchanged basic information as we walked. Mark said very little, if anything. Charity Childress was entering ninth grade, as I was. Her family had moved to State City a year before; her father was a professor in the Art department at State University.

"You might find that Southside Junior High is not the most congenial environment," she said. "People tend to group together in cliques, and it's hard to break into them—even if you wanted to, which I don't."

Charity's accent sounded peculiar to me. It wasn't un-American at all—you couldn't call it British—but it wasn't Midwestern. It sounded studied, affected. "Rather" came out as "rah-ther," and "idea" as "idear."

I wanted to ask Charity who was the young woman was, whom she had been kissing, but I didn't think it would be polite to demand information. I figured Charity would tell me when she was ready to. The two of them looked nothing alike, so at first it didn't occur to me that they could have been sisters. The older one had looked so much more a young woman than a girl that I wondered whether she might be Charity's tutor, or a governess of some kind—as though any fourteen-year-old girl in Iowa in the 1960s would have had a governess.

"Are you two the only children in your family?" Charity asked me.

I bristled internally at the term "children," but I forced myself to smile.

"In a manner of speaking."

"We are, too. My sister and I are, I mean."

Partly, my mind was still on the backstory I was creating for that young woman. "Was that your sister... saying goodbye to you?" (I wanted to say, "You look nothing like her," but I wasn't sure that that was quite the thing to say, so I didn't.)

"Yes. She's so beautiful, isn't she?"

§

Southside Junior High was a sprawling two-story concrete building, built in that mid-twentieth-century institutional style, with a parking lot to one side and a playing field on the other. Many of the students were milling about outside the main entrance. Since neither Mark nor I knew anybody, we went directly into the building, where a stenciled cardboard sign in the main entrance-way directed the seventh graders to a special orientation assembly in the gym. Mark split off from me and Charity.

My first-hour class was English, in room 116, according to the schedule I had received in the mail the previous week, so that's where I headed. Charity was still with me.

"Have you got English first hour too? That's my favorite subject." Charity gave me a big sidelong smile as though she were inviting some kind of conspiracy. "Do you like poetry?"

"Not really. I don't know much about it."

"I'm a writer," Charity said. "I love to write poetry. I'm going to be a journalist when I grow up. Do you know what you're going to be yet?"

"A bum."

I was already uncomfortable, walking with this awkward and plain girl. I hoped she wouldn't attach herself to me right away—but naturally she sat down right next to me in first-hour English.

I began one other long-term acquaintance on that first day of ninth grade, although it was several days before I spoke to him. My first encounter with Mitch Rosen was a mimeographed sheet that was handed out to all the ninth-graders during home-room period on that first day: "A Message From Your Class President."

This is our last year at Southside, so set
an example for the younger kids. I know the

temptation is hard to resist, ha-ha, but
don't be as rough on the seventh-graders as
the ninth-graders were on you two years ago.
See what you can do <u>for</u> them rather than <u>to</u>
them, and see what you can do to give back
to the school in other ways. And keep up
your studies! Your grades are really going
to start to matter, now, and they will matter even more when we get to State City High
next year. So buckle down and get to work--
but let's have fun!

I wasn't actually introduced to Mitch Rosen. I didn't have a single class with him all that year. But at lunch in the cafeteria that first day I set down my tray at one of the long tables—this one was mostly occupied by a group of boys who looked like ninth-graders, all of them utter strangers to me, of course—and I heard someone near me call, "Hey, Rosen." I looked up to see who responded. Rosen was tall—almost as tall as I was. He had curly black hair and a hooked nose. He was a good-looking kid. He smiled a lot and had big shiny white teeth. His clothes were that bit nicer than the other kids', though not so much better as to stick out. Pressed chinos and a pastel-colored short-sleeved but-ton-down shirt.

He sat down not far from me—across the table and a couple of people over. I immediately got the impression that he was holding court. I knew already that he was the class president. It's nothing you can easily describe, but you can tell when other kids defer to a leader. When they make a statement, they glance over at him to see if he smiles or nods. If they're in doubt about some-thing, he's the first guy they'll ask for clarification.

Rosen looked nice. Friendly and benign: I suppose those would be the right words. He was athletically built, lean, but not tough-looking. Certainly not mean-looking. He didn't act pomp-ous at all, or throw his weight around. He just sat relaxed and confident in the role of "first among equals."

I said nothing at the lunch table that first day; I just watched and listened. Rosen didn't say much either, although he smiled and nodded a lot. Mainly he let the conversation go on around him, only occasionally putting in a comment or a laugh.

I didn't say anything at lunch the next few days, either, but the vicinity of Mitch Rosen appeared to be where most of the action was, so I made a point of sitting near his crowd—this group of apparently élite boys—to listen and observe, to get an idea of what kind of people I would have to deal with at this school. In return for my silence, none of these other boys acknowledged me. I was fine with that. Truth to tell, I was staying quiet for fear of drawing attention to myself. I was afraid that if I were acknowledged, it would only be to attack me or make fun of me or tell me they didn't want me sitting with them.

It must have been the second week of that first year that I set my tray down near Rosen, as usual, and this time he smiled at me and said, "Hi, Gabby."

That shocked me for an instant, because my middle name is Gabor—the Hungarian for Gabriel—and I lived in fear that these kids would find out and call me Zsa Zsa or "Dahling" with that burlesque accent, which was what had happened in Waukoshowoc. It took me a second or two to realize that Rosen had just given me a nickname—indeed, the traditional nickname for a silent person. He obviously meant to be friendly, so I didn't take offense.

"Andy Palinkas, right?" No doubt he made it his business to learn names.

He turned to the other kids sitting nearby. He said, "This guy looks like he's thinking about blowing up the school, doesn't he?" I must have had a somewhat cold, glowering aspect; at any rate, since I was naturally suspicious of other people I never made much effort to look friendly. "What's the story, Gabby?" Rosen grinned at me again, clearly inviting me, so I had to talk.

"Well, what do you want to know?" I was wary. "I just got here. From Wisconsin."

"Packers fan, eh? Good for you. Gosh, they just completely *dominated* last year. But I like the Lions this year. They got Plum from the Browns; they got the defense. Should be a good fight between them and the Packers."

"Yeah, it should," I said. "We've got the defense too. And you can never forget about the Bears."

"Hey, too bad about the Braves this year," Rosen said. "They're good. Too many other good teams, though. Looks like the Dodgers are gonna do it. That's my team. If they can get along without Koufax. I guess they lost him for the season—but he was a big surprise, wasn't he? He's my favorite."

"Yeah, Koufax," I agreed. I forced myself to say a little more, to show that I was willing to meet Rosen halfway. "He could be huge. If they can fix that finger of his, he ought to win twenty next year."

"Gabby" I was, from then on, as far as Rosen was concerned. Later, he would find that I could talk plenty.


# 6 THE CHILDRESS FAMILY

Rosen and I never became real friends. We pretty much lost interest in each other after that initial conversation. I remained on the periphery of that lunchtime clique. I would sit near, but only occasionally and briefly would I join the conversation. Rosen and I would say "Hey" to each other when we passed in the hallways, but that was about it. In ninth grade I hardly talked to anyone.

Sometimes Charity and I walked together to and from school. I was reluctant to walk with her because I was afraid the

other kids would assume we were a couple. But they didn't. Probably nobody noticed. I usually enjoyed the conversations we
would have as we walked. Charity was bright, anyway, and we
could keep up with each other intellectually.

I anticipated that Mark would start kidding me about spending time with Charity. He never did; never mentioned it at all—
but out of that fear, I once said to him, off-hand, as we were
both in our room one evening, "You know, Charity isn't my girlfriend." Mark didn't look up from the chess problem he was
studying. He shrugged, and said, "What do I care?"

Not that I would have minded having a girlfriend. But boys
matured a little later, in the early 1960s, than they do now. Most
of the boys my age were starting to notice girls, but most of us
still hadn't worked up the nerve to approach a girl in a serious
way. In that respect, at least, I was pretty normal. I was starting
to take an interest in girls—real girls, as opposed to Ava Gardner
or Brigitte Bardot—but only theoretically.

I didn't find Charity at all attractive, and I didn't want anybody else to think I had such poor taste. I don't mean to say that
Charity was hideous. She was what old women would call "inter-
esting-looking." Then there was the way she dressed. Not dirty:
Her clothes and her person were always clean. But she put herself together like she didn't care. Or almost like she was self-
consciously dressing as sloppily as she could get away with. In
those days, girls still had to wear skirts to school, and Charity did,
but they would be wrinkled almost as though she had slept on
them to create wrinkles. She wore thick white socks instead of
nylons—which a lot of other girls her age did, too, but Charity
would seldom bother to pull hers up all the way, or ensure that
they were the same length, and she wasn't religious about shaving
her legs.

Charity did have one extremely attractive blouse that she
would wear to school about once a week: silk, of blue and silver

paisley. Those weren't her colors, not with her dark brown hair and yellowish skin, but the blouse was a special piece for her, she told me, because her sister Grace had made it for her.

Charity and I had that in common: a superior sibling. But Grace was older than Charity, not younger, as Mark was, which made it not quite as bad for Charity as it was for me.

I only ever saw Grace from a distance, at first, because every weekday morning Grace and Charity would walk off in opposite directions. It was still difficult for me to get my head around the idea that Grace and Charity were sisters, because physically the two of them were so different. The only point of similarity was the mouth. They both had exceptionally wide smiles that ended with an odd little tooth-sucking pursing of the lips. They were both slender, but Charity was a stick, while Grace had some slight curves. Charity usually dressed any old how, while Grace always put herself together perfectly.

I don't just remember that Grace wore those tailored skirts and dresses; I remember some of the specific garments. Always high heels, on school days, and light makeup, and she usually had her hair waved, or she wore it in a simple updo. After that first day, I usually saw Grace carrying one of those green Ivy League-style bookbags over her shoulder as she left her house in the morning, as Charity did, and I suspected that maybe Grace was a college student or even a schoolteacher—living with her parents because she wasn't married yet, as some young women did, back then. Grace was small, and she had the face of a teenager (including a zit or two, sometimes) but otherwise she looked grown-up enough to have been a teacher.

I wasn't introduced to Grace that year, but she would always wave to me if we happened to come out of our front doors at the same time, or if we saw each other coming home in the afternoons. I don't think Grace and I ever exchanged a word beyond "Hi" that year, but she would always give me a big smile along with the wave, and the first time she did that, I saw the braces on her teeth and concluded that she almost certainly was still a high school student.

Charity and I had known each other for a few weeks before I asked her off-hand about her sister, and that's when she told me that Grace was two years ahead of us: a junior at State City High. She mentioned that Grace was actually just one year older than we were—so she would have been fifteen at that time—but she had been skipped ahead a year—gone straight from kindergarten to second grade—because she was so intelligent.

Charity didn't talk about Grace a lot—at least not to me—but when she did, it would be to report another of her sister's accomplishments. She mentioned several times what a wonderful dancer Grace was, and how she was going to be a professional ballerina. Grace was also a terrific flute-player, according to Charity; she played piano and violin besides; she made all her own clothes. She knew how to spin, weave, sew, and knit; she was as good a cook as her mother and would probably be even better before long.

One thing Charity said about Grace, that I remember especially vividly (and I'll never forget the tone of her voice, or the look on her face, when she said it, as though she were talking about an imaginary ideal, almost):

"Grace is perfect. I wish I could be her."

Charity told me she was learning to play the clarinet, but she didn't think she was any good.

"I don't like anything as much as writing," she said, "and I'm fairly good at that. Thank goodness, Grace doesn't show me anything she writes. I'd probably get a complex about that, too.

"I write essays and short stories, mostly. I had an article published in *Jack and Jill* when I was nine, and one in *Golden Magazine* when I was eleven. My parents teach me. They're much better than any English teacher I've ever had."

Charity wrote for the Southside Junior High newspaper—and she told me about the monthly newspaper that she published just for her family: *The Childress Chronicle*.

I read about Charity and Grace's parents before I met them. Charity, one morning on the way to school, presented me with a copy of *The Childress Chronicle*, plus a few of her poems.

*The Childress Chronicle* was four sheets of plain typing paper, printed in aniline purple ink, evidently from a ditto machine, and stapled together: a newsletter rather than a newspaper. The copy was produced on an ordinary typewriter, but the mast-head and the headlines were of various styles of calligraphy: Gothic, Italic, others. I supposed that Mr. Childress supplied Charity with the dittomasters and ran them through the machine at his office. Charity confessed that Grace had done the headlines for her.

"Grace is a wonderful calligrapher. She did all that with a stylus. She did a few of the illustrations, too. I expect you can tell which ones."

I still have that copy of *The Childress Chronicle*. Or rather, my parents had it, stowed away in one of those boxes in their basement, and I reclaimed it when I was cleaning out their house a few years ago.

*The Childress Chronicle* was much like any other family newsletter that a child might produce—although with much better production values, thanks to Grace's calligraphy and illustrations, and Charity's reporting, which I thought was well-written indeed, as she had suggested it would be. Mostly it was brief articles about anything noteworthy that any of the Childresses had done in the past month.

"Professor Joseph Childress starts his second year as Chairman of the Art department at State University this fall. In addition to his duties as head of the department, he teaches..."

"Rae Childress looks forward to an exciting political campaign! She's Committeewoman of the Democratic Party in State

City's 19th precinct, and she will coordinate local efforts for Harold Hughes for Governor and E.B. Smith for Senator..."

Those were the two lead stories. It struck me that in this particular edition, anyway, there were no stories about Charity herself except for a mention that she was helping her mother stuff envelopes and knock on doors for the Democrats. However, she did include an uninspiring editorial, preaching to the choir, parroting some broad and essentially meaningless slogans that purported to prove that the Democrats were the party to vote for. This surprised me a little. It seemed to me that Charity might have brought some original thought to this topic. But maybe there wasn't any political debate in that household. Maybe she was just told, at home, what to believe. At any rate, this editorial was clearly calculated to please at least one of her parents.

*The Childress Chronicle* included a page-long feature on Grace—written in interview format—in which Grace described her ballet lessons and talked about her goals for the coming fall. The third page contained the main story. It was headlined, "Joseph And Ra'el: The Greatest Love Story Ever" with a sub-head that read, "Part IV: The Toughest Test Of Our Marriage".

```
"The toughest test of our marriage
would have to have been World War II,"
says Ra'el Childress.  "Having our two
daughters was our greatest joy, but we
almost missed out on that because of
the war."
     "It's true," says Joseph Chil-
dress.  "The war almost wrecked our
marriage--not because I was in danger
of being killed, but simply because I
was obliged to serve."
     "Your father was and is a Quaker,
and a pacifist, and he considered
claiming the exemption he was entitled
to as a 'cradle Quaker,'" says Mrs.
Childress.  "I understood that he
```

wanted to take a principled stand, but
I told him I would be disappointed if
he did.  This was a war against Hitler,
and I'm Jewish by birth, as you know,
so you can imagine that I felt very
strongly about it."

"There are times when you have to
compromise," says Professor Childress.
"Your mother had reason to believe that
claiming the exemption would be for one
thing pointless and for another would
be something I would regret later in
life. And she was correct.  I was qual-
ified for a commission--that is, I
could enter the service as an officer--
so I went to Officer Candidate School."

Professor Childress joined the
Army intelligence services and worked
with secret information to help the Al-
lies win World War II.  He still isn't
allowed by the government to talk about
most of what he did.  He and Mrs. Childress were apart for more than two
years from the beginning of 1943 to
late 1945.

"It was rough," he now admits.
"Your mother and I had serious disa-
greements about whether or not I should
serve.  But what sustained me was the
thought that I was fighting to defend
my wife, and whatever children we might
have together after the war."

"In the long run," says Mrs. Childress, "the war made me admire your father more than ever.  I was never so
proud of him as when he was wearing his
uniform and fighting against Nazism and
hatred.  His military service made our
marriage much stronger than it had
been."


Professor Childress was one of the handsomest men I have ever
seen. Evidently Grace got most of her looks from him, while

Charity favored her mother more. Dr. Childress was rather short—maybe five-six—and slender, blue-eyed, blond-haired, with chiseled features. I thought of him as English-looking, but maybe I thought his features were English because he was English in his manner.

He looked like a caricature of the tweedy East Coast professor type that I had only ever read about in books. He was the first man I ever saw wearing an ascot. (And those ascots looked great on him.) He wore his hair a bit longer than was normal for that time and place, and Mom explained that that was because he was from Back East where men wore their hair longer, like the English. Dr. Childress talked a little bit like an Englishman, although now I know that he had a Boston Brahmin accent.

I didn't know much about what his relationship with his children was like. Now that I think of it, I don't recall that I ever saw him interacting with Grace or Charity except briefly and minimally. On the very few occasions, over the next few years, when I was in the company of that whole family at once, I can only remember one time when he said a word to either of his children. I can hardly remember him speaking to his wife, either. From what his daughters told me about him, it's clear that he did have conversations, and engage in activities, with each of them, and that they appreciated and admired him—but I got the impression that they admired him at a distance.

He didn't speak to me or to Mark, either, beyond a bare greeting. He'd give us a nod or a wave if he happened to see us outside. I'm positive he never set foot in our house. For that first year, at least, I don't think he ever had more than the briefest conversation with either of my parents.

I sometimes thought I would like to get acquainted with Dr. Childress, but I had no idea of how to approach him. I couldn't get up the nerve to ask Charity to introduce me to him properly. I had some small artistic ambitions—I liked to draw, anyway, and

I designed baseball uniforms and ballparks—but I knew I wasn't good. I would have liked to ask a real art professor for guidance, and maybe for his opinions of my work, but I was afraid of looking like some kind of fool if I proposed such a thing.

Dr. Childress was more forthcoming with my mother. Right from the start, if he saw Mom, he would call across the street, "Good morning, Paivi Palinkas! All's well, I hope?" in what struck me as a surprisingly grand, breezy voice. Mom would giggle, every time. I could tell that she was a tiny bit taken with him. But Mom never had much to do with him, because—again, this is largely conjecture here, because I don't know—it appeared to me that he and Mrs. Childress mostly led separate lives. It was Mrs. Childress who cultivated Mom's acquaintance.

Women tended to age faster in those days than they do now. Mrs. Childress was only a year or two older than my mother, but she looked considerably older. She had a noticeably wide mouth—that's where Grace and Charity got it from—and wiry, frizzy, greying black hair. Her face was a bit lizard-like, as Charity's was, and a bit ape-like besides.

She was the same height as her husband, and probably outweighed him. She tended to wear gingham housedresses, unless she were going out, in which case she would wear brightly colored dresses and large, broad-brimmed picture hats: red, purple, dark green. She had that deep smoker's voice, and a heavy New York Jewish accent: "sor" for "saw"; "oal" for "all"; "hara" for "horror." When I heard it, I realized that Charity's accent was an amalgam of how her two parents spoke.

Charity once told me, "My mother was so beautiful when she was young. Of course she still is [she was not], but she was such a knockout judging from her old pictures."

Charity took a breath and a sigh, and went on. "Apparently neither of their parents approved of the marriage... well, they were different religions and all. And I guess my father's parents

**75**

felt that she would lead him into a way of life that was... rather less conventional than they would have liked. And my mother's parents, on the other hand, they felt that my mother was somehow betraying her birthright. I think it's such a romantic story, don't you?"

Maybe it was, but it seemed to me at the time that the romance had worn off long ago. I never saw Charity's parents being physically affectionate. Come to think of it, I rarely saw them even talking with each other, save for a couple of memorable occasions. The impression I had—from observing them, from what I could tell of their body language—was that they were being decorous with each other, respectful, but without any noticeable warmth.

My parents would hug each other now and then, or sit close together on the sofa. Maybe Dr. and Mrs. Childress did so in private, too, but it was something I couldn't imagine them doing. Long ago, I supposed, they must have been attracted to each other because they were tantalized by the danger inherent in going against their parents. But by this time, it seemed to me, they didn't have a lot in common except for their daughters—and evidently their daughters were enough to sustain the marriage.

Just by the way, religion was never any kind of an issue in our family. Mom's parents came from Lutheran stock, but they had raised her without any religion. Dad had been baptized Roman Catholic, but he never discussed Catholicism. We never went to church; Mark and I never had any formal religious instruction. So far as I know, neither set of grandparents had had any problems with Mom and Dad getting married.

I often noticed nice cooking smells coming from across the street. Charity told me her mother was a pretty serious cook—and as I got to know her over the years I discovered that Mrs. Childress was good at quite a lot of things. She wasn't without her positive qualities. Rae Childress wasn't my sort, though. I didn't like her.

She talked loudly. She didn't hesitate to express her opinion on any given subject—only it was usually not an opinion, but the Received Wisdom of Ra'el Milstein Childress. Her favorite response to anyone else's opinion was, "Stuff and nonsense!"

I suspect that Mrs. Childress got on my mother's bad side right away—even if Mom didn't admit it to herself—when she brought us over a cake by way of introduction. It was still September of 1962, a day or two after Charity had shown me the latest edition of *The Childress Chronicle*. I came home from school that day to the smell of cigarette smoke in our living room—a smell I have always loved, perversely—so I knew there had been company, since my parents didn't smoke.

When I walked into the kitchen and asked who it had been, Mom told me, "Mrs. Childress, from across the street. She brought us a cake." And I swear Mom looked a little put-out, as though it annoyed her that she would have to serve us this nice rich dessert.

Mom was strange about food. If she found that one of us liked a particular dish—not just me—it would be a long time before we saw it on the table again. If a neighbor brought us a cake or something—and I'm pretty sure it happened with this particular cake too—she would throw it out after a couple days, when there was still a good bit left of it. She would claim "it was stale," but in reality, I'm convinced, she would throw it out to prevent her fat son from eating too much of it.

Anyway, on this occasion, Mom went on, "I think she was trying to recruit us. I mean, sure, she was partly just being neighborly and trying to make us feel welcome, but practically the first thing she asked me after I'd invited her inside was, 'Are you Democrats?'"

Which we were; at least, my parents were. My first political memory was the Presidential election of 1956. That was when Dwight Eisenhower was running for his second term, against Adlai Stevenson, and I was eight years old. My parents were big for Stevenson. It was a serious matter to them.

I had seen Eisenhower's picture in the papers. He looked like a nice old man. I asked Mom, at dinner one night, "Why don't you like him?" Mom said, "Oh, he's not so bad. He's just not that bright. Stevenson is so much more intelligent. He seems like he knows what's going on. Besides, I don't dislike Eisenhower so much as I can't stand Nixon." (Richard Nixon, who was Eisenhower's Vice President.)

Why could she not stand Nixon?

"Well, because many years ago—right around when you were born—Nixon went after this man named Alger Hiss, and accused him of being a Communist. And Alger Hiss was a... well, a very well-thought-of, and educated, and respectable young man, and Nixon accused him of spying for the Russians, and Hiss ended up going to jail. I've never been able to stand Nixon ever since then."

Dad looked like he didn't want to contradict, but I suppose he felt he had to. "But, honey, Hiss was guilty."

Mom scoffed, "Oh, well," as though Hiss's guilt were of no consequence whatever—or at least ought to be overlooked for the sake of the larger point, whatever that might have been.

I remember now that I told that story to Charity, on the way home from school, the very day after her mother had brought us over that cake—because I had to mention that I had enjoyed the cake. I added, "Apparently your mom was trying to recruit my mom." Charity asked me, in response, whether my family was at all politically inclined.

"So I suppose you're interested in politics too?" Charity asked me as we walked.

"Not really," I said. "I don't know much about the issues. But getting elected to public office might be neat."

"Were you involved in school politics at all? Back in Wisconsin? Are you planning to run for anything here? Like maybe Student Senate, when we get to City High?"

We were approaching our respective houses. Ordinarily we would have split up, but on this day Charity and I ended up sitting on the Childress front stoop to continue the conversation.

"I don't think so," I replied. "I almost did, once, when I was in—it must have been fourth grade, so I'd have been nine years old—and the teacher brought up the concept of class officers. Well, being class president sounded like fun. If only for the prestige of it. I mean, in fourth grade, class president doesn't get to do anything except be the class snitch—you know, he's supposed to tattle to the teacher if anyone misbehaves while she's out of the room. Not much to it besides that.

"But the prestige appealed to me. You know, just the idea of getting some sort of recognition from my classmates. Anyway, I came home from school that day and I told Mom, 'We're going to be electing class officers this week!' All excited, right? And do you know what was my mother's immediate reaction? The very first words out of her mouth? She gave me this... *pitying* look—like she was, I don't know, like she had *contempt* for me—and she said, 'I hope you don't vote for yourself, Andy.'"

Charity stared at me. Then she said—almost whispered—"What a strange, strange thing to say to your child!"

"Well, that's my mother. I haven't had much to do with politics, since then."

"Grace and my father are pretty apolitical too," Charity said. "My mother and I have all the political energy in the family. I love working with her on this campaign. Two years ago I was helping her go door-to-door for Kennedy. That was so exciting!"

"My parents were all for Kennedy too."

"But not you?" Charity smiled a little as she asked that question, as though she knew the answer and couldn't decide whether to be put off by it, or amused, or interested in my reasons if I had any.

"I was neutral," I said. "I tried to understand why my parents were so crazy about Kennedy, and why they didn't like Nixon, but as far as I could tell, it pretty much came down to personalities, didn't it? Kennedy is just a lot more charming than Nixon. And better looking, of course."

"You might say that," said Charity.

"I caught hell from my mom when I said that to her. She got real upset with me. She was all, 'Oh, how can you say that? There's a night and day difference between those two!'"

Charity smiled again.

"Yeah," I said, "and when I asked her to explain what that difference was, specifically, between Kennedy and Nixon, she just went, 'Oh, well,' like she does when she can't think of anything. And then—this conversation took place at the dinner table—for the rest of the meal, she'd look over at me, and go 'Tsk!' every couple of minutes."

Now Charity looked serious.

"You don't like your mother, do you?"

I didn't say anything.

"I'm sorry," Charity said. "I should learn not to ask questions like that if I'm going to be a reporter."

What I probably would have told Charity, if that conversation had continued, was that I had felt sorry for Nixon, back when he ran against Kennedy. I had had the feeling that a lot of people were supporting Kennedy because of his looks, and his charm. He was charming, no question about it. Nixon probably had got picked on at school too, when he was little.

§

It was the following summer—1963, the summer before I started tenth grade—when I began to pay more attention to the rest of the world.

I didn't see a lot of the Childress family that summer. In June, they all took off for a month-long vacation Back East. Charity told me they were going to see her mother's family in New York and her father's in Massachusetts, and then they would spend a few weeks on Cape Cod. Then in July my family took the "grand-parents' route," too, visiting the Dahlgrens in suburban Minneapolis and the Palinkases in Pittsburgh. For the rest of summer vacation, I was pretty occupied catching up on my APBA Baseball and my other related projects, plus reading.

While I was reading books or "sitting around pitching dice," Mark was absent for much of the day, most days. He had friends he spent time with: swimming at the municipal pool, or riding their bicycles. I didn't care to ask him for an accounting. I figured if he told me what he had been doing, it would only depress me. And he practiced his accordion for hours a day.

I used to hear music from the Childress house, too, that spring and summer when the weather was warmer and the family was home. I learned from Charity that it was usually her father, playing piano. Sometimes I would hear him accompanying a flute that sounded smoothly and confidently played—baroque tunes mostly, so far as I could tell. Sometimes I would hear more tentative, erratic sounds from a clarinet, playing scales over and over again, or elementary melodies.

Some mornings, that summer, I would see Grace skipping out of the house wearing a cotton shift over a leotard—on her way to a ballet lesson, evidently—but on other days I don't think I ever saw her in anything that could be called casual. She never wore jeans, shorts, or pants of any kind. Sometimes she would wear a linen or seersucker skirt and white blouse, but more often a sun-dress—usually in a pastel color to set off her complexion.

She usually had her hair up, in a bun or a French twist. High heels unless she was wearing her ballet slippers. I certainly never saw Grace in tennis shoes, and I don't recall ever seeing her without makeup. Charity usually wore shorts and a halter-type blouse, that summer—the halter somehow emphasized the fact that she barely had any breasts at all—and her hair hung straight, unless it was tangled.

George Orwell wrote that when you reach a certain age—maybe fifty or so—you start thinking about things that you saw or heard in your youth that you'll never see or hear again. A restaurant where most of the customers are happily smoking. A metal bell clanging to let you know that you have a phone call. A teenaged girl wearing a demure, conservative pastel sun-dress with high heels.

I bet you'll never see a "mom and pop" drugstore again, either—by which I mean a single, family-owned drugstore, as opposed to a chain like Walgreen's or CVS. I have no way of knowing if the last one in the United States has closed down, but I would bet there are hardly any left.

As far as I know, the last independent drugstore in State City was Roy's, which was a tiny store: much, much smaller than the big chains that you see today. Roy's stayed in business in the heart of downtown State City for many years because it specialized in products and services that the bigger drugstores couldn't or wouldn't provide. Old Mr. Roy would custom-mix perfumes and grooming products; he could handle any kind of special orders. If you wanted a particular type of hair tonic, Charlie Roy would know that the very best of its type was manufactured in tiny artisan batches in a private home in Timbuktu—and he knew the address, and could buy it for you.

Roy's also carried—or could order—magazines and newspapers from almost anywhere in the world. You would go in there and find *Der Spiegel* and *Paris Match* in the magazine racks. If you wanted *The Sunday New York Times*, or *The Village Voice*, you would get it through Roy's, although you would get it the following Tuesday or Wednesday.

We took *The Sunday New York Times*, every week. I know it's mean of me to think this way, but I suspect that in part, my parents took it as a way of showing off. "Status signaling." Sure, they read it. I read it too, sometimes. But it did occur to me at the time that maybe we kept *The Sunday New York Times* in our house to remind ourselves—and to show others—that we were enlightened and sophisticated. *The Sunday New York Times* was part of the décor of our living room, like a vase or a painting.

I usually didn't read much of the paper, but I would always look at the *Magazine* section. It was in June of 1963—sometime during summer vacation, anyway—when I saw on the cover of *The New York Times Magazine* a photograph of a bald-headed Asian man, wrapped in robes, sitting cross-legged on the ground, enveloped by flames. The caption read, "A Buddhist monk sets himself on fire in a Saigon street. Why?"

In the summer of 1963, Americans were just starting to become aware of Vietnam (we spelled it Viet Nam, at first), because our government was getting more involved in Vietnam militarily. It was in the news a lot. We'd had "military advisers" there since the Eisenhower administration, but in 1963 we started hearing about Americans getting involved in real shooting in Vietnam. One big issue at that time was that the Buddhist majority in South Vietnam was being persecuted in various ways by the Roman Catholic Diem family, which ran the puppet government that the United States was supporting. The monk, apparently, had set himself on fire to protest the Diem government's treatment of Buddhists.

It struck me at the time that self-immolation seemed pretty extreme, in the service of a cause that I would have considered not worth the trouble. I didn't know the word "vainglorious"

**83**

then, but that was the word I would have used. What an inflated notion of himself this crazy old man must have had!

After I read that article, I said to Mom, "How nutty do you have to be, anyway, to pull a stunt like that?" Mom tsk'd at me, and said, "Maybe he was standing up for his principles. Maybe he wasn't just thinking of himself."

It then occurred to me that Jesus of Nazareth had done much the same thing. He could have avoided execution easily enough, but—at least according to legend—he had chosen martyrdom to fulfill his destiny. But did Jesus do that for altruistic reasons, or because he was insane? Or did he do it because he was after all God made Man, and had come down to Earth precisely to do what he did?

If it had been Jesus' destiny to die so—or the monk's destiny, for that matter—how could he have chosen to do it? Do any of us have free will? Or are we simply doing what we can't help doing? Could it be that on account of the way each of us is constituted, physically and psychologically, we can't help acting the way we act? Could it be that due to the equally helpless actions of those around us, every single nanosecond of our lives has effectively been predetermined?

Those questions have bedeviled me all my life. If you're fated, or destined, then you have no free will, correct? Or you might think you have free will, when in fact every single choice you make—from your decision to get married to your decision to belch rather than hold it in—is scripted by a hand that can't be stayed, nor altered from its course.

It must have been August of 1963, the month or so before school started, when Mrs. Childress started inviting herself over to our house pretty regularly, to chat with Mom. Once a week, at least, I would find the two of them sitting at the kitchen table talking—Mrs. Childress would be chain-smoking her Pall Malls—or they would be outside on lawn chairs if it was nice weather. Mrs. Childress would bring over cookies or homemade candy, of which I would eat only a little, to avoid Mom's displeasure. Mom would provide coffee or iced tea, and would listen as Mrs. Childress held forth—sometimes on local gossip, but more usually on politics. In that summer and fall of 1963, I heard them discussing President Kennedy frequently—sometimes Jackie, too—and Mrs. Childress would talk about who was going to be running in November's City Council elections.

State City used to have some terribly hard-fought City Council elections back in those days. "Urban renewal" was the big catch-phrase. In State City you were either for or against it. The way it was represented to me—by Mrs. Childress, so I didn't get the unbiased version—was that the people who supported urban renewal wanted to make the city nice, wanted to make the business district a place that people could be proud of. Those who opposed urban renewal—so Mrs. Childress explained to me—were greedy local businessmen who didn't care how crummy the downtown got, so long as they made money. These people were "despicable," Mrs. Childress said.

Mrs. Childress specifically referred to old Charlie Roy as one of the "despicable" people who were opposing the urban renewal plan, which struck me as just plain wrong, because Mr. Roy was a nice guy, not despicable at all, and certainly not opposing the plan out of evil intent. But what did I know?

For all that she wasn't terribly informed about politics, Mom was impressionable. A few afternoons with a personality like Rae Childress would have an effect on most people. Usually, if I were nearby when Rae finally got up and went home, Mom would smile a little and roll her eyes at me. But she was apparently sold, on whatever Rae was selling her.

I had never seen Mom as energized as she was that fall. For about eight weeks, up to Election Day, she was making phone calls on behalf of the City Council candidates that she and Mrs.

**85**

Childress were supporting; stuffing envelopes; discussing progress and strategy with Rae over our kitchen table. Of course, Mom and Rae would talk about other things, while they were working. Rae told Mom quite a lot about her background—and her husband's. Mom would report this information to me and Mark and Dad at dinner, most evenings.

Mom once said to us the same thing that I had been thinking all along. I don't know for sure whether she and I were right, but Mom said:

"I get the impression that Rae and her husband have a distant marriage. She has her politics, and I guess he has his painting, but I don't think they do much together. I wonder if they don't resent each other a little, after all."

"I'd be resentful, if I were married to her," Dad said.

"Oh, stop. Maybe she was different when she was young."

On another evening, Mom said, "I worry about poor Charity. She's kind of an ugly duckling, isn't she? It must be hard for her, being the plain one in the family, when her sister is so obviously the pretty one. Andy, you should be extra nice to Charity. Do you ever think about asking her to any dances or school parties?"

I didn't care to be advised in that way. I wasn't all that interested in Charity. In any case, I wouldn't have had the courage to ask any girl to anything, at that time.

Besides, by then, I was starting to think about another girl.

**BOOK II**

# 7 STATE CITY HIGH

In the fall of 1963, I entered tenth grade—which meant that Mark and I were in separate schools again, much to my relief. Mark was in eighth grade at Southside Junior High, and I went to State City High, which was more or less north of where we lived, in the opposite direction from Southside, and a little farther away: about a fifteen-minute walk.

State City High was more grown-up-looking than Southside. It looked like a school, not a prison. Southside was a fairly new building and it had that awful cement-blocky institutional architecture from the 1950s, but State City High was from around 1900: red brick, built on a hill with a huge lawn in front of it and a collonaded entranceway. I would have to call it a grand building. Inside, it was nothing special—high schools all pretty much look the same on the inside—but the outside was impressive.

I continued to not have many friends, at State City High, and hardly any close ones—but that was mostly my own doing. I was suspicious of others, still. I kept my distance from everyone, emotionally. I did make one new friend, though.

Arno Prick—or Hasno as some of the boys called him—was my age, but he had gone to Northside Junior High, so I hadn't known him before. He was funny-looking: no other way to put it. He was of middle height, gaunt, with a short, broad face and a square jaw—not a large jaw, but wide, with knobby hinges.

He had an unintelligent face. Whether or not it's socially acceptable to admit it, one can sometimes tell whether or not a person is bright from his or her physiognomy. Arno Prick looked like a dimbulb. And he was. He was slow-talking; he seemed fascinated by anything I said to him. If I told him about a book I had read, or my dice-sports hobby, he would nod, open-mouthed, like whatever I had just told him was quite remarkable to him. Or maybe he couldn't quite believe that I was crazy enough to pursue a hobby like that. His own particular interest was cars; he was part of the auto-shop clique. High schools all have pretty much the same cliques: the jocks, the drama crowd, the music nerds, and so on. And then there's the group of boys who seem to spend every spare minute working on cars.

Prick's parents were fairly intelligent. Professor Prick had been a German soldier, a prisoner of war, and as a college-educated engineer he was useful to the Americans, so he was allowed to stay in the U.S. after the war. But apparently he hadn't known enough about English slang to change his name. He married an American girl he'd met when he was waiting out the war at Camp Scottsbluff, where evidently he'd been allowed some minimal interaction with the locals. He ended up getting his doctorate, moving to Iowa, taking U.S. citizenship, and teaching at State University. But his son gave you the impression that he had been dropped on his head as a baby. Arno Prick and I were in "Bonehead Math" together, so I know how he did in that subject anyway: not well.

I was more adept in math than poor Prick, but not by much. I hated math. I was willing to concede that it was probably important to learn simple arithmetic, and I was a whiz at that because I kept all those baseball and football statistics, so I could do long division in my sleep. But I didn't see the point of going beyond that unless I were headed for a career that called for a knowledge of higher mathematics—which I wasn't. I didn't have much idea what I was going to do with my life, but I knew it wasn't going to be anything to do with math or science. Consequently, I had gotten A's in arithmetic as a kid, but C's and D's in middle-school math. Much to my parents' despair, of course.

The other subject that Prick and I took together was French. Prick could speak German somewhat, because of his father, so even if he wasn't bright he at least grasped the basic concepts of language. If only for that reason, he was real good at French.

So was I. I had been at the top of my first-year French class at Southside, and Prick and I were far and away the two best students in this second-year class. Which is not to say much. The rest of the kids in that class barely knew anything beyond "Bonjour." They couldn't even say that in a proper accent.

Shirley Webster was the French teacher. Madame Webster. She was a sunny woman: no other adjective is more accurate than that. She was in her early thirties at the time; pretty, in a sloppy bohemian way, with long straight red hair and a nicotine-stained overbite. If it had been a few years later, the word "hippie" would have been in vogue, and might have been used to describe her. The kids all liked her. She was friendly and informal and almost like one of us. But she absolutely could *not* teach French—mainly because she couldn't speak it. She had a ridiculous accent. Consequently, so did every kid she taught—except me and Prick.

It was almost comical to hear Madame Webster speak French. She had a strong rhotic "r," being from the Midwest, and she couldn't handle the French guttural "r," which sounds almost like a strong "h." The "ü" sound, in words like "*poilu*" or "*déçu*," was utterly beyond her abilities: She would say "pwaloo," and "daysoo." "*Sur la table*," on Madame Webster's tongue, was rendered "soor la tobble." I daresay her former students are all identifiable as hers, to this day, if ever they visit France.

My parents both spoke French. They had met in a French class at the University of Wisconsin. When I was little they would speak French if they didn't want me or Mark to know what they were talking about. When I was starting to learn French, in ninth grade, they corrected my pronunciation. (I didn't always mind constructive criticism from them. It stuck in my craw to take it, but sometimes I had to admit it was for the best, and this was one of those times.) So I had a proper accent, which I taught to Prick—he and I sat side-by-side in class, and worked together—and consequently, Prick and I were the only ones in Madame Webster's class who didn't utterly butcher the language. I don't think Prick or I missed a single test question, either, that year or the next.

In Bonehead Math, instead of working on our equations, Prick and I would sit together at the back of the room, whispering away in French. We didn't know any of the "bad" words, at that time, so we would tell each other dirty jokes in French using the clinical or "proper" words, which could be found in the French-English dictionary in the school library.

It's a wonder that Prick and I both passed math, that year. Once, we wrote a pretty decent pornographic short story in French, during math class, passing the paper back and forth, each of us writing a couple of sentences or a paragraph at a time. If we didn't know a word, we would use the English, then look up the French in the school library later. Thus we improved our vocabulary, way faster than our classmates did. The math teacher never caught us. I could probably recite that whole story today—in French.

It wasn't an erotic story, because neither Prick nor I knew enough about sex to write plausible erotica, but it was funny-pornographic, gross-pornographic. We imagined all kinds of go-ings-on between various teachers, various students, mostly the ones we disliked.

Besides Madame Webster, only a few teachers stand out in my mind, from my time at State City High. One of them was the boys' gym teacher and football coach: Harley Vance.

We never saw Coach Vance wearing regular street clothes, except when he showed up for evening functions like plays or choir recitals—which he always did. During school hours it was always red shorts, white t-shirt tucked into the shorts, gym shoes, thick white socks. A whistle on a cord round his neck, a clipboard in his hand almost always. A red warmup suit on cold days.

Coach Vance was tiny: hardly more than five-foot-nothing. Which is probably why he made you wonder whether he was waiting for someone to give him shit about something. I suppose he wore the t-shirt partly to show off his physique, which was impressive. He must have been about forty-five, but didn't carry any fat that I could see. He had a hard, scowling, deeply lined face with enormous bulging ice-blue eyes that startled you, they were so large and light. He rarely spoke: he barked. Teachers al-most always called students by their first names, but Coach Vance would use your last name, as though you were an army recruit or a prisoner. And the kids called him "Coach," not "Mr. Vance." I usually called him "Sir," a title that it wouldn't have occurred to me to use to any of my other teachers.

He was not nice. He would insult you if you screwed up. "Palinkas, if you had one more brain cell, it'd be lonely." He seemed especially hard on the fat kids—and I should know. Dur-ing our unit on judo, when he demonstrated a move, he would invariably use me as his throwing dummy. Maybe because I was big, and he wanted to show the class that a little man could throw a big one. Luckily—and entirely coincidentally—I had once read an article in a sports magazine that contained introductory information on judo, including how to absorb the shock if you were thrown. So I knew to slap the mat with my hand as I went down—hard, really making it pop. Maybe that's why Coach kept using me. For the impressive noise.

A rumor persisted that some kid—"just last year, or maybe the year before"—had lost his temper and gone after Coach Vance. The rumored attacker had been a great big tough kid, whose name, for some reason, nobody remembered. Vance, the legend insisted, had knocked him plumb unconscious with one punch. But I never believed that story. Not even the craziest kid in the world would have been crazy enough to even look the wrong way at Coach Vance.

He had been an All-American boxer and wrestler at State University, and would have gone to the Olympics for sure if the war hadn't gotten in the way. A lot of the boys disliked him, but he had his adherents. These were mostly the football team and the wrestlers. I avoided the jocks—we were all pretty well separated, socially, by our interests, and I seldom exchanged a word with an athlete in my three years at State City High—but in my few conversations with one or another of them, it would come out that most of the athletes thought the world of Coach Vance. "He wants to make us good, is why he's tough on us," one of them told me.

I wasn't friendly with Coach Vance, and I certainly didn't look forward to his classes with anything but resignation, but to do him justice he wasn't a bad guy. I had no ill feeling toward him. He knew his business. He was good at what he did, and I can see why he might have been some students' favorite teacher. He would nod to you if he passed you in the hallway, which most teachers didn't do. He never missed a band or orchestra concert, choir recital, talent show, or school play.

Equally memorable, and the teacher I liked best during my time in high school despite her shortcomings, was Dr. Helen Pritchard. She took her job seriously too, but in a different way from Coach Vance, whose name she never uttered without adding a visible sneer.

Coach Vance was all about the school, and about his students in the context of the school. Dr. Pritchard was dedicated to her students, too—but mostly insofar as they related to her classes and her drama club. I never saw her at a football or basketball game—she would have disdained the very thought—nor, come to think of it, did I ever see her at any event organized by any other teacher.

Every now and then, at the beginning of a semester, some student would make the mistake of calling her "Miss Pritchard." She would reply, "Now, let's get my name straight. It's Doctor Pritchard. I worked hard for it." She would say that with a little smile, but you could tell she meant business.

She was about my parents' age, and she looked like a little grey mouse—except for that awful acne-scarred complexion of hers. I felt bad for her, about that, and I remember thinking at the time that maybe that was why she couldn't attract a husband—but in retrospect I suppose it's just as likely that she was not interested in attracting a husband. I never asked.

Some of the kids loathed her. She was strict: not unduly so, but she gave you plenty of work and expected you to get it done. I got along with her, because she made the work interesting and I didn't resent having to do it. She was so enthusiastic about literature, and made me want to read more because she would explain to us, before we had to read it, why a particular book was important in the grand scheme.

In her theatre class, she would describe to us what a production of *Romeo and Juliet* would have looked like in Shakespeare's own time. When she assigned us to write a paper—a book report or whatever—she would tell us, "I do *not* want you to simply tell me what happened in the book. That's an insult to me and to you. I assume you've read the book; you don't have to prove that to me. I want your opinions."

# 8 THE CALL TO ARMS

The class that I had with Dr. Pritchard, that first semester of tenth grade, was American Literature. At State City High, sophomores were required to take English 10—but they had the option of taking a test the week before school started. If they passed, they would be exempt from that class. They could then fulfill their English requirement by taking more advanced elective classes.

I was a bit surprised that my parents allowed me to take that test, since I was aware that they disapproved of my efforts to call attention to myself, or to get ahead of myself, but maybe it was the way I put it to them, that convinced them. I said:

"I'll be bored in English 10, and I'll get a C. Let me test out of it, and I bet my grades will be a lot better."

Anyway, I took the test, and passed it, and so apparently did Jimmy Axton, because Axton and I were the only sophomores in American Literature that fall.

I had been off-hand friendly with Jimmy Axton at Southside, where I had noticed that Axton was the only kid who did worse than I did, in gym class. Axton was almost as tall as I was, but skinny. He wasn't uncoordinated, but languid and weak.

I had been in another couple of classes with Axton, the previous year. Axton was a lot more like a girl than like a guy. That's not to say that he camped it up, or talked funny, or was over-particular about his appearance. He just wasn't masculine. He was hopeless at sports. He hung out almost entirely with girls— and not the way a womanizing guy would. He would whoop and giggle with the girls, and raise his voice in excitement, and croon "Awww" if something struck him as particularly evocative or sweet or tragic. When Axton interacted with boys—which he rarely did—he was shy and soft-spoken. He became much more animated around girls.

I was sheltered, but not entirely naïve. I was pretty sure I knew what the deal was with Axton.

American Literature was my first class of the day. On that first day of school I had arrived in the classroom a little before time and had found myself a seat on the other end of the room from the door—and to my considerable surprise, I saw Grace Childress walk into the classroom. I still remember she was wearing a teal-blue dress that was more tailored and businesslike than what a high school girl would ordinarily have worn in those days. She was walking alongside Jimmy Axton, talking with him, which I thought was odd to begin with, since seniors seldom took any notice of sophomores at all—certainly not on the first day of classes.

Grace caught sight of me at once and gave me this big silent pop-eyed open-mouthed greeting. I noticed that the braces had been taken off her teeth, probably right at the end of the summer. Then she gave me a little wave; she actually bounced once or twice on the balls of her feet as though she were excited to see me. But then she kept talking with Axton, and sat down next to him, some distance from me. The two of them continued to chat till class started.

That was the pattern, all through that semester: Grace and Axton would come in together to American Lit, most mornings, and they would sit side-by-side, in conversation, till Dr. Pritchard took her place at the front. Grace would always catch my eye, across the room (which wasn't difficult, since I was usually anticipating her arrival) and she would smile and wave at me.

The first book we studied in American Lit was *The Terrible Tragedy of Pudd'nhead Wilson*, which is one of Mark Twain's lesser-known works but much under-rated in my opinion. It's still one of my favorites, maybe because I associate it with that class, and with that time. Anyway, Dr. Pritchard assigned us each to write a report on the book. "I want you to choose a topic," she told us. "Anything about the book that caught your interest, anything you especially liked or disliked about it. Use that as a starting point, and give me at least two pages."

This was maybe the second week of the fall semester, and it was later that same day, in the middle of the afternoon, when I walked into the school library as Grace Childress was preparing to leave.

(I remember Grace telling me once, later that year, that she loved the library because it was so old-fashioned, with all its dark wood trim and the smell of old books, and she was right. It was nice for a high school library.)

Apparently Grace had a study period during fourth hour. I had one fifth hour, so our paths crossed. Grace was at the main desk, checking out a book; I was returning one, so there I was standing right next to Grace for the first time in my life. So far, we had never done more than greet each other, from a distance. I felt I had to grab the opportunity to talk with her—I don't think it's accurate to say that I was crushing on her, then, in anything more than the abstract, but she was so remarkable-looking that I had to try to get acquainted with her—so I asked Grace, "Have you decided what you're going to write about for American Lit?"

Grace laughed as though I'd actually said something funny—I still can see her covering her mouth to stifle it—then she whispered, "You know what? I haven't, yet! Isn't that terrible? I'd better think of something fast! Maybe I'll write something about

Roxy. About what happened to her. That was so sad, so awful, when she was sold down the river!" Grace looked right at me, almost appealingly—as though inviting me to commiserate with her about Roxy. "What are you going to write about?"

I told Grace that what had struck me about *Pudd'nhead Wilson* was the strange code that apparently prevailed Down South, about how to settle disputes.

"Did you notice," I asked Grace, "how if someone assaulted you, or insulted you verbally, you'd be called a coward if you had that person prosecuted, or sued him? You were supposed to fight a duel with him instead. But if the person you were disputing with was of a lower social caste than yours, you were stumped, because, you know, gentlemen couldn't fight with their inferiors. Anyway, I thought that might make an interesting topic. The rules about whom you can fight and whom you can't."

Grace looked at me so seriously, and said, "Oh, that's such a good idea! Plus, it's a different topic from what most of us will be writing about, I should think! It's remarkable that you would focus on that issue, so immediately. You'll have to let me read it when you've finished."

Yes, Grace absolutely said that. High school students did not volunteer to read each other's homework: certainly not then, and I daresay not now, either. Telling another student that you were looking forward to reading his class paper? Forget about it. But Grace said it.

Grace and I exchanged farewells; then she walked off to her next class. I went through the rest of that day in a sort of ecstatic fog. I had always been interested in Grace, from afar; I had always thought she was so pretty and exotic. Maybe I had a little crush on her already, in the utterly unrealizable way that I had had a crush first on Ava Gardner, and then on Brigitte Bardot, years before. But I had learned, almost as soon as I had taken notice of her, that Grace was two years ahead of me. Hell, at first sight I had assumed she was even older than that. It would have been ridiculous for me to have acted on my initial attraction.

All of a sudden, though—now that I had felt the full force of her personality—the conceptual, emotionally detached attraction that I had felt toward her was gone. It had been obliterated by a new emotion. The practical objection—our age difference—was forgotten, or at any rate dismissed.

I was in love—besottedly, obsessively in love. Nothing would do but I would have Grace Childress for my very own.

What was it that did the job? The only way I can explain it is to say that Grace had a personality that could just *blast* whomever she was speaking with, the way the spray from a fire hose can knock a person down. It's so hard—impossible—to put my finger on what it was specifically. Part of it was her looks, certainly. That impossibly shimmery red-blonde hair; the short, slender dancer's body. She had those amazingly twinkly, lively blue eyes—a deep, pure blue. A bluebird's blue, contrasting with her reddish-blonde hair the way a bluebird's back and wings contrast with its orange breast. Even when Grace had waved to me from a distance, over the past year, I had noticed the exceptional animation in her eyes, in her whole face.

When Grace talked to me, or even just greeted me, she would turn those eyes right on me. When our paths crossed, at school or in the street, her face would light up as though her whole day had been improved just because she had caught sight of me. If Grace were conversing with me—or with anyone, so far as I could tell—she would give absolute focus. Or at least she would give me to believe that she was focused on me, hanging on my every word, paying total attention to me because I was the most fascinating person she had ever known and she couldn't imagine wanting to talk with anyone else, at least for the time being.

Starting on the following day, and for the rest of that fall semester, I re-located myself in American Lit class. I spotted an empty seat in the very front row, at the left end of the room from the student's perspective, that was directly in front of Axton—and diagonal from Grace, so that I could easily turn around in my seat and talk with her.

The girl who sat to my right, directly in front of Grace, was Julia Swinford: another unforgettable. She was a senior like Grace, a plain girl with dishwater hair and not that good of a complexion. I googled her recently and found that she's a lawyer now. A litigator, apparently part of a pretty prestigious firm. She still looks about the same as she did in high school. Still has that fishy frown that she used to wear as her default expression.

Julia was bright, well-read. She made a point of letting me know that she had already read everything that was on our reading list for American Lit, and then some. She liked to speak French—she would say things in French and expect me to understand them—and when I tried to speak French back to her, she would maliciously correct me. Not in a helpful way, but in a mocking, sneering way. I was good at French for a tenth-grader, but I was only in my second year of learning the language: nowhere near her level yet. For example, I hadn't learned the subjunctive, and it apparently amused Julia to spring it on me.

As far as I ever saw, Julia only acted happy and animated when she was talking with Grace. She and I, and Grace and Axton, formed a regular conversational foursome every morning while we waited for Dr. Pritchard to start the session. I suspect that Julia was unpleasant to me because she sensed that I was crushing on Grace—and maybe she saw me as a rival.

I don't mean for sure that Julia desired Grace sexually. Maybe she did and maybe not. A teenaged girl will sometimes develop an extremely intense, romantic attraction to another girl that isn't necessarily sexual. That may have been what was going on in Julia's case. I remember, so often, when the four of us were chatting together before class, catching sight of Julia gazing at

Grace with such an ardent, longing expression: staring, mouth slightly open. Almost worshipful—or maybe not almost. I bet Grace never even noticed it.

Usually the four of us would sit together in the cafeteria at lunch, too. I would be trying to keep up my end of the conversation; Julia would be sneering and putting me down; Axton would do that nervous laugh of his.

In the course of those conversations, I found out that Grace and Axton always came in together in the morning because they were both taking a ballroom dancing class that fall, outside of school, before first period. I remember Axton telling me that he was the only boy in that class and the other girls had to take turns at being boys. Grace told me that she also had ballet classes right after school, as well as music lessons two or three times a week.

Grace tended to talk about herself a lot—but not in a way that was at all off-putting. It was charming, ingratiating. A person can often charm others by acting enthusiastic about herself. That's what Grace did. She would tell us about herself and her interests and activities, or tell us little stories about her childhood, with such energy, with considerable gesture and vocal dramatics. And she would ask me questions about myself. That's one of the keys to being considered a good conversationalist.

The other key is to not simply ask questions—if all you do is ask questions, you'll make the other person feel like he's being grilled—but to talk to the other person about himself. Make statements (complimentary, of course) about the other person; act like you have that other person in your thoughts. Grace did that, with me, almost every day.

I got so intimately acquainted with Grace's person, during that semester, from sitting with her and talking with her on those two occasions every day. Outside of American Lit class, outside of lunch, my thoughts would be all about the next American Lit class, or the impending lunch. I became familiar with all of the faintest irregularities in Grace's complexion. I knew that her nostrils weren't exactly the same shape. I noticed that her right ring finger had evidently been broken once because it was crooked toward her middle finger, above the second knuckle.

Grace had a distinctive personal aroma that I have never forgotten. I can't re-create it in my mind—I wish I could—but I remember it. She smelled faintly of sweat, almost all the time, but it was a sexy, spicy kind of sweaty smell. Grace was so energetic, and she danced for hours every day, so no wonder. You wouldn't see Grace seriously dripping, like you might see a guy all sweaty after a workout, but she usually had a faint sheen of perspiration, and that smell. It wasn't pungent, as it might have been on a guy. It was a girly smell. On Grace, it was adorable.

Her aroma was sexy—to me—but I couldn't have called Grace sexy. She was untouchable. She never had a boyfriend that I knew of. I got the impression that she didn't even think about that sort of thing, as though she preferred not to know about the icky parts. Grace was almost a work of art: a priceless vase, or a figurine—only with animation and a personality.

You know what else? I'll bet anything that Grace didn't know this about herself. She may well never have known it, never have guessed it, not even years later. Grace was so over-the-top perfect, to a point where she was almost a parody of herself. She was so consistently gracious, so invariably cheerful, so perfectly put together at all times, that she was almost not human. She would talk about her accomplishments so matter-of-factly: how (as Charity had already told me) she made her own clothes, played three or four musical instruments, danced—I can't even remember what-all else she could do. She mentioned things like batik and macramé that I didn't even know what they were.

Once, the four of us got into a discussion of religious beliefs, and Grace said, "I'm not completely sure what I believe. I've read the Bible all the way through, and..."

How many human beings, let alone teenaged girls, have read the entire Bible? Grace just casually mentioned having done so, as a natural part of that conversation, with no elaboration or explanation, as though she wouldn't have thought it unusual, as though she supposed that plenty of other people our age had read the entire Bible.

I never saw her grim; I never saw her sad. Even when something was wrong, Grace would be smiling. Yet she would speak to me so seriously, with such vivacity, looking me square in the eye. She would often say, "My father says..." or "My father taught me that..."

Grace once mentioned to me that her father sometimes used the "plain speech" when he talked to her. I remember the two of us puzzling over why the correct form, in plain speech, was "thee is," or "thee has," or "thee goes," instead of "thou art," "thou hast," or "thou goest." Why would they use "thee" as both the subjective and the objective? Why would they use the third-person instead of the second-person form of the verb? I remember Grace promising me she would ask her father about all that, but she must have forgotten. I can't remember that we ever did find out the explanation.

Grace told me, "I don't think I've ever heard my father use the plain speech with anybody else—except with his own parents, sometimes, and then he only uses it when they're kidding with each other. On the other hand, he only uses it with me when he's being very serious. And only when we're in private. I don't hear him use it to my mother, or to Charity."

So, yeah, apparently Grace idolized her father. She hardly ever talked about her mother at all.

I remember her saying, once, "I'm more my father's daughter, and Charity is more her mother's daughter. Not that they don't love both of us and not that we don't love both of them. It's just that it's inevitable that a parent will feel a certain affinity for one child, or that a child will choose to take after one parent more than the other."

I bet it was from her father, more than from her mother, that Grace got her emotional makeup—that is, insofar as I got to understand her emotional makeup. Even though Grace was always so cheerful and quick to laugh, she conveyed extraordinary *gravitas*. A seriousness, an earnestness, that was almost excessive. Every Friday, in American Lit, Dr. Pritchard would have scheduled one kid or another to come to the front of the classroom and read a poem, or part of a short story. Something of our own choosing. Grace was especially fond of Longfellow, whom I couldn't stand. One of my most enduring memories of that year is the time Grace read us "The Village Smithy."

She read it in such an emotionally intense tone—almost overwrought; I could almost hear a sob in her voice—that one of the other students snickered aloud. Chuck Haviland. Haviland was a year behind Grace and a year ahead of me. Another Big Man On Campus type, somewhat like Mitch Rosen, only Rosen tried so hard to be likable, while Haviland threw his weight around by being scornful and sarcastic.

When he laughed, I whipped around in my seat and glared at him like I was ready to kill him right there. Haviland flinched, probably more from reflex than from actual fear; then he recovered, every bit as quickly. He laughed again. At me.

Two things I took from that incident. First, while it was unlikely, it was at least possible that I had just thrown a scare into an older kid, if only for an instant, just by looking like I might be dangerous. Second—I had to admit this to myself, even in the moment—I had had an urge to cringe and snicker at Grace's performance as well.

The following week, Dr. Pritchard heard me read aloud for the first time. I read a section of *Pudd'nhead Wilson* to the class; I did the various accents and all. I must have performed pretty

**103**

impressively because after I had gotten through it, Dr. Pritchard gave me a big smile, and said, "Andy, have you ever thought of joining the Drama Club? Or the forensics team?"

I had fooled around with acting as a kid, doing classroom skits and so on, but I had never acted seriously. I didn't even know that there was another meaning for "forensics" other than "crime-solving." This was the first time I had heard that the word also related to rhetoric. I knew there were debating tournaments, but till then I had not known there were contests for things like poetry reading, dramatic interpretation, and so on.

Forensics hadn't been available to me in junior high, either in Waukoshowoc or in State City. In any case, I had spent those three years trying to keep my head down. Still, I did like to perform. I did like attention. I did want to do something that was somehow cool, and have it noticed. When Dr. Pritchard suggested speech and drama, I was immediately attracted. A tournament was coming up in a few weeks, she told me, on the State University campus. Why didn't I sign up for it? I did, then and there. I took that selection from *Pudd'nhead Wilson* and entered myself in Humorous Prose.

I dreaded telling my parents that I was going to do this thing, though. I anticipated maternal opposition, and I got it. I can hardly remember a time when Mom didn't use "No" as her default setting. I would sometimes propose activities that upon consideration she wouldn't find objectionable, but her first instinct was almost always to say "No."

"I worry about your grades, Andy."

Always my grades. Never anything about developing whatever poor talents I might have had. In general, Mom had always made it pretty clear to me that ambition was bad. Never did she suggest anything about "following my bliss" (if I had had any to follow). Just my goddam grades. Of course she only had my well-being in mind, and I should have been grateful for her concern—

or at least I should be grateful now, in retrospect. Only I wasn't, and I'm not.

I was able to advance the argument that I had already entered the tournament, that it was a done deal, that I couldn't very well let Dr. Pritchard down by withdrawing from this event, and even if I did, withdrawal wasn't likely to help my grades—not in her class or any other—now was it?

"Well, all right," Mom finally said—with a big sigh to indicate what a concession she was granting—"but we'll see how it goes. I don't want you getting involved in too many of these things and not paying enough attention to your schoolwork."

It's such a pity that there's no professional forensics. I have no doubt that if it were something that one could pursue as a career, I would have been a Jack Nicklaus or a Henry Aaron: not merely a star, but a star with a long career at the top. I wasn't particularly good, that first year—I didn't win any trophies or ribbons—but I learned a lot.

Many people, when they hear "forensics," think "debate," but that's not right. Debate is about as different from other forensics events as basketball is from wrestling. I probably could have been halfway good at debate, but the debaters were all the kinds of kids I didn't like to associate with. They tended to be supercilious, intellectually overbearing. They also tended not to have much humor.

Rosen was on the debate team. He was the only debater with whom I was on friendly terms. Another debater I got to know slightly was Chuck Haviland—the junior who had snickered at Grace. He was another Student Government type. Tall, athletic. Popular. But somehow from looking at Haviland, the first time I saw him—even before the snickering incident—I had had to mistrust him. Haviland had a mean face. There's no other way to describe it. He was smiling almost all the time, but it wasn't a likable smile. He looked like the type who would get his kicks by mocking people. Mean, like Julia Swinford—but he was more outgoing than Julia.

I tried almost every forensics event, other than debate, over the next three years. If I had fun with any part of my high school career, it was forensics. Even acting in plays—which I got rather good at, and which I'll touch on later—wasn't as much fun. Partly it was the individual nature of forensics, and partly it must have been the thrill of competition. Here, finally, was something I knew I could do well, and stand a reasonable chance of winning at it, or at least placing high.

Also, as I discovered, at forensics meets you got to hang out with some of the smarter kids from all over the state, and some of them were interesting—if a bit geekier than the average. Forensics was a way to get introduced to good literature, and to various ideas that maybe you hadn't considered yet (because the kids who did Original Oratory would talk about anything, from banking to vegetarianism). You would learn acting technique. You would learn, through observation, some of the most common errors in rhetoric and elocution, and how to avoid them. Plus, I enjoyed the camaraderie that was born of common interest, rather than forced juxtaposition.

I remember one girl from a school in Davenport, whom I developed a tiny crush on—even while I was crushing on Grace. We competed against each other at the first tournament of the year, and I thought she was good and she thought I was good. Mary Hurd was her name. She was short and a tiny bit on the plump side—you couldn't call her fat—with long curly brown hair and light blue eyes the color of morning glories.

Evidently, she had had polio. At that time, with the vaccine only available for about seven or eight years, you would still see one or two kids, in most high schools, who had to use wrist-crutches. Mary Hurd was one of them. She always wore floor-length dresses to cover up her legs, which I suppose were atrophied, and this made her look even more charming because the dresses gave her a bit of a fairy-princess aspect.

At that first tournament of the year, in the first round of Humorous Prose, she performed before I did: a funny monologue about Stonehenge, of all things. I was impressed. I gave her a smile and nod when she had finished. Then I performed my piece: that selection from *Pudd'nhead Wilson*.

Mary Hurd mouthed, "Good job," as I sat down, and that was enough. We got to talking after that round, and hung out as we could, between the next two rounds. From then on I would seek her out at every tournament for the next three years.

I don't know how Mary felt about me, but I always felt better just from seeing her. Whenever I saw her at a tournament (after that first one), I would go right up to her and give her a big hug—lifting her off her feet, crutches and all, and giving her a whirl before setting her back down again, while she would be giggling up a storm. Even during that year, despite my feelings for Grace, I had a bit of a longing for Mary Hurd—and I would continue to have, for the two years following.

It's funny. I didn't try to think of some way of corresponding with her, or developing a long-distance courtship. Davenport was sixty miles away, and I was too young to drive. Maybe I could have written her letters—but in that first year I wouldn't have been interested, and in succeeding years she always seemed to have a guy hanging with her. That didn't stop me from giving her the big hug, but it cramped my style otherwise. Anyway, ever since, I have regarded Mary Hurd as an opportunity lost. That was one girl who *liked* having me give her a hug.

Grace, though, was so much nearer to hand and infinitely more alluring. Why, how, could I have been so divorced from reality that I tried to *court* Grace—I mean, tried to get Grace to think of me in romantic terms? I have always been a bit eccentric, but this was downright delusional. This was a level of craziness that I never knew I had in me till it showed itself.

All through my high school years, I got acquainted with a few girls—not many, but a few—to whom I might have paid more attention: girls with whom I could have had nice times. Not sexual, maybe, but just friendly-like. Or I could have been some girl's boyfriend in a naïve, virginal sort of romantic way, as was much more common then than it is now. But would I have dared to go after a girl who might have been attracted to me in return— knowing the parental restrictions I would have to work around, the maternal snooping, and so on?

Not to mention, would I have wanted to belong to a club that would have had me as a member? If any girl had shown attraction to me, I'm afraid I would have rejected her, because that would have meant that I was settling for what I could have, rather than reaching for a star. Any girl who might have been attracted to me—well, clearly there would have to have been something wrong with her.

I had not yet learned that having a girlfriend makes you more desirable to other girls—just as having a job makes you more desirable to other prospective employers. Looking back, it just flat-out amazes me how ignorant and unobservant I was, how much obvious information I flat-out failed to see.

# 9 THOSE FOUR DAYS IN NOVEMBER

It seems to me that every American who was of school age on the day John F. Kennedy was assassinated has approximately the same story to tell. The principal or some other school adminis-trator gave the announcement over the intercom, or walked into each individual classroom to announce it, and classes were immediately dismissed in some cases, or the kids and the teachers limped through the afternoon's lessons as best they could and the kids walked home in a semi-daze, not knowing what to say to each other.

It's funny how I never discussed that day with anyone, afterwards. Not with Mark, not with my parents, not with Grace or Charity. Not a word. It was as though the events of that day just *were*, and no word could be added to them.

I was sitting next to Arno Prick in Bonehead Math, after lunch, with only about five minutes left in the period, when the intercom came on and we heard the principal, Mr. Pope. His secretary always made the daily announcements, so as soon as I heard Mr. Pope's voice I knew something bad was up. He was speaking slowly, and couldn't keep the tremble out of his voice:

"Students, and teachers, this is Mr. Pope. I have terrible news. We have received word that President Kennedy has been shot. He was in Dallas, Texas, riding in an open car, and was apparently shot by a sniper. We have no definite word on his condition but we understand he is badly hurt. Please resume your day's work, and I will let you know if anything else develops."

Bonehead Math was almost all boys, and the teacher, Miss Zwingli, was standing there stunned, so we all started talking at once. A couple of the boys wondered aloud whether the Russians might have been involved, or whether it was some other organization—but just about all of us seemed to assume that this had been the result of some kind of conspiracy.

Miss Zwingli, at the blackboard, didn't order us back to work. Instead, she tried to join in the discussion, but within a few seconds she exclaimed, "Oh, his poor children!" She sat down at her desk as though she were collapsing. She started to sob—and that, I believe, was more upsetting to the class than the President's assassination. Her crying shut us up completely, till she had composed herself.

"You don't know; he might be okay," said Prick, after Miss Zwingli had blown her nose and put her handkerchief back in her purse.

"No, he's not. I have a feeling," said Miss Zwingli. Then the bell rang. Of course there was pandemonium in the halls, everyone talking at once, it seemed like.

"What's going to happen now?" asked Prick. He and I were walking down a flight of stairs. His destination was the auto shop; I was headed for the library for my study period.

"Well, if he dies, it'll be Lyndon Johnson," I said. "I don't know anything about him."

"No, I mean to the country," said Prick. "Everything's gonna go crazy. You think? Like maybe the Russians will take over?"

"No. This is just history happening. We'll go on. Like we always do when a President dies." Prick and I split up then, and I went to the library where, again, nobody was making a pretense of being quiet. It's odd, but I felt pretty calm. I hardly ever actually studied during study period, but on that day I sat in the library and did my math homework for the next day, just to keep my mind off of what else was going on.

The sixth hour was Coach Vance's gym class. When we were suited up, and in the gym, a couple of the boys asked Vance if he knew anything else. He just shook his head.

"I can't believe it," he said. For once he was speaking very low. "Line up in fives. Jumping jacks."

A few minutes later, Vance broke us up into four groups, to play half-court basketball. When my team had the ball I would try to stay out of everyone's way, and when the other team had it, I was at least slightly useful because I *could* get in the way. The class was about half over when we heard the intercom come on again, and every kid stopped still.

Mr. Pope's voice, again: "I'm sorry to have to tell you that President Kennedy is dead. Apparently he was taken to the hospital but he died a few minutes after the shooting. We don't know yet who did it but obviously it was someone who doesn't respect America very much. Again, I'm sorry to give you this news. I wish I could dismiss for the rest of the day but I'm afraid I'm not authorized to do that, so please go about your business as normally as you can."

Coach Vance was white in the face. He took a few seconds to collect himself, then he said, "Fellas, I'm not allowed to lead you in prayer, but we all need to just sit quiet and think for a few minutes." So we all sat on the floor, silent. After about five minutes, Vance said, "Okay. Go take long showers."

In French class, we didn't even pretend to work. Madame Webster and the students just talked, in English, about who might have done it and what it might mean for America—with no conclusions drawn.

Grace and Charity and I walked home together, that day. We didn't say a word to each other. Not a word. I'm probably remembering it that way for the sake of a better story, but I don't recall any of us saying anything: just walking together and maybe walking a little closer to each other than usual, the way people do when they have heard terrible news.

Most people who recall Kennedy's assassination will talk about the profound emotional reaction they had to the event. I'm afraid I didn't have one. I felt a little stunned, naturally, because it was an event for which I wasn't prepared, but I wasn't particularly horrified, or panicked, or even sad. It seemed to me that this was the kind of event that could happen. One had to allow for the possibility, and once it did happen there wasn't much to do about it except go on. My main thought was an abstract, detached awareness that a hugely important historical event had occurred, but I didn't feel any great emotion.

It was a cold, rainy day: gloomy enough to be almost dark by the time we got home late that afternoon. I murmured, "See you later" to Grace and Charity. I can't remember whether they said anything in response. I do recall watching the two of them going up their front walk and into their house, still walking close together, before I went into mine.

I assumed that the rest of my family had heard the news, and I knew that they had, as soon as I walked in the front door, since Mom, Dad, and Mark were all sitting on the floor, huddled around the radio. (We still didn't have a TV. It would have had a bad influence on me and Mark.)

Dad looked pale, and shocked. Mom had obviously been crying. I couldn't judge Mark's reaction. I don't mean to say that Mark was unemotional; he certainly was capable of great emotion at times. But in my observation he tended to keep a straight face and an even expression unless he were really stressed about something, and on this occasion he looked suitably grave but not particularly moved.

I asked, "Do they know yet who did it?"

Mom's expression changed from woe to wrath in a blink; she had turned her venom on me before, but never like this. "Oh, what do you care?" she wailed. "You were for Nixon! I hope you're happy!"

I must have stared back at Mom; I couldn't quite believe I had heard right. I could see Dad wince, but he didn't say anything either. I must have stood there about ten seconds before I could think of anything to say, and even then all that came to my mind was, "I don't think that was called for," but I was so gobsmacked that I couldn't even say that. I just kept looking at her.

Then Mom said, "I'm sorry, Andy, I shouldn't have said that." And maybe she was sorry; she probably was. Still, that's the kind of remark you remember. And that's my chief memory of that day.

You'll also hear, from anyone who lived through it, about the lasting impact Kennedy's assassination had on our society—so again, I won't go into that to any great length. I will say that up to that incident, I had sensed a general feeling of optimism, almost euphoria—at least among the people I knew—about where the country was going. We were going to solve our social problems and colonize outer space; we would either co-opt Russia and China or make them irrelevant; we would make unimaginable technological advances and have plenty of time and resources for education and the arts, too. That's what a lot of us believed, in the early 1960s, and Kennedy had a lot to do with that.

I don't think most people understood Kennedy's policies much, if indeed he had a coherent policy. What people loved about Kennedy was that when he spoke, he made you feel that you, personally, were good. Same effect as attending a Pete Seeger concert. Whether he was giving a speech or holding a press conference, Kennedy had such a presence that you had to feel proud of him. People tingled at the sight of him, at the sound of his voice.

The White House had such glamour and sophistication to it, when the Kennedys lived in it. That was largely due to Jackie. America hadn't had a young and sexy First Lady since Frances Cleveland in the 1880s. It was Jacqueline Kennedy—or so it was popularly believed—who turned the White House into a salon where great musicians were invited to perform, and poets given state dinners. Jackie, every bit as much as her husband, made us all feel prouder to be Americans.

So what if it were a baseless, superficial pride? Still it was palpable—and that pride, that optimism, that enthusiasm largely died with JFK. It sounds simplistic, I know, but I believe it to be true. Following Kennedy's death—for the rest of my time on Earth it seems to me—Americans have been basically cynical, pessimistic.

You know what else died with JFK? Poetic public speeches. You heard some of the last of them coming from the Rotunda of the U.S. Capitol on the Sunday, two days after the assassination. The one I remember best was by Sen. Mike Mansfield of Montana. About halfway through his speech, as we listened on the radio, Mom started sobbing. She ran out of the living room, down the hall to her and Dad's bedroom. She stayed in there for some time while Dad and Mark and I continued to listen.

> There was a sound of laughter; in a moment, it was no more. And so she took a ring from her finger and placed it in his hands.
>
> There was a wit in a man neither young nor old, but a wit full of an old man's wisdom and of a child's wisdom, and then, in a moment it was no more. And so she took a ring from her finger and placed it in his hands.
>
> There was a man marked with the scars of his love of country, a body active with the surge of a life far, far from spent and, in a moment, it was no more. And so she took a ring from her finger and placed it in his hands.
>
> There was a father with a little boy, a little girl and a joy of each in the other. In a moment it was no more, and so she took a ring from her finger and placed it in his hands.
>
> There was a husband who asked much and gave much, and out of the giving and the asking wove with a woman what could not be broken in life, and in a moment it was no more. And so she took a ring from her finger and placed it in his hands, and kissed him and closed the lid of a coffin.

A piece of each of us died at that moment. Yet, in death he gave of himself to us. He gave us of a good heart from which the laughter came. He gave us of a profound wit, from which a great leadership emerged. He gave us of a kindness and a strength fused into a human courage to seek peace without fear.

He gave us of his love that we, too, in turn, might give. He gave that we might give of ourselves, that we might give to one another until there would be no room, no room at all, for the bigotry, the hatred, prejudice, and the arrogance which converged in that moment of horror to strike him down.

In leaving us these gifts, John Fitzgerald Kennedy, President of the United States, leaves with us. Will we take them, Mr. President? Will we have, now, the sense and the responsibility and the courage to take them?

I pray to God that we shall and under God we will.

§

The following Monday, the schools were closed. Mom phoned across the street to ask Rae Childress if we could come over to watch the funeral. Mom wasn't the sort to do that—to ask for another family's hospitality—but we didn't have a TV and evidently Mom felt it was something we all had to see. So there we were, all assembled in the Childress family's living room, on the sofa, in the armchairs, and some of us in the wooden chairs that Dr. Childress carried in from the dining room. The four teenagers sat on their big dark greenish-brown velveteen sofa: Mark on the far right, me at his left, Charity at my left, and Grace on the other end.

That was the first time I had ever been in that house; I can think of only a very few times I was ever in it after that, and never for more than a minute or so. All I remember of the inside of their house was what I saw of it on that day.

I liked their house. It wasn't remarkable but it had a certain formality and a certain cheer and humor to it, for want of better words. Even though that was a sad day and the weather continued rainy and gloomy, the Childress living room had a welcoming look. It was done in warm colors: yellows and oranges, and some browns and greens for contrast.

Otherwise, the house wasn't remarkable. It was two stories to our one, and it had a bigger footprint than our house, but the furniture was what I would have expected to see in any middle-class home at that time and place. It was color-coordinated, though, which ours wasn't. On one wall was a framed still-life of flowers in a vase, that looked well-executed to my uneducated eye; I assumed that was by Dr. Childress.

It was rather a small painting, maybe twelve inches by fifteen. I didn't know much about art at the time, but from reading the encyclopedias I had learned a little. I remember thinking that the still-life looked almost like a Renoir but not quite; almost like a Seurat but not quite. On another wall I saw a multicolored fabric hanging, done in a way that I wasn't familiar with, but which I now know was macramé. On one of the bookcases—and it's funny that I don't remember what any of the book titles were—was a framed photo of Grace and Charity, evidently taken about three years before: Grace sitting behind Charity with her arms around her, protective; Grace smiling a huge smile in defiance of her braces; Charity looking a bit somber. That's about all I remember, now.

The funeral, the procession, the burial: That's another story that's been told over and over again, and if you saw it, you remember it. The muffled drums; the riderless horse; Mrs. Kennedy with that heavy black veil; the President's brothers next to her; Cardinal Cushing saying the funeral Mass; the interment; the folding of the flag; the salute; the last playing of "Hail to the Chief." Probably nobody who saw that spectacle will ever hear "Hail to the Chief" without thinking of Kennedy.

The most memorable part of the procession, for me, was not when little John F. Kennedy, Jr. stepped forward from his place on the sidelines and saluted the coffin. It was the sight of the five-foot Emperor of Ethiopia, Haile Selassie, marching next to the nearly seven-foot President of France, Charles DeGaulle—both in full military uniform—and Dad remarking, "Hey, look! There's Haile Unlikely, and Big Chuck."

Mom tsk'd at that, and sighed, "Oh, Steve." Joe and Rae Childress both glanced over at Dad, although I couldn't see the expressions on their faces if any. I was paying more attention to Grace's and Charity's reactions to what was unfolding on TV. Charity looked so solemn—but Grace didn't, or at least she looked less so than Charity. Now and then Grace would catch my eye and give me the tiniest hint of a smile, surreptitiously, almost as though she and I were sharing a confidence, only I didn't know what that would have been.

Was Grace trying to buck me up, assuming I felt some emotion that I didn't in fact feel? Or was she giving me a smile of commiseration and comradeship, as though she sensed that I wasn't as deeply affected by this moment as perhaps I should have been, and was she trying to convey to me that she wasn't, either? Maybe she was trying, wordlessly, to say, "Yes, I agree with you, but we have to put the right face on it so that we won't disgrace ourselves, don't we?"

The latter is much more fun as a fantasy: the idea that somehow Grace and I understood each other, emotionally. That we were a pair in some ways.

At one point, Grace leaned over and picked up a plate of cake from the coffee table and passed it to me. Mrs. Childress had prepared one of her poppy seed cakes, as well as a saffron cake with candied peel. She was a wonderful baker; I don't understand how the rest of her family all stayed so slim. From hearing Mrs. Childress talk, a person might have got the impression that she was all about politics and didn't think about much else, but she did have a bit of the old-fashioned Jewish momma about her after all.

She'd put a plate of cheese and crackers and salami out there for us, and a pot of coffee, and that cake, and nobody else in the room was touching the food. I suspect they were making a point of not touching it because it would have been unseemly to eat during JFK's funeral procession. But it was there, on offer, and delicious, and so all through the ceremony and the procession I was sipping coffee and eating that cake.

Grace was the only other person eating—and every time she would take something, she would then pass the plate over to me, as though she especially wanted to keep me fed. Finally, Mark took something too, but mostly it was just me and Grace—and especially me. I know, the woman did offer it and I did eat. It's no excuse. I could have refused. But it was awfully good cake, and Grace Childress—*the* Grace Childress—was passing it to me! How could I refuse cake from a plate that Grace had touched with her own fair hands?

When I was handling the plate I made sure to touch it in the areas where Grace had touched it.

Dad went back home after a while—said he had work to do—and Mom looked at him reproachfully, as if to say, "how could you?" The rest of us stayed, but at one point, Charity got up, presumably to answer a call of nature. For a minute or two there would be nobody between me and Grace. I had to somehow seize this opportunity to have some kind of a conversation, so I leaned over and said softly, "Is that your father's work there on the wall?"

Grace giggled.

"No!" she managed to exclaim and whisper at the same time. "That's mine! Would you like to take a closer look?" She stood up and made toward the painting, so of course I did the same.

"It's actually not as impressive if you're right close to it," Grace admitted, in library voice, when we were standing right in front of it. "When you stand at a distance, all those little points of color blend together so that it looks realistic, whereas up close, like this, you can see that it's really just dots."

"Must have taken you a long time," I said. We were still almost whispering, not to disturb the rest of the company.

"Long enough," she said. "I've still got a lot to learn. If you want to see good work, I should take you upstairs."

Grace turned to her father, who was across the room, and raised her voice to a normal speaking level.

"Father, is it all right if I take Andy up to your studio? We won't touch anything."

Odd, I thought, that she called him "Father." People only did that in books or movies about colonial times, I had thought. But apparently not.

Dr. Childress smiled a little.

"I'm much flattered," he said, and turned back to the TV.

I was curious enough about her father's paintings that I almost forgot to feel thrilled that Grace, herself, was leading me into the inner sancta of her house. I almost forgot, but not quite. The staircase was in the small alcove between the living room and the kitchen; I was close enough to Grace to smell her as she led me upstairs. Maybe it was the juxtaposition of Grace's pheromones and (presumably) her bedroom that gave me the sudden urge to grab her and kiss her right there.

I didn't do that; the impulse only flitted across my mind for an instant. But I surely thought to do it. When Grace turned her head to make sure I was following her, I focused for just that instant on the exact spot on her lips where the initial contact would take place, imagining how soft it would feel and how her mouth might taste, and how I might inhale her scent even more deeply as I was kissing her... but it was only a thought.

Grace, when we got to the top of the stairs, pointed out the music room (evidently a re-purposed bedroom, which contained an upright piano) and her father's studio—which, I saw, faced our house.

Several of Dr. Childress's paintings hung on the walls of his studio. A couple more were on easels—including a painting of the rear of Mom's Fairlane, evidently observed from the window, accurate as to the general shape of the car but in a stylized magenta (as opposed to the maroon that really was the car's color) contrasting with the yellow of our house and the blue of the sky, which were also painted in exaggerated shades.

I wish I could say that Dr. Childress's paintings showed signs of exceptional talent, but (at least to my teenaged eyes) they didn't. They were landscapes, for the most part, and he did have a flair for color, and for juxtaposing colors, but the objects portrayed—the houses, the telephone poles—looked slapdash to me: chunky, boxy, blocky.

On the wall next to the window hung an unframed canvas, a portrait of a young woman seated on a stone bench in a flower garden: a slender, black-haired woman with one brown eye and one bright blue eye, smiling subtly and looking off into the middle distance. It was the only painting on display that had a human figure in it. The flowers in the background were mostly reds and blues; her dress, of brown and rust tones, clashed with them. I supposed that that was intentional. Her hands were folded demurely in her lap. Again, I didn't think it was anything special; I wouldn't have called it the work of a master. But the contrasting eyes were a clever idea.

"Is that your mother, when she was younger?" I asked. "Except both your mother's eyes are brown."

"Oh, you're so close!" Grace laughed. "It's actually a combination portrait. It's me and Charity. Only we're a little older than we are now. Isn't that clever? You see, it's Charity's coloring, but the facial structure is mine, and the mouth is mine. And the eyes, I love the eyes. He managed to combine her eyes and mine just perfectly, didn't he? And I should say that girl's posture is a little more like me than like Charity, but he definitely captured both of us, didn't he?"

He had. With Grace's explanation, I had more respect for the painting. I still didn't think, admittedly speaking from ignorance, that it displayed any technical excellence. But Dr. Childress had combined his two daughters into a credible portrait.

"I sometimes keep my father company when he's painting," Grace said. "I sit in the rocking chair there, and I work on my knitting or my needlepoint. So he's done a lot of sketches of me, over the years."

"Gosh, you do everything, don't you?" I said.

"Well, I don't wrestle or play football. Anyway we'd better get back downstairs. We're missing history."

It was on my mind to ask, "Wouldn't you rather stay up here, and wrestle?"

Instead, we went back downstairs, where the TV was showing us the gravesite, at Arlington National Cemetery, where the casket had been placed on a framework above the open grave. The honor guard was removing the flag and folding it.

Rae Childress, speaking in a voice that was uncharacteristically soft, for her, but clear, recited:

Death, be not proud, though some have called thee
Mighty and dreadful, for thou art not so

Dr. Childress, speaking at about the same volume, recited the next two lines:

For those whom thou think'st thou dost overthrow
Die not, poor Death, nor yet canst thou kill me.

They stopped there, although I was halfway expecting them to go on and recite the whole sonnet—the two of them, two lines at a time, turn-about. But we all sat still, then, while the guardsmen folded the flag and presented it to Mrs. Kennedy.

Mom, Mark, and I left, late that afternoon, with Mom thanking Rae Childress profusely, and Mark and me echoing. As soon as Mrs. Childress had shut the door after us and we were headed down the front steps of the house, Mom was all, "Andy, I'm ashamed of you! All that cake! Even if it hadn't been in the middle of a funeral, you made a human garbage can of yourself. That was so embarrassing for the rest of us."

So what I remember most about JFK's funeral was how I disgraced the family with my beastliness.

It was Campbell's soup, and sandwiches, for supper that night. All during the meal Mom was shooting daggers at me as though I ought not to be getting any supper at all because of how I had been such a swine, and had shamed our family.

"I didn't make dessert tonight because we had all that cake this afternoon," Mom announced as we were finishing up.

Ah, so now I had deprived the rest of the family of dessert, through my unspeakable behavior. I wanted to go down to the basement and hang out by myself, but that would have smacked on the one hand of masochism—sitting on the cold stone floor—and on the other hand it would have looked as though I were exiling myself voluntarily, by way of penance, as though acknowledging that I had misbehaved, when I wasn't sure I had. Although I was forced to ask myself, "Good Lord, what must Grace think of me now?"

So I went down the hall to Mark's and my bedroom. I clearly recall remarking to myself that the excitement was over and that in the morning it would be back to the same old routines. It

would be still nearly three years before I could escape this goddam drab poky house where I was nothing but an albatross to
my family. Three years before I could get far, far away, someplace
where nobody would keep reminding me what a loser I was, or
telling me what to do or what I wasn't allowed to do. Where
nobody would know that I had a younger brother who was better
in every way than I was.

§

The State City High School newspaper was called the *Cat's Paw*.
State City High's sports teams were the Wampus Cats, because
State University's sports teams were the Rivercats, but whoever
came up with that name for the newspaper must not have been
aware that a cat's paw is a tool: a person being used by someone
else, usually for nefarious purposes. Or, who can say? That is
what newspapers are used for, as often as not.

Anyway, the December 1963 edition of the *Cat's Paw*, which
came out right before Christmas vacation, contained a great
many eulogies to Our Martyred President, from faculty and students. Grace and Charity and I had a conversation about one of
them. The one that I found the most memorable—not because
it was the best-written, but because it may have struck a spark
that would lead to a conflagration later on—was by Mitch Rosen,
representing the sophomore class.

> Not often does someone come along, that a whole
> generation can look up to no matter what their own
> political persuasions, religions, or color. John F.
> Kennedy was such a man. With his cheerfulness,
> his optimism, and his faith in the American people,
> President Kennedy truly showed us what each of us
> could potentially make of our own lives.

It's easy to say as a matter of form that we admired President Kennedy. But let's go a little farther. Let's think about why he was so admirable. Not for his smiles and his good looks and his witty remarks. Not even for his style. Not for his beautiful wife and two charming children.

For his guts, for one thing. For the way he rescued the survivors of PT 109. For the way he battled and defeated illness and injury. For the way he stood firm against Castro and Khrushchev.

Mostly for the way he made us feel our responsibility to our fellow man. The way he reminded us that we owe something to our neighbor and our community, and to the Family of Man. He said "Ask not what your country can do for you; ask what you can do for your country." Let that be the question we ask ourselves as we go through our lives, in memory of our greatest modern President.

He also said, "Let the word go forth that the torch has been passed to a new generation..." For his sake, for the sake of his memory, let's each of us carry that torch with a humble pride.

Rosen and I certainly weren't enemies, but we weren't exactly friends either. Even though he was a sophomore—a station that could hardly be lower—he was acting too much like a leader for my taste. His exhortations—maybe I'm being unfair here, I don't know—came off to me as bossy, sanctimonious. It was like the rest of his personality: possibly well-intentioned, I would concede, but maybe a bit too aggressively so, ostentatiously so.

Know what else I didn't care for, about Rosen? That "Rupert" sweatshirt of his. Not too many American kids knew about Rupert, back then. He was a British comic strip character, a white bear who wore yellow checkered trousers and a red turtleneck sweater. I had heard of Rupert only by accident, long before, when I had been very little. Rosen had this sweatshirt that he wore quite often, with Rupert Bear's image on it. That struck me as precious, right? Like it was a way of saying, "I'm a fan of this obscure character—and I was even in England once, and I got this sweatshirt!"

Yes, I know, that's dumb of me. You know where I get that kind of thinking from? My mother. She was always concerned that if any of us ever slipped up and let people know that we were a little better off financially than they were, or a little better educated, it would be taken as a sign that we were trying to high-hat them. (This, despite our displaying *The New York Times* in our living room.)

Like for instance, way back when I was nine or ten years old, playing with some other kids, I referred to my bad feet as my "Achilles feet." I told them, "Achilles only had a heel, but I've got Achilles feet." Then I had to explain the reference to my playmates. Mom overheard me, and afterwards, she chided me—not angrily, but she did want me to know that I should be careful about displaying my erudition that way. I honestly wasn't trying to show off—I thought the other kids had probably heard of Achilles—but that's how I got the idea that one could show off that way, and that's probably why I resented Rosen for his Rupert sweatshirt.

The day this edition of the *Cat's Paw* came out was another of those rare days when Grace, Charity, and I all walked home together. As we were walking, I said something like this:

"I don't get all this praise for Kennedy. I mean, sure, it's bad that he got shot, but I don't understand what he did as President that was so great, except that he was good-looking and he had that glamorous wife. And Rosen, talking about how Kennedy taught us that we owe something to the rest of society: I don't buy that. I think Rosen's being a suck-up. Saying what he thinks the teachers and principals and parents want to hear, so that they'll talk about what a fine, upstanding young man he is."

Charity looked downright indignant. She whispered, "Oh, Andrew, that is awful. You should be ashamed." As though I had hit her. Or worse. As though I had strangled a kitten.

Grace, in that so-sweet tone of hers, said, "I don't think that at all. If that's how you feel you have every right to say so." Grace, too, was looking seriously at me—but almost (I thought) as though she were admiring me. I don't think she was admiring me, but that's how my wistful mind took it at the moment.

# 10 LOOK TO THE RAINBOW

The annual school musical would be cast, and would go into rehearsal, right after Christmas break. On one of the last few days before Christmas, as I was leaving her class, Dr. Pritchard had asked me, "You're going to audition for *Finian's Rainbow*, aren't you?" I hadn't thought about it. I knew I was an okay speaker, and I was pretty sure I could act—but I had reservations about acting in a musical. I hated the sound of my own singing voice. No doubt it wasn't as bad as I thought it was, but it was bad enough. Then Dr. Pritchard added, "We never have enough boys—and there's a part that's just right for you."

I suppose I should have gone ahead and auditioned for the play, after Christmas, and gotten the part, and presented Mom with a *fait accompli*. Instead, I mentioned to her that very afternoon that Dr. Pritchard had urged me to audition for *Finian's Rainbow*. I got exactly the reaction I had expected:

"I'm not so sure, Andy. You're already doing all those speech contests, and this would mean rehearsals every night for who-knows-how-long. I worry that you don't have time to study."

I admit I wasn't calm in my reaction. Rather energetically—well, okay, shouting—I reminded Mom of what my first-quarter grades had been: B's in chemistry and gym (Coach Vance was a kinder man than he looked), A's in everything else. "That's what my semester grades are going to be, too. For God's sake, the smartest kids in the school—I mean kids with higher grades than I have—all have extracurriculars of some kind. Not to mention that you don't get into a good college without extracurriculars!"

Mom had to admit that last point, anyway. Finally, grudgingly, she dropped her objections—but only because Dad and Mark both told her I ought to be allowed. Mark, by the way, was on Southside's basketball team, with no kick from Mom. But Mark was a perfect student. I don't think he ever got a B in anything, his whole career.

I don't mean to suggest that Mark was a goody-goody, or totally submissive. Not at all. He had a temper nearly as volatile as mine. He didn't get visibly angry or tearful as often as I did, but when he did, he would go absolutely apeshit, screaming and throwing stuff. He would resist, too, if he felt that a parent or teacher were being unreasonable. But Mark was a much better student than I. No getting around that. Mostly because he followed orders.

In a junior high school or middle school, whichever you call it, a lot of the teachers are there because they couldn't cut it at the senior-high level. In any community, the junior high will attract the worst teachers. They tend to assign useless busy-work projects—as in this case, "Make a flour-and-salt map of Saudi Arabia." On the day the assignment was due, thirty kids would turn in their little topographical maps, which the teacher graded and maybe displayed at the back of the room for a day or two, then presumably threw away unless a kid wanted his back.

Me, given a project like that, I would do it badly or not at all—so it's hardly a wonder that I had gotten mostly Cs and Ds all through junior high. Mark, though, when he got that assignment, he made a little flour-and-salt map that belonged in a gift shop. He literally pulled an all-nighter getting his map as accurate as possible. At one point early in the project, he flipped out and burst into tears because it wasn't going along perfectly. But the final product surely was fine work.

That's by the way. I showed up at the school auditorium to audition for *Finian's Rainbow*, after classes on January 13, 1964. I must have done okay, because on the following morning Dr. Pritchard posted the cast list on the Drama Club Call Board (a big bulletin board she had set up in the school's entrance hall, opposite the athletics trophy case, as though in defiance of Coach Vance)—and there was my name, opposite the part of Senator Billboard Rawkins. It was the part that Dr. Pritchard had had in mind for me all along: the comic villain, the bigoted Southern Senator who tries to enforce segregation in the mythical state of Missitucky.

Also on the cast list was Grace Childress. She and I hadn't discussed this show at all. I had known that Grace was a dancer, and that this show had a character named Susan the Silent, who communicated entirely by dancing—but I hadn't made the connection in my mind. It had never occurred to me that Grace would be cast in that part, since she had never said anything to me about being interested in drama.

Seeing Grace's name on the cast list was like having a second Christmas. The fall/winter semester was almost over; in another week, Grace and I wouldn't be in American Lit together anymore—and apparently she and I wouldn't have any classes together in the spring semester. But now, thanks to this show, I would be spending time with Grace at rehearsal for six weeks or so—plus maybe walking her to and from rehearsal, with nobody else around. The first-hour bell hadn't even rung yet and already I was thinking this had to be the luckiest day of my life.

I'll never forget the exchange when I walked into American Lit, about two minutes later. It was one of the few times I hadn't gotten there before Grace, and as soon as I had stepped into the classroom, Dr. Pritchard gave me a big smile and said, "Congratulations, Andy. You'll make a great Senator." Almost as though it had been a surprise to her.

Grace turned around in her seat to look at me; she gave a little delighted gasp and exclaimed, "Oh, are you Senator Rawkins?" Like it made her day, finding that out. I can still hear it; I can still see the expression on her face, how her eyes lit up like she was truly happy and excited for me. I damn near levitated, right there, and floated to my seat at the front of the room.

I sat down as usual, in front of Grace, next to Julia Swinford, who (also as usual) barely acknowledged me. Then Dr. Pritchard said to me, "Andy, you've got a little brother, over at Southside, don't you? Do you think he'd like to have a chorus part? We could always use a few more boys. Does he sing?"

Mark could sing rather well, but I wasn't going to let Dr. Pritchard know that. I was already dreading the day when I would begin my senior year and Mark would be a sophomore in the same school, and would show everyone how much better he was than I, at everything. (And a lot less weird.)

So I said to Dr. Pritchard, "Well, I had a hard enough time getting permission to be in this show. Our parents are pretty concerned about our studies."

"Would it help if I called your mother?" Dr. Pritchard asked. "I could let her know that it wouldn't take up too much of your brother's time."

"Yeah, but he's on the basketball team, besides. I really don't think it'd work."

I can't be sure, but I suspect Dr. Pritchard sensed my discomfort. At any rate, she dropped it.

Another reason why I didn't want my brother hanging around during rehearsals was because if he did, I might feel obliged to spend time with him—which would have interfered with something else I had in mind.

I figured that if I played it cleverly, Grace and I could end up keeping each other company, during rehearsals. We both had a lot of off-stage time. From that time spent together one-on-one, who knew what might develop?

Sure, I realized that the difference in age—even more, the two-year difference in our scholastic careers—might be a hindrance. But I refused to admit what I must have known deep down: that the difference wouldn't be merely a hindrance, but an absolute deal-breaker! Like a kid choosing to believe in Santa Claus—or an adult choosing to believe in God, for that matter—I forced rationality out of my head for the sake of wistfulness. I could make this happen, I told myself.

This would be the chance of a lifetime to find perfect and permanent happiness: to hang out four nights a week, for six weeks, with Grace Childress. If I couldn't woo and win her in that time, I told myself... and that thought stopped me.

I was about to think, "Then I'm not Andrew Palinkas." But that was the one insurmountable difficulty that I had to admit to myself: I *was* Andrew Palinkas! Could I imagine Andrew Palinkas winning Grace Childress?

Oddly enough, I could. Enough to fantasize, anyway. These were fantasies that went beyond the ridiculous—including one in which Grace and I had actually gotten married, I at fifteen and she at sixteen, via a special legal dispensation that was granted in view of our extraordinary love. Mostly, the fantasies were idyllic rather than sexual. They involved a lot of kissing and caressing and soulful gazing—and that was about as far as it got. I'm surprised, in retrospect, that I was able to fantasize about going even that far with Grace. Because she was untouchable.

On the day when rehearsals were to start, when the bell rang to end seventh period, I practically flew out of my chair and raced out of French class—not lingering behind to chat with Prick, as I usually did, which must have surprised him. I wanted to get to the auditorium as fast as I could, preferably to be there when Grace got there. I didn't want to lose even a few seconds that I could have spent in her company. Grace and Axton were already there, sitting side-by-side in about the middle-front of the orchestra seats. I sat down on the other side of Grace, and we waited for Dr. Pritchard to kick things off.

I had known that Dr. Pritchard was a strict teacher, but I wasn't prepared for her little speech on the first afternoon of rehearsal. I hadn't done any serious acting before. I hadn't thought about the discipline that's required to put on a good show. I felt just a bit resentful when I looked at the mimeographed paper that Dr. Pritcherd had handed out, which listed not only the rehearsal schedule, but deadlines for being off book. At the bottom of the page, in capital letters, she had added: FAILURE TO BE OFF BOOK BY DEADLINES MAY RESULT IN DISMISSAL FROM THE CAST.

Dr. Pritchard repeated this orally. "If you don't learn your lines by those dates, you'll be out," she said. She wasn't much of a smiler in her classes, but now she was downright grim, like she was angry at us already. "If you miss a rehearsal, you had better be *seriously* ill. And you had better phone me beforehand and tell me so—or if you're on your way to the hospital, have someone in your family tell me so. If you miss a rehearsal without a very good reason, you'll be out."

Grace and I looked at each other, and we both widened our eyes. I took it as an especial honor that I was exchanging that little confidential glance with Grace.

We started the first rehearsal with blocking—that is, determining where on the stage each actor should be during each scene, and where he would move to, if he moved. This can be pretty tricky and time-consuming, especially in a musical where there are a lot of ensemble numbers with dancing and other movement involved. Since I didn't appear in the play till partway through the first act, I sat in the auditorium, front and center, watching Dr. Pritchard up on the stage, moving people around. Grace, as Susan the Silent, would have to flit about the stage, interacting with the other actors here and there, while all the time remaining fully visible to the audience. The opening scene of *Finian's Rainbow*, through the first song, took a good hour to block.

Dr. Pritchard finally called a ten-minute break. I wandered up onto the stage and sidled over to Grace before anyone else could—and she motioned me to follow her into the wings, then led me through the stage door into a corridor. I was thinking, "My God, does she already have the same idea?" Then in another instant I told myself that that was impossible—but just the fact that Grace apparently wanted to talk to me in private was impressive enough.

Once we were alone in the corridor, Grace said to me, "Now, watch this. Dr. Pritchard wants me to choreograph all my own dance routines, and I have two ideas in mind. One is a classical ballet approach, and the other is more modern. I hate to mix ballet and modern moves, but I'm afraid I'm going to have to, to some extent. Now, you tell me which you prefer..."

She started showing me various dance moves, there in the hallway. I had no idea how to distinguish modern moves from ballet moves—I still don't—but I watched. I told Grace which approach I preferred.

Grace did that little exclamatory gasp of hers. "Oh, Andy! I'm going to make them give you co-credit in the program, for choreography!"

She did, later on. I still have a souvenir program, and in the crew credits it says, plain as day, CHOREOGRAPHY: Grace

Childress, Andrew Palinkas. Thank goodness, Grace hadn't been so self-denying as to have given me first billing: I'd have been mortally embarrassed.

I remember how effortless Grace's dancing seemed, as I observed it during rehearsals. Obviously she put a ton of effort into it, worked her tail off—but it looked like it came so easily to her. The only time during the show when she looked at all uncomfortable was at the end of the play, when the Leprechaun makes a wish that she could talk, and then Grace had a few spoken lines. She seemed to seriously hate speaking on stage. She delivered those lines pretty stiffly, I have to say. But dancing-wise, she nailed it.

I nailed Billboard Rawkins, too, although I say it as shouldn't. My part was a challenge, in some ways, but the only component with which I had any big problem was the singing. I had just one song, with the three "Passion Pilgrim Gospeleers." All three of those kids could sing a little, and I totally couldn't. I could barely carry a tune. I had no idea how to project my singing voice the way I could my speaking voice.

But as an actor, yeah, I ripped. I had to maintain the accent, and the demeanor—and then there was that scene where I literally changed color on stage. That is, I turned from a white person to a Negro—which was considered the polite term for black people in the 1960s. (I won't reveal how that was done, so as not to spoil it for anyone who might one day attend a production of that show.)

*Finian's Rainbow* has a lot of parts for Negroes, and we didn't have but two of them in the whole school, only one of whom— Nia Garthwaite, her name was, short for Antonia—was in the show. So we had a whole bunch of actors who—for dress rehearsal and all four performances—had to paint their faces, arms, and (if female) legs with brown greasepaint every night, and take it off again afterwards. The State City High Drama Club produced a bumper crop of zits for a couple of months thereafter.

I have no idea whether Grace was twigging to the fact that I was so crazy about her. Grace was so unassuming, or at least she gave the appearance of being completely without guile, and I was doing my damnedest not to be too obvious about it—but it seems to almost defy ordinary sense, to imagine that Grace didn't see it. When we were both off-stage, I tried to stay as near to her as I could, as often as I could—although I was obliged to share her with other members of the cast and crew.

I wonder: Is it possible that her parents thought that if they named her Grace, she would feel obliged to live up to the name? Or was she genetically hard-wired to act the way she acted? Grace never condescended to anyone. Whomever she happened to be talking with, she would act as though nothing else mattered to her besides that conversation. This drove me bats, naturally, because I couldn't bear to see Grace giving that much attention to anybody but me. She did, though. I don't think I ever saw her *not* act that way to anyone else.

One of the Passion Pilgrim Gospeleers, with whom I sang that one song, was Jimmy Axton. He was one of the kids who hung out with Grace a lot, besides me. He lived near us, so on most nights the three of us would walk home from rehearsal together. If it were especially cold, Grace's mother, or her father once or twice, would pick Grace up after rehearsal, and Axton and I would catch a ride with them. I remember Grace telling me that she knew how to drive but hated to—she was scared to—so she never drove if she could help it. I always thought that was so strange, since I had the impression that under that nicey-nice exterior, she was probably fearless. I don't know why I thought that, but I did.

Another of the actors—a senior, like Grace—was hanging around Grace as much as I was. Unlike Axton, he clearly had the same idea that I had. He wasn't a very good-looking kid, or very interesting, but he was a senior, so naturally I saw him as a serious competitor, one to worry about. It got pretty annoying, being part of that foursome of Grace, me, Axton, and this other guy— Larry Boylan—while wishing I could eliminate the two other guys. Nothing painful. Just blowing them up or something.

During one rehearsal, while we were waiting off-stage, I asked Grace where she was planning to go to college that coming fall, and she told me she wasn't going to college at all—not yet. She wasn't sure whether or not she would be admitted, she said, but she had applied to a summer dance workshop at the Vaganova Ballet Academy in Leningrad (as the city was then called)—and after that... well, she had also applied to various conservatories, all over the world, mostly in France.

"Just think: I might not be back in the United States for four or five years! And I haven't even been taking French here at school; I've been taking Spanish! Luckily Julia has promised to teach me some French."

I hadn't considered, till then, that I might completely lose touch with Grace, following the end of the school year. I figured it was likely she would go to State University, or if she went else-where she would at least be home in the summers. So it was a rough knock, hearing that. It hit me in the guts. It really was a feeling somewhat like taking a physical blow. It galvanized me, though. Maybe a sane, sensible person would have accepted re-ality, but I was neither sane nor sensible. All I knew was that my time, in which to win Grace, was now limited, and that I would have to take the initiative.

Anyone but me would have recognized the wise course. Any person with even a drop of self-awareness would have said to himself something like this:

"Look, Palinkas, she's two years ahead of you, and at this stage of your lives that's an awful lot. Plus, she's a major talent—

a prodigy—with very likely a career as a professional ballerina in front of her. She's going to be studying at one or another of the most prestigious academies in the world. *In. The. World.*

"One thing she is *not* going to do: She is not going to conduct a long-distance romance with some snot-nose little boy who's got two years of high school still left to get through. Are you stupid?

"If you want any chance of getting with this girl—ever in your life—now is not your time. Your only play—and it's such a slim chance as to be negligible, but it's all you've got—is to be casually friendly with her for the rest of this year, then send her a letter or two while she's overseas. Never, never suggest to her that you have any ulterior motive for staying in touch. Then, *maybe*, ten years from now when she's twenty-six and you're twenty-five, you *might* have a *very* remote chance. Any other course would be not only absolutely fatal, but ridiculous."

Clearly I was not only stupid and crazy. I was also psychologically incapable of employing that strategy: a strategy so plain that any other teenager in the whole world—even some hypothetical teenager with about half of Arno Prick's IQ—could have seen that it was my only chance. It didn't occur to me that I would have to play a waiting game.

§

On opening night of *Finian's Rainbow*, when the curtain came down after we had all made our bows, Jimmy Axton gave a big loud whoop, grabbed Grace in a bear hug, and lifted her up in the air: much the same type of hug that I always gave Mary Hurd at speech contests. I should have seen it that way—as nothing more than a gesture of collegial exuberance—but, being crazy and dumb, I didn't. Instead, I felt once again as though I had been kicked in the guts.

I asked myself, could it be that there was some bizarre romantic tension between Grace and Axton after all? Another completely irrational thought, I admit. A complete crazy-ass thought. Even if nothing of that sort were in play, it enraged me to see anybody handling *my* girl in that manner.

I strode over to Grace and said, "I've got to get a hug too." I threw one arm round her shoulders—rather abruptly, I have to admit—*and she pushed me off.*

I don't remember that she said anything—just that she pushed me off, wiggled out of my grasp. The hurt of watching Axton hug Grace was nothing at all compared to that. I suppose I should have anticipated it. I should have known better than to try such a move.

I did know better! I did it, knowing that trying to hug Grace would come off all wrong and make me look clumsy and clueless at best, and creepy at worst. I knew before I did it that Grace wouldn't like it and wouldn't react well to it. But I *would* go ahead and try to hug her. I couldn't *not* do it.

The next evening, when we were in the green room getting ready to go on, I asked Grace flat-out why she had pushed me off the night before. "After all," I said, "I just wanted to give you a hug; I wasn't planning on doing anything more than that."

"I'm not a hugger," Grace said, very serious. "I'm a handshaker. Now, Charity is a hugger. So is my mother. My father, not so much. I guess I'm like him. In that regard."

"But you didn't mind when Jimmy did it..."

"But with Jimmy it's different because we're such old friends. We've had all those dance classes together, and then we walk to school together every morning... holding hands..."

Grace laughed, and I wondered then—I wonder to this day—*why* would she have added those last two words, except to push my buttons? If she had been trying to push my buttons, it must have been because she knew that I had feelings for her beyond friendship—feelings that she clearly meant to encourage, even if she didn't reciprocate. Or at any rate she meant to aggravate my feelings of jealousy and frustration. Is it possible that she was *not* trying to perturb me by adding those two little words, "holding hands"? I can't imagine that she didn't know what she was doing—but I'm crazy. It could be my own paranoia that's putting such a spin on the matter.

This little incident made me even more determined to win Grace for myself. What I would do with her, once I got her, I had not even a vague idea. What I wanted from her wasn't too clear. Sexual favors would have been out of the question—so far out of the realm of possibility that I didn't even think about them. (Never mind that I had had a fantasy about the two of us being married.) I knew that Grace was going away—perhaps never to be seen again in State City—but somehow that wasn't even a detail in the picture.

The picture? It wasn't a picture. It was an infinite black canvas of obsession and despair.

We performed *Finian's Rainbow* four times over a weekend: Thursday through Sunday in early March. The cast party was held on the Friday following. The Spring Dance was scheduled for the day after that. At the party—it was held at Larry Boylan's house—I took Grace aside and asked her, first off, if she would care to sign my program from the show. We sat down together on the floor, in a corner, and she took my program. She inscribed it thus, in that perfect swooping hand of hers:

Roses are red
Violets are blue
Sugar is sweet
And so are you
—Grace

That—I thought when I read it—was almost bizarre: such a hackneyed and insipid inscription from such a bright girl. Frankly, if only for an instant, it made me wonder why I was so fascinated with Grace. But only for an instant, because at the same time, it made my heart soar. You know, at fifteen, a boy doesn't realize the connotations of "sweet." He hasn't learned yet that when a girl calls you sweet, that's almost always code for "nice, but not attractive in *that* way."

I thought Grace was telling me that she was into me.

Thus, I felt at least a degree of hope as I took a big breath and told Grace I had something else to ask her.

"Pop the question, eh?" Grace replied, and she laughed.

Again, that struck me as so weird. Grace could not have been unaware of the implications of that phrase, so it seemed to me that she used it deliberately, as a way of acknowledging that she suspected that I was going to make some kind of strong move. I know: ludicrous. How could she imagine that a pipsqueak sophomore would dare so much?

I could barely get the words out, but I forced it: "The Spring Dance is tomorrow night, and I wondered, if you hadn't already been asked yet, if you'd like to go with me."

It was the first time I had ever asked a girl to do anything. It might have been the most scared I had ever felt in my life. When I had started performing before an audience, I had been surprised at how confident I had felt. A little nervous, sure. But afraid? Never. I have never—then or now—felt more at home (or more comfortable, I should say, for "at home" wasn't always desirable) than when I was on stage. But this. Asking a girl for a date—*this* girl! Nothing puts your ego on the line like asking a girl for a date.

Grace's response shocked me. I had expected a flat-out "Oh, thank you, Andy, but I really don't think I'd care to. That's so sweet of you to ask, though." Well, she did say the last bit.

"Why, Andy, that's so sweet of you to ask. I think I could; I'll have to ask my parents, of course. Why don't you call me tomorrow and I'll let you know for sure?"

It was my first experience of that kind of response, and I only partially grasped that this might be a polite and gradual way of refusing. I still can't believe I was so dumb—but I was pretty sure I had heard a "yes."

I might have borne it better if Grace had replied, "*Eeew!* Are you kidding?" There's no way, though, that Grace, being Grace, would have done such a thing. So I had to go home that night congratulating myself for having bagged Grace Childress as my date for the Spring Dance.

When I left the party, shortly after that conversation, Grace had been chatting with Boylan, and I hadn't dared to risk horning in on their conversation to ask Grace to walk home with me. I suppose I could have waited for Grace to leave—but I was afraid of what I might see or hear if I stayed.

The next morning, per instruction, I phoned across the street to the Childress house. Our phone was in the kitchen—most home phones were, in those days—hard-wired to the wall, next to the basement door. If you wanted privacy on the phone, in our house, you had to sit on the basement stairs with the door shut behind you (not completely shut, since the phone cord was in the way) and hope that nobody heard you if you talked softly.

So that's what I did. I dialed across the street, hoping like hell that Grace, and not some other family member, would pick up. She did. She sounded thrilled to hear my voice on the other end—I can't imagine that she would ever have sounded any other way—so I asked her, "Are we on for tonight? How about I ring your bell at eight o'clock, and we can walk over together?"

Grace replied, "Well, I've talked it over with my parents, and I think it would be better if we just each went to the dance... and I'll see you there."

I was done in—sucker-punched—and just barely intelligent enough to be one hundred percent sure that Grace's parents had had nothing to do with it.

I asked, "Can't I at least walk you over?" I knew I was begging. "You don't have to spend the whole evening with me. But I could walk you; no harm in that, right?"

"Why, we're all going out to dinner, and my parents will drop me at the school afterwards. Don't worry, I'll see you there."

I must have gone pale by the time I emerged from behind the basement door, or maybe the hurt in my stomach was visible in some other way, because Mom, who was working there in the kitchen, immediately asked me what was wrong. I told her. I was in too much pain not to. I couldn't have pretended that there was nothing to tell.

"Well, maybe Grace wants to be more of a free spirit," Mom said. That might have been a reasonable enough explanation, but I wasn't having it.

"Why don't you ask Charity?" Mom suggested. "You could still dance a dance or two with Grace." It hadn't occurred to me that Charity might want to go. I had never talked with Charity about any dances or parties. I assumed she had always stayed home from them, as I had.

"I could," I said to Mom, "but it'd be awfully short notice and I'm sure she'd know she was a substitute. It might not be very polite of me."

"That's true," Mom said. "I had a boy ask me to a dance once, when I knew I wasn't his first choice, and I was mad at him all evening and had a lousy time. Maybe you should just go to the dance and spend as much time with Grace as you can, without imposing on her, and see what happens."

What happened was that I didn't spend a lot of time with Grace. We met up at the school gym. Grace was wearing this sea-green party dress that I assumed she had made herself. She had

141

her hair up in a modified beehive. She danced the first couple of dances with me, all right. It was that body-shaking dancing that was done then, like the twist and variations thereupon. I would never have been able to imagine Grace doing that sort of dancing if I hadn't actually seen her do it, that night in the gym. Then she went over to Boylan and started dancing with him.

The two of them danced together for most of the rest of the evening. Grace was chatting with Boylan with every bit as much animation as she had ever shown to me. I didn't notice that he was any better than I was, as a dancer—not that anyone danced well, at that age and in those days—but evidently his conversation was sufficient to hold Grace's attention.

A couple of times, in the course of the evening, Boylan magnanimously stepped back, and allowed me to have the dance. Thank God, Grace chose to sit out all the slow dances. If I had seen her and Boylan doing a slow number, there's no telling how I might have reacted. But from this—the fact that Grace would *not* take any of the slow dances with Boylan—I allowed myself a faint lingering hope. Maybe she was making it clear that she wasn't much interested in Boylan, either.

I continued to lurk near Grace, all through the evening. Maybe I shouldn't have, but I did. If a slow dance came up when I happened to be partnered with Grace, I would leave the floor with her, and keep talking with her, and Boylan would drift over to us and join the conversation, so that Grace would be his for the next fast dance.

There was no way I was going to dance even one dance with anyone else. If I ever needed someone to haul me to the curb and tell me to stop acting like a goddamn idiot, I suppose it was then—but who was there to do it?

On my own, I was not capable of controlling what I knew was useless and undesirable behavior. Maybe if Coach Vance had been one of the chaperones at that dance, and maybe if he had somehow happened to have noticed my behavior and figured out what was going on, he could have walked over to me and said, "Palinkas, knock it off. Now." That would have been that. Not that it would have won me any points with Grace, if I had handled the situation differently, but maybe I could have preserved an atom of dignity.

Around 10:30 that night, the three of us—Grace, Boylan, and I—were standing by the refreshment table. Boylan and I were both trying to provide Grace with a glass of punch at the same time. Grace escaped the dilemma of having to accept one offer and refuse the other by saying to Boylan, "I should get home now. I promised my parents I'd be home early."

At the time, I asked myself: Had Grace really made that promise, and was she being dutiful to her parents? Or was she finding the situation uncomfortable? Or was she, quite sensibly, leaving the party while she was still having fun?

Grace didn't invite either of us to walk her home, but she was unable to shake either one of us loose, so she ended up walking home with Boylan on her right and me on her left.

Although this had been the Spring Dance, it was mid-March, and thus still winter in State City. It wasn't terribly cold, but the snow on the ground was pretty deep. The sidewalks were mostly shoveled incompletely, one shovel's width wide, so that sometimes both Boylan and I—but almost always I, at least—had to tramp through snow, leaving Grace to take the sidewalk. Thank God, Grace was sure-footed. She never slipped, so at no point did she have to take Boylan's arm. If she had done that, I'm not sure how I would have dealt with it. Never in a billion years would she have taken *my* arm.

As we approached her house, Grace finally spoke to me: "Andy, you're so silent! Are you all right?"

"Actually, no," I said. "I'm a little mad at you, matter of fact." I knew better than to say that. But I couldn't stop myself.

**143**

Grace said, "Oh, dear." And the three of us walked up her driveway to her front porch. She giggled and said, "Well, good night, gentlemen," and went inside.

Boylan and I shrugged at each other, and walked back down the driveway, side by side, not speaking. Boylan didn't know that I lived directly across the street, so I walked with him to the end of the block, resolving to take the opposite direction, whichever way he turned. At that point he said, "Oh, are you going that way? Good night, then." I echoed, "Good night," and I walked away, without looking back. I was pretty sure Boylan wasn't going to double back to Grace's house—but if he was going to do it, I sure didn't want to see it. I kept walking for a quarter-hour or so before I decided it was safe to turn around and head home.

When I got near our house I started cutting through other people's yards, tramping through some deep snow, so that I could approach our house through the back yard, and let myself in by the back door. Thus, I wouldn't have to see Grace's house. I didn't want to be forced to notice whether lights were still on in there, or whether there was company. Once I had got indoors, I avoided looking out of any window from which I might catch a glimpse. Our house was dark; Mark and my parents were already in bed. I undressed in the dark and went right to bed too—pulling the covers clear over my head. It took too long for me to fall asleep.

# 11 THE ATTACK

It was time to regroup, to assess, to plan—or so I told myself, the next day. Any sane person would have informed me that in reality it was time to retreat, but it didn't occur to me to retreat, to bide my time for ten years or so. I'm amazed that that thought never crossed my mind. It didn't. At that point, all I knew was that I had to strike—fast.

What I eventually did, never had any chance of working to my advantage. I fantasized a positive outcome in my head, over and over again, as though by so doing I could cause it to work out right. But I must have known—I *must* have—going in, that I was going to make an idiot of myself.

Why, then, did I do it? I don't know—except that I must have been hard-wired to act that way.

I forced myself to wait for a couple of days. I didn't have any classes with Grace, in that second semester, and now that the musical was over, I didn't have much other opportunity to spend time with her, except at lunch. Our lunch group had become a fivesome, with Boylan joining Grace and me and Axton and Julia Swinford, so if I wanted to have any substantial conversation with Grace I would have to seek her out to do it. Somewhere around the middle of that next week I stopped by Grace's locker and asked her, "Can we talk after school? There's a project I want to discuss."

Grace widened her eyes at me and gave me another of those huge smiles—then she looked conspiratorial. She said, "How mysterious! It can't be today, though. I've got ballet class right after school. How about tomorrow? I'm so intrigued! What could this project be?"

"Well, it concerns you. I'll tell you more later."

"I know! You want to intensify my French lessons so I'll be ready for the conservatory in the fall! That's so sweet!"

"Well, we could do that—but it's not what I especially wanted to talk with you about. It's... a delicate matter, and I'd just as soon keep it confidential. And if it doesn't work out, I'm hoping you can keep it to yourself too. If it does work out—well, you can tell the world for all I care!"

**145**

Grace looked so earnest—and at the same time, she looked so amused.

"I can't wait till tomorrow, to find out what you're talking about! I'll see you after school then—for our rendezvous. That sounds so romantic, doesn't it? Rendezvous!"

I took advantage of the extra twenty-four hours to sit down in the basement, that evening—it was the only place where I could be sure of a few minutes' privacy—and write down a list of things I wanted to tell Grace. That's right: "talking points," as though I were preparing a speech to a jury, which in a sense was pretty much what I was going to do.

It was mainly words of flattery, and partly to tell Grace what my feelings were for her, and to add that I hoped I could know that they were returned. Scarlett O'Hara tried that approach on Ashley Wilkes. Look how far it got her, though! And she was a hell of a lot more alluring than I was. I'm sure other people have tried it and made themselves similarly ridiculous. But I like to think that nobody ever made a bigger fool of himself than I did.

The next day, when the bell rang, ending French class, I bolted out of my seat. I told Prick, "I gotta run, man, sorry; lemme catch you tomorrow."

Sure enough, there was Grace, waiting by her locker, assembling all the stuff she had to carry home: her bookbag, her flute in its case. Thank God she had already put her overcoat on, or I would probably have tried to help her on with it as though we had been on a date. As it was, I asked Grace if I could carry her books, in addition to mine. She passed the bag to me—again with that huge smile of hers.

For a few glorious, never-to-be-forgotten minutes, I was carrying Grace Childress's bookbag. Carrying *the Grace Childress's* bookbag, slung over my shoulder for all to see, as Grace walked alongside me. Not many kids carried a bag of that sort: it was identifiably Grace's.

It was only as we exited the building and walked along the footpath that I remembered that my own overcoat was still in my locker: I had forgotten to go get it before racing over to Grace's locker. Luckily it wasn't all that cold out; I wasn't uncomfortable, in my shirtsleeves—but I certainly would not go back for it, and I knew I would get a ration of shit if I came home that evening with no coat.

"What will you do in the morning when it's sure to be cold?" Mom would demand.

Instead of walking Grace in the direction of our street, I walked her over to the area out behind the school where there were tennis courts, a couple of baseball diamonds, and a practice football field—all of them still partly snow-covered, and very wet. I immediately saw that I had made another mistake.

"I'm sorry, I wasn't thinking," I said. "I'm making you get your shoes all muddy."

"It's okay. I was going to clean them tonight anyway."

I led Grace to the tennis courts, which at least were solid clay. She and I stood there, side by side, looking out across the baseball diamonds, me still carrying two sets of books, and finally I was starting to feel pretty cold.

"I wanted to talk to you" (my voice was practically croaking as I said this) "about... well, you know, you and I have become... well... you're about the best friend I've ever had, so I hope you'll indulge me in letting me tell you this, and hope you won't think I'm presuming..."

Grace's face lit up in dawning comprehension. She looked all serious and concerned and empathetic.

"Ohhh, Andy. It's Charity you wanted to talk about. Isn't it?"

Oh shit, I said to myself. She would think that. Or pretend that she thought that. I'll never know, now, will I? Was she putting me on? Or maybe, now that I think about it, Grace was gifting me with a last-moment chance to back down and escape with

**147**

my dignity. It's academic, because even if I had guessed, at the time, that that was what she was doing, I wouldn't have taken the out that she was offering.

"No. I want to talk about you."

"What about me?"

"Well, it's more about me in relation to you." It took me a few seconds to go on. My mouth and throat were as dry as they have ever been, before or since.

"Excuse me," I said. I reached into my pocket. "Sorry, but I wrote down some things I wanted to say. I hope you don't mind if I keep this list in my hand while we talk."

"Why, no, of course not!" Grace looked more perplexed than ever. I glanced at my notes.

"Apparently I didn't make it clear enough, these past few months. I mean, I've been trying one way or another to... well... I don't know whether you know it or not, so I'll just ask: Are you aware that I've been... *after* you?"

"After me?"

"For the past few months... I've been..." (I groped for a delicate phrasing) "amorously pursuing you. You didn't know that?"

Grace continued to look at me with the utmost solemnity.

"No. I knew you liked me, but I didn't know it was anything more than that."

"So what do you think about it?"

This had been the point at which I had planned to launch full-tilt into the main body of my little speech. But I was too flustered to remember to look at the notes, there in my hand, and at any rate—all of a sudden—I didn't think it would do me much good to start waxing lyrical.

As long as I had insisted on being fool enough to go through with this business, I should have actually composed a speech, rehearsed it word-for-word, stayed on text and on message no matter what. Then, while I might have gone up in flames anyway, at least I'd have done it with some style.

"Andy, I don't know what to say. This is just so unexpected. And..." (Grace giggled) "I don't know what to expect now!"

Now I was totally on the defensive.

"Well, don't worry. I'm not going to do anything about it if you're not interested. I'm not going to... you know... try to kiss you or anything."

"Why, I don't think I would want you to do that."

"I don't, you know, I don't... force myself on people... I mean I try not to..."

"Oh, Andy, let's not talk about that. You're an extremely nice boy. Let's leave it at that for now."

"You don't have to say anything one way or the other," I said. I was freezing inside and out, by this time, but I barely noticed the cold, because I was so pumped full of fear-endorphins. "I just wanted to lay it out for you, you know... and let you know... what was going on, because I'm aware that I... that I act kind of strange around you..."

"Why, no, Andy, you don't act strange around me that I can tell. You're always so kind and polite."

Well, bless her heart. That made me feel even more foolish. I wish that Grace had said I acted brutal around her, that she was frightened and horrified of me—thoroughly grossed-out, besides. If she had felt all that, she might eventually have become a little more attracted to me, anyway.

"Well, if I am, it's because I want to be, when I'm around you. But... I don't know, I was thinking that you must have guessed that I... felt a certain way about you..."

"No, it never occurred to me. I can't believe you're telling me this." Grace giggled again. I might almost have preferred it if she had started running and screaming for help. "I can't believe you're serious."

That's when I lowered my voice to a near-whisper and added to it a soft, slow, dramatic intensity that would have done credit to my own mother.

"I have never been more serious in my life."

"Well, I don't know what to say," Grace replied.

I said again, "You don't have to say anything." I was trying to sound all strong and confident. "Just... give me a chance, is all I'm asking for. To... prove myself, for want of a better way to put it. Will you give me a chance?" Which didn't sound strong and confident at all, and I was entirely sensible of it.

"All right," said Grace. She sounded perplexed. "I should probably start home, now. You don't have to keep carrying my books. They must be heavy."

"But I'd like to."

So instead of doubling back to the school to get my overcoat, I walked Grace home from school. In full view of anyone who cared to notice. I got to be seen walking Grace Childress home from school, carrying her books.

I knew I had blown the scene. Hell, I had known in my heart that it was a no-go before it got. Still, I was walking Grace Childress home from school, carrying her books. I don't know how many kids saw me, if any. How I hope, to this day, that at least a few of them did.

Grace was walking on my right. Her left hand held her flute case, so I couldn't take hold of it, but still I held my books under my left arm, while at the same time my left hand held the cord of Grace's bookbag, which was slung over my left shoulder, in case her left hand became available at any point. This was uncomfortable and awkward, but I had to do it.

As we walked, we dropped the subject we had been on. There wasn't much more to say about it, after all. Grace started asking me about my various classes—and that was a painful reminder to me that I was still a sophomore. I forced myself to do no more than answer her questions, as casually as I could. I only hoped to avoid saying anything else that was weird.

I didn't mention Boylan, by the way, during that conversation. I wanted to—I wanted to get an idea of what Grace thought of him, if she thought of him at all—but I knew that that wouldn't help. The itch was always there, though: the urge to ask Grace how she could think of spending any time with *that* gink when she could be exclusive with *this* gink.

I should have not mentioned *anything*, at that point. I should have shut up, except to respond when Grace spoke. I should have realized that I'd gambled hugely and lost, that I should chalk this up to experience, never speak of it again, act as though it had never happened. If Grace ever brought it up, I should feign amazement and insist that she must have dreamt it. I couldn't help it, though. As we were getting close to her house, I said:

"Anyway, I guess I've said all I can say on... what we were talking about. I just wanted to tell you what was going on... and see how you felt about it."

"I think let's be friends. It's much too early in my life for me to think of that kind of thing. Right now I'm simply trying to get through high school, and I'm not interested in getting romantically involved—with anybody."

That was better than nothing, those last two words.

"Well, sure." Now I was trying to sound eminently reasonable. "And you know I'm... well, I'm ready for you, if the situation changes and you ever do feel that... that you're ready for me."

"Thank you so much for carrying my books, Andy. You're so old-fashioned! I'll see you in school tomorrow!"

When I walked into our house, Mom said to me, "I just happened to be looking out the window, a minute ago. Did I see you carrying Grace's books for her?" I had to admit that she had.

"Are you two an item, now?" Mom was smiling. I believe she was even farther out of touch with reality than I was. She must

**151**

have been absolutely in some other world. Or maybe Mom was deliberately ignoring reality, for my sake, because she somehow could sense how much I wanted it to happen.

"I wouldn't say that, for sure. It's hard to tell what the situation is. We'll have to wait and see."

Mom didn't say a word about my overcoat.

§

I might have found it easier to deal with, if Grace had made a point of ignoring me after that. But she didn't. She was as accessible as ever, as though nothing had happened. She still left her house early, most mornings, for a music, dancing, or gymnastics class. During the day, between classes and at lunch, Julia was trying to claim a monopoly on Grace—her sneers at me became almost snarls—but on Tuesday and Thursday afternoons, when she had no after-school lessons, I started making a point of walking Grace home. Sometimes Charity was with us, and sometimes not. Sometimes Julia would be along—coming over to Grace's house to study with her, I supposed. But I was always there for the walk, twice a week. Only once more—on a day when we happened to be walking just the two of us—did I offer to carry Grace's books for her, but she declined.

"I have to build arm-strength."

Some of the other kids had started noticing that I would make a beeline from my locker to Grace's at the end of the day on Tuesdays and Thursdays after French class. Once Haviland, as a joke, came over to my locker and said, "Hey, Andy, hold on, I want to talk to you about something," and when I told him, "Let's talk tomorrow, okay? I've gotta run," he grabbed me by the arm and pretended he was going to detain me physically. I broke free and absolutely swung on him. I missed, thank goodness—I probably didn't really want to hit him, just make him back off—but I bet my rage surprised him. He shrank back, I think at first in genuine surprise and maybe a little fear, but then he laughed and pretended to cringe and whimper in terror.

I apologized to Haviland the next day, explaining that "I was feeling weird yesterday," but from then on Haviland kept a distance from me, like Lord knew what I might do next.

Haviland was older than I was, and a good athlete. I'm sure he could have whipped me in a fair fight—but probably he thought I was too crazy to mess with. And he probably wouldn't have wanted to fight me anyway, because I amused him so.

For the next few weeks, I tried to keep my conversations with Grace friendly, with no mention of the talk we had had at our "rendezvous"—and in any case I seldom had Grace all to myself. But after six weeks or so—by the beginning of May—I wasn't able to control myself any longer. I was walking Grace home one afternoon—one of the few times when we had nobody else with us—so I asked her, "Have you thought about it? I mean, what we talked about, before?"

"Why can't we just be friends?"

"Because I'm afraid that's not enough for me. You... well, you think I have a crush on you, right?"

"Well, yes."

"But I'm afraid it's gone a little deeper than that, now." (The fact that I conscientiously eschewed the "L" word is pretty strong evidence, it seems to me, that I had a clear idea of how foolish and unrealistic were my ambitions.)

"Oh, dear." Grace simpered. We kept walking.

"I don't know what to do. You said you'd give me a chance and I've been doing whatever I know how to do to... I don't know... to show you whatever good points I might have." (I didn't believe I had any.) "And you know, it's frustrating, when I'm doing the best I can—and I don't want to accuse you of doing anything wrong, because you haven't—it's just that... well, this means everything to me and sometimes I think you're making light of it, and probably laughing up your sleeve at me."

At this, Grace stopped walking and mimed laughing up her sleeve, ho-ho-ho. Then she said, "I always thought that was such a strange expression. What are some other expressions that strike you as... unusual?"

"You're trying to change the subject."

"Maybe I am. But I get so interested in words."

A couple of days after that, Chuck Haviland passed by, while I was at my locker, and he asked me, "Hey, Palinkas, who are you taking to the prom?" He had a couple of his mates with him, and he was standing at a safe distance, grinning at me.

I looked mystified, because after all I was only a sophomore, and sophs weren't allowed at the Junior-Senior Prom unless they were the date of an eleventh- or twelfth-grader. So I asked Haviland what he meant, and he said, "I thought you had a date, you know. Grace. Ha-ha! Jeez, you sure know how to pick 'em!"

I wasn't particularly insulted for myself. Embarrassed that Haviland knew, and that he was joshing me about it, yes—but that didn't bother me so much. Rather, I was good and steamed at him for implying that I was somehow showing poor judgment, or poor taste, by being interested in Grace. I forced myself to shrug, and I gave Haviland a little smirk. For once, I wasn't letting him get to me. But it was at that moment that I realized that once again, I had made myself a laughingstock—possibly for the whole school—and I had nobody to blame but myself.

Haviland had given me an idea, though. It would certainly have been within the rules for me to go to the prom as Grace's escort. I don't suppose there had ever been a sophomore boy at one of these shindigs, in the history of the school—but that's not to say it couldn't happen. Besides, although the prom was still a few weeks off, I had to ask Grace before Boylan could, assuming he hadn't done so already.

So I asked her, that same day, and she refused. Nicely.

"It's nothing to do with you, but I feel that I've outgrown high school dances. I just don't care to go at all."

That was better news than I had expected. It meant that Grace probably wasn't giving Boylan any more encouragement than she was giving me. Indeed, I never saw the two of them together in those last weeks. How can I know? Maybe he had approached Grace as I had done, and maybe she had given him a similar response. Only, if that had happened, Boylan had apparently had the good sense to retreat.

In all this time, Charity's attitude towards me seemed to change. I don't know—I never asked—how much Grace had told Charity about our dealings, but I'm sure Charity could sense that something was up. Shortly after my first baring my soul to Grace, Charity had started to look at me in a way that seemed reproachful to me, or at least disdainful. Sometimes if I spoke to Charity, like in a class, she would ignore me.

When it became clearer and clearer that I was wasting my time on Grace, and that Grace was starting to find my persistence a bit annoying, Charity would look at me out of the corners of her eyes when she and I passed in the hallways, and shake her head a little, and I'd hear a slight laugh in her voice when she said, "Hi, Andy," as though she meant to add, "you comically pathetic person." Charity and I hardly had any conversation, in the latter part of that semester.

Never did I get any of that derision from Grace herself— although as the spring wore on, I would notice that Grace's greeting would sometimes be polite rather than cheerful.

One morning in late May, though, I passed by Grace's locker between classes as I often did—oh-so-casually in case she happened to be there—and Grace greeted me in the old way, with that huge smile and her eyes open wide. She seemed almost ready to jump out of her skin from happiness and excitement.

"I just got the best news! It was in the mail this morning! I got placed in that workshop in Leningrad, so I'll be leaving town a couple months earlier than I'd thought I would—right after graduation in fact."

Which left me two weeks to close the deal.

"And have you decided where you're going this fall?"

Grace didn't answer, which I took to mean that she had decided—and had decided not to tell me where. I persisted.

"Why not stay here and go to State? I'm sure you could study dance all you wanted, here, and meanwhile you'd have an education so that you'd be ready for something else when you couldn't dance anymore."

Grace smiled—rather tensely, it seemed to me.

"No, I don't think so."

"Then we'll have to write to each other. I'll torment you with verbose love-letters."

I was trying, in my ham-fisted way, to be light-hearted. That was the first time I had ever said "love" in Grace's hearing. At the word, Grace looked severe, although her face still wore a tight, tense smile.

"Verbosity is fine. But love letters, I'd rather not get." Grace took a deep breath. "Andy, really, I think it's time for us to stop seeing each other unless you can keep off this subject."

"Look." (I was trying to sound utterly reasonable, and the Soul of Patience.) "All I'm going to do, when you're away, is write to you. It's not like there's anything else I can do, anyway. And naturally I'd like it if you wrote back. You don't have to answer every letter, I mean, if it starts to get to be a chore for you, you can stop, but you know, it would be a favor to me if you would let me write to you, because it would... you know, give me something to hold onto..."

I was fully aware of how pathetic I was sounding. But I could not shut up.

"If I could stay in touch, maybe... well, maybe it would have a cathartic effect, writing to you..."

Grace giggled, at that.

"Okay, that wasn't a very smart choice of words. But, like I say... It would give me something to hold onto and... and I'm beginning to repeat myself."

"Andy, you know where I stand." Now Grace was speaking softly and not smiling even a little. "We can be friends... or we should stop having anything to do with each other."

At that point I was afraid I might start crying—to which almost anything would have been preferable—and I had to do something to stop myself. At the same time, I realized that if there was one blessed thing that I *had* to achieve, out of this whole ridiculous enterprise, it was to hold Grace Childress in my arms and lock lips with her, seriously, one time in my life, and there was never going to be another chance, most likely.

Not that this was a chance, exactly. It was more like an assault. Quicker than it takes to remember it, I threw my arms around Grace and tried to pull her to me, with one hand on the back of her head, ready to draw her face against mine.

I wish to God I could forget that, but I can't.

Grace ducked and wriggled out of my grasp immediately. This time she actually looked scared, and I was afraid for an instant that she might scream, but instead she whispered, "Please," and backed away from me. "I don't think we should see each other ever again."

"No, that wouldn't work. I swear. I've got to be your friend, at least."

"Only if you promise not to mention this, ever again."

"I promise," I said. Grace walked away. Believe it or not, I had better sense than to follow her.

For the rest of that day, I had the worst ache in my guts. I mean physical pain, cramping and all. I stayed out of Grace's way: made a point—for the first time that year—of *not* getting into her sight.

It wasn't just my guts that hurt. I can't explain it, but the injury to my psyche translated into something that wasn't exactly a physical pain, but at the same time, physical pain is all that I can call it. It felt as though I had been beaten up by a much bigger kid, without having been literally bruised or battered.

By nightfall, those various aches had worn off, somewhat. Probably my psyche was defending me, somehow, by perversely reminding me that I still had two weeks left, that I wasn't beaten yet, that somehow I would still find a way to get... oh, I still had no notion of what I wanted to get, but whatever it was, I still had two weeks to try to get it. I felt, that night, faintly optimistic— almost euphoric.

I suppose I understand how Hitler must have felt in the spring of 1945—when everyone but he was perfectly aware that the war was utterly lost and that Germany was doomed, but he was still asserting that somehow, due to any of a number of possible reasons, Germany would still win by a nose. I don't suppose Hitler, either, had any notion of what he could hope to win at that point.

I still walked Grace home from school as often as I could, and when Grace and I were alone I kept my word and didn't bring up my feelings. But Grace became less and less talkative as those two weeks went by. Clearly, she was enduring my presence, forbearing to tell me exactly what she thought of me. I wonder, now, why she didn't surround herself with other friends, to neutralize me, but so far as I could see, she never made any effort to avoid being alone with me.

It was through my mother, at the dinner table one evening, that I heard about the Childress family's plans for that summer.

"That Rae Childress," Mom told us. "I don't know about her. You know what she's doing for the summer? She, and Joe, and even Charity? They're going Down South, to Mississippi. To be civil rights workers. She told me she didn't know yet what that would consist of, but that's what they're doing. While Grace is in Leningrad." Mom shook her head. "Sometimes I have to wonder about that family. I guess it's commendable, what they're doing. I have to say it's... not my idea of a vacation."

"It would make sense," Dad said. "I mean, it figures. Quakers and Jews. They tend to be interested in such activity."

"It surprises me that they'd put their daughter in danger," Mom said. "But maybe they know what they're doing. And I suppose Charity would be enthusiastic about it, too, from what Rae has told me about her—and from what Andy tells us.

"Anyway, Andy, Rae asked if you could be in charge of mowing their lawn and watering their flowers through June."

§

On the next-to-last day of the school year—a Thursday—Grace hardly spoke a word to me as we walked home. When she looked at me—which was seldom—it was sidelong, unsmiling. I clearly saw a glint of resentment in her eye—something I never would have imagined I would ever see from her.

As we turned onto our street and got near Grace's house, I said, almost murmuring, "You don't like me anymore, do you?"

"I wouldn't say that. Maybe I'm just tired of... all that."

"Well. You only have to put up with it for another day."

Grace actually curled her lip the least bit, when I said that.

That was the moment when I finally, fully, realized the enormity of what I had done.

Grace turned away, without a goodbye, and strode up her front walk to her house.

The 1964 yearbooks had been published a week before; I had already gotten mine signed by most of the kids and teachers I

**159**

had wanted the signatures of. This was not many. I got Charity's signature, and Axton's, and those of a few teachers and a few other speech and drama kids—and Prick's. There was one friend I had made, such as he was. I almost forgot to ask Prick to sign my book. He signed it, "To one of the nicest guys I know." Which astonished me.

I hadn't got Grace to sign yet, though. I had been afraid to ask—afraid she might flat-out refuse.

On the morning of that last day—a Friday—the final issue of the *Cat's Paw* came out, with the senior wills, the predictions, and a list of where each graduating senior was headed in the fall. Grace's prediction—I don't know who wrote it; I suppose a committee of kids got together to write predictions for the whole class—was, "Grace Childress will end up as a member of the Rockettes, till her arches fall—and then maybe she'll marry Rudolf Nureyev. Sorry, Andy."

Grace's will was the shortest of the entire class of '64: "I, Grace Childress, will my dear little sister to the tender mercies of State City High." I could almost hear Grace saying that, with that laugh in her voice, but I was struck by the brevity and the lack of originality—although I shouldn't have been. Grace—as she had told me before—had outgrown this kind of thing, if indeed she had ever had much tolerance for it.

On the "Where They're Headed" page, I saw that in the fall, Grace would be attending the Conservatoire de Paris. Julia Swinford was going to Radcliffe, but I had known that.

School was scheduled to be dismissed at noon, that last day. I had cleaned out my locker the day before, so I had a few extra minutes to stake out Grace's. Sure enough, there she was, crouched on the floor, bagging the last of her stuff. Her back was to me. Julia was crouched down next to her; I could see that she was signing Grace's yearbook. I hung off, a few yards away, hoping neither of them would see me.

Julia had tears on her cheeks. They both stood up, and embraced; Julia appeared to be actually sobbing. She held Grace really tight, for several seconds. At last they broke apart, and I heard Julia say, "See you at the ceremony tonight, then." She was clearly trying to get herself under control. Then she turned her back to Grace and scurried down the hall, as though she wanted to get away from Grace before she lost it completely.

I sidled up to Grace. I must have looked pretty sheepish; I sure felt that way, anyway. Grace didn't have much stuff to carry home—but I asked her, "May I help you with all that? It looks like a lot."

"No, thank you."

Grace wouldn't look at me.

"Would you sign my yearbook for me?" I put my yearbook in front of her, and held out a pen. Grace opened the book to the inside of the front cover, signed her name in the top left-hand corner, and handed book and pen back to me, still not looking at me.

"Grace Childress," she had written.

That was it. From someone who had once written that I was sweet as sugar. I realized that that was all I deserved.

"May I sign yours?" I asked.

"Of course."

Her voice was barely a whisper. She sounded resigned. She handed over her book.

I wrote, "I hope you will remember my feelings and not the way I expressed them. Good luck always."

We walked out the door of State City High side-by-side—Grace, for the last time. I would have to serve two more years.

We walked down the path that divided the school's front lawn, toward the street, toward home. It was hot: the first hot day of the year. I could smell Grace's musk, stronger than ever—and noted to myself that I was smelling it for the last time.

"I know where you're going. This fall."

Grace said nothing; she continued not to look at me.

"I could find out your address, there, in Paris. Or I could write to you in care of the school."

Still silence, but I could see that Grace was tensing.

"But I won't. Don't worry. I wish you all the best."

"Thank you."

"I'm sorry I was such a pest to you. I suppose I knew I was... but I couldn't help it. I couldn't just do nothing. It wasn't in me to let it go."

More silence.

"We're still friends, aren't we?" Knowing, as I asked it, that I was merely requesting this concession for form's sake. I knew that Grace and I were no longer friends; could never be friends again. My doing.

"Of course," Grace said again—using the same resigned, grudging, weary tone she had used when she had agreed to let me sign her yearbook.

We kept walking, silently. I was aware that I probably now had less than five more minutes with Grace, for the rest of my life—and that I was beyond being able to make anything of them.

"You're leaving when?"

"Tomorrow." Grace was still using that flat, dull tone, looking away from me. "We're all getting up way early and driving to Chicago. They'll drop me at the airport, then Charity and my parents will head Down South for a month." Her voice regained a wee bit of its old cheeriness; she even managed something like a smile, when she added, "And I'll be in Leningrad!"

It says something, about how poorly I was getting along with Grace and Charity at that time, that neither of them had shared with me any of the details of this planned vacation. I knew no more about it than what Mom had reported over dinner, a few nights before. Maybe the fact that Grace hadn't told me about it, previously, was some indication that she didn't think it was worth talking about. Or maybe her parents hadn't finalized their summer plans till after Grace had gotten fed up with me.

Grace and I walked the rest of the way without speaking. When we got to her house, on the sidewalk just before she was about to turn and go up her front walk, I said "Goodbye," put my right arm round Grace's shoulders, and squeezed her to me for an instant—and no more, because she gave a tiny but awful little moan, as though of utter dismay and revulsion. She was tensing up to resist, but I released her before she could start wriggling. I walked across the street and into my house, not looking back. I stayed indoors or in the back yard for the rest of the day.

That night, I knew, Grace would graduate in the Grand Ballroom of the State University Memorial Union. (The size of State City High's graduating classes had long ago gotten too big for the families of all the graduating seniors to be squeezed into State City High's auditorium.) I stayed in Mark's and my bedroom, sitting up in bed, reading, with the radio on. I kept my face away from the curtains, so as not to see the Childresses' car pulling into their driveway later on. At last, Mark asked me to turn off the radio so he could sleep. Then, as I had done after the Spring Dance, I turned out my bedside light and pulled the covers tight over my head so I couldn't hear or see anything.

I slept late the next morning. By the time I was out of bed, Grace and her family had gone.

### BOOK III

# 12 THEOLOGY AND POLITICS

It might sound romantic if I could say that from then on, I was working toward the day when I would see Grace Childress again, but that wasn't in my mind. Not even for a moment, after we said goodbye. I knew I had lost her forever, that she would fall in love for the first time (and for the last time, even if it wasn't with the same person) with someone other than me. That she would marry someone else, be seen naked by someone else, lose her virginity to someone else.

I never asked Charity or Mrs. Childress for Grace's address, in the years and weeks that followed. I didn't want to be told, "She asked us not to give it to you." And to give them a letter to send to her: no. Too humiliating for me—and its only purpose, at that time, would have been to annoy her. Come to think of it, I don't believe I ever so much as spoke Grace's name to any of the other Childresses, unless they mentioned her first, and they hardly ever did that. Grace was gone, irretrievably gone. In the immediate term, with her and the rest of her family out of town for much of the summer, I was able to put Grace to the back of mind—to some extent—more easily than I had feared.

She was still there. When I played my APBA Baseball games, if I were managing a team, Grace was there in the stands, rooting for us. A Presidential campaign was on, that summer of 1964, which reminded me that I still wanted to be President of the United States one day, myself. I started working on inventing a simulation game that would re-create a Presidential campaign. I did actually complete the invention, but I never tried to sell or publish it because it was so awfully complicated. It led to some dandy fantasies about myself as a Presidential candidate, though. Every one of those fantasies included Grace as my future First Lady. Naturally it makes me cringe, to remember all this and re-late it—but if you can't be honest, don't write memoir.

Grace has never left me. Grace has been with me, every day of my life since we first had that little conversation about *Pudd'nhead Wilson*. Since before that.

That was a fascinating year, 1964. Not just because of that *débâcle* I'd gone through with Grace. No doubt it was an amazing year for Grace, too, in Leningrad and then in Paris, but even here in Absolutely Nowhere, Iowa, life was interesting enough. Not with regard to my home situation. That was about as boring as boring could get, and it certainly wasn't much fun. But 1964 was fascinating in terms of what was going on in the world. The sense of danger that the Cold War brought was certainly a part of that. The way the Space Race was heating up: that was another part. America had resolved to put a man on the moon by 1970, and at that time we had ideas of maybe colonizing the moon, or build-ing huge space stations that could each contain the population of a small city.

As I mentioned before, that global sense of optimism had seemed to die with President Kennedy, as quickly and violently as he had died, but 1964 still had a sense of fun and adventure about it, along with the fear and uncertainty: a nervous gaiety, as though we somehow knew that Kennedy's assassination had been the spark struck—and that greater conflagrations were sure to arise from it.

Most Americans think of the Beatles when they think of 1964, but they were only the most prominent piece in the amazingly broad and complicated mosaic of pop music in that year and subsequently. The British Invasion that followed the Beatles: the Rolling Stones, the Dave Clark Five, and so on. The folkies, who had been around for a couple of years already but came on my radar that year: Bob Dylan, Joan Baez, Judy Collins. In sports, Cassius Clay, as he called himself at first, was the sensation of the moment—even if he was generally despised. And the cars. Thunderbirds. Those great big Buicks, Mercurys, Oldsmobiles. I loved the sight of those cars, and I couldn't know, at the time, that in a few years they would all be downscaled and we would never see those huge boats again.

I spent a lot of time that summer following the Presidential campaign. It wasn't because I was especially interested in politics—despite my fantasies about winning office. I think I was interested in the campaign out of intellectual curiosity, more than anything else—but it may have been playing the part of Senator Rawkins, in *Finian's Rainbow*, that got me started thinking about civil rights legislation, which turned out to be a major issue in the race between Barry Goldwater and Lyndon Johnson.

I remarked to my mother that it seemed to me that a reasonable person might see two sides to the civil rights issue. Mom gave me one of her pitying looks. "Andy, sometimes I wonder about you."

Another way I disappointed my mother that summer was that I thought it might be fun to get a job. I wasn't particular. Any kind of a job, to earn some extra pocket money. I had brought the matter up to Mom that spring—as the school year was ending—and she had said, "You should leave that sort of thing for kids whose families don't have as much as we have. You don't have to work. Why should you take a job that could go to some kid who needs it?"

Then she said, "If you want something to do, why not volunteer, at a hospital or someplace?" Which was all nice and high-minded, but it was the money I wanted, not the occupation.

She added, "At least that would be more useful than sitting around pitching dice." Which seriously pissed me off.

"Sitting around pitching dice." I had constructed several fairly elaborate fantasy worlds, all based on various dice games, and even if they were meaningless to anyone but me, I felt that they were accomplishments of a kind.

Anyway, when I tried to tell Mom that a job that made money might be to my taste, but volunteering in a hospital wasn't, she said, "I wish you cared more about other people. Sometime I'd love to sit down with you and listen while you explain to me why you... why you don't seem to care for anybody but yourself."

I spent the summer "sitting around pitching dice," mowing the Childresses' lawn once a week, and reading *Don Quixote*. That was my big project for the summer. Maybe I was immature and clueless for my age, but I couldn't help making the comparison between Don Quixote's situation and mine. I knew perfectly well that I was vainglorious. I suspected that I was actually insane. It was obvious to me that I habitually withdrew into fantasy because it was so much more bearable than the real world. Sure, my acquaintance with reality was a little stronger than Don Quixote's, but not by a lot.

The comparison of Grace with Dulcinea of Toboso occurred to me too, certainly, but I had to conclude that they weren't quite equivalent. Grace—or so I told myself then—was not a figment of my imagination. She was not someone I had made up. But I could see that in a way—every time I pitched those dice, for example—I was doing with Grace what Don Quixote had done with his Dulcinea.

I would take the book with me when I went across the street to the Childresses' back yard, on days when I didn't have to mow or water. They had a good-sized yard, well shaded, that faced onto some other family's back yard. A family with no small children, apparently, since it was so wonderfully quiet back there. I could only faintly hear the sound of what little traffic there was in that neighborhood, and even more faintly the sound of children playing, off in the distance.

I would prop myself against one of the Childresses' elm trees, out of sight of the rest of the world, for at least an hour or so, most afternoons, and read, with Grace's head in my lap, and I would hold her hand or stroke her hair, while she slept or smiled up at me. At times, I would imagine leaning down to kiss her. I wasn't unhappy.

Mom wondered why I was so fascinated with *Don Quixote*. She knew nothing about the book except that it was Spanish, and that it was about a man who rode around on a horse, accompanied by another man on a donkey, and that he did crazy things like trying to fight windmills, thinking they were giants. I told her a little about what I had read so far.

"Okay, I can see why you would like it, I guess," she said. "We'll have to call you the Knight of the Sad Countenance."

"Better than being the Knight of the Incontinence," I replied, and I believe Mom and I were both just about helpless, laughing, for several minutes.

The Childresses stayed Down South longer than they had expected to. Mom got a postcard from Rae, later that summer, asking her to have me keep watering their plants, and mowing their lawn, for the rest of the season because they were too swept up in History to not stay involved in it till the fall semester began. I still remember a paragraph from that postcard:

"You would not believe the incredible hatred and ignorance we are experiencing down here. And the forbearance and the nobility of the Negroes we've befriended. It has never been harder to be an American. We are both proud and ashamed, and we're so thrilled that we've had the privilege of participating in the making of history."

When they got back, Rae showed up at our house to bring Mom the full account. When I wandered into the dining room, where she and Mom and Dad were sitting (it was very rare for Dad to join the two women like that, but I'm sure he was curious about what the Childresses had been up to), Rae brought her chequebook our of her purse, and asked me how many times, in all, I had mowed their lawn.

Dad immediately said, "Oh, you don't have to pay Andy for that; it's something you do for a neighbor."

I about shit. Teenaged boys got paid for mowing lawns. Period. It was a matter of course. Maybe they weren't paid much, but they were paid. I deserved to be paid. Give Rae Childress credit. She did the right thing. She insisted on paying. So my parents agreed that I could accept one dollar for each of ten mowings, although I had mowed probably twelve times and the going rate for a lawn of that size would have been at least two bucks, plus some extra for watering the flowers. So Rae took a ten-dollar bill out of her purse. I had to feel dirty, accepting it.

After Mrs. Childress had left, Mom said to me, "Andy, I really didn't care for that look you gave Dad, when he said Rae shouldn't have to pay you. You made us both ashamed."

Over the next few days, oh, boy, did Rae Childress give us an earful about the family's experiences Down South. Either I was there when she came over to visit, or Mom would report the conversation to the rest of us at the dinner table. It was mostly anecdotes to prove that ninety-nine percent of white Southerners were stupid, evil, and homicidal.

Rae was preparing to play a big part in the election campaign that fall. By then, she was one of the vice-chairs of the State County Democrats, and she was to oversee the getting out of the vote in several precincts. My parents were all for Lyndon Johnson's re-election, too, it goes without saying.

So was I, at first, if only because Mom and Dad—and Rae and Charity Childress—were all so insistent on the idea that Barry Goldwater was literally a madman and actually *wanted* to blow us all to Kingdom Come. But as I continued to read about the issues (because the more you know, the more you question) I found myself sympathizing with Goldwater and his positions. I felt that he was preaching freedom and self-reliance. That struck a chord with me. Mom was disappointed in me, to say the least, when I told her that. Downright angry, I believe.

I recall one time—it was in early September, maybe the day before school started back up—Mom and Mrs. Childress were sitting in our front yard as they often did, and I was sitting with them, and I mentioned to Rae that I was starting to think Goldwater would be the better choice. She laughed and said, "Stuff and nonsense! You just want to be different. You don't really believe that."

Mom didn't defend me. "Oh, he's always been that way."

§

My first memory of eleventh grade is of the kid who sat down next to me in the second period of the first day, which was Dr. Pritchard's Shakespeare class. He was runty. If you looked carefully you would realize that he wasn't unusually small, just medium-small—but he was skinny, and his face hadn't started to mature, so he looked smaller than he was. He had that too-alert, too-energetic, rather peppery manner that a lot of small guys have, like they have to prove something to you. His hair was clipped like a tennis ball. He had little grey eyes that slanted away from his nose rather than toward it as mine do. He didn't have much of a nose to speak of, either.

He held his hand out to me, and in a plainly Southern voice he said, "Ah'm Gus Guidry"—which was odd, because teenaged boys in that time and place didn't introduce themselves. They waited for you to learn their names by osmosis. You would become acquainted by repeated contact rather than formal introduction. But I shook Gus Guidry's hand and told him I was Andrew Palinkas. He said, "Howdy, Anj. Ah'm a coonass, me. What kinda ass are you?"

I must have looked perplexed, because Gus Guidry explained that a "coonass" is an inhabitant of the Acadiana region of Southern Louisiana—a Cajun, in other words. His family had just moved to State City from Lake Charles, he said. His voice, which was squawky and raspy, was still breaking. He had a slight lisp. He talked almost constantly. One of those jumpy, hyper people who can't bear to keep quiet. He was starting to tell me why his family had left Lake Charles when Dr. Pritchard called the class to order.

We caught up again at lunch that day. I found out that Guidry's name in full was Gustave Toutant Guidry, after Louisiana's main Civil War hero, Gen. Pierre Gustave Toutant Beauregard. Also, that Guidry's father had recently retired from the U.S. Army, as a Lieutenant Colonel, after twenty years of service, having risen from the ranks instead of going to West Point. Guidry added that last bit with an air that made it clear he expected me to be impressed.

His mother had been teaching at McNeese State College and had accepted an associate professorship in the English department at State University. It was through his mother, Guidry told me, that he had discovered Shakespeare, and from his father that he had inherited a love of musical comedy.

"You're in luck," I said. "Dr. Pritchard is not too bad of a drama coach and she's always looking for guys. She'd probably want you for forensics, too, if you're interested in that."

"Hell yes." I sensed that Guidry was exaggerating his Southern accent, for effect. "That'uz the on'y thang that saved mah *sanity*, down there in Lake Charles, was speech 'n' drama."

"You'd probably have got my part in the musical we did last year, if you'd been here," I said.

I started to recount my triumph as Senator Billboard Rawkins, but Guidry interrupted me to say, "I'd have wanted to play the leprechaun. I've got no interest in playing some evil Southern cracker." He began to sing, "When I'm Not Near the Girl I Love," which sounded pretty dreadful in that bizarre voice of his. I was impressed, though, that he was familiar with the show and its score.

So we hit it off, right away. Guidry didn't make a lot of friends. He wasn't disliked, but he was regarded as an object of fun. He was prickly, and tended to take offense at chaffing. Sometimes he would rage at you like Donald Duck, when he was good and mad. But I could understand that attitude easily enough, Lord knows, so if he bristled at another kid's off-hand remark, I at least empathized.

He did get kidded a lot, at first. Quite a few of the students made fun of his voice and his accent, and one guy, at lunch in the cafeteria one day, suggested that maybe Guidry was getting set to organize a Ku Klux Klan chapter here in State City. Guidry was not amused.

"Now let me tell yall something," he said to the whole table-ful of us, with his full Louisiana drawl on, "Ah don't hold with inny of that shit, and neither does innyone in mah family. Mom found a job Up North here so that we wouldn't have to live in that environment. Dad was in the Army for more'n twenty years, and worked with men of all colors. He always taught me there ain't no difference among races other'n outward appearance."

Guidry looked around the table with eyebrows raised, and his voice dropped to a dramatic stage-whisper.

"Kennedy's assassination was the clincher for our family. When our neighbors, some of 'em, were goin' around smilin' on that day, and the days after it, like his death was a good thang... that right there's when mah parents decided it was time to go live elsewhere."

Mitch Rosen was sitting across the table, and one or two people down. He gave Guidry a big grin and said, "You're not a Goldwater guy? I thought the South was solid for Barry!"

Guidry sighed. "Ah can see Ah'm goin' to have to dispel some notions."

"Gabby Palinkas, there, he's our Goldwater man," said Rosen.

Guidry looked a bit shocked. He put down his fork and looked at me with the gravest disappointment. "That so?" I felt immediately defensive, as though indeed I had somehow engaged in a shameful betrayal.

"You a segregationist?" Guidry asked, more in sorrow than in anger. I had to explain to Guidry that I had studied the civil rights issue, and had concluded that Goldwater was acting on a sound principle.

"Goldwater doesn't oppose the Civil Rights Bill because he opposed civil rights for black people," I said. "It's because the bill exceeds the government's mandate—and that ended that, as far as Goldwater was concerned."

Guidry, again with that dramatic whisper, demanded, "What else is government for, if not to better the lot of the common people?"

"I wish its purpose were to *protect* us from folks who are trying to better the lot of the common people," I said. Rosen grinned and chuckled at this, but Guidry looked even more in-dignant than when he had first heard that I was for Goldwater.

Still, Guidry and I became good pals, mainly because he was a prattler and I didn't mind listening. He was proud as could be of his Southern heritage, even if he didn't care for the politics. He claimed at least distant kinship to several heroes of the Late Unpleasantness, including not only Gen. Beauregard, but Na-than Bedford Forrest, Jubal Early, and Alexander Stephens. I suspect that at least some of those claims were more wishful thinking than reality. But he did have a ton of stories. And a ton of show tunes in his head, which he repeated so often—almost compulsively—that it was physically tiring to be around him for any length of time. Which I was, since we were both in the Drama Club and the Forensics Club. Charity was in Drama too, that year. During rehearsals for the fall play, she and Guidry would take turns excoriating me for my political views.

Prick and I hadn't had anything to do with each other over the summer—we didn't live near each other and didn't have many common interests—and by the time eleventh grade started, he had taken to hanging out more with the auto-shop crowd, which was regarded as a hoodlum element, or juvenile delinquents as they were called back then. To be fair, most of them were law-abiding. They smoked cigarettes and wore side-burns and smelled of motor oil, but seldom if ever got into any trouble. Prick and I still sat together in French and math—we helped each other in the former and helped each other to goof off in the latter—but in that junior year we had each of us solid-ified into a different clique, so we were at a certain social remove.

Besides speech and drama, my big interest in the fall of 1964 was trying to get Barry Goldwater elected President—or at any rate to help him carry Iowa, which didn't look too likely. Two or three afternoons a week, at least, after school, I would walk downtown to State County Republican headquarters—which

**175**

was like any local political headquarters at that time and place: crummy vacant office space that had been rented for the two months of the fall campaign. There, I would sit in a metal folding chair at a big plastic-topped folding table, stuffing envelopes; making canvassing calls on the phone; doing whatever else had to get done.

Mom gradually curtailed her head-shaking and tsk-ing at this awful behavior of mine, as the fall went on. She would come home from the State County Democrat headquarters—also two or three afternoons a week—full of good cheer and predictions that Johnson couldn't possibly lose. If she and I happened to be working downtown on the same day, Mom and I would usually arrange to meet up and drive home together. She seemed, finally, to be willing to put up with my perversity. Still, every now and then, she would remind me that she couldn't, for the life of her, understand why I was for "that nut."

The people I worked with, at Republican headquarters, didn't seem all that nutty to me. Mostly they were old ladies, perfectly respectable old ladies. They all thought I was such a nice young man. I was, too—around them. It was a pity that these weren't people I found particularly interesting.

Democrats tend to be more personally fascinating than Republicans; there's no denying it. I wouldn't say more likable, certainly. Republicans, as a rule, seem to make more of an effort to be pleasant. If only they didn't tend to be so bland. In some ways, though, the Republicans were more the kind of people I wanted to be. The women were neater, the men more prosperous-looking and better-dressed.

Rosen was politically active too—as a Democrat. To hear him tell it, he was cheerfully doing the grunt-work (as I was for the Republicans) and ingratiating himself with precinct leaders, especially the female ones. In this respect he and I were quite similar. Rosen was much more focused and goal-oriented than I was, as a general thing, although I worked hard on this campaign. I was less interested in making contacts for the future, than in getting Goldwater elected—although it was pretty clear from the start that that was hopeless.

When I was working for Goldwater I got to know Adina Owens somewhat. She was in my grade, and I had known her by sight the previous year but hadn't spoken to her—partly because I had been obsessed with Grace, and partly because I was sure she wouldn't have been interested in speaking to me. She had been in the chorus of *Finian's Rainbow*, but I hadn't had any classes with her. This year, she was in my American Government class, but we sat at opposite ends of the room.

Adina was half-Chinese; her father was a white man who had come back from World War II with an Asian bride. She was exceptionally pretty and not obviously Asian. She could probably have passed for someone who was basically white with some remote ancestry from some other race. She had the long dark hair, but it had a little wave to it—it wasn't straight like Asian hair—and she had a light golden-brown complexion, but her features were more Caucasoid than Mongoloid.

Adina Owens was so all-American that it was as though she were trying to overcompensate for her non-white blood. She was a cheerleader, so she tended to hang out with other cheerleaders, and athletes. She favored tartan wool skirts and angora sweaters, and always a slender gold chain round her neck, with a Protestant cross pendant.

She wasn't charming in the way that Grace had been. Grace would charm people by acting as though she sincerely were interested in them, genuinely prepared to be their friend. Grace probably really did mean it, when she was nice to people. Sure, I sometimes suspected that Grace's manner was to some extent a matter of *noblesse oblige*, but on the whole I'm pretty sure that on her inside, Grace truly was as nice as she acted.

I didn't see any actual malice in Adina, but I got the impression that she didn't like people much, whereas I believe Grace did. With Adina, I always got the feeling that she was afraid of catching other people's kooties. Her smiles seemed tight, forced, condescending.

People had loved Grace. At least I had. Julia Swinford had. Jimmy Axton had, and maybe Larry Boylan had. I wonder whether anyone loved Adina, aside from her immediate family, although I'm sure plenty of people admired her.

Sometimes, at State County Republican Headquarters, Adina would sit across a table from me as we stuffed envelopes. It was mindless, repetitive work, so we chatted, although we seldom found a subject for deep discussion. I tried to get Adina talking about subjects she liked, or teachers she disliked, but she didn't care to commit herself.

I would prod, though. I would kid her. Like, once I said, "C'mon, Adina, there must be one teacher you seriously despise; you can tell me."

Adina barely smiled. "No, there honestly isn't. I can't waste my time and energy disliking people. That doesn't do anyone any good, and the Bible tells us it's not good for our souls, either, in the long run."

That observation made me less interested in her. It's not like Adina ever made my heart leap, the way Grace had done, but I had been attracted to her—if only because I knew that I ought to be. She was pretty, and very much a "nice girl": that is to say, a girl whom any boy would be proud to show off to his parents.

Adina and I had almost nothing in common. Now that I knew the foundation of her values, I actually disdained her—or told myself I did. But all of a sudden, even though I found her less compelling than I had, a moment before, I resented her for not being attracted to me. For not flirting with me. For being what she was: a cheerleader who—if she dated anyone—would date the best-looking guy on the football team, or some other *élite* type of guy, and certainly not a fat loser like me.

I don't know if I was more angry at her, for clearly not having any feelings for me, or angry at myself, knowing that I was not appealing enough to win the affections of a girl like her. Probably I thought at the time that it was the former, although more likely it was the latter in reality. But whatever its source, whatever its direction, I could feel the anger welling up in me, fast.

It took me a minute to come up with something witty—or something that I thought was witty—and even at the time of delivery I knew that a decent person wouldn't have said it, because it served no purpose except to create strife, but I wasn't a decent person, so I said it:

"Well, God doesn't need to dislike anyone, because he's supposed to be all-good and all-powerful. But you're not God, so you're excused, if you want to dislike someone. I don't see how you could get through life, not disliking at least a few people."

"God doesn't want me to dislike anyone. And God's a Christian, like I am."

That statement was irresistible bait to me. I couldn't help, then, asking her, "How can anyone know there's a God, in the first place? And how do you know he's a Christian?"

If I had been smarter I could have asked her whether it wasn't a philosophical impossibility for God to be a Christian.

I mean, if you're a Christian, you believe that Jesus is your personal savior, and that Jesus is God incarnate. In that case, wouldn't God, as a Christian, be saying that he is his own personal savior? And if God is all-good and all-powerful, does he need saving at all? Saving from what? A power even higher than he is, that could damn him to Hell if he doesn't repent his sins and accept Jesus?

"I just know there's a God, and that he's a Christian." Adina was now looking downright beatific. "I've found such comfort in God, and I'm sorry if you haven't. I'll pray for you." She gave me this little simper.

When Adina said she would pray for me, it pissed me off. As though it were an act of aggression. I wanted to hit back. It has always struck me that when someone says, "I'll pray for you," it's like "I curse you." Usually if someone promises to pray for you, it means she's going to pray for something to happen to you, and usually it's something you don't want to have happen, like a religious conversion. In that context, there's something malicious about saying, "I'll pray for you."

There's also something malicious, I think, about saying that you're certain of your faith, that you know what's going to happen when you die—and not only when *you* die, but when some other person dies. Later in life I found that people who follow other religions—Eastern or New Age—will do the same thing. They'll say, "I *know* we'll be reincarnated, I know that it'll happen to everyone."

There's a certain malice in that, a certain "Ha-ha, it's going to happen to you whether you like it or not," that I find unseemly. It's not only Christians who do this, but (in my observation, at least) it's almost exclusively women who do it. I wonder why that is.

I asked Adina, then (I was perfectly civil about it, for I wanted to know) "So, do you really think the world was made in seven days, and that Adam was just made, and didn't evolve?"

I expected Adina to say that she didn't believe in evolution, that she believed everything in the Bible absolutely literally, but she didn't do that. Instead, she said, "I don't understand why we spend so much time trying to figure out whether evolution is true or not. Why are we bothering? I think we should spend more time being grateful. Grateful for being here, and for the world around us, and for the sacrifice that God made for us."

"Wait," I said. "What sacrifice did God ever make for us?"

Adina smiled again, and shook her head. "Gosh, you really do need to hear some good news," she said. "Let me quote you from the Bible. John 3:16. Probably the most important verse in the Bible; in fact, if you had to boil the whole of the Bible down to this one verse, it would probably be enough.

"'For God so loved the world, that he gave his only begotten Son, that whosoever believeth in him should not perish, but have everlasting life.' That's all you need to know."

"I don't see as how that's much of a sacrifice," I said. "God can do anything. What's a son to him, especially if he didn't do any more than make him up, out of thin air? He could make a billion of them."

This time Adina couldn't think of anything to say off-hand, and I didn't have the sense to let it alone. I kept on.

"Besides," I said, "being crucified is an awful way to go. You know that, right? Why would God let that happen to his son, if God is so good and kind? He sounds like a sadist to me.

"What's more, how can you say God is good? If God is... I don't know, the ultimate, the Alpha and Omega, then how can he be good or bad? Whatever he does, it's... well, it's immune to any discussion of good or bad, isn't it? If what he does is good, then you have to admit that he's capable of doing bad, and that there's a definition of good or bad that exists outside of God. Right? I mean, some higher power that's even higher than God, that gets to determine what 'good' is."

"You're just being difficult," said Adina. "We all know what good is."

"So, was World War II good?" I asked. "All those people getting killed? Okay, it got rid of Hitler, but why did God make Hitler? And your mother. You told me your mother died of cancer when she wasn't even forty years old. Was that good?"

"It's all part of God's plan," said Adina. "Those are things you're not supposed to question."

"So if it's all God's will, and God's plan, and God can do anything he decides to do, and it's all good by definition, then why is it important to God for me to praise him for doing it, and tell him that everything he does is so wonderful? Isn't he sure of himself? I mean, does God have low self-esteem or something, so that he needs for me to worship him? And if I don't, he's going to get back at me by sending me to Hell? Is that it?"

"It's not important to God that you worship him," said Adina. "It's important to you. God doesn't send anybody to Hell. You send yourself, because if you reject Jesus you're without God. Only through Jesus can you come to God."

"Okay, but if God is all-knowing and all-powerful and all-everything, then I must always be with God because God always has the choice to do whatever he wants with me, right? You're saying that God has a will; God has plans—and in that case, he must have choice. He has to choose to do one thing rather than something else. Which means he's capable of doing some other thing that's maybe somehow less good than what he actually does do. So whichever he does—one thing or something else—there must be somebody or something—some higher power, I mean—that determines which is the better choice."

"That doesn't follow at all! God does whatever he does, and it's good."

"Automatically good, whatever he does?"

"Yes."

"So it's good that God gives me the choice to worship him or not, and if I don't, I have to go to The Bad Place?"

"But that's not God's choice. That's yours."

"So supposing I choose to do something really, really bad. Like, kill you. God chose to let that happen, right? He could have stopped me if he'd wanted to. But he chose to let me kill you."

"We all die," Adina said. "I know that if I die, God will take care of me."

"But suppose I do even worse than that? Suppose I go around killing anybody I feel like? Or here's something that might even be worse: How about if I kill a bunch of people who haven't accepted Jesus yet? They're all going to go to Hell now, because I killed them before they had a chance to repent! Why would God allow that?"

This seemed to stymie Adina, at least for a moment, which was all it took for me to come up with another point.

"What about people who live in the middle of nowhere, like, I don't know, some place in Africa, and they haven't heard of Jesus?" I asked. "Are they going to Hell? They haven't accepted Jesus, but is that their fault, if they never had the chance to?

"Maybe Hell isn't so bad for them," said Adina. "Anyway, I can see that you want to argue for the sake of arguing. Maybe we'd better talk about something else now if we're going to talk at all. But we can talk about this another time if you'd like to know more about it. I'm sorry that you don't have the peace in your life that I have from knowing Jesus—but I *will* pray for you."

"If you do, I'll never forgive you," I said. I was smiling, but I almost meant it. Adina looked at me like she thought I had meant it, too. Like she felt both indignant, and threatened.

As soon as we had had that discussion, I knew there was no way I could ever have a date with Adina, even if I had been a cool enough guy for her to be interested in me.

I would have loved to have had a similar discussion with Grace. Probably Grace would have had fun with it too. But Adina wasn't Grace; Adina could never have carried Grace's ballet slippers.

I had deliberately provoked Adina, with that discussion. I hadn't had to start with her, when she said God was a Christian. I could have shrugged, nodded, and asked her what her favorite dessert was. What good did it do either of us to argue this point?

What good did it do either of us, for me to cast doubt on her beliefs? If I had convinced her there was no personal God, let alone a Christian God, would it have made her a better or happier person? No. It was a way of throwing sand, breaking her toys, flipping her skirt.

It could be that I pursued that argument as a way of insulating myself: to ensure that I would never be in a position where I might make friends with Adina. That would spare me the pain of being rejected, if I had ever subsequently tried to make myself more than a friend.

Adina and I left Republican Headquarters, that night, at the same time. As we stepped out the door of the headquarters and onto the sidewalk, there on Old School Street in downtown State City, I asked Adina if she were going in my direction, and would she care to walk along with me. She said, "No, thanks," and turned in the opposite direction.

Then as though to put the clincher on it, as she turned her back to me, I reached out and gave Adina a playful little backhand swat on the butt—right there in the street.

Adina was too astonished to yelp. She gasped, and turned around and gaped at me. Her mouth was open like a steamer trunk. Then she turned again and stalked off, at speed.

I didn't understand, fully, why it was so bad, what I had done.

I had thought—honest, at least a part of me had thought—that I was doing no more than being flirtatious in a mischievous way. I had seen such behavior in movies, after all, so I knew it was done. I'll grant you that a psychologist, being wise after the fact, would see that little swat as a gesture of aggression and anger, and perhaps even of hatred—and might have compared it to the times when I had tried to embrace Grace, or the times when I had tried to attract girls' attention when I was four years old. But I had expected Adina to take it as fun, or funny: as though Dean Martin or Frank Sinatra had done it to her.

Believe it or not, I was astonished at Adina's reaction. But I couldn't chase after her and try to make it better, and the next day I wouldn't have known how to apologize, even if I had had the inclination to try. I tried to tell myself, "You put that stuck-up little chippy in her place." But I never believed that. For the rest of that fall, Adina never spoke to me; she wouldn't so much as look at me if she could help it.

# 13 THE CROSSTOWN RIVALS

I'm pretty sure that Charity sensed, that fall, that I had Adina in my thoughts. It's not like I was crushing on Adina, but I certainly was allowing her to live in my brain because of the way I knew I had disgraced myself with her. Charity wouldn't have known that, of course. One morning I was sitting with Guidry and Charity at a table in the library, talking low, and Adina happened to walk past. I wasn't staring at her, I swear. I maybe glanced up as she passed. Charity snorted. Like, way more contemptuously than that giggle she used to throw at me when she'd sensed that I was crushing on Grace. When Adina was out of earshot, Charity whispered, "What would you want with a girl like that?"

"I wouldn't," I said, but I didn't suppose I was fooling Charity. "What would she want with a guy like me?"

Charity shook her head and tsk'd, almost identically to the way my mother did it.

"Say, what's got into you?" I demanded.

"Oh, I'm sorry, I'm just in a mood. And maybe a little angry at girls who are so... so *attractive*."

"Aw, you're attractive enough," I said. Charity pouted, and a couple of minutes later she gathered up her books and walked off without saying anything more. Guidry looked at me with some disdain.

"Couldn't you have been a little nicer to her than that?"

"If she wants to be more attractive, she should do something about it, and if she did, I'd probably mention it," I replied.

I never allowed myself to take an interest in any other girl, that year. That was largely because Grace was still on my mind, and no girl could ever compare with Grace. But that wasn't all of it. I knew—I knew for a certainty—that I would never see Grace again. I did find other girls attractive; I would have liked to have had a girlfriend. But I made no effort to find one. One reason might have been that I feared that Adina might have told a few people about what had happened—or that she would tell, if she saw me trying to get close to any other girl.

I suspect, though, that the overriding reason was simply that I knew I wasn't going to be able to attract anyone; that I would make a complete idiot of myself if I tried to. So I didn't try to.

It rankled, that no girl seemed to be interested in me in that way. It made me mad at myself that I didn't have the gumption to try to attract anyone—or that I knew I was too repulsive to attract anyone. Either way, there was nothing I could do about it. It didn't make sense to try to talk to anyone about it.

Guidry had no more luck with girls than I had, but he didn't seem to let it bother him; at any rate he never complained to me. He would sometimes remark that this or that girl appealed to him, but always in a joking manner. He never seemed particularly interested in anyone. Prick once told me that he wished he had a girlfriend but couldn't see why any girl would want him for a boyfriend.

"'Course I'll want to get married one day," Prick told me once. "But first I guess I have to get to be the kind of guy that a girl would want to marry, right?" He laughed, self-consciously I thought. I might have replied, "Yeah, me too, but how do we do that?" but I'm afraid I thought Prick wouldn't be bright enough to have that discussion.

I would see Rosen walking or chatting with one girl or another, but nothing serious. He evidently didn't have a girlfriend in the romantic sense, but he would hang out in the hallways or the cafeteria with mixed groups, not just boys, or go from one class to another with one of the better-looking girls for company.

I suspected that Charity was crushing on Rosen, that year. If she sometimes observed me looking at Adina, I sometimes saw her giving Rosen the eye. That wasn't surprising. Rosen was a good-looking guy, personable—maybe too personable—and a real Mr. Popularity. He was even more of a go-getter, that junior year, than he had been before.

I don't believe Rosen reciprocated Charity's admiration. He liked her well enough. He called her Li'l Sis. Rosen had a nickname for practically everybody. He still called me Gabby. He befriended Gus Guidry, too, and called him Johnny Reb. Rosen was cultivating the entire student body that year, because he was getting ready to run for President of the Student Senate in the spring. He palled around quite a bit with the current President: Chuck Haviland, who was now a senior and who had been elected to that office the previous spring.

It was impossible to hate Rosen, or even dislike him, because he never did anything offensive. He was too nice, too sure of himself. That was annoying, but you couldn't escape the possibility that he was as nice as he pretended to be. Or that he was that sure of himself. He appeared to be driven by a purpose, at any rate, which was more than I could claim. That's a quality I had envied and admired in Grace, and to a lesser degree in Charity, and in my brother Mark—and in Rosen. I couldn't help it.

Speaking of Mark, he was then in ninth grade at Southside Junior High—continuing to excel at everything, naturally. But that year, my junior year, I was a straight-A student too, except in Phys. Ed., if only because it was sometimes easier to get an A than to get a B. I seemed to be developing an aptitude for history, political science, and English as well as French—plus speech and drama. All in all, I wasn't terribly miserable that year. Except for sometimes thinking that if Grace had not been skipped ahead a grade when she had been younger, she would still be there, and only one year ahead of me academically. If only I had played it cool the year before, Grace might have been more receptive to my attentions in the fall of 1964. Who knows?

Guidry, Charity, and I were all involved in drama and forensics, so the three of us spent quite a lot of time together. That was a good year for drama. Dr. Pritchard had us doing a couple of unusual plays, like *A Chain of Jade*. That's an obscure Chinese play that we performed in its original manner: stylized, with elaborate gestures and tones that had to be worked into the delivery. A challenging play. In December we did a stage version of *Dracula* that Dr. Pritchard had written herself. But the musical, which we rehearsed beginning in February, and performed in mid-March, was the big production of the year.

*South Pacific.* I had asked Dr. Pritchard for a non-singing part, so I was Commander Harbison, which is a small role, but I had fun with it. Guidry was Stewpot, another small part. A couple of other juniors got bigger parts—like Nia Garthwaite, who played Bloody Mary.

It must have been a challenge for Dr. Pritchard, trying to find parts for Nia. Most plays either have lots of parts for black people—like *Finian's Rainbow*—or none at all, or there's one Negro and that's the maid or the butler. Dr. Pritchard would always find some way to give Nia a decent part. In this case, Nia was playing a Tonkinese person, but Dr. Pritchard must have figured nobody in State City would know the difference.

It wasn't till *South Pacific* that Nia and I started to get acquainted. Once at a rehearsal she said to me, "I was afraid to talk to you, when we did *Finian's Rainbow* last year. You know, I assumed you really believed like your character."

"I do."

"Oh, you're bad!"

From then on we were friendly, though not close.

Adina Owens played Bloody Mary's daughter, Liat—darkening her skin with makeup, for the performances, to be closer to Nia's color. Adina had grave reservations about the suggestiveness of the scenes between her and Axton, who played Lt. Joe Cable. (It looked pretty funny—precious Jimmy Axton playing the tough macho marine—but nobody else had the voice for it.) When we were blocking the scene where they meet and fall in love, Adina objected when Dr. Pritchard placed them in a way that made it look like they might actually be about to have sex— or might just have had sex—although of course she didn't put it that way. What she said was, "I don't want it to look like I'm a fast girl who went all the way with Jimmy."

That made us all giggle, and I whispered to Guidry, "Even if that were true, what would it amount to, in Jimmy's case?" Which caused Guidry to whoop out loud and earned him a dirty look from both Adina and Dr. Pritchard.

Dr. Pritchard wasn't Guidry's favorite teacher. She was a martinet as a director, and Guidry chafed at this, which was odd since he came from a military family and had a no-nonsense way about him, but there it was. I got an idea of what caused his attitude during one rehearsal when he made a suggestion about how one of the dance scenes should be staged, and Dr. Pritchard said to the whole bunch of us, "You notice Gus thinks he's directing this show." Guidry apologized, sarcastically. Bad blood existed between them thereafter—not only for that show.

A day or so after that incident, while we were both between scenes, Guidry and I got to talking, first about that situation and then about Dr. Pritchard in general. Guidry said:

"I realize that Helen tries to put on precise and authentic shows that are a little unusual, and I give her credit for that. Helen's ambitious and hard-working and I give her credit for that too—but she makes a ton of amateurish and rookie mistakes that embarrass the Sam Hill out of me."

I had to agree. I would note decisions that Dr. Pritchard made, with regard to staging, costuming, and makeup, that made no sense to me, or that seemed sloppy and thoughtless. I respected and appreciated the way she would let actors find their own way to play a part, but sometimes she would fail to step in and correct them when they badly needed correcting.

"Y'know what I find objectionable about Helen?" Guidry went on. "She. Has. Reached. Her. Level." Guidry had a way of stamping out words one-by-one when he wanted to sound dramatic. "She's as happy as a clam doing these halfway-decent high school productions, when she could've pushed herself harder and become a professional director, maybe moved on to regional theatre and even gotten to Broadway eventually."

"Maybe she prefers teaching school."

"Maybe, but I doubt that that was her plan, originally," said Guidry. "She's ossifying here at this li'l ol' Midwestern high school, where she's not developing her talents past a certain point—where she's developing attitudes that actually lower the quality of her productions. Y'notice how she always puts down Coach Vance? And the athletes? At the school I went to, in Loysiana, the drama teacher would go after the athletes—after all, they weren't all of 'em busy at sports at the same time of the year—and some of 'em, they'd surprise you. They could act. Now, Helen, here, she's too stuck-up to do the same—which if she did, she might have better shows."

At the cast party after *South Pacific*—Guidry had volunteered to have it at his house—Guidry took me aside and invited me into his dad's study, along with Charity. While all the other kids and Dr. Pritchard were in the front room, celebrating, Guidry sat in his dad's leather-upholstered swivel chair, leaning back like a big businessman, while Charity sat in the guest chair and I leaned against a file cabinet, listening to Guidry's plan to take the State City High Drama Club private, so to speak. He would organize a production, come late April or early May, that would coincide pretty closely with the regular spring play—except he was going to try and get it cast, and into rehearsal, before Dr. Pritchard could get started on her play.

"Then she'll be shit out of luck, won't she?" said Guidry, and he grinned and threw his arms open in triumph, "because we'll have bagged most of the best actors for our show. Who the hell knows? She might have to stoop to recruitin' a few football players after all."

Guidry helped himself to one of his father's cigars, from a box on the desk—it was an A&C Grenadier—and passed the box to me. Guidry lit us both up with a Zippo lighter. It was the first time I had ever smoked anything, and I didn't exactly like it—certainly not enough to become a regular smoker—but it was fun doing something forbidden.

Guidry told us he had decided on *Pygmalion*, which has a good-sized cast. If he had been able to pull it off, he would have left Dr. Pritchard with very little talent left with which to stage a play of her own.

"I have you in mind for Higgins," Guidry said to me. "You're just the type. I'll direct, and I was thinkin' I'd take the part of Alfie Doolittle, besides. Maybe, Charity, you could play Eliza—and Nia would do fine as Mrs. Pearce. Maybe we could get Axton to play Freddy, or Pickering."

Dr. Pritchard's spring play was going to be *Seventeen*, which is a funny but slight comedy that has largely to do with teenagers. It was always my observation that most teenagers would rather play grownups—because that's what they can't wait to be. I, for one, wasn't looking forward to being in *Seventeen* in any capacity, although I was planning to audition for it because Dr. Pritchard would have expected me to. I figured I would end up playing the father, or some smaller role, since I was too big and heavy to play the seventeen-year-old hero.

I was flattered by Guidry's suggestion, and tempted. With Guidry springing this idea on me, it didn't occur to me that *Pygmalion* would have been an overwhelming project for us to attempt independently. It's an expensive play to stage, because it requires elaborate sets and costumes—and the changes of scenery (not to mention the construction) require serious manual labor. It's not a show to be taken lightly.

But Guidry figured that out. A few days later, he told me he had had another idea. *Cat on a Hot Tin Roof*, he said, could be done with a much simpler set. He would be Brick, I would be Big Daddy, "But frankly I don't see our friend Charity as Maggie the Cat," he admitted. "We'll have to find someone else. Maybe she could be Mae, or Big Mama. 'Cept she ain't all that big."

Again I was tempted, but I said to Guidry, "Look, I know you have your problems with Helen, but I have to admit I feel loyal to her. She's been real good to me, and she's given me something to do that I enjoy. I'd be letting her down if I joined some rebel organization—as much as I like your ideas."

Guidry looked a little annoyed, but he thought about it and nodded, finally, as though he understood my argument.

"What might be better," I said, "is if we got up a company that could work alongside the Drama Club, and not compete with it. Maybe we could do sketches and scenes, you know, variety-type shows rather than plays. That way we could act in Helen's shows and still do the kind of stuff we like. Besides, that way, she might be willing to share resources with us, like props and costumes—if she sees us as somehow complementing what she does instead of trying to undermine her."

"Not a bad idea," said Guidry. "We could do a full production in the summer, which'd give us somethin' to keep us occupied, 'stead of lettin' our talents run to seed for three months."

Thus, a few days later, we formed the Crosstown Rivals. We never said whom we were rivals of, and State City doesn't even use "crosstown" as a direction as some cities do. As it turned out, we weren't rivals of anyone. We didn't compete with Dr. Pritchard and her productions. It was a synergistic relationship, after all, because as I had suggested, Dr. Pritchard ended up letting us borrow sets and props now and then. We, in return, promoted her production of *Seventeen*.

The Crosstown Rivals consisted of me, Guidry, and Charity, plus three or four other drama kids who would join us on an *ad hoc* basis if we needed a bit actor for a scene or skit. We went to Mr. Pope—the kids called him Principal Poop—and offered to provide a skit for the wrestling team's final pep rally. Mr. Pope also allowed us to perform in the cafeteria at lunch and after school.

What we did was a hodgepodge: a few improvisations, plus a few tightly scripted sketches—each of us wrote a couple—as well as a few dramatic scenes from classic plays, and some individual readings and declamations. Guidry was fond of political satire, and we did one fairly funny skit in which I was Hubert Humphrey and Guidry was Lyndon Johnson, ordering me about in various outrageous ways while Charity played Lady Bird, trying to mediate. Guidry also did an embarrassingly earnest interpretation of excerpts from President Kennedy's speeches.

Guidry wrote a couple of parodies of TV shows, which I understood imperfectly because—since I so seldom had the opportunity to watch TV—I was completely unfamiliar with the shows he was trying to make fun of.

My own strength was satiric portraits of the faculty and administration. I could do a passable impression of Principal Poop.

He was a bit heavyset, and had a slightly pompous manner that wasn't too far removed from mine, so it wasn't much of a stretch. Guidry could play Coach Vance pretty well, as well as Mr. Titone, who was the basketball coach and chemistry teacher. Guidry worked up a terrific sketch of Mr. Titone as a mad scientist who was trying to invent a performance-enhancing drug for our sports teams, while I played Principal Poop (wildly ambivalent and nervous about such a project) and Charity played Dr. Pritchard, making contemptuous remarks about athletes in general and urging Mr. Titone to invent something that would help her drama club. We performed that one at that final wrestling rally, to general hilarity.

Another time, in the cafeteria at lunch, we did a skit for which I put on a wig and a dress and portrayed Madame Webster, imitating her ghastly accent—and in French class that afternoon Madame Webster was still chuckling. I do wish, though, that the incident had inspired her to take a special summer course in pronunciation. I'm sure State University must have offered something of that kind.

It was early in May. The Drama Club was in rehearsal for *Seventeen*, and I was the father, as I'd predicted I would be. I was also getting ready for the last of the year's speech contests. On this day, Guidry and Charity and I were having lunch in the school cafeteria and kicking ideas around, as to what the Cross-town Rivals' major production would look like that summer, when Mitch Rosen came over and sat down with us, instead of with his usual crowd of *élites*.

"Listen, guys," Rosen said. "I've got an idea of how we can help each other. I've started my campaign for President of the Student Senate, and I was thinking, I need some people to give my campaign a little pizzazz in the next few days. I wondered if maybe you guys would want to write up a few bits—things that you could do here in the cafeteria, maybe—to make people aware of my campaign. I mean, to remind them to participate in the process. That's important, right? Getting people to participate in a democracy."

"Yes, it is," said Charity. She smiled at Rosen—too brightly, I thought. "That's a wonderful idea."

"But how would that benefit us?" I asked.

"Well, you get to back a winner!" Rosen laughed loud and hearty to show that he meant it. "Seriously, when I'm Student Senate President next year, I'm going to try to make a few changes in the way the student government is run, and I'm going to need a lot of help in presenting my ideas to the rest of the student body. And it occurred to me that if I had you guys on my side, next year, you could step up to the plate with little acts and routines that would help us to, you know, encourage people to participate with us."

"I suppose that would depend on what you were going to try to do, once you get to be President," I said. "And I still don't see what's in it for us."

"It'll give you experience," said Rosen. "You'll get a lot of practice speaking and acting—which is what you guys like to do anyway—and you'd get involved in the political process too. And I know you guys are all political. If you're thinking about careers in public service, this could be a way where we could all help each other to get ahead. Don't you think?"

"I'd need to know what you stand for," I said. "Not that that matters much, in student government, does it?"

Rosen gave me another of his exaggerated haw-haws—this time, I daresay, to pretend that he wasn't offended.

"Tell you what," he said. "When you get home tonight, look in the *Examiner*." (*The State City Examiner* was an evening paper, in those days.) "They're running a feature about my campaign. That should answer your question."

So I did—and it did.

# City High's Rosen Hopes To Focus On Community Service

*By Wendy Fritz*
*The State City Examiner*

When Mitch Rosen gets elected President of State City High School's Student Senate this month (so far he's the only candidate in the race) his main focus will be getting the student body more involved with serving the community.

Traditionally, high school presidents have as their main duties the oversight of the usual activities, such as Homecoming, Sadie Hawkins Day, and organizing pep buses for out-of-town football and basketball games. But this City High junior also wants his classmates to help him boost the school's reputation all over State City.

"I hope to make State City High a byword for community service," explains Rosen, who has just turned 17. "For example it would be great if we could raise money for local causes as well as for purely selfish things like dances and parties. It's great to have fun, but we also have to remember that most of us have been given a lot by the local community, and we ought to think about what we can give back."

The son of Jacob and Silda Rosen, of 817 Mayfair Road, Mitch Rosen isn't taking his election for granted. "I don't have any opposition yet," he says, "so it's probable that I'll be elected." Mitch points to his years of experience in student government—he was president of his ninth-grade class and has served in the State City High Student Senate in both 10th and 11th grades—as well as his many victories as a member of the school's debate team. Last fall, he headed State City High's Young Democrats in their efforts to get out the vote for President Johnson and Governor Hughes. He's also a starting forward on the State City High varsity basketball team.

"If I'm elected, I'll feel very fortunate and grateful for the opportunity to represent State City High to the community as a whole," he says. "All my life I've felt that there's nothing more important than to be involved."

As President of the Student Senate, Mitch says, he will work to involve students more with the community, especially with underprivileged or elderly State Citians.

"In terms of how they spend their spare time," he explains, "teenagers tend to just pay attention to whatever is in front of them. It will be my job to make sure they have the opportunity to choose something interesting to do with their lives."

As for Mitch's own life, after high school, he's undecided. He says he wants to go to college but is undecided on which school and what to study.

"I want to experience a lot of options," he says. "One thing is for sure: After college, the Peace Corps. I might not be an Albert Schweitzer, but I want to feel that I've done as much as I can for others."

First thing the next morning, I walked into State City High's main office and took out a nominating petition for Student Senate President.

# 14 RUNNING

I had only two days left before nominations closed, and I needed thirty signatures to get on the ballot. At first it didn't look like I would be able to do it. I had spent my first two years at State City High avoiding most people, and the kids I associated with were the sort who would already have signed Rosen's petition. During my study hour that day, and at lunch, I only got four or five signatures—but right after lunch was French class, and when I told Prick what I was up to, I was surprised at how he reacted.

"I didn't know you were allowed to do that," he said. "I thought you had to be, like, some kind of important guy to run for office like that." Prick looked at me with what I thought was admiration—as though he had suddenly discovered that I belonged to an even higher social caste than he had imagined up to that point.

"Oh, don't worry," I said. "I'm still a bum. Us bums need some representation too."

Prick signed my petition right then and there, and took it on himself to pass it around the classroom. Madame Webster was too amused to object. She just smiled at me and said, in her awful accent, *"Eska voo saray notra Barry Goldwater?"* I replied, *"On va bien voir."* Most of the kids in the class, I believe, felt that it would be un-neighborly not to sign. At any rate, I got ten more names right there. Prick then asked if he could take my petition down to auto-shop. When he brought it back to me at the end of the day, he had collected another fourteen—so I had my thirty.

"Some of 'em didn't even know who you were till I described you," Prick said. "And some of 'em thought you were a kind of a snob 'cause, you know, you're in the Drama Club and you don't hang out with people like us, but I told 'em you were a nice guy and helped me out in French class, so they signed."

On the following day, I had no trouble getting three more people to sign, for good measure. I handed in my petition at the school office that morning, a Friday. A couple of hours later—it was my study period and I was sitting in the library—Haviland walked up to me, bowed with sarcastic ceremony, and handed me a note. It turned out to be from Mr. Pope's secretary, informing me that all candidates for school-wide office, and their campaign managers, were to meet in the Principal's office immediately after school, to discuss the week-long campaign that was to begin on Monday.

Haviland laughed aloud as I read the note—which earned him a look from the librarian. "Do you have a ticket?" he asked me—softly, but still in a tone that managed to convey his contempt. I looked at him uncomprehending.

"You know, a ticket. Haven't you got anybody running with you for Vice-President, and Secretary-Treasurer? You're supposed to."

I hadn't even thought about that.

"I'm just running for President. I don't have to run as part of a ticket, do I?"

"No, strictly speaking you don't have to," Haviland was grinning at me like his face might break. "Have you even got a campaign manager?"

"Not yet."

"Well, I strongly advise you to get one." Haviland shook his head—bemused, I guess. "Do you think you have *any* chance?"

"If you worry too much about the odds," I said, "you won't get much accomplished."

Which sounded smart, and it's exactly the kind of thing Rosen would have said, which made me immediately ashamed that I had said it. What I should have said—one of those *esprits d'escalier* that occur to you when it's way too late—was, "If half the kids in this school were persuaded to vote for *you* last year, Ass-Wipe, it ought to be a pushover for me."

On one point, though, Haviland was right, and I hadn't even considered it. I needed a campaign manager—or at least I needed someone who would pretend to be my campaign manager long enough to introduce me to the school assembly the following Friday morning.

So, as soon as I could track him down, I asked Guidry.

"Ah don't know why you're doin' this, Anj." This must have been a momentous pronouncement for Guidry, because once again he was exaggerating his drawl. "Ah have to tell you, Ah thank Mitch Rosen is exactly the man for the job, and he's who Ah'll be votin' for. As a friend, Ah'm willin' to he'p you put up your campaign posters an' all, next week, but in good conscience Ah cain't be the one to give you your introduction."

Charity was my next choice—she was almost as good a speaker as Guidry—but I knew, before I stopped by her locker and asked her, what her answer would be. She laughed at me the way she used to when she knew I was eating my heart out for Grace: part pitying, part mocking, part contemptuous.

"Maybe if I'd known you were going to run, I'd have talked you out of it. I have no idea why you're doing it. Maybe you could explain it to me?"

"Gladly."

But then I had to stop to think for a moment, because I had not properly systematized, in my own mind, my reasons for having suddenly decided to run.

"I don't think Rosen is the right guy for the job," I said—slowly, because I was trying to think and talk at the same time, which is difficult. "He's too big for his britches, and he wants to lord it over the rest of us—and show off to all of State City what a good little boy he is. What I'm going to promise is, if I'm elected, I'm going to let people alone. Instead of preaching about how virtuous I am and how they all ought to be like me."

(To be fair, Rosen hadn't explicitly done that, but the tone of the *Examiner* article had certainly reinforced that impression, for me.)

Charity gave me a big sigh of patient suffering. She added a shake of the head and a smug, patronizing laugh.

"Obviously you won't be telling people to be like you. Do you have any idea how you're generally regarded in this school? You're just *weird*. Most of the girls are afraid of you, at least a little. Gus and I, and Arno Prick, are the only friends you've got. Maybe Nia would be your friend, and maybe Jimmy Axton too, but they both think you might come at them with a knife, or something. Nobody's going to vote for you, except maybe as a joke. Not even me, I'm afraid. Mitch is admirable—I think—and he actually wants the job, and he'll make a wonderful President.

I know that deep down you're a very nice guy, but you're not someone I'd feel comfortable having represent our school to the rest of the community."

It was on the tip of my tongue to demand, "How the hell do you know what the other kids think of me? Do you go around the school asking people? Have they appointed you their spokesman?" But then, before I could say anything, I realized that Charity was almost certainly right—even if she didn't have any empirical evidence to back it up, even if she couldn't actually show me a girl who said she was afraid of me, or a student of either sex who thought I was any weirder than any other kid. It would have done me no good whatever to say anything in response. Except "thank you," which I did say before I turned on my heel and walked off.

"And you still look like a fucking lizard," I muttered, wishing that I had had the nerve to say it to Charity's face.

I couldn't help thinking of Grace, once again. If her parents hadn't skipped her ahead a year, she would have been a senior about to graduate, and if I could have gotten her to introduce me to the school assembly, that would have lent me enough *gravitas* to have swept Rosen plumb off the stage. I bet she would have done it, too. Even if we hadn't been boyfriend and girlfriend, she might have done it. I fantasized, at least for a few minutes, as I walked from Charity's locker to my next class, about how Grace would have looked on the podium, barely tall enough to be seen over the lectern, so prim and so perfectly put together, so earnest in her manner as she charmingly exhorted the student body to vote for *her* friend, Andy Palinkas.

But only in my daydream. And thus it was that that afternoon in French class I offered the job to Prick—explaining that all he would have to do was show up at Mr. Pope's office after school that day for the briefing, and then introduce me at the assembly the next Friday.

"I dunno, Andy. I never do any of that stuff. I mean, I never stood up in front of people like that. And if I was to talk to the whole school? I'd look like a moron. And I'd make you look like a moron, too."

"Nah, you won't," I said. "You'll do great. Besides, I've got nobody else."

I still feel lousy about having done that to Prick.

§

State City High's main office was pretty big, with a chest-level reception desk that ran the length of the front of the room, with always two or three clerks or secretaries working right behind it, and then the secretaries' private desks behind that, all of which formed a layer of protection for the three windowed private offices at the back—for Mr. Pope; Mr. Havermeyer, the assistant principal; and Mr. Rolf, the dean of students. I arrived at the main office that afternoon to find Chuck Haviland, Mitch Rosen, and Adina Owens already waiting near the front desk, where the secretaries were. Also waiting were a small, thin, dark-haired girl named Catherine Haynes, and Wendell Bell, who was a tall Negro kid—the center on our basketball team, and the only other Negro student at State City High besides Nia Garthwaite.

I didn't know either of them well. Catherine Haynes was sneaky-pretty: the kind of girl you don't notice at first but if you take a good look at her you might remark that she's better-looking than you had thought. She was short and slight; she had a very ruddy complexion, long straight dark hair, and bright grey eyes. I had always been afraid to try to make her acquaintance. I hadn't ever exchanged a word with her, I don't think—but I was annoyed, all of a sudden, that she was part of Rosen's posse.

Rosen immediately switched on his big smile, and held out his hand. "The more the merrier, right, Gabby?"

I certainly don't think Rosen believed I was any threat to his election. If I had had to guess, I would have said he was probably more pleased than annoyed that he had someone to run against. It wouldn't have been quite as impressive, in his own mind, if he had run unopposed. It would have looked like he had pursued an office that nobody else considered important. Which would have been pretty near the truth.

Rosen explained that Adina was running for Vice President, Cathy Haynes was running for Secretary-Treasurer—and Bell was the campaign manager for the three of them. Adina wouldn't even deign to look at me at first. After I had shaken hands with Rosen, Cathy, and Bell, she managed to say "Hi," very softly, still not looking at me.

"I guess Adina takes this a little more personally than I do." Rosen was still grinning. "Come on, Adina. Gabby doesn't bite." But Adina still couldn't even smile.

Prick arrived, out of breath. I imagined that he had almost forgotten, and he must have run all the way from auto shop. Rosen and Adina both looked like they wondered what he was doing there. Haviland laughed aloud: one vicious syllable. Prick looked embarrassed, and I didn't blame him.

I still don't blame him, and Lord forgive me. I still beat myself up, for having put him in that position.

Mr. Pope's secretary, Mrs. Rodgers, then led us past the front desk and herded us into The Pooper's office, which was not large, so it was pretty crowded and there were only enough chairs for the two girls and Haviland to sit down. The other boys all stood by the door (I kept reminding myself not to lounge against the frame) as Mr. Pope gave us all what I assumed was the standard talk about how he wanted a nice clean campaign, and a high school election was in some ways democracy at its finest, and he wanted us to keep that in mind and live up to the ideals of student government, and dah-de-dah-de-dah.

On Monday morning, Mr. Pope advised us, we could begin campaigning. The candidates would speak at an assembly the following Friday morning. The voting would take place on that Friday afternoon.

"And that's it," said Mr. Pope, standing up. "Mr. Palinkas, would you and your campaign manager mind staying here for another minute? The rest of you, we'll see you on Monday." Haviland stifled another laugh. He and Team Rosen departed.

"Please, gentlemen, have a seat." Mr. Pope motioned me and Prick to the now-empty guest chairs. He sat back down at his desk and looked solemn.

"Mr. Palinkas, what exactly do you think you're accomplishing here?"

"I didn't hear you ask Rosen that question. Don't I have as much right to run as he does, without being asked about my motives?"

"Well, I think I know Mitch's motives," said Mr. Pope. "After all, he's been involved in student government for years. Apparently you decided to get into the race on the spur of the moment. I'd had no idea that you were at all interested in this sort of thing. And you, Mr. Pr... Arno, you're one of the last people I would expect to have anything to do with student government. What got you interested?"

Prick writhed in his chair and grinned down at his shoes.

"I'm not, that much." Prick was speaking to the floor. "But Andy needed someone to introduce him next week at the assembly, and he's a good guy."

"I see."

What Mr. Pope saw, pretty clearly, was that this was strictly a vanity move on my part and that I had dragged Prick into it willy-nilly. Which were not exactly mistaken perceptions.

"Well, humor me, Mr. Palinkas. As I say, Mitch has made no secret of his motives. But I'm curious. Why are *you* running?"

"Maybe for the same reason he is. For ego. Rosen can make all the sermons he wants to, about 'serving,' but he's doing this so he can tell himself he's a big shot. That, and because he figures it'll look terrific on his record."

Mr. Pope thought for a moment.

"Are you sure you're not just trying to rain on Mitch's parade?" His tone wasn't at all harsh, or even unkind.

"What if I did? That's not why I'm running, but if it were, that would be as good a reason as any, right?"

Mr. Pope did that steepling thing with his fingers, which is supposed to make you look powerful and wise.

"You have the right to run for whatever reason," he said. "That's what democracy is all about. I was just trying to get an idea of what your agenda is, what your platform is, what you plan to do if you win this election."

"Be a good President, I hope."

Mr. Pope sighed. He sounded exasperated but was clearly surrendering.

"That's all we can ask, I guess. Have a good weekend."

As we walked to our lockers, Prick muttered to me, "Hope he's not mad at us."

"He's not mad at you, anyway," I said. (I almost added, "He knows you're only a stooge," but I fought it back.) "He's not even mad at me. He just thinks I'm making a fool of myself, and who knows? I probably am. Anyway, you don't have to do anything—although if you wanted to come to school early on Monday and help me put up signs, I'd sure appreciate it."

I spent most of my waking hours that weekend in the basement, making campaign posters—which in my case consisted of taking sheets of construction paper and lettering them "Pálinkas for President" in crayon, in contrasting colors, as neatly as I could, which was not very. Or I clipped pictures out of the old magazines we had stacked in the basement, and pasted them onto the construction paper. For example, on one poster, a picture of the Harris Bank lion was accompanied by a word-bubble saying, "I'm not lion! Pálinkas is a real tiger!" On another, Nikita Khrushchev declaimed, "If Pálinkas had been President of Hungary, I wouldn't have messed with him!"

The accent over the "a" in my name was there because I had decided that after all, a somewhat exotic name might be a net plus for my image, and the diacritical mark would emphasize its exoticity. The name is spelt with that *aigu* in the original Hungarian, where it's pronounced (more or less) "PA-lin-kash" instead of the Americanized "pa-LINK-us." The former sounded more elegant. Besides, the other kids would ask me about the accent, if they saw it on a poster, which would give me an opportunity to talk about the race and why they should vote for me. So I figured.

Again, Grace came to my mind. If she had been there, she would have brought her talents to my poster-making. They might have been rather girly-looking, I suppose, but I could have lived with that.

That Friday evening, after supper, I was down in the basement working on those posters. Mom came down to transfer clothes from the washer to the dryer, and asked me (in a perfectly friendly way) what I was up to, so I told her.

"And you didn't talk to us about it?" Mom sounded somewhat put out, if not downright dismayed. "I'm not sure that's such a good idea, Andy. Sometimes I don't like the way you put yourself forward. It's not becoming—the way I see it."

"Why not? If I honestly think I'm the best one for the job, why shouldn't I run?"

"Well, did someone ask you to?"

"No, it was my own idea."

"Then how do you know anybody's going to vote for you? I mean, are there any issues you're running on?"

"I've got to give them someone to vote for, other than Mitch Rosen. Did you see the article about him in the *Examiner*, night before last? If you didn't, dig it up and take a look."

Mom thought. "Yes, come to think of it, I did see that. He does sound a little... I don't know, a little full of himself. But at least he sounds like he's trying to do some good. I hope that's why you're running."

I didn't say anything to that.

"I wish you had told us earlier," Mom said. "Maybe we could have helped."

Or talked me out of it, I said to myself. Or suggested several planks for my campaign platform, based on her own broad general knowledge. I could imagine.

"Well, what do you plan to do, if you're elected?"

"I won't have to do anything. I will have accomplished my mission, which is to keep Mr. Perfect out of that job."

"Oh, Andy, really!" Now Mom was seriously indignant. "You're doing all this out of spite? Oh, Andy. I am *sorry* for you."

Mom started the dryer and flounced back upstairs. This was one of those five-star flounces where I definitely heard that sting from the invisible orchestra.

She must have complained about my abhorrent conduct to the rest of the family, because within a few minutes Mark was coming down the basement steps, looking faintly amused.

"Mind if I see what you're up to?" he asked.

"Such as it is. I guess Mom has already told you what a horrible person I am."

"But I knew that," said Mark. He sat down cross-legged on the concrete floor, as I was. He looked over the couple of posters I had completed, and I felt myself tensing up—because I knew that if Mark had been running for any office, his posters would have been a lot better. More neatly executed, more artistic, more imaginative. I almost asked him to leave me alone, but couldn't think of a diplomatic way to do it. Mark picked up a piece of construction paper and a magic marker. I kept on clipping likely-looking pictures, pasting them down, and writing quickly considered captions above the pictures.

Half-an-hour later, Mark passed me over another poster—lettered, as I might have known it would be, in a perfectly legible manner, with slightly stylized lettering, thus:

*Principled*
*Able*
*Loyal*
*Independent*
*Noble*
*Kind*
*Affable*
*Simply the best!*

"That's real nice," I told Mark, and I meant it. "Thanks. Can I use it?"

"Sure, that's why I did it. Want me to do a couple more?"

So he did—and sure enough they were as good as, or better than, anything I had done. Except for my Khrushchev poster. I did think that one was clever. Only I should have gotten Mark to do the lettering for me.

§

I got to the school at about 7:00 on Monday morning, just as the janitor was unlocking. Rosen was waiting on the front steps.

Charity was with him, as were Adina Owens, Cathy Haynes, and Wendell Bell. Rosen gave me a big smile when he saw me. He and Wendell each held what looked like long cloth scrolls.

"Here we go!" he crowed. "Good luck, Gabby!" He shook with me again.

I debated whether I should go inside on my own, and let Guidry and Prick catch up with me if they even showed up at all, or wait for them so that they wouldn't have to go looking for me. I decided on the latter, mainly because it would look pretty pathetic if I were in there putting up posters on my own while Rosen's five-man team was papering the school.

It wasn't till almost 7:30 that Guidry showed up, then Prick about a minute later. Guidry was careful to reiterate, "Now, Ah'm gonna he'p you put up the posters, but that's as far as Ah go. Jes' so y'know."

For the next hour, before the bell rang for the first class of the day, we put up our posters. Rosen had brought an enormous banner that he and his pals hung above the main staircase. It ran along the wall for about fifteen feet, and must have been about four feet high with three-foot letters: ELECT MITCH ROSEN. Nothing friendly or cute about it, I'll say that: more of a command. Which wasn't a bad idea. I, of course, had not thought to produce a banner like that. My posters were each made of a single eleven-by-fourteen-inch sheet of colored construction paper. They looked nice, if I say so myself—both Mark's and mine— but they were small, and hard to read from a distance. They looked even smaller next to the Rosen posters. Rosen had one other big banner, which he and his pals taped up over the entrance to the library. His other posters, more numerous than mine by far, and all of them bigger than mine, went up at various strategic spots in the halls and stairwells.

As I was going into my first-hour class that morning, a short, skinny tenth-grader with heavy black-rimmed glasses, who was a reporter for the *Cat's Paw*, stopped me in the hall and handed me a questionnaire, which he said would be used for a special pre-election edition of the newspaper, and could I please get it back to him by the end of the day?

**NAME:** Andrew Pálinkas
**Brothers/Sisters/Age or class:** Brother, Mark, class of '68.
**What annoys me:** Officious people.
**Nickname:** Gabby.
**Most prized possession:** My APBA baseball game. (Don't ask me, unless you feel like listening to me go on and on for hours.)
**People would be surprised to know that:** I have bodies buried under my parents' house. Or maybe people wouldn't be terribly surprised, at that.
**Secret ambition:** To manage the Milwaukee Braves.
**I can't go without:** Books.
**Favorite class or subject:** Advanced Acting.
**Favorite food:** Spareribs and sauerkraut.
**Favorite breakfast:** That's not something I think about.
**Favorite color:** Purple.
**Movie:** "Tom Jones."
**TV show:** I don't have one.
**Music:** The Shadows.
**Book:** "Vanity Fair" by William Makepeace Thackeray
**Actor:** David Garrick.
**Actress:** Lillian Gish.
**Words of wisdom:** "Avoid running at all times."

Yet there I was, running. I wondered if anybody would notice that little play on words. I didn't have a favorite TV show because I didn't have a TV, but I couldn't bring myself to say that. I meant for my response to suggest that I was above having a favorite TV show.

I had never given much thought to what my favorite kind of music was. I had always liked the Beach Boys, but somehow they didn't strike me as a group an Alpha Male would like. If I had confessed that my current favorite song was "Sugar Shack" by Jimmy Gilmer and the Fireballs (which it was), I would probably not have heard the last of it. The Shadows appealed to a tougher crowd. It wasn't a band for girls.

I chose David Garrick and Lillian Gish to be different, so I wouldn't be making a conventional choice, and because I knew that I might well be the only kid in the school who knew who David Garrick and Lillian Gish were. So, yeah, I was showing off. Besides, if anyone asked me who David Garrick and Lillian Gish were, I would know that they had read my profile—and I could show off my knowledge by answering them. Ditto with Thackeray. Ditto with *Tom Jones*.

Those two were true answers. *Vanity Fair* is still my favorite novel of all time—the greatest ever written in the English language if you ask me—and if *Tom Jones* wasn't my absolute favorite movie it was at least the movie I had felt the best about having gone to.

*Tom Jones* had reached State City in the summer of 1964—right after Grace had left town. This was in the days when there were only so many prints of a movie. It would be released in the largest markets in the fall, and might take as much as a year or even two to get to a little town like State City. When I had mentioned to Mom that I wanted to see it, she had said, "I don't know, Andy." It seems that the ad for it, in *The State City Examiner*, bore the warning in large letters across the bottom: "Not Recommended for Children." I had just turned sixteen, and I pointed that fact out to Mom. On the following Saturday, whether Mom liked it or not, I walked the couple of miles to the theatre. I then walked home again and reported to Mom that *Tom Jones* had been way fun and that she and Dad should see it.

Mom's immediate reaction was to start with "Oh, Andy..." but then she must have realized for once that it wasn't worth making an issue of. The next night, she and Dad went to see the show, and at Mark's request they brought him along, having decided that he, too, was old enough to place his sensibilities at risk. Mom actually came home laughing:

"Thank you, Andy, for recommending it. We had so much fun! And we might have missed it if you hadn't told us."

Aside from filling out that questionnaire, there wasn't much more for me to do. I had made some "Pálinkas for President" buttons—just circles of colored construction paper—and for the rest of that week I carried a bagful of them (and some straight pins) around with me at school, handing them out to any kid who wanted one. But a lot of kids told me, "No thanks." Besides me and Prick, I didn't see but two or three kids wearing them. Jimmy Axton did, and Nia Garthwaite. A lot more kids were wearing similar badges that said "I've Chosen Rosen."

Otherwise, classes went on. I didn't campaign much, because for one thing I had no clue how to do it; for another, I felt it was unseemly to walk up to kids I'd had no interaction with previously, to urge them to vote for me. Which is a ridiculous attitude for any politician to take. You might think it was snobbery on my part, but it wasn't. Simply diffidence.

I'd like to believe it was about my dignity, too. Lord knows, I could be brash and overbearing at times, but to go up to someone, glad-hand him, ask for his vote, when I had never spoken to him before? That struck me as crass. Demeaning to me, and an insult to the other person.

Meanwhile, Rosen was doing everything I should have been doing—or so it was reported to me. I didn't pay him much attention. I noticed, here and there in the hallways, that he would be stopping and chatting with groups of kids he didn't normally associate with—tenth-graders, kids from the less prestigious cliques—maybe three or four of them at a time, just schmoozing, so far as I could tell.

The special election edition of the *Cat's Paw* came out on Thursday, and there was my questionnaire, and Rosen's right beside it:

**NAME:** Mitchell Barron Rosen

**Brothers/Sisters/Age or class:** Sisters Ida ('59), Ruth ('60), Melissa ('63)

**What annoys me:** Pets.

**Nickname:** Main Man.

**Most prized possession:** The diver's watch I got for my bar mitzvah.

**People would be surprised to know that:** I'm distantly related to Leonard Bernstein.

**Secret ambition:** To man the first space-station.

**I can't go without:** People.

**Favorite class or subject:** Advanced Economics.

**Favorite food:** Pasta.

**Favorite breakfast:** Familia.

**Favorite color:** Red and white! What else?

**Movie:** "Mary Poppins."

**TV show:** "Profiles in Courage." (Too bad it's ending!)

**Music:** Bob Dylan.

**Book:** Anything by Isaac Asimov.

**Actor:** Burt Lancaster.

**Actress:** Julie Andrews.

**Words of wisdom:** "Never stop striving."

Mainly, I was pretty sure that Rosen was trying to impress people with his sophistication—whereas I, if only subconsciously, was trying to confirm my reputation for weirdness. His choice of Bob Dylan, for example: While it may well have been truthful, it was a way of signaling. A way of establishing his credentials as a hip, cultured person. And it's not generally known, now, but in the simple 1960s, Familia—which was an imported Swiss breakfast cereal—was fashionable among people who liked to consider themselves refined, discerning, in-the-know about nutrition, and appreciative of good food from faraway places. Familia is still available, I believe. A close kin to granola but not so sugary.

It was remarkable, I thought—and it was telling—that pets would be the first thing to pop into Rosen's mind as a major annoyance. As far as I'm concerned, anyone who doesn't like animals is to be suspected of Lord-knows-what.

When I saw those answers, I decided, okay, I was weird, but better to be weird than all "look how high-minded I am" like Rosen. Once again, apparently, I held a minority view.

The Rosen ticket had Wendell Bell to introduce them to the school assembly. It should have occurred to me to ask Nia Garthwaite to introduce me, to show that I was every bit as much into diversity as they were, but I had never heard Nia say anything about politics or student government. I had no reason to suspect that she would support me, much less be willing to serve as my sponsor on stage.

All I had was Prick. There he was, on Friday morning, looking as good as he knew how to look—and looking indescribably uncomfortable—in a blue blazer he'd outgrown, and a white shirt with sleeves that almost covered his hands. If there's one thing in that campaign that I feel guilty about, it's having put Prick through that. I have read, since then, that a surprisingly high number of people list speaking in public as their greatest fear of all. That doesn't make a lick of sense to me, because I've always been—and am, to this day—more at ease performing for an audience than when I'm taking part in ordinary social conversation. But there we were, candidates and campaign managers, plus Chuck Haviland, who was moderating, all of us seated on a temporary rostrum at one end of the gymnasium. (The auditorium couldn't have accommodated the whole student body.)

Rosen and his posse were all the "beautiful people" types, the *élites*, the "preppies" if such a term had been in vogue in State City at the time. Prick was the kind of kid whom those kids would have sneered at: a hoodlum, a gear-head, a loser, hardly worth looking down on. Plus, no kid had ever improved his image or his social standing through association with me.

Prick was sitting beside me, there on the platform, literally shivering. He was red in the face, as I understand happens to some people when they're terrified. It didn't make him feel any more comfortable, I'm sure, when Haviland introduced him to the crowd as the speaker who would introduce me—and a soft but unmistakable ripple of chuckles and giggles swept through the audience when he stood up and walked to the lectern. I don't know how he managed to get there. He looked as though he was forcing himself, and he probably was.

Prick stood in front of the lectern twisting his fingers and blinking hard behind his glasses. Well, there were a thousand people in the gym—students and faculty—some sitting in the bleachers along the sides, some sitting on the floor of the basketball court. All those people, and Prick had never come close to doing this before. For a moment I thought he was going to freeze and not be able to get any words out. He did freeze, too, for about three seconds. Then he leaned his head forward so that it almost touched the microphone—a common mistake for people who aren't used to microphones—and he caused a terrible feedback with the first sound he made, which made him jerk his head backwards. This brought more laughter from the assembly.

Prick looked over to Haviland for help. Haviland stood up again and pointed to a spot about twelve inches in front of the mike. "Put your head right there," he said to Prick. "The mike will pick your voice up." The mike picked up Haviland's voice, too, which caused another titter, and Haviland sat back down, grinning.

Prick peered out at the crowd for another moment, also grinning, but from terror.

He finally muttered "Hi," into the mike, and looked relieved that the mike didn't rear up and throttle him. "I want to... I want to introduce the guy I think would make the best Student Senate President." Even with the mike, he was barely audible.

Some boy shouted "Louder!" More titters from the audience.

"I don't know anything about the issues," said Prick, a little louder, "but this guy's my friend and he's a good guy and... vote for Andy Palinkas."

Prick turned away from the mike and brushed past me in his hurry to get back to his chair. He was looking at the floor and his face was even redder than it had been.

"Sorry," he muttered to me.

Haviland absolutely guffawed. I wanted to grab Haviland, drag him to the floor of the rostrum, and kick him and stomp him literally to death, right then and there. Instead I turned away from the audience to pat Prick on the shoulder as he retreated. I said, "You did great," but I'm not sure Prick heard.

I didn't have much more experience with microphones than Prick did, so I was a few words into my speech before I found the right volume and distance. Once I had started talking I found that I couldn't quite focus—couldn't be totally into the part—as I would have been if I had been acting, or performing in a speech contest. Maybe it was because, when I wrote the speech, I realized that what I had to say could be covered in about one minute—and that it would be ridiculous to fill time with high-minded clichés.

But then, after the first few paragraphs, I conjured up Grace. She was there, sitting on the platform right behind me—it had been she who had introduced me, a minute before, rather than poor Prick—and now she was there, listening, glowing with admiration, that wonderful smile on her face, but subdued, serious, as she weighed the import of my words.

Good morning. I'm Andrew Palinkas, I'm running for President of the Student Senate, and that is all that I'm running for. If I'm elected, I will preside over the Student Senate, make sure that the meetings are orderly, and cast the deciding vote where the President's vote is needed.

It's customary, in elections for offices in student governments all over the United States—and all over the world for all I know—for candidates to talk about what they're going to do for their school, or for the student body, if elected. I, on the other hand, promise to do nothing for you. On the other hand, I will do nothing *to* you.

As President of the Student Senate, I will let you alone. I will preside and I will execute. That which is not the Student Senate's job, will not be done.

Let me make it clear that the office I'm running for is one that I believe ought not to exist. I oppose government for its own sake, and the very idea of a student government is ridiculous since we have no power. The only point of student government that I can see is to make certain people feel important. Other than that, the student government's job is to administer and execute whatever matters the administration assigns to it, such as dances, pep buses to athletic events in other towns, and whatever else you've got. That being the case, I would prefer that the Student Senate be called the Student Administration. A governing body, it is not. A governing body, it should not be.

I'm not interested in leading. Nor do I want to be led. My parents didn't raise me to be a herder of sheep—and I hope your parents didn't raise any of you to be sheep.

**217**

I will run the Student Senate as efficiently as I know how to, and do my best to ensure that the Senators do their job without annoying the rest of you. But if you want me to do an especially good job of leaving you alone, I have got to have your vote. Thank you all.

The applause was lukewarm at best, although I heard a few laughs at the conclusion. Wendell Bell's introduction of Rosen contained a catalogue of Rosen's accomplishments from seventh through eleventh grades—which I had to admit to myself were impressive. Then Rosen got up to speak. I'm not reproducing his entire speech with word-for-word accuracy here. But I'm amazed at how well I remember it, even at a remove of more than fifty years. I would be pretty certain that what I write here is about ninety percent accurate.

> Good morning. You all know me. Most of you know what I've been doing with myself for the last few years. I was president of my homeroom in ninth grade, and I've been in the Student Senate for all of my time at State City High. If you followed our basketball team this winter you'll probably remember that I had a little to do with our success—not much, but a little. I'm also on the debating team, and the Quill and Scroll society.
>
> But when I think about what I want to do as President of the Student Senate, I like to compare it to what I do when I play violin in the school orchestra. When I decided to run for Student Senate President, I asked many of you, my schoolmates, what were some of the most pressing problems that face us here at State City High. One thing that a lot of people mentioned to me is the problem of cliques—these people stick together and won't associate with those people, and so on. They tell me it's too bad that we have so many cliques at State City High, and they wish everyone could be more friendly.

I like to think of our student body not as a bunch of cliques that don't communicate, but as an enormous symphony orchestra that works together. You have a string section, a woodwinds section, a brass section, a percussion section—and then you have instruments that don't really fit into a particular section, like the piano, the xylophone, the bell, the organ, and the human voice, but even those instruments that don't quite fit in, can contribute to an orchestra. Then within each section you have different instruments. Even if you have several people playing the same instruments, each one will have his or her unique way of playing.

When I made up my mind to run for Student Senate President, I thought about my campaign in terms of the first-chair violin, who's called the concertmaster—and who serves as a leader under the conductor. I'll admit I'm not a good enough violinist to be concertmaster of the State City High orchestra—that would be Billy Howser [light laughter]—but I think my experience, ability, and dedication will make me a pretty good President of the Student Senate.

Some people complain that the Student Senate doesn't have much of a function besides organizing social events such as dances and pep buses. One of my goals as President of the Student Senate will be to change that. I will set an example for leadership in the school and the community, and I'll encourage the rest of the Student Senate to do the same. Irregardless of our race, colors, and creeds, we all are privileged to be students at State City High, and we all want to make our parents proud of us. Through my work in various community groups, I've become aware of the countless options that are available to us if we want to help the community, and as president I will use that knowledge to further our school's involvement in the community.

Moreover, I want you, the student body, to involve yourselves with each other, making State City High a true Camelot, if you will, in the spirit of the late President Kennedy. A society in which each individual cares about the group, and the group cares about each individual—instead of the few small groups that we have now, that tend to stick to themselves and don't seem to care much about the rest of the school. Finally, I want you, the student body, to show your best face to the community: to show the people of State City that its teenagers are not the "troubled teens" that you read about in supermarket magazines. We didn't have to live through a depression or fight a war, and we can thank our parents for that.

And we can repay our parents by making them proud of us, here at school and when we interact with the community. My opponent just said that he didn't want the President to be an activist. I disagree. I believe it was President Theodore Roosevelt who said, "The Presidency is a bully pulpit." As Student Senate President, I'll use the bully pulpit to represent our school to the community—and to encourage each of you to do the same, through volunteerism and involvement in whatever causes are important to you and your family. And always, always, I will use the bully pulpit to be your advocate, the spokesman for each and every one of you, to the administration, to the board of education, and to the broader community of State City.

We may not all be playing the same instruments; we may sit in different sections; but together we can all make beautiful music. And it will be an honor and a privilege to lead you. When you mark your ballot today, mark it for Mitch Rosen. Thank you for listening.

Loud applause. Adina and Cathy then spoke briefly, but I was paying no attention. I repeated to Prick, in an undertone, "You did great. Thanks, man." Prick gave me a wan little smile, and I started thinking of how I might rebut Rosen's speech during the question-and-answer session. For once, I regretted not having gone out for the debate team. If I had bothered to learn the rudiments, I suppose I could have picked Rosen apart pretty easily—maybe even to the point of making a few converts.

Very few questions were asked, though. The only one I remember—I can't recall who asked it, or if I even recognized his face in that crowd—was, "What makes you think you'd be a better President than Rosen?"

I did have to fight back the urge to say, "For one thing, at least I know that 'irregardless' isn't good English, and I know better than to say 'last' when I mean 'past'"—but having resisted that temptation, all I could do was repeat my general line.

"I'd be a better President because I'd tend to my knitting," I concluded. "But it's up to you—all of you who are voting—to decide what kind of a President you want to have. Do you want one who does the job, does it well—or do you want someone who arrogates to himself the authority to act as your representative to the community?"

I actually did say "arrogates." I immediately wanted to kick myself for having said it: partly because I knew most kids wouldn't know the word; partly also because Mom would have been annoyed if she had known I had used it. Showing off my erudition, you see.

The assembly lasted through first hour, that morning. Haviland sent us on our way with the admonition, "When you go to vote, remember the wise words of Charlie Chan: 'Mind like parachute. Only functions when open.'"

The polls were open through sixth period; a few Student Senators were excused from seventh, to count the ballots. The results were to be announced immediately after school, in the cafeteria. This wouldn't be a formal assembly like a pep rally; it was optional, for anyone so emotionally involved in the election that he was willing to stay after school to get the results.

**221**

Okay, I showed up. Maybe I shouldn't have—but if I hadn't, I'm sure a few students would have gotten together the next morning to kid me into thinking I had been elected.

It must have been seventy to eighty kids who showed up. A few of them actually looked earnest, hopeful, as though it mattered to them. I wandered into the cafeteria on my own. I hadn't asked Prick to come with me, because I felt it would have been an imposition. He hadn't volunteered. The Rosen party came in a few seconds behind me, to loud cheers. Then the outgoing President and Vice President, Chuck Haviland and Scott Louis, came in together, with Principal Poop trailing behind. Haviland carried a folded paper. Louis was an officious type, and he was sticking close to Haviland as though he figured he had better be ready to prevent anyone from snatching the paper, like anyone would have done that. Kids were all milling about; Haviland and Louis and Mr. Pope had to thread their way through them to get to the approximate center of the cafeteria, where Haviland clambered up onto a table and stood there waiting for silence.

"Here are the results," he said. This great big shit-eating grin started creeping across his face. There's no way I could have proven it, and maybe it was no more than my paranoia, but I got the clear message, even though he wasn't looking in my direction at all, that he was enjoying this because he was having a good laugh at me.

"The Secretary-Treasurer for next year is Cathy Haynes..." Cheers from the assembly. "The Vice President... is Adina Owens..." More cheers. "And the President of the Student Senate for next year... is Mitch Rosen. Congratulations, Mitch." Several guys around Rosen whooped, and slapped him on the back. Rosen hugged Adina and Cathy and shook hands with Wendell Bell. Haviland got off the table as quickly as he could—still grinning all over his goddam face, but not looking at me—and started making his way over to Rosen.

I was closest to Adina, so I went over to her first, and held my hand out. "Good campaign, Adina, and good luck. And congratulations."

Adina didn't smile at all. She wouldn't even look at me. "Thank you," she said. You could only just call it a handshake; she barely brushed my hand with her fingertips before she withdrew them. That pissed me off, but good.

"You'll knock 'em dead," I told her. I made a point of giving Adina as big a smile as I knew how to. Then, before I walked away, I gave her a swat on the butt—knowing, this time, what I was doing and how she would take it. I saw her mouth fly wide open again, and her face go bright red, in the instant before I turned my back to her.

Rosen was finishing up shaking hands with Haviland and Louis when I got over to him, and he immediately grabbed my hand and clapped me on the shoulder.

"You ran a good campaign, Gabby," he said. He was seriously pumped, and I couldn't blame him. I envied him: not the office, but the emotional high. "All in good fun, right?" he added.

"I'm sure you'll do great," I told him. "Good luck." I didn't want to be rude, but Haviland was already on his way out. I got out of Rosen's grip and elbowed my way towards the door as fast as I could, catching up with Haviland in the hallway. He had been moving fast. I almost had to physically stop him.

"Hey, Haviland, don't you usually announce the totals?"

Haviland laughed in my face. "Ordinarily, yes," he replied. "Sometimes we don't want to embarrass one of the candidates."

"Well, tell me."

"Confidentially?" Haviland was plainly having fun. "It was five hundred eighty-six... to eighty-four. The highlight of the count was when you got three votes in a row. So, congratulations. You made twelve percent. Barely, but nice going." Haviland offered his hand, ironically. I shook it without thinking.

I walked home at my usual pace. When I came in the front door, Mom was in the living room, on the sofa, reading *The State City Examiner*. She glanced up at me and said, "I take it you didn't win. Or you'd have been running. How did you do?"

I could have said that the vote totals hadn't been published, which would have been strictly speaking true, but I gave her the figures that Haviland had given me. Doing my damndest to look like it hadn't hurt, which did cost me some effort.

Mom sniffed. "That's about as many votes as you deserved." She resumed reading the paper.

# 15 SUMMER REPERTORY

Charity walked along with me to school the following Monday, and she told me, "I voted for you after all. Not that I agree with you, but I admire you for taking a stand."

I thanked her, although I might have preferred it if she hadn't voted for me. I would have hoped that all eighty-four of my votes had come from people who actually wanted me to win. Plus, I suspected that Charity hadn't pulled the trigger for Rosen because he had never responded to her interest in him. But I suppose that suspicion was typical of my own pettiness.

Then from out of nowhere, Charity asked me, "You're not going to the prom next weekend, are you?"

"No, I'm not."

I almost added, "Who would go with me?" but for once, I caught myself. I also thought, but forced myself not to say to Charity, "There's nobody I'd care to ask."

"I'm not comfortable at dances." I said. I haven't been to one since the Spring Dance before last. In '64."

"I didn't go to that one," said Charity. "But I remember Grace told me you looked very handsome."

It was the first time Charity had mentioned Grace to me, all that year; the first time I had heard Grace's name spoken, since she had left. My heart dropped right down into my guts. It almost took the wind out of me. Part of me wanted to ask, "How is Grace, by the way?" Part of me didn't dare to, and part of me didn't want to. I think I covered that all up, though. At least, I tried not to sound like I was affected.

"That can't be true," I replied. "I seem to recall that she was wearing her glasses that night, so she couldn't have said that, unless she was putting you on."

Charity gave what looked like a forced half-smile. I knew that what I had said wasn't as funny as I had meant it to be; it was just useless self-deprecation.

"I'm not going either," she said. "I've never been interested in... dances and all that foolishness."

Clueless I may have been, but not entirely so. I certainly could have asked Charity to the prom. But a number of factors weighed against my doing so.

First, plain and simple, I was not attracted to Charity. If I would go to all the trouble and expense of going to the prom, I would do it for a girl I wanted to be boyfriend-and-girlfriend with, someone I could be proud to have on my arm. If I took Charity to the prom, I figured, people would assume we were a couple, and that was about the last thing I wanted. Moreover, I suspected, people would think that it was a good match: the geeky guy with the plain girl. A rather amusing match, too. At least, I'd have found it so, if I'd been observing. That would have been more humiliation than I could have handled.

Another huge factor: It would have been a betrayal of Grace, and of the feelings I had had for her—still had for her—to have gone out with Grace's plain little sister as a substitute. It would have insulted Charity, and given her false ideas, if I had taken her to the prom despite my feelings. Call it hypocrisy if you will, but I told myself that one reason why I didn't ask Charity to the prom was that I respected her.

Another reason had nothing to do with Charity; it had to do with Mom. I knew all too well what would happen if I tried to go to the prom. Mom would give me leave to go, but she would meddle endlessly beforehand, giving me unwanted direction in dress and deportment, assuming that Charity was really my girl-friend, gossiping about it with Rae Childress—and no doubt she would insist on my coming home after the dance, missing the after-party, which would last nearly till dawn.

Even if I could have gotten a date for the prom with a girl I wanted to be with and be seen with—*especially* if it were a girl I wanted to be with and be seen with—would I have set myself up for the humiliation of having to admit that Mommy had put a curfew on me? I think not.

That Monday afternoon, during sixth period, the final hom-eroom session of the year took place—to elect two Student Sen-ate members from each homeroom (homerooms consisted of about thirty kids) for the first semester of next year. When the supervising teacher, Mr. Titone, opened the floor to nomina-tions, before anyone had nominated anyone else, Nia Garthwaite put her hand up and proposed me. I heard a few giggles, and Mr. Titone raised an eyebrow, but another kid immediately seconded. A few minutes later, when the ballot slips had been collected and the votes counted, Mr. Titone announced that I had been elected. Since he read off my name first, I had the impression that I had received the most votes of all the candidates.

Most of the students started clapping—and most of those who were clapping, were looking over at me. Even Mr. Titone was smiling.

He said, "You'll keep 'em honest, Andy."

Word got around fast. Rosen came over to me in the hallway as I was walking to my seventh period class, which was Bonehead Math, with almost as big a grin as he had worn when he had won the Presidency the previous Friday, and shook my hand again. "It'll be great working with you," he said.

"Don't speak too soon," I replied, but I was grinning back; I couldn't help it. I tried to tell myself it didn't matter that I had been elected—but it did.

When I brought the news home to Mom that afternoon, she looked startled at first. Then she smiled a little—and a little reluctantly, I thought, but maybe I'm too quick to put a negative spin on it. She said, "That's fine, Andy. Congratulations."

The next day—probably trying to be conciliatory—Gus Guidry approached me with his plans for taking our acting company into the summer, and maybe arranging public performances, locally.

"We could work up some new sketches," he said, "and we could turn it into a real full-length show. We could perform— well, on the University campus, in the Memorial Union, or outdoors on the Student Common. Or we could use the City Park. There must be all kinds of places we could rent for nothing, or for real cheap at least."

"Sounds great," I said, "but the publicity would be the big expense. It'd cost a fortune to advertise in the papers, not to mention putting up handbills all over town would take forever unless we hired people to do it. Have you got the money for that? Because I don't."

"God-damn."

"But why don't we go where there'll be people already?" I asked. "We could work up one act for adults and one for kids, and perform at the public library—like on Saturday mornings when they have Story Hour. We could contact church groups, and... hell, I don't know, maybe garden clubs, hospitals, nursing

**227**

homes, then there's the schools for handicapped kids that are open all summer. Not for money: just to get a reputation. Then eventually we could start some kind of professional company."

Guidry thought about this for a few seconds. "Captive audience," he said. "Might work. Specially if they're old and frail; we can intimidate 'em into applauding. And terrorize the children. Maybe do some dramatizations of Edgar Allan Poe. Scare 'em so they'll never forget it."

Over the next few days, Guidry and Charity and I started working up two coherent hour-long shows—one for kids and one for adults, as I had suggested, although we used some of our material for both. We had a scene from *Pygmalion*, and one from *Hedda Gabler*. Charity wrote brief stage versions of a couple of children's stories. We developed some mimes. Charity chose a few poems by Emily Dickinson and George Eliot to recite. Guidry knew some Scots-Irish folk tales that had been translated to a Southern setting—"Grandfather Tales," Guidry called them—and some stories about the Civil War, most of them involving his hero, Nathan Bedford Forrest, which we figured would be especially fascinating to little boys.

I focused on poetry. I chose "The Cremation of Sam McGee," and "Casey at the Bat," for kids. For adults, I chose "anyone" by E. E. Cummings, and "The Lady's Dressing Room" by Jonathan Swift, among others. I had to finally admit that Guidry and Charity were right, when they urged me to replace the Swift poem with something else, because it had the word "shit" in it. One member of one audience or another, sooner or later and probably sooner, would have been sure to fly into a tizzy about that. But I resolved to use that poem in speech contests during my senior year, if Dr. Pritchard would allow it.

In the following weeks—the rest of the school year and the first few weeks of vacation—the three of us worked on the show, rehearsing and refining. My parents, for a change, couldn't think of any objections to our performing—at the library and at nursing homes and so on. Dad said, "That's a real good idea," and Mom said, "It's a *great* idea!"

The only time we had any controversy with my parents was when we performed the adult version for them and for Mr. and Mrs. Childress, outside in the Childresses' back yard. Mom half-seriously—or maybe all-seriously, though she was smiling when she said it—suggested that I might not want to perform "anyone" for old people, since it was so sad and might make them think about death. I said I figured they were probably old enough to handle it.

"Your mother's a dear woman," Guidry told me the next day, as we were assembling at his house to give the same performance to his family. "Just the finest kind."

"Yes, I suppose she is," I said, "as long as you don't have to be her eldest son."

Guidry gave me a sharp look, as though I had said something obscene. I never mentioned my family situation to him after that.

Now that I think of it, it occurs to me that I might have done better in life if I had had a confidant to whom I could have made remarks like that.

Grace, maybe, could have been that person. I know Grace would have listened, if I had ever come to her with a problem, and she might have had good advice, besides. But I would never have dared to confide in Grace, in that way. I would never have dared to reveal my defects and neuroses to her. Of course that's exactly what I ended up doing.

Mom, meanwhile, had an equally high opinion of Guidry. "He's a good kid," she said to me, at about this time. "He's a little eccentric, but a good kid. You do seem to have some nice friends."

The Crosstown Rivals didn't last long, but we got a lot done in a few weeks. We were ready to give our first real performance by mid-June. We lined up gigs at the State University School for Crippled and Handicapped Children (we still had schools like that, in those days before mainstreaming, and they were in session during summer break); at the Public Library, at a few retirement homes, and at several different wards at State University Hospital—children's and adults' psychiatric units, burn unit, geriatric unit—plus performances on the State University Student Common and in City Park. We performed in public parks in a couple of smaller towns near State City, too. I suppose we must have played close to twenty engagements in about six weeks.

I got to drive to some of them. I finally was granted a driver's license that summer: at seventeen. Most kids had got theirs at sixteen, but my parents had insisted that I wait a year to get mine. For no reason that I could see, other than to stick to their concerted strategy of retarding my social development. Getting a driver's license is a real big thing for most kids, but it wasn't for me. After all, my license was granted to me only grudgingly, at a time in life when it could not have been a big thing because most of the other kids my age already were driving.

In August, all three families took vacations: the Childresses to Europe (I didn't dare ask if they were going to see Grace; I assumed they would), the Guidrys to visit their relatives Down South, and the Palinkases to Pittsburgh, stopping for two days in Chicago (where we saw the Field Museum, the Art Institute, and a Cubs game) along the way. Then summer was over.

### BOOK IV

# 16 sun moon stars rain

Mark and I were once again in the same school, that fall of 1965. Predictably enough, after the second or third day of classes, Mark reported to me that some older kid had asked him, "Are you weird like your brother?" Nice of him to tell me that. But Mark seemed to get along okay. I stayed out of his way, made a point of keeping my distance from him, in school. I figured I was doing him a favor. He seemed to have friends. Whenever I saw him in the library or the cafeteria, he would be with a few other kids from his grade—boys mostly, but sometimes girls. Come to think of it, I just did not see my brother alone, at any time when we were both at State City High. I didn't bother to acquaint myself with any of his friends, but he had plenty of them.

Right at the beginning of the year, Mark told me that he was going to give speech and drama a try, too. This was about the worst news he could have told me. There was nothing I could say about it, nothing I could do but accept it. What was I going to do? Say, "Look, Mark, I'd rather you didn't"? In this one area where I thought I had worked out some sort of a reputation for myself, Mark was going to show me up yet again.

How do you sabotage someone's performance in a speech contest? For one thing you don't, whether the guy's your brother or your deadliest enemy. For another, it's not like football, where you can weight a guy's shoes or put HEET in his jock or pay someone on the other team to injure him. You just have to play your own game, and hope the other guy fucks up.

Mark chose to start out in Humorous Interp. He even chose a piece that I had used the year before: a monologue by Anton Chekhov called "On the Harmfulness of Tobacco." That's a difficult piece because it's smile-funny, chuckle-funny, cringe-with-vicarious-embarrassment funny, rather than laugh-out-loud funny. It's got nothing to do with tobacco. The character who delivers the speech is the world's most henpecked husband, who is supposed to be giving a lecture on the subject mentioned, but instead he goes off on tangent after tangent about his miserable family life.

Mark performed it for me several times, in our bedroom, and he wasn't bad. Public speaking is like anything else: It takes practice and experience to get good. I judged he was no better than I had been, as a tenth-grader, but he wasn't any worse either. I might have advised him to choose an easier piece, but I didn't—and the reason I didn't was because I was afraid I might give him the impression that I was jealous: that I was warning him off of a piece with which I had had some success, for fear that he would win more accolades with it than I had done. That impression would have been correct.

I had decided to focus on Poetry Interp, my senior year. Mom had done me a favor, as it turned out, when she warned me about performing a sad poem like "anyone" in front of old folks. That suggestion—silly as I had thought it was at the time—

reminded me that if there's one big advantage you can give yourself in a high school speech contest, it's choosing material that has to do with death. Judges tend to react well to that subject, because death-related material gives kids a chance to emote in clumsy, unsubtle ways, and morbid kids are drawn to forensics the way tough kids are drawn to football and wrestling.

I performed "The Lady's Dressing Room" for Dr. Pritchard, in private, at the beginning of my senior year, and she loved it—especially the part where I looked out in anguish to the imaginary audience, letting a sob into my voice as I stammered, "Celia... Celia..." and then dropping to a mortified whisper, "Celia shits!"

Dr. Pritchard damn near fell out of her chair laughing—but she warned me that that poem probably wouldn't fly in a speech contest. Quite apart from the word "shit," for which one judge or another was sure to disqualify me, it was a long poem—it took more than ten minutes to recite—and it was written in an antiquated English that would have to be spoken with extreme care and precision. I could have performed it, but it would have been a severe test, and simply not worth the trouble since I couldn't hope to win a prize with such a ribald piece.

"The judges want 'serious,'" Dr. Pritchard reminded me. "They want to be Deeply Moved." (I could hear the capitalizations in her voice.) "You've got one great poem, with 'anyone,' but it's short, so you'll need to perform it along with another poem that complements it."

So I chose "After Apple-Picking," by Robert Frost. I performed that poem for Dr. Pritchard in a low-key, subdued, somewhat bemused manner, as though I were recounting a disturbing dream and trying to give it interpretation in my mind as I was telling it—and anticipating subsequent dreams (as well as the Big Sleep) with some dread. "After Apple-Picking" is not a dramatic poem, so I had to recite it with considerable energy—and the challenge lay in conveying that energy while speaking in a soft, confidential voice.

Then I gave Dr. Pritchard my interpretation of "anyone."

What struck me odd was that I had recited "anyone" over and over again, that past summer, and it hadn't had much of an emotional effect on me. I had been taught—by Dr. Pritchard herself, in American Lit, my sophomore year—that "anyone" was a poem about conformity, about the small-mindedness of small-town America. I had brought that information to my performances with the Crosstown Rivals.

That poem hadn't been the strongest item in my repertoire, that summer, to be honest. I hadn't put a lot into it. I hadn't given my interpretation as much thought as I should have given it, so I hadn't had a clear idea of what I was trying to communicate—and thus I didn't communicate anything very well.

But when I considered "anyone" in conjunction with Frost's poem, that fall, I thought harder about it, and I took a new perspective on it. It *wasn't* a poem about conformity and small-mindedness, I concluded.

One day, in the school library, I found a recording of E.E. Cummings reciting his own poetry, including "anyone". I listened to it, and found that he spoke it in a way that I could not understand at all: in a tired, droning voice, excruciatingly slowly, paying no attention to the meter—even though the meter is one of the most interesting characteristics of the poem. That made me think a lot more about how *I* thought it should be recited. The more I thought, the more I came to think that I understood Cummings' poem more perfectly than Cummings had, himself!

When I first performed it for Dr. Pritchard, it was the first time I had performed it since that summer: the first time I had performed it since I had seriously *thought* about it. I was doing it cold—and it came out completely differently from how I had done it before. It just came to me, this new interpretation, and came out of me without my hardly having to think about it.

The poem starts with dactylic trimeter. Then you'll encounter subtle metrical changes throughout, which work together synergistically to form a sort of song. I emphasized the sing-song nature of the poem, speaking rather rapidly. I spoke softly, in a tone of wonderment, almost. Smiling at first, as though I were telling a funny/ironical story. Then, as the song progressed, I spoke as though I were revealing a great mystery.

> anyone lived in a pretty how town
> (with up so floating many bells down)
> spring summer autumn winter
> he sang his didn't he danced his did
>
> Women and men (both little and small)
> cared for anyone not at all
> they sowed their isn't they reaped their same
> sun moon stars rain

I leaned slightly forward, into my audience, establishing more eye contact with Dr. Pritchard, giving her a little conspiratorial smile as though I were telling her something she maybe shouldn't be hearing:

> children guessed (but only a few
> and down they forgot as up they grew
> autumn winter spring summer)
> that noone loved him more by more

I slowed my pace. My tone became a bit sad and sentimental, and just slightly awed, as though in admiration of the devoted couple:

> when by now and tree by leaf
> she laughed his joy she cried his grief
> bird by snow and stir by still
> anyone's any was all to her

I shrugged, then recited the next verse at the original some-what faster pace, as though bringing the audience forward briskly into the story:

> someones married their everyones
> laughed their cryings and did their dance
> (sleep wake hope and then) they
> said their nevers they slept their dream

My eye contact with Dr. Pritchard became more intense, as though I were making sure she was listening and understanding, although I maintained the brisk pace and the song-like rhythm. I let a mystified tone creep into my voice, as though I were trying to puzzle the story out for myself as I related it:

> stars rain sun moon
> (and only the snow can begin to explain
> how children are apt to forget to remember
> with up so floating many bells down)

I paused; inclined my head; cast my eyes down for a moment. I paused just a second or so longer than I had between any of the previous stanzas, then I went on again in a slower, softer way, as one does when imparting a sad but inevitable outcome:

> one day anyone died i guess
> (and noone stooped to kiss his face)
> busy folk buried them side by side
> little by little and was by was

With another fatalistic little shrug, I picked the pace back up just a touch but maintained a quiet, sadful demeanor, still speak-ing rather softly:

all by all and deep by deep
and more by more they dream their sleep
noone and anyone earth by april
wish by spirit and if by yes.

As I began to speak the last stanza, I slowed my pace dramatically, and all on their own—I never would have anticipated them—tears actually sprang to my eyes and started running down my cheeks. Real tears that came spontaneously. I wouldn't have wanted them to come. But they did, as slowly and almost wonderingly I concluded the poem:

Women and men (both dong and ding)
summer autumn winter spring
reaped their sowing and went their came

And my tears blinded me as I whispered the last four words like the far-distant tolling of a church bell:

sun... moon... stars... rain

"I'm sorry," I said to Dr. Pritchard—I could only just get the words out—and I wiped my eyes on my sleeve. "That never happened before."

"My God, Andy, don't apologize. Never apologize for that kind of emotion! If you can bring that to your performance, you'll win everything there is to win this year."

"I wasn't acting. It just happened."

Every time I performed that poem, that year, the tears would come, sometimes as early as the sixth stanza but never later than the last one. Fifty-plus years later, when I recite that poem, the tears still come—every time. Explain it if you can.

# 17 MORE POLITICS

We had a small family crisis that September. Right after Labor Day, Mom took to her bed with an illness that she couldn't quite describe, except that "I feel so awful." For weeks, she stayed in the darkened bedroom almost all day, emerging for calls of nature but only rarely for meals. She lost a lot of weight. None of the rest of us could cook, and Dad was reluctant to take me and Mark to a restaurant while Mom stayed home in bed. The level of cuisine in our household, which was never high, sank to an almost unbearable nadir for a while, till Dad gave Mom a little talking-to and she agreed that she would get out of bed if only she didn't have to venture outside.

By the beginning of October, Mom was spending more and more time on her feet, doing housework or preparing meals— although by that time I had taught myself to cook, somewhat, and sometimes I made dinner. Sometimes Mom would sit in the living room, reading or playing solitaire. She only left the house when it was absolutely necessary.

Mom did go to see our family doctor, finally.

"He said I'm healthy as a horse," she reported to us. "He said it's nothing organic: he called it non-specific anxiety disorder."

Non-specific it may have been, but I could guess at the source of it. Rae Childress, at the end of the summer, had announced her candidacy for City Council, and she had invited Mom to be a precinct coordinator for her campaign. That would have meant canvassing a few streets, passing out literature, finding out who Rae's supporters were, making sure they all got yard-signs, seeing if they would need absentee ballots, and making sure that they voted. Mom had been happy to do this sort of work, the past three Novembers. To hear Rae Childress tell it, the stakes were pretty high this time.

Three of the five city council seats were up for election that fall, and it's not important to go into the details, but there was one slate of three candidates (to which Rae belonged) that was in favor of the proposed federally funded urban renewal program that would dig up the downtown and pretty much rebuild it from scratch. Running with Rae were a Congregationalist minister named Bob Cadwallader, and a plumber named Tim Chelius. The slate of Cadwallader, Chelius, and Childress advertised themselves as "The Three Cs for Change!"

Another slate of three candidates opposed them—and opposed the plan.

Rae was over at our house one afternoon when I came home from school—a day or two before Mom took sick, this was—having coffee with Mom on our front lawn, and I sat with them long enough to hear Rae refer to the other three candidates as "the Slob Group," since (this was her version, anyway) they were in favor of a dirty, down-at-heel downtown while she and her cohorts were in favor of a prettified, vibrant downtown.

The "Slob Group" consisted of a beer distributor named Clifford "Doc" Erickson, and two men who were fathers of kids I knew. One was Dubose Garthwaite—Nia's father. He was a tall, husky Negro with remarkably high cheekbones (he probably had some Indian blood, as many American Negroes do), processed hair, and a loud, hearty voice. He looked like he might have been a professional heavyweight boxer once. He hadn't been, but he had been a First Sergeant in the U.S. Army, and now he owned a slightly raffish blue-collar bar downtown called Topsy's—I suppose because he'd been a Top Sergeant. The bar was located in the area that would be razed if the urban renewal plan were implemented.

Most likely, Mr. Erickson and Mr. Garthwaite knew each other because Mr. Erickson supplied Mr. Garthwaite's beer. They were both rough, blunt-spoken, working-class types: considerably below the Childresses and the Palinkases on State City's social ladder. But the third member of the "Slob Group" was an entirely different animal: Mitch Rosen's father, Jake.

Rosen's was the biggest men's clothing store in State City. Still is, today. Manny Rosen—Jake Rosen's father and Mitch's grandfather—had founded it, back in the 1910s. While the store was in no danger of being displaced, the proposed urban renewal plan did look like it could drastically reduce both pedestrian and vehicular traffic around Rosen's. So Jake Rosen opposed it.

"It was clever of them, I have to hand it to them, to find two Democrats to run on that slate," Rae said to Mom that afternoon. "Erickson's a Republican, so of course he would be against the plan, and Garthwaite... well, he's a Democrat, but he's a dumb N. God forgive me for saying it."

Mom's facial expression didn't change, but her head moved back an inch or so as though she had smelled something.

"I know, I know," said Rae. She waved her free hand, the one not holding her cigarette, as though to clear the air of the euphemism. "It's not nice to say it, but it's a plain fact. And a lot of people will vote for him because he's a Negro and they want to be able to pat themselves on the back for electing a Negro to the City Council. But Jake Rosen, for God's sake! You'd think *he* would know better."

I got to talking about the election with Mitch Rosen, in the school library the next day. This was the way he explained his perspective (as best I can remember):

"I'm a lot more progressive than my dad. He's not all that political. I guess he can't afford to be, because he has to stay on good terms with everybody. And I have to say, I'm not completely on his side on this issue. I think all the businesses downtown ought to sacrifice a little, for the common good. But he seems to feel that the redevelopment would hurt him pretty badly. Maybe not right away, but years down the line. Dad's always thinking ahead.

"I'm not sure; I'll give him a break on this one because I don't know the downtown as well as he does. But you know, just between the two of us, if I could vote? I'd vote for Dad because he's my dad—but then I'd probably vote for two of the candidates from the other slate."

Rosen gave me a big wink and added, "I'd leave Mrs. Childress off."

It was about halfway through Mom's illness—around the end of September, when she was still spending almost all her time in bed—that I had a fairly long talk with her. The first we had had in quite a while. One afternoon I passed by my parents' bedroom and she called out to me—in a very faint voice, almost a whisper—to come in and sit with her for a few minutes and tell her about what was going on in the outside world. It was all dark and close, in there. It didn't smell bad; I mean, Mom still washed, and all, but it was like the air hadn't moved in that room for weeks. I was tempted to say to Mom, "Damn it, there's nothing wrong with you! Get on outside and find out for yourself!"

I didn't say anything of the sort; I was a big enough jerk to think it, but not to say it. I went and sat in a chair next to the bed where Mom was lying propped up, and I told her about how my classes were going, and about the City Council campaign, which was getting pretty hot and causing plenty of talk around town and in school. I told her about the conversation I had had with Mitch Rosen.

Mom said, "I hardly know Mr. Rosen at all. Daddy says he's nice enough."

"Well, and he doesn't strike me as a guy you could call a slob," I said.

"Maybe he's not," Mom said, "but the two other stinkers he's running with certainly are. Oh, no, I shouldn't say that. Especially about Mr. Garthwaite. I'm sure he's had... I don't know, probably he's had door after door closed in his face all his life long, just for being a Negro. So I shouldn't judge him.

"You know, it's funny, Rae Childress said the darndest thing to me a few weeks ago—well, you were there. But after you'd left, she said to me something like, 'I can forgive those other two because they're idiots, but Jake Rosen ought to know better.' And then she said, 'He's not a good Jew. I'm convinced of that.' Isn't that strange? Doesn't that sound strange to you?"

It did. Not that I knew much about Judaism, but as far as I knew Mr. Rosen didn't go around doing awful stuff.

"Did you ask her what she meant by that?"

"Well, I assumed she meant that he wasn't taking the position that she thought he ought to be taking." Mom smiled and almost laughed. "I don't know, maybe he eats bacon in secret. Except the Childresses don't... I don't know what you call it, they're not kosher? Of course Mr. Childress isn't Jewish at all. And you know how Rae is about celebrating Christmas."

How was Rae about Christmas? Not fanatical, but close to it. She took Christmas pretty seriously. Every December, the Childress family had a big elaborate Christmas tree in their front window—it certainly wasn't a vulgar one, but a big one, tastefully decorated—and Christmas lights wrapped round the little dwarf pine that stood in their front yard. Rae would distribute her Christmas cakes and cookies all over the neighborhood.

I don't know the explanation for that: why a Jewish woman from New York would be so into Christmas. I wouldn't be surprise if there were an interesting story behind it, but if there is, I'd have to invent it, now.

242

Here's what's funny: Charity told me once—I'm pretty sure it was around Christmastime of our junior year—that her father hated all the fuss that her mother made about Christmas. I'm guessing it was to do with his Quakerism. As nearly as I can remember, this is what Charity told me:

"Dad thinks the Christmas tree and all the decorations have turned Christmas into a pagan ritual. He says Christmas is a celebration of money and materialism. He says it's because of a conspiracy of everyone in the business world to—'browbeat' was the word he used—to browbeat people into spending money and ignoring the religious significance. And..." (Charity looked pretty displeased.) "He says it's mostly Jews who are behind it."

That struck me as interesting, at the time. It didn't especially surprise me that Dr. Childress would take a position against the commercialization of Christmas, since I had heard from Grace and from Charity that he had some firm opinions. But that thing about the Jews: I was saying to myself, "Why did he marry a Jewish girl, then? Or does he have something against Jews because he doesn't love his wife anymore?"

I'm still puzzling about that.

Anyway, after Mom had told me what Rae had said, about Rosen not being a good Jew, she said, "It's as though Rae can't make up her mind whether she wants to play up being Jewish, or try to live it down."

Which I thought at the time was a more insightful remark than Mom usually made.

I said, "I can't imagine that she could ever fool anyone into thinking she was anything else. Not with that accent."

"Well, and she's so overbearing," said Mom. "I shouldn't say it, but it seems to me that a lot of Jewish people are like that. You know, the other day while you were at school, she came knocking at the door and I actually hid in here. Pretended not to be in. I'm not proud of it. I hate putting her off, but I don't want to work

**243**

for her! I guess I'll vote for her—I do think it's important that her slate gets elected—but I don't feel right about ringing door-bells for her. I don't think she'd work well with others."

I hung out a little more with Prick, outside of school, that fall. His parents had let him buy a 1955 Chevrolet Bel Air con-vertible that was in barely salvageable condition, and he was re-storing it. Sometimes after school I would walk back to his house with him, to help if I could. I knew as much about cars as Prick knew about politics, so I wasn't much use, but I was there if he needed an extra pair of hands. Just for fun, we learned the French words for "struts," and "spark plug," and so on.

It's funny: I didn't do enough work on that project to learn much about cars, but I enjoyed the experience—because for once I was letting Prick be in charge, doing the grunt-work for him, while he did something he was good at. It was a way of paying him back, maybe, for that damn speech.

Speaking of that, the first speech contest of the semester was supposed to take place in mid-October. Nia Garthwaite and I were both signed up for it. It was a big one, a statewide compe-tition, taking place on the campus of State University. Nia was doing Humorous Interp and I was doing Poetry Interp. She and I were both in Dr. Pritchard's Honors Acting class, and we both had parts in the fall play, which was *The Frogs*—and we were both looking forward to *Oklahoma!*, which would be the winter musi-cal. With one thing and another, I got to be better friends with Nia, that fall.

One afternoon, Nia invited me over to her house so that we could practice together, and exchange critiques, and that was how I met Nia's mother. Nia and I each performed our pieces for her. Mrs. Garthwaite wasn't a remarkable-looking woman at all. Maybe forty, pleasant enough to look at, medium height and build, just an ordinary Negro lady. I remember the dress she was wearing that day. It had a zig-zag black and white geometrical pattern, sharply tailored. A nice dress, a little more formal than what you would have expected a woman of that time and place to wear around the house.

All the time I was in the Garthwaites' house, I have to confess, I kept looking around for any differences that might exist between it and any normal white household. I didn't find but one, although all I saw of the house was the living room, dining area, and kitchen. The only thing I saw that was at all unusual was a portrait of Jesus on one wall of the living room in which he was unmistakably a Negro, with dark brown skin and short kinky black hair and beard. Around him were other men, presumably apostles, some of them black and some white. I didn't get close enough to it to see if it was a print or an original.

Nia's piece was a satirical version of the "Hänsel and Gretel" story, in which Gretel ends up on trial for murdering the old witch. Mrs. Garthwaite seemed to get a kick out of it. Then I recited my poetry. Mrs. Garthwaite sat there open-mouthed, not saying anything for several seconds after I had finished.

Finally, she said, "You have got *talent plus*, young man." She was almost whispering. "You're going to go a long way in the theatre; I can tell that."

Since Mom was still sickly and only getting out of bed now and then, I suggested to Nia that we perform our pieces for her, too, the following afternoon.

Mom was up, in the kitchen, when I walked into the house with Nia, and I was struck by the way Mom greeted her. Mom, I must say, was one of the most gracious people to a stranger I have ever known in my life. Completely open, unassuming, always with a big smile for everyone—such as she bestowed on Nia, that day. Although she was directing the main force of her smile at Nia and not at me, it seemed to me—and this could be entirely my imagination—that she seemed to be glancing at me, incidentally, with a touch of maternal pride.

Lord knows I had learned to read the subtlest changes in Mom's expression, but this was a reaction that I had never caused before. I could tell it. It struck me, after the fact, that I had seen a similar swelling of pride in Mrs. Garthwaite the previous day.

After Nia had left, Mom said to me, "That's such a nice girl. Are you dating her?"

I wasn't, at all. Nia and I hung out sometimes at school, sat together at lunch sometimes, worked together in speech and drama—but that wasn't "dating."

"I think it would be so nice if you dated a Negro girl."

I didn't object to the idea of dating Nia, except that she was kind of silly and frivolous in her demeanor. She was quite pretty if you like them chubby, but I didn't. Nia was nice—very nice— but she didn't strike a spark with me. Plus, let's face it: Most teenagers, boys and girls both, are going to be disinclined to date anyone their parents urge them to date.

I told Mom, "We're just friends. I like her, but I don't really want her for a girlfriend."

"You might want to think about it," Mom said. "Or at any rate ask her to do things with you, socially, in case she doesn't have very many other friends. I don't know how the other kids treat her, but you should always give her a real fair shake. Or give any Negro a real fair shake, because not everyone will."

"Mom, Nia is one of the most popular girls in the school. Everybody likes her."

"Well, that's good, but still..." Mom thought for a moment. "It's too bad you don't get to date more."

"I'm picky," I said, which was maybe true, but it wasn't the reason why I didn't date much. It wasn't that I was still committed to Grace, although she remained in my mind. I knew I would never see her again, and I didn't object to finding some other girl, but I didn't try to. At least, I didn't try very hard. I believed

I was too creepy and obnoxious to attract anyone—that the only way I would ever get a girl's attention would be if she observed me being creepy and obnoxious.

Mom had another little think. "You know, I always thought it was too bad about Grace. Too bad that she didn't give you a chance, I mean."

I had to laugh—not scornfully, but because Mom was over-rating me for once.

"Oh, Jeez, Mom. Talk about living things down! I'm still trying to live that one down. As if Grace could ever have been interested in me, that way. That just wasn't going to happen. If only because of the age difference."

"Well... maybe not, I suppose."

At that moment it struck me that Mom was trying to be kind to me, and maybe didn't totally loathe me. Clueless she was, yes; unrealistic; utterly out of touch with the way teenagers think and interact—but at least she didn't think it inconceivable that Grace might actually have come to be attracted to me. In her dumb way, Mom was praising me.

It did occur to me that I could have done a lot worse than to date Nia. It wouldn't have done me any harm socially. Quite the opposite: it would have given me a leg up. There wasn't a kid in the school who didn't like Nia.

But Nia wasn't Grace. She wasn't even Adina. She was a nice girl, but she wasn't a nine or a ten. I could certainly see myself being friends with Nia—I already was friends with Nia—but being her official boyfriend? Holding hands with her in the school hallways? Kissing her on the dance floor? Maybe parking with her on Saturday night? No. I would have known I was settling for her, and it would have rankled. Still, Nia and I continued to practice together, and generally hang out now and then.

247

# 18 A GREAT MANY TEARS

For that first speech contest of the year, I was allowed to borrow Mom's Fairlane and drive myself and Mark to the State University campus. Then, feeling big-brotherly for a change, I led Mark over to the Liberal Arts Building, up to the room where the contestants were to register and find their room assignments for the first three rounds.

One of the first people I spied, in the mill of students gathered in the hallway, was Mary Hurd—wearing one of her floor-length dresses as usual. This one was low-cut enough to show a little cleavage. Once again I swooped Mary up in my arms and gave her an even bigger hug than usual, while she shrieked and giggled. Yes, I admit it: I was showing off in front of my little brother. I then introduced Mark to Mary.

I told Mary, "Mark's gonna continue the Palinkas dynasty in the history of Iowa high school forensics." Mary laughed again, and asked Mark what his event was.

"I'm doing Humorous, too," she said. She turned to me. "I found this great piece by Dorothy Parker; I'm sure you'll get to hear it at some point this year. Mark will probably hear it today."

Sure enough, according to the schedule, Mark and Mary would be in the same room for the first round, which would mean she would get to hear him perform, and probably would report to me that he was a real star, which would put me off my own game if I heard about it.

I could imagine it. With horror. Mark would come in first or second in Humorous, or at least make it to the finals, while I might have an off-day—aggravated, no doubt, by comparisons of his performance to mine—and we would both be on a roll for the rest of the year, in different directions. He would be bringing home trophies at the rate of two a month, while I would never again come anywhere near to an award of any kind.

I found the room in which my first round was to be held, and I walked in feeling totally unready to perform. I was well rehearsed, but I could tell that my concentration was off, that my thoughts were on Mark's performance (which had not taken place yet) rather than on my own. It took a conscious effort for me to get my mind back on my own game.

My maiden performance in Poetry Interp wasn't as good as it could have been—I was a little nervous, a little flat—but those tears came to my rescue at the end of "anyone". When the round ended and I had heard the performances of the six other kids in the room, I was pretty sure that I had done enough to win the highest score in that group, anyway, even if I hadn't been at my best. If I stepped up my game a little in the next two rounds, I would go on to the semi-finals in the late afternoon, and maybe even to the finals in the evening.

I came out of that room and started walking in the direction of my next round, which would be in the same building but down the hall and down a flight of stairs. In the stairwell I ran into Mary Hurd coming the other direction, apparently *en route* to her next round, laboriously pulling herself up the stairs one at a time with her crippled legs and her wrist-crutches. Her eyes were shining and her face was bright red—but not from exertion, I could tell. As soon as she saw me, she started fizzing and snorting like she was trying to hold back laughter. She wasn't succeeding.

"Oh, my God," she cried—finally. Then she started laughing out loud and collapsed against me for a moment. "I have never... ever... been in a round like that. And I want to say I hope I never am again, but it was so funny, I wouldn't mind if I was. Oh, my God. Oh, your poor brother!"

**249**

I stood still, waiting for Mary to catch her breath. At last she went on, a little calmer.

"The worst of it was, I think it was a little bit my fault, what happened. I mean, obviously I distracted him. See, I was the first one to perform, and your brother was *looking* and *looking* at me... not looking like he was interested in the performance, you know, but *looking* at me..." (She demonstrated an open-mouthed moon-calf gaze of infatuation.)

"And I felt like I'd done pretty well, but then it's your brother's turn next, and..." here Mary turned even redder, and buried her face in her hands. "Oh, my God," she moaned. "Oh, my God."

"Well, what? Was his fly open?"

"Would that it had been only that! First of all, he just froze, when he was trying to give his introduction. Looked like he was blanking on the words for a couple seconds. Of course that can happen to anybody. Then finally he got started, but he was still... you know, he wasn't sure of himself. And after he'd got about a minute into it, he was still... in obvious distress. It looked... well, I certainly don't have any first-hand experience of this, but I've been *told*..." (Here Mary Hurd blushed even redder and giggled some more) "that a guy's... stuff... can sometimes get shifted around in his underwear so that it's not comfortable..."

"Oh, sure, that happens all the time. You have to adjust yourself, as discreetly as you can. Or live with it, since nobody else is going to know."

"Well, while he was speaking he was also... trying to... *jockey for position*, somehow... and... and he wasn't able to fix the problem let alone do it... discreetly, like you said... And at the same time he was trying to say his piece, like nothing else was happening, only I don't think any of us were paying much attention to his speech. Only to the dance." Mary took a hankie from her purse and wiped her tears.

"Does it get even better? Did he drop dead of mortification?" I was hoping he had.

"Well, some of us started looking at each other—we couldn't help it—and he noticed, and that got him even more rattled, and it was only then that he happened to glance down and notice that his barn door was wide open—not that he didn't have his underwear on, of course, but still. And at that point he *screamed* out *'God damn it!'* right there in the middle of his speech, and then he said to the judge, 'I'm sorry, I can't go on,' and he bolted out of the room."

"Oh, Jeez." I only had a couple of minutes before my next round was to begin, so I told Mary I would catch her later. I ran downstairs and scouted the halls for Mark, but didn't find him. I looked in the men's room, and there he was, washing his face at the sink. Evidently he had been crying.

I said, "Mary told me you had some trouble. You okay?"

"Obviously it won't do me any good to go to my next round." Mark wouldn't look at me; kept looking in the mirror.

"Ah, go on, do the next two rounds. Maybe you won't win, but the experience will be good for you. Just so you'll do better the next time."

"I can't. I'll forget my lines and choke up again."

"If you lose a line, improvise till it comes to you. Or jump ahead to the nearest point you remember. If you're cool about it, nobody will know it happened."

"No, no, forget it." Mark was looking like he might fall apart again. "I'll walk home. Or something. This isn't my day."

At that point I had to get to my next round, so I did, and I did great. I nailed it in my third round too. I made it to the semifinals, then to the finals—and finally, around eight o'clock that night, in the main lecture room of the Liberal Arts building, it was announced that I had won first prize in Poetry Interp: best in the whole state. After I had walked down to the well of the lecture room to accept my trophy, and returned up the aisle with it, there was Dr. Pritchard waiting at the back of the room to clap me on the shoulder. She said, "Well, Andy, you've finally got yourself a little hardware for the Palinkas family trophy case. You earned it. This is going to be your year. I heard about Mark, though. That was too bad."

I never told Mark this, but I drove home that night feeling all, "Ha-ha! *One thing*, you shit, *one thing* I can beat you at!"

I was exultant at winning, but almost as strong as the exultation was the relief. The outcome that I had dreaded, hadn't happened. I had neither had to chauffeur Mark and his trophy home in triumph, nor witness his gleeful announcement to our parents, nor feign delight and pride at my brother's accomplishment, while I stood there empty-handed (or, worse yet, with a Semi-Finalist certificate). No. I drove home with only my trophy for company. My trophy. Not quite as magnificent as if I had been driving Grace to the high school parking lot, for a little "alone time." But, damn, it was mighty close to that.

Mom was in bed with the lights out when I got home, but Dad was up, reading, in the living room. He said, "That's great, Andy," when I showed him my trophy, but he said it very softly so as not to disturb Mom. He gave me a big smile. "You can surprise Mommy with that in the morning. She's gonna be real proud of you."

But Mom was awake. She heard us, and called out, "Andy? Did you win something?" I went into her room, where she had switched the bedside light on and was sitting up in bed, and I handed her my trophy. Mom beamed at me.

"I had a feeling, today," she said. "You're going to go far this year." Mom set the trophy down on the bedside table and reached out her arms, and I bent down and got a hug.

"So, tell us about it," she said. Dad and I sat down on the bed, and I had to explain that there wasn't much to tell—Mom and Dad had seen my performance already—except to relate that I'd swept the field before me, and had said my piece better each time I'd performed it. I didn't say a word about what had happened to Mark.

"It's funny how you get on a roll sometimes, when you're performing," I said. "I can't explain it, but there's nothing like it. Oh, and Nia got to the semis, in Humorous, and my friend from Davenport, that girl with the crutches, she came in first in Humorous, so it was a pretty good day, all in all."

"You seem to like that Davenport girl," Mom said. "Too bad she lives so far away."

"O cursèd fortune," I replied, which got a laugh out of Mom and Dad. But what I immediately told myself was that it was just as well that Mary Hurd didn't live in State City—or I'd have made a play for her and made a fool of myself again.

I walked the trophy into Mark's and my room. Mark looked like he had recovered. He was sitting in bed as usual, working on another chess problem. I set the trophy on my dresser; Mark barely looked up.

"What place?" he asked.

"First."

"Hm. Congratulations."

"Thanks."

I didn't say anything more; I didn't want to make Mark think about his own performance.

Mark never competed in a speech contest again. I had four more statewide and regional tournaments, that semester, and five more in the spring of 1966. Added all up, in those ten tournaments, I took two First-Place trophies, a Second, and a Third, in Poetry Interp; a First and two Thirds, in Dramatic Interp—and gold certificates in both events, at the Iowa High School Speech Association tournament. (I tried Extemporaneous Speaking, once, without winning anything.) Not a bad haul for one year.

§

On the Sunday before Election Day, that November, Mom was still feeling too ill (she said) to attend the candidates' forum—which was to be held that evening in the State City High School auditorium. (It didn't need the gymnasium. The attendance was less than for my own *débâcle* the previous spring.) Dad and Mark and I went. We listened to Rae Childress and her slate, and Jake Rosen and his slate, presenting their positions on urban renewal. Mr. Rosen looked something like his son, but greyer and shorter. He had a little moustache, like my dad. He took a moderate view: He said he favored beautification efforts but wasn't prepared to go along with a full-fledged version of the federally funded urban renewal plan such as the "Three Cs" were proposing.

"My main objection to that plan is that it will impede the growth of downtown State City," Mr. Rosen said, "In an ideal world, that might be a good thing. Some people want to keep this city small. If we could do that and still maintain the prosperity of the downtown, I might not object. But I'm skeptical."

The other two members of the "Slob Group"—Mr. Garthwaite and Mr. Erickson—were more strident in their opposition. Mr. Garthwaite had a noticeable "blaccent" (although we didn't know that term at the time), plus the rather overblown, pompous, orotund way of speaking that you often heard from Negro politicians in those days—but he didn't strike me as a "dumb N." He seemed to me to be arguing sensibly against forcing businesses out of downtown—even if temporarily—for the sake of a program that he wasn't sure was going to do the downtown any good in the long run.

"This proposed plan disturbs our peace," Mr. Garthwaite said. "It's pestiferous to the honest businessman and it interferes no little with commercial prosperity—all in the name of some airy-fairy concept that the town radicals call 'progress.'"

Then Mr. Erickson got up and remarked that "Among the 'Three C's'—and I'll leave it to your imaginations to decide what the C stands for—" (This elicited a loud "Ooo!" from the audience) "we have one candidates whose business is located on the outskirts of the city limits, nowhere near downtown; another whose church is likewise located away from downtown; and a faculty wife from New York City who has only lived here for two or three years. All three of them—make no mistake—represent the vanguard of creeping socialism."

In her rebuttal, Rae Childress—quite politely, I thought—said, "I have to correct Mr. Erickson. I've now lived in State City for more than four years..." A few of the audience broke into ironic applause. She smiled. "Which is a little longer than our friend Mr. Garthwaite has lived here."

As Dad and Mark and I were walking out, Dad said, "Rae handled that as well as she could have, but I have a feeling it's going to count against her."

When we came home and reported the event, Mom apparently felt some remorse, because the next morning she called Rae on the phone to report that she was feeling somewhat better and might be able to help a little on Election Day at least.

Consequently, on Tuesday afternoon, Mom was ensconced at the little desk in our kitchen, making calls from the lists that the poll-watchers had sent over to her, of likely Childress supporters who hadn't voted yet. Across the street at her home/headquarters, Rae was presumably doing the same, and no doubt she had many other such callers all over town.

Nowadays it would all be done by computer. In 1965, each poll-watcher at each precinct polling place would have in front of her a typed list of names of people considered likely to vote for her candidate, and as each of them came to the polls, the watcher would cross another name off the list—and then in late afternoon, the watcher would drive the list over to the home of whoever was making the phone calls, or put it in a taxi. So Mom sat at that kitchen desk from about five till about 8:30 that night, making call after call. We all just made sandwiches for dinner, as we could. The polls closed at nine, and as I looked out the front window I could see Mrs. Childress backing her car out of her driveway. Charity was in the passenger seat. Presumably they were on the way to what they hoped would be a victory party with the other two Cs at their downtown headquarters. I could see a light still on in the upstairs studio where I supposed Dr. Childress would be working away—even on this evening.

Mom and Dad briefly discussed driving over to the party themselves, but Mom said, "I'd feel guilty showing up there. I didn't do enough." So we switched on the radio and listened to the results coming in on KSCR.

The news from the first few precincts indicated that the final vote would be close. It was touch-and-go for the next two hours. At about 11:00, KSCR announced complete unofficial results. The difference between first and sixth place could have been covered with a dime. Jake Rosen (4,174) was first past the post, barely ahead of Tim Chelius (4,137) and Bob Cadwallader (4,072), and those three were the apparent winners. "Topsy" Garthwaite (4,046) and "Doc" Erickson (4,045) almost tied for fourth—and Ra'el Childress (3,946) brought up the rear.

"That's about as clear as mud," Dad said, as he switched off the radio. "Two out of three ain't bad. And the two least objectionable of the three Cs got in."

Mom said, "Poor Rae. I feel so guilty now."

"Don't see why you should," Dad said. "You didn't really want her to win."

"But I did vote for her. If I was for her, I should have worked harder for her."

"You know what probably happened," Dad said. "She probably alienated quite a few people with her personality—plus the fact that she hasn't lived here that long. I'm guessing that some of the people who were for the three Cs decided, well, Rosen's a decent enough guy and he's the most reasonable of the Slob Group, so they voted for Chelius and Cadwallader, then substituted Rosen's name for Rae's."

Mom thought for a moment. "So it couldn't have been because she's Jewish."

Charity looked awfully pale and haggard in school the next day. Her eyes were puffy, as though she had been up all the night, possibly crying for part of it. She avoided looking at me. I came home from school that afternoon to find Mom and Rae sitting at the kitchen table drinking coffee over a plate of cookies that Rae had brought over. Rae gave me a great big hearty smile— and for that instant I could see how Grace had had the very slightest resemblance to her mother after all. They both had such a huge smile, when they wanted to use it.

Rae told me, "Dig in. I've been baking cookies all day, to give them out to some of my supporters. And to keep my mind off what happened. Obviously State City isn't ready for a woman on the City Council."

I wanted to give Rae back her usual "stuff and nonsense," because I had read that State City was the first city in Iowa to elect a woman Mayor, back in the 1920s.

"We hardly deserve cookies," Mom said. "I didn't do much."

"You were sick," Rae said. "You did what you could, dear, we all know that." Then Rae glanced over at me, for an instant. "It probably wouldn't have made enough of a difference anyway. Still, a couple of extra hands, you never know..."

It was about a week after the election—or not even: the Monday of the next week, in the evening—when Mark and I were lounging on our respective beds, doing homework (or pretending to, in my case), and I was feeling put out that so far no girl had invited me to the Sadie Hawkins Dance that was coming up on November 13. There was still the rest of the week to go, but I had a feeling that most people already had their dates lined up. I suppose I shouldn't have expected any girl to ask me—none ever had before—but maybe I felt that now that I was older, more established at State City High, it wouldn't be completely far-fetched for some girl to be interested in me.

It was then that Mark asked me, "Are you going to the Sadie Hawkins dance with anyone?" So I knew right away that someone had asked him, because he wouldn't have brought it up except that he wanted to tell me the good news.

"Nobody's asked me yet," I said. "I suppose you're going."

"Yee-up." Mark looked at his book and began jotting notes.

"Who?"

"Charity."

# 19 A CERTAIN WORD: DEMOCRACY

It goes to show you how completely Mark and I stayed out of each other's business, when we were growing up, that I had had no idea he was friends with Charity at all. I hadn't had any clue that they had ever spent any time together, other than incidental contact. Sure, when Mark told me that Charity had asked him to the dance, I was off-hand curious as to how it had happened—how they had come to be that friendly with each other—but not curious enough to ask either of them for the backstory.

The next morning at school, I sought out Nia at her locker, between classes, and greeted her (trying my best to look non-threatening), then I said, "Say, Nia, I'm not going to go to the Sadie Hawkins dance with you unless you ask me pretty soon. Time's a-wastin'."

Nia looked dismayed—and I don't know if she meant it or if it was an act. "Oh, Andy, I'm sorry," she said. "I've already asked Wendell. Gosh, if I knew you wanted to go..."

"Oh. Okay."

"Oh, Pookins, I would've asked you," said Nia. "I wanted to. But I didn't know if you would think it was right if..."

I tried to shrug. "Whatever," I said. I was trying to act like I didn't mind. But I must have looked like I was mad at her because Nia backed away from me a step or two.

I said, "Okay, later, I guess," and I walked off to class.

From then on, for the rest of the year, Nia didn't actually cut me or snub me, but she didn't seek my company. I didn't approach her in any way, either, because I didn't want to impose.

Nia and Wendell hung out together for the rest of senior year, although I could sense that there was nothing in it. I'm pretty sure they dated because they were the two Negroes in the senior class—a basketball player and a cheerleader to boot—so it would have been expected of them. I'm not even sure they liked each other all that much. So far as I know, their relationship didn't last beyond graduation.

I stayed home on the night of the Sadie Hawkins dance. I deliberately went to bed early, hoping to fall asleep before Mark got home. It was one of those nights when you try to fall asleep but you can't because you have an itch here, a twitch there. It felt like hours of lying in my bed, rolling and thrashing this way and that, but I must have finally dropped off, and Mark must have stayed out way late, because whenever he did get in, I didn't notice. Mom and Dad certainly wouldn't have allowed me to stay out so late, at his age.

On the following Monday, Prick finally had that Bel Air of his road-worthy. He'd driven it to school that morning. That afternoon, after school, he took me for a spin in it. We took it out on Highway 1: drove out to Kalona and back, about an hour in all. It was a perfect afternoon for a drive. Cold, but not so cold that we couldn't have the top down. The road to Kalona is hilly, with broad vistas of trees and pastures that reminded me of Grandma Moses paintings.

It occurred to me that if I had spent the previous two summers working on something that paid, I might have had a car of my own, and who knew? Maybe I could have found a girl to take for a drive like this one. But that seemed, for the moment, like something that I wasn't likely ever to experience.

I'd never seen Prick so happy. He wasn't an articulate guy, so he didn't say much of anything, but I could tell by the expression on his face, as he drove, and the vibe he was putting out (for want of a better description) that he'd realized a dream: getting this car and getting it into shape, all on his own. He'd accomplished something. I'm a selfish bastard, so I'm not often happy for someone else's sake, but I was happy for Prick, then.

"You've got her running real well, so far as I know anything about how cars run," I told Prick. He was doing close to 90 miles per hour, really hitting it since there was hardly any traffic on the highway in the late afternoon. "You're good at this, aren't you? Gotta hand it to you. Maybe this is what you ought to do with yourself. Mechanic."

"Yeah," Prick said. "I guess it's one thing I'm halfway good at. I'm not smart like you, but I'm smart about stuff like this. It's what I like, you know? School?" Prick made a short raspberry. "Never saw the point of it, for me. Maybe for guys like you."

"School's not for me, either," I said. "I'd love to not go to school. I mean, I realize I have to do it, because whatever I end up doing with myself, I'll probably have to go to college, but I'd rather not. I've always hated school."

Prick glanced at me for an instant. "You're kidding."

"What?" I laughed a little. "You think I *like* school?"

"Well, I figured you did *now*, anyway," said Prick. "Maybe you weren't always good at it, but you *got* good at it. I mean, you're one of the best guys I know, about plain old *dealing* with school. Now. And you're one of the cool kids, now. It's great that you did that."

That amazed me. Sure, that was only Prick talking, and what did he know? But I had to say to myself, maybe I should listen to what Prick was telling me, after all. Even at that age, I understood that other people sometimes have a clearer perception of you than you have of yourself. Even if, like Prick, they're not bright. They can see what you can't. I was one of the cool kids, now. I didn't believe it, exactly, but I liked hearing it.

§

Prick dropped me off at my house, a few minutes later. I walked in the front door to find Mark and Charity lying entwined on the living room couch, sucking face. They must have heard me coming in the front door, so they must have made a point of affecting not to have heard, of not acknowledging my presence. Not that I wanted them to acknowledge me, particularly, but evidently they wanted to make it plain that they were oblivious to all but their new-found love.

I could hear Mom moving about in the kitchen. I figured she had to be aware of what was up. I was right, because I passed through the living room as quickly as I could to get clear of that scene, and when I entered the kitchen Mom smiled archly at me, as much as to say, "Isn't it cute how they're showing off for us?"

For months thereafter, it seemed that Mark and Charity had no greater pleasure or desire in life than to pound it into everyone else's heads that they were a couple. More days than not, they would be on our living room sofa doing the grossest, sloppiest kissing I had ever seen, much worse than anything I could have imagined if I'd cared to imagine it.

I had thought about kissing a lot, two years before, when I had been obsessing about Grace. I had practiced it, too—on my pillow, at night, as I drifted off to sleep, or when I was lying half-awake in the morning. I kissed Grace all the damn time, in my fantasies; I had come to suppose, at last, that I knew something about kissing. Maybe I *did* know as much about kissing as it's possible to know when you have never kissed anyone in your life.

I knew, in theory, about "French kissing," but these two... oh, Lord, it was like seeing two dogs tongue-wrestling. Only, dogs would have been more discreet. I would do my best not to be in the same room with it, but sometimes it was hard to avoid—and Mom had no choice but to let it happen in public, because she could not very well have advised them to go off and do it someplace by themselves.

I had never been the least bit attracted to Charity. I wouldn't have wanted her for a girlfriend. The idea of kissing her actually squicked me. That's not the point. The point is that Mark got her. He got a senior girl when he was a sophomore. The quest that had ended in humiliating failure for me, was so easy for him.

Charity still wasn't at all pretty. But from then on, for the rest of that school year, you couldn't call her all that plain anymore either—if only because she was better groomed, dressed more neatly, wore makeup. She had started taking the trouble to make herself as attractive as she could make herself—for Mark.

At least I now had the bedroom to myself, most evenings. I wasn't treated to the sight of Mark working on advanced calculus, or some incredibly complicated chess problem. No, indeed. He and Charity would be studying together, either in our living room or at her house, or he would be playing his accordion to the accompaniment of her clarinet. They would improvise tunes in our basement—which consequently was no longer my private hideaway—or across the street. It was klezmer-style tunes, mainly, and jazz. It wasn't bad.

By entering that relationship with Mark, Charity stepped out of my circle of friends, as small as it was. No enmity: we just stopped having anything much to do with each other. I spoke not a word to Mark or Charity about their romance, for the whole of that school year. I did my best to ignore it.

Student Senate was no big deal for the first couple months of that semester. We met once a week, at a different hour every time so as not to unduly interfere with our classes, in whatever classroom happened to be vacant at that hour. We didn't do much besides vote to fund a pep bus to this or that out-of-town football game—and organize the infamous Sadie Hawkins dance. (The senior class had been responsible for Homecoming, but I had kept my distance from it.)

Either Mr. Pope or the Dean of Students, Mr. Rolf, sat in on every meeting of the Student Senate. Usually they just kept watch and said nothing. I don't think Mr. Rolf ever spoke at any of our meetings. Mr. Pope would occasionally pass along some information he felt we needed to know, or he might informally ask for opinions on this or that piece of school policy. Mr. Pope wasn't a bad guy, as principals go. He did always treat kids with respect. I didn't blame him—let alone hate him—for what happened that year.

I should have made a habit of attending Board of Education meetings, now that I was a member of the student government. None of the rest of us did, so it never seriously occurred to me that I ought to do it. Membership in the Student Senate was an honor rather than an office. So it came as a surprise to me, in the meeting right after Thanksgiving break, when Mr. Pope asked to speak at the start of the meeting.

It was in the afternoon, sixth hour: that is, the next-to-last hour of the day. We were in the "business room," on that day:

the room that was used for classes in typing, shorthand, and other secretarial skills. Thus each of us Student Senators was sitting at a desk with a manual typewriter in front of us. Rosen sat at the teacher's desk, presiding. Mr. Pope usually sat at the back of whichever room we were using, but this time he started the meeting standing, next to Rosen's desk.

"You should know," Mr. Pope told us, "that the Board of Education has been discussing ways to increase and encourage a spirit of volunteerism among State City students, especially on the high school level. At their meeting last week, Mitch, here, suggested an idea that I thought was ingenious, and innovative.

"Mitch and I stayed behind and talked with some of the Board members after that meeting, and we all agreed that rather than the Board laying down the law, so to speak, we ought to give you—the Student Senate—the opportunity to put something into place, yourselves. Some minimal requirement of volunteer community service that would be part of the required course work every year from now on. This would be a recommendation that you would pass along to the Board of Education so that they can make it official."

I looked around and could not discern in my fellow Senators any unusual facial expressions or body language. I heard no gasps, no cries of indignation or outrage. Evidently, I was the only Senator who wasn't liking what he was hearing.

"I asked Mitch to draft a proposal," Mr. Pope went on. "I should advise you that this is something you had probably better go ahead and act on, because if you don't, the Board of Ed almost certainly will. So, I'll leave you to it."

As Mr. Pope had been speaking, Rosen had brought out a stack of mimeographed papers, and we Senators passed them along, each taking one. The draft proposal read as follows:

VOLUNTARY SERVICE AS REQUIREMENT
FOR PROMOTION AND GRADUATION

Each year, a certain number of hours of
community service hours shall be required of all students of State City
High, as follows: 20 hours for seniors,
15 hours for juniors, 10 hours for
sophomores. For the spring semester of
the 1965-66 school year only, the requirement shall be 8 hours for seniors,
6 hours for juniors, and 4 hours for
sophomores.

From June 1, 1966 forward, beginning
each summer in June, students may earn
their community service hours for the
upcoming or ongoing school year, during
summer break. All summer hours must be
properly documented by September 15 of
that year. Hours completed after school
begins must be documented within one
month of the service activity.

Volunteer supervisors who sign forms
must be from non-profit agencies or
from individuals who directly received
service. These people cannot be relatives, by blood or marriage, of students submitting the forms. If a student does not complete the community
service requirement for the recently
completed school year, the student must
make up the missing hours as soon as
possible. Failure to do so will make a
student ineligible for promotion to the
next grade. Such a failure will be
listed on his transcript.

To encourage reaching out into the
larger community, students may receive
community service credits for volunteering during school hours (e.g., as-
sisting in a lower school classroom or

tutoring a student). These hours may count toward total hours, but they may NOT be used to meet the minimum number of required hours per grade level.

*Guidelines.* Community service is defined as giving of one's time to improve the quality of life for community residents in need, particularly low-income individuals in such fields as health care, child care, literacy training, education (including tutorial services), social services, housing and neighborhood improvement, public safety, crime prevention and control, free domestic services for the aged and handicapped, and community improvement. Community service CANNOT be:

--Lobbying or political campaigning
--Entertainment, such as music, theatre, or dance
--Efforts directed to serve only a family member
--Direct fundraising activities
--Any activity that results in financial profit

Questions about meeting service requirements or whether service fits the guidelines should be directed to the Guidance Office. When in doubt, students should first check with a counselor before performing the service. Compliance forms will be submitted directly to the Guidance Office.

All students are encouraged to earn extra Volunteer Service Awards by completing over 50 hours in a calendar year: 50-75 for a bronze award, 76-150 for a silver award, and over 150 hours for a gold award. For this year only, bronze awards will be given for 25

hours of service, silver for 40 hours,
and gold for 60 hours.

Evidently, Mr. Pope had gone over this with Rosen well in advance of the meeting; possibly they had cooked this up between them from the beginning. I could feel myself preparing to leap out of my chair and start screaming. I forced myself not to. Instead, I put up my hand.

"Point of information," I said. "Mr. Pope, do you mean that the Board is going to make us do some kind of work, outside of school, in order to be promoted or graduate—just like we have requirements for math and science and English?"

"The Board hopes that the Student Senate will adopt some minimum of volunteer service," said Mr. Pope. "Rather than the Board mandating it. I think you should look at this as an opportunity, rather than a requirement."

"An opportunity is something you can choose to take, or not," I said. "It sounds like this is something we're going to be compelled to do, and to call it 'volunteer service' is about the most disgusting form of hypocrisy I can think of." I could feel my face getting hot. "As for inviting the Student Senate to set the requirements, that's like the Board is saying, 'Do this, or we'll do it for you.'"

Mr. Pope shrugged. "I'm sorry you see it that way."

"We better just do it, man," said Wendell Bell. "This is tiny. Just a few hours, you'll hardly notice it. It'll only be worse if we don't do it and the Board decides the conditions for us."

"Okay, order, please," said Rosen. "I'll admit that this is a revolutionary idea. As far as I know it's never been tried in any public school district in the United States. Mr. Pope was talking just now about opportunity, and I say to you that this proposal presents us—the people here in this room—with an *amazing* opportunity. Not only a once-in-a-lifetime opportunity, but a truly unique opportunity.

"It's an opportunity to make history not only for State City, but to set an example for all of America. We can be the student government that put this idea into place, and created a standard for other schools in other towns. And I predict that if we do, it'll become the norm, the standard operating procedure, for every public school district in the nation. Not overnight, but maybe thirty or forty years from now. And *we* will be able to say we were the ones who did it.

"As President of the Student Senate, I can't put this proposal forward as a motion, but I'd welcome it if..." Adina Owens put up her hand.

"I so move," Adina said. Somebody seconded; I forget who. I was almost literally blind with rage.

"At this point," said Rosen, "I'd like to turn over the chair temporarily to our Vice President, Adina, so that I can speak to my own motion."

It wasn't his motion at all, since Adina had formally proposed it, but Rosen had authored it (no doubt with some help) and he was eager.

You can imagine. Rosen went on for about three minutes, to the effect of, "It's just past Thanksgiving. Christmas and Hanukkah are coming up, and at a time like this we need to think about all that we have to be thankful for, and what we owe to the community that has provided us with a nice town, a nice school. It's time for us to start thinking about giving back to our community; time for us to learn and appreciate a spirit of voluntarism and to understand that we are part of a greater community and that service to others is the highest service. Our late and beloved President Kennedy said, 'Ask not what your country can do for you; ask what you can do for your country.' I say we should ask that we ask what we can do for the community of State City."

I wanted to kick Rosen right in the fucking balls. Looking back, I wish I had been crazy enough to do it.

As it was, all I did was raise my hand and ask to speak against the motion. I didn't do a good job of that, because I wasn't prepared. The proposal had come like a sucker punch—which I'm pretty sure was what Rosen, and maybe Mr. Pope, had intended. No doubt Adina had been in on it too. It was all I could do to keep my voice at a normal volume, and say anything that was faintly coherent. I was ready to start yelling deliriously like Yosemite Sam. I didn't know any techniques for physically calming myself down. The best I could do was to stand up and choke out my basic points, barely making them articulate.

"For one thing, this is hypocrisy," I said. "Calling this voluntary service, or calling the students volunteers. This is as voluntary as a bank robbery. It's something that's being forced on us, and calling it volunteer work is absolutely shameful." I'm sure my face was about purple.

"Second, you're imposing values on us," I said, and I looked first at Rosen, then at Adina, then at Mr. Pope. "Maybe some of us don't think it's important to do this kind of work. Maybe some of us have other stuff we'd rather be doing."

"Some students have things they'd rather be doing other than going to math class," said Mr. Pope. "It's the same thing."

I almost told Mr. Pope to shut the fuck up while I had the floor. Again, I wish I had. Or at any rate, I wish I could have done it, then re-wound and given myself a do-over, so that nobody else would remember that it had happened.

"If Mitch feels that he owes the community something, that's his business," I said, "and if he wants to pay it back, he can. But he can't tell the rest of us that we owe anything. I, personally? I don't owe the community the warm steam off my pee."

Several of the boys laughed, and so did one or two of the girls, although most of the girls gasped. Rosen got this glassy grin on his face, and Mr. Pope looked thunder but I believe he was too astonished to say anything.

"All this is," I said, "is a few do-gooders trying to show that they have the power to impose their values on the rest of us, and boss everybody else around."

I looked around the room, and tried to make eye contact with each Senator. "This is how authority figures operate," I said. "They force the people they're oppressing to implement some new rule or program—and then they can say we're doing it to ourselves, of our own free will, and they call that democracy. That's a ridiculous game and I'm not going to play it.

"If the Board wants to force this on us, they can—but we've got to make it clear that that's what they're doing. We have to let them know that we're wise to what they're up to, and that we'll resist. I beg you all to vote against this motion."

Rosen took back the chair from Adina, and she got up to speak, looking oh so solemn and dignified.

"First of all," she said, "I want to thank Mitch for letting me have the honor of sponsoring this motion. Without any question, this is going to be the most important decision that the Student Senate is going to make in my three years at State City High, and I want to make sure that we do the right thing—not just for us, but for students who are to come after us, and even for our own children and grandchildren.

"We hear so much these days about *rights*. Civil rights, the Bill of Rights, the Right to Work. It seems that everybody is concerned with their rights—and I say it's right that they should be." She smiled at her own miserably lame wordplay. "But what our Founding Fathers forgot, when they put together our Constitution, was that with freedom comes responsibility. In addition to a Bill of Rights in the Constitution, they should have put in a Bill of Responsibilities."

I about screamed aloud. Was I the only person in the room who was aware of the implications of *that* little pearl of wisdom? I was afraid I might be.

Adina went on for a couple more minutes, about our responsibility to the greater community, both individually and as a group of students. I was literally twitching in my chair as she talked, forcing myself not to leap to my feet and shout her down.

"For those of us of religious faith"—here I thought she looked significantly at me—"to serve the community is part of our spiritual responsibility to a higher being, whether that's God, or some other god like Buddha or Mohammed... or Yahweh." I noticed Rosen grinning behind his hand.

Somewhat to my surprise, a couple of other Senators spoke on my side. Leland Cole was a nerdy-looking guy, a junior, and he made the "time is money" argument.

"We're being told that we have to give up our time outside of school," he said. "That's time that we could be using to make money to pay for college, or maybe for stuff that might not be important to strangers but might be important to us as individuals. It seems to me that in a way, this is a kind of robbery."

"Hear, hear!" I cried, and a few of the other kids giggled.

"Why isn't it good for us to be taught that it's important to help others?" one tenth-grade girl asked, and quite a few other Senators clapped. I could have answered her question, I suppose, but at that point Rosen said, "Listen, we need to wrap this up before the period is over, so, if there's no more discussion..."

"Hold on a sec," I said. "I move that the question be postponed and made the special order for next week's meeting." The only thing I could do at this point was buy some time. From the number of speakers and the volume of clapping, it appeared to me that this proposal was going to pass, if voted on immediately. I figured if I had a week to work on a few people, I might change enough minds. Maybe I could get the proposal referred to a committee, and let it die there without being acted on.

"Second the motion to postpone," said Cole. Rosen looked slightly exasperated.

271

"Those of you who are for this proposal would probably be glad of a postponement too," I said. "Whether you're for or against it, we need time to go over it and see whether it can be improved, whether it's proper and legal, and we all need time to really think about this. About whether this is fair and right. Even if you do think it's fair and right, you have to ask yourself whether you're sure it'll work."

Once again, Rosen turned over the chair to Adina, which to my mind was a pretty blatant abuse of the privilege.

"I think it's important that we vote on this question today," Rosen said. "If we wait another week, we might not have time to get going on the implementation process before the semester break—and if that happened, it would be hard for us to enforce voluntary service on this year's class at all. So in effect we'd be legislating only on behalf of future classes, which would make us look like a bunch of hypocrites—at any rate it would take away a lot of the moral authority that this will have if we, you know, if we practice what we preach.

"Like I said before, this is a unique and historic opportunity that we ought to consider a privilege. How many school boards would have given the student government the authority to implement a program like this one? We ought to feel grateful for this chance, and we ought to vote on it now, so at this point I'll call the question."

"No, there's a motion to postpone on the floor!" I shouted. "That takes precedence."

"We only have ten minutes left," said Adina.

"That's okay," said Mr. Pope. "You can run over into next period if you have to."

Adina shot me a dirty look. "In that case we should vote on Andy's motion." She almost spat the words at me. "Mitch, you can have the chair back."

"The motion is to postpone consideration of the question until next week's meeting," Rosen said, in only a slightly less unpleasant tone than Adina's. "All those in favor, 'Aye.'" (Came the chorus, louder than I had anticipated.) "Those opposed?" (The noes sounded louder; they always do sound louder on account of the "o" sound.)

"The noes appear to have it," said Rosen.

"Division!" I cried. Rosen had no choice but to ask Cathy Haynes to call the roll.

Of the thirty Senators, one was absent; we voted 16–13 in favor of postponement. The two "Cabinet members," Cathy and Adina, voted against, so it was 16–15. I was praying (atheistically) that Rosen didn't know enough about parliamentary procedure to know his own powers. In vain.

"The chair can vote to make or break a tie," Rosen said, looking right at me and then over at Mr. Pope. "I vote no; therefore the vote is tied 16–16, so the motion to postpone fails. Hearing no more debate on the main motion, the chair declares debate closed—with just one reminder. Like Wendell said a few minutes ago, this motion is probably a lot more lenient than anything the Board of Ed would come up with themselves, so keep that in mind as you vote. Cathy, you want to call the roll again?"

If I had known more about correct parliamentary procedure, then, I probably could have delayed it. I could have insisted on a motion to end debate, which would have needed a two-thirds vote. I could have found a way to talk it to death, or amend it to death, or something. But, again, I wasn't prepared.

The motion passed, 18–13. I told myself it could have been worse. If I could change three minds, I could get one of those three to introduce a motion to rescind, or to reconsider, at the next meeting. Well, no: four minds. Rosen could tie a 16-15 vote. But I was pretty sure I wouldn't be able to do anything about it in the long run.

I felt as though I had been physically beaten up. That is, I felt tired, actually weakened, and slow and slightly nauseated: much the same effect as if you'd taken a really hard blow in the solar plexus. It wasn't like the pain of physical emptiness that I had felt, sometimes, on account of Grace. It was a feeling of having been personally violated.

I took my time walking home that afternoon. I could hardly speak to Mark or my parents at first—but I couldn't keep this to myself for long. At the dinner table that night I told Mom, Dad, and Mark the whole story, as completely as I could recall it.

This started out as pretty frustrating exercise, because when I revealed what the Board of Ed had proposed, Mom said, "Why, I think that's a fine idea!" and I almost broke off my narrative in order to jump down her throat and tell her she was an idiot. I barely stopped myself; then I went on to describe the prepared motion that Rosen had given to Adina to introduce, and Dad said, "I don't like the sound of that." When I described how it was pushed through, even Mom said, "I have to admit, that doesn't sound quite right."

Then she added, "But still, Andy, I don't understand how you could oppose something like that. Maybe the way they forced it on you wasn't the best way to do it, but..."

"But how else are they going to get kids to vote on something like that?" Dad asked.

"Exactly," I said. "It was sheer hypocrisy to make us vote on that. It was insulting. If they wanted to force us into some kind of slave labor, let them do it themselves instead of pretending that we were doing it ourselves of our own free will!"

"But the thought behind it was good," Mom said. "People don't think of other people enough."

"I think they think too much of other people," I said. "Always minding other people's business, always trying to make people do stuff they don't want to do."

"Well, but why wouldn't you want to help other people?"

"That's not quite it. What I don't want is, I don't want to go around looking for people to do stuff for, for the sake of doing stuff for other people. Or for the sake of sacrifice. For one thing—oh, I should've brought a copy of the resolution home to show to you guys, but what it said was, it said specifically that this 'community service' couldn't be for your own family. It didn't exactly say that it had to be for people you don't know, but that's what they were getting at."

"If there weren't a provision like that," Dad said, "then a lot of kids would be mowing their own lawn or babysitting their own little sister and calling that community service."

"And isn't your little sister part of your community?" I asked. "If it comes to that, who the hell is the school, to tell me that I have to do household chores in my own house, let alone somebody else's? And why should I mow a stranger's lawn rather than my own? If I want to do it, fine. Or if it makes sense for me to do it, fine. But if I don't want to do it, I shouldn't have to—just to prove that I'm altruistic when I'm not."

"You mow somebody's lawn because he's too old and sick to do it himself," said Dad.

"Yes, of course," I replied, "but the Board of Ed has no right to tell me I have to do it. And neither does the Student Senate, and they should be ashamed of themselves. I was disgusted to be in that room today next to those people."

"I agree it doesn't sound like it was handled very well," said Mom, "but if it's something you would do if Daddy or I asked you, why not just do it because it's the right thing?

"But it's not the right thing," I said. "The Board of Ed basically handed down an order, because they can, and eighteen members of the Student Senate voted for it so that they could feel good about themselves—or to show that they're obedient little sheep."

"But wouldn't it make you feel good to help other people?" Mom asked.

"No! Not if I was being forced to, by a bunch of jerks! Why would I feel good about being enslaved?"

"That's a pretty strong word," said Dad.

"This 'community service' crap," I said, "is nothing more than a high-minded-sounding way of cutting down our free time. And you know it is."

"Maybe that's a good thing," Dad said. "Keep kids busy and tired, and they won't get into trouble."

"Listen to you!" By this time, I was yelling. "You're talking like teenagers are all a bunch of criminals that need to be chained up, breaking rocks. Is that what you really think? Is that what you think of me, or Mark, or any of the kids we hang out with?"

"But that's not what this new rule is saying," said Mom. "It's giving you the opportunity to do good! Not break rocks."

"It's not an opportunity if you *have* to do it," I practically shrieked. "That's like stealing your purse and calling it an opportunity to help poor people."

"But what difference does it make, if you don't object to helping people in the first place?"

"Because I don't owe it to anybody," I said. "If I say I don't want to, that should be explanation enough."

"But you *should* want to," said Mom, with considerably more energy, getting to her feet. "If you don't want to help people who aren't as lucky and as well-off as you are... then you don't deserve the life you have!" Mom picked up her plate and almost tipped over her chair in her hurry to get to the kitchen. A few seconds later, I could hear her in there, sobbing.

That pretty much killed the conversation at the table for the next several minutes. Finally, I said to Dad (Mom was still in the kitchen; I could hear her loading the dishwasher, slamming the plates and silverware in), "Look, I am not going to go along with this. Period. I don't know yet what I'm going to do, but I'm going to fight back somehow. I'm not going to be buffaloed."

"But after all, what do you do with your spare time as it is now?" Dad demanded. "Sit in the basement and pitch dice? I don't see you doing much besides that."

"Speech, drama, Student Senate..."

"But that's all stuff you want to do..."

"So that's bad? And even if all I ever did was sit in my room and pitch dice, as you so politely call it, that should be my business. Not anybody else's. If I'm missing out on something super-wonderful by not going out and living for others, then that's my loss. I don't see how anybody has the right to say they know what's good for me, better than I do. Not the Board of Ed, and not the Student Fu... the Student Senate. I don't know what I'm going to do, yet, but I'm going to do something. I'm not going to let them get away with this!"

Dad looked down at his plate—then he said, rather loudly and clearly, but still looking at his plate, not at me, "Andy, Mommy and I would be very disappointed if you took this any further. You've made your protests, and that's fine, but now it's time to go along."

I would have kept arguing, but even I—and I'm not that bright—could see that it wouldn't do me a bit of good at that point. At least Dad didn't order me to apologize to Mom, which I had been afraid he would.

"I'm going to have to resign from the Student Senate. Which I don't want to do, but I have to, now."

"Why so?" Dad looked genuinely surprised.

"Because the Student Senate is supposed to work on stuff that's the students' business, like organizing dances and such. We're not supposed to be used as a tool by the Board of Ed. And if I stay in the Senate after this, I'm saying that I approve of what they've done, or at least that I've agreed to be part of it."

"That's taking the easy way out," Dad said. "Do you see real Senators or Congressmen resigning when a bill gets passed that they don't agree with?"

If I had been older, if I had been thinking more clearly, been faster mentally, I might have replied that a Senator or Congressman would have a duty to resign if he felt that the body were behaving immorally or illegally, and that if he stayed a member of the body, he would be partaking of that illegal or immoral behavior. (The fact that no Senator or Congressman ever does resign on those grounds, because he doesn't want to forfeit his personal powers, perks, and privileges, is the best proof that I can find of the corruption of the system.)

It was a full two days before Mom stopped tsk-ing at me whenever I entered her presence. Dad didn't say any more about the incident; he may have thought it was forgotten. Mark hadn't said anything about it in the first place.

For the next several days I tried—desultorily, I admit—to talk a few of my fellow Senators into changing their votes so that I could introduce a motion to rescind. I focused on people like Wendell Bell, who seemed to be supporting the measure only to avoid a worse scenario, but I got nowhere with any of them.

A few days later, the Class of 1966 Graduation Committee voted that regardless of whether the community service scheme was approved and enforced, no senior would be permitted to take part in the graduation exercises without having completed the minimum hours of "volunteer work." I couldn't help thinking that Adina (who chaired that committee) had pushed this through so that if anyone did manage to obstruct her and Rosen's agenda, she would have that much leverage at least.

During Christmas break, on the Monday after Christmas Day, Mark and Charity—in Mrs. Childress's car, with Charity driving—went over to University Hospitals and Clinics to sign up for volunteer work. They both requested to be assigned to the burn unit. To show off how hard-core masochistic they could be about their voluntarism.

Privately, I wondered why they hadn't volunteered to be drowned in diarrhœa. That would have provided happiness to a lot more people.

Thus, a new routine developed. Every Saturday morning, Charity would come over to our house, all bundled up in her winter overthings, to have breakfast with us. She and Mark would then leave, holding hands, and go across the street to borrow one of the Childresses' cars, or if both cars were required by adults, they would tramp through the snow to the corner and stand there, kissing, waiting for the bus. Every time they left our house, Mom would look at me and "tsk." I took to getting up extra early on Saturday morning so that I could be done with breakfast before anyone else and would be out of "tsk" range by the time Charity came over. Which meant that once a week I relieved Mom of the trouble of having to organize the orange juice and coffee, but I neither expected nor got thanks for that.

I didn't ask exactly what it was that Mark and Charity did at the burn unit. I never spoke to either of them about it at all. I assume they both found the work satisfyingly ghastly.

# 20 OKLAHOMA!

Also shortly after Christmas break, each class homeroom held elections for Student Senate for the second semester. I chose not to run for re-election, but several kids told me they'd written my name on their ballot paper anyway. On that same day, Dr. Pritchard asked me to stop by her desk in the English faculty room, after school, to discuss the upcoming musical.

"Of course we're going to have open auditions as always," she told me, when I was sitting next to her desk that afternoon, "but I'd like to have an idea of what part you'd want."

"Obviously, Curly's out of the question," I said. "That's for Jimmy Axton. I'd love to play Will, but he's got those two songs and I don't have the voice or the confidence..."

(In *Finian's Rainbow*, two years before, Senator Rawkins had had to sing only a few lines, in one song that a group of actors performed. I had been barely able to croak out the notes. Commander Harbison hadn't had to sing at all in *South Pacific*.)

"You never thought about Jud Fry?"

No shit, I had thought about Jud Fry. That was *the* part I had been thinking about all year, ever since I had found out that *Oklahoma!* was going to be the musical. But I hadn't wanted to get my hopes up.

"You'd have to do the ballet," Dr. Pritchard added. "You know which one I'm talking about, don't you?"

In *Oklahoma!* there's a "dream ballet" at the end of the first act, illustrating the romantic triangle of Curly, Laurey, and Jud. In most productions, it's performed by trained ballet dancers substituting for the actors. I couldn't help thinking that Grace could have danced it.

"We're going to have to modify that scene, because we don't have any serious ballet dancers this year," Dr. Pritchard said, "and I know we don't have enough boys. We might even have to have a couple of girls playing farmers and cow-men, although I hope it doesn't come to that. But I'm probably going to have to have you—I mean, Jud—and Curly and Laurey all doing the dance scene themselves."

I figured Axton could probably handle the dancing well enough. But if I couldn't sing, I *totally* couldn't dance—not with my nearly useless feet. I had never had a dancing lesson in my life, save for square dancing in gym class.

"I'm pushing you, Andy. I want you to play the Dream Jud too; I want you to dance and sing for a change. You can do it if only you make yourself."

The auditions were a formality. I was cast as Jud Fry. Axton, as I'd predicted, was Curly. Adina Owens was Laurey. Guidry was Will. Charity was Ado Annie. Mark got a chorus part. I would have wished that Mark hadn't auditioned at all, but I couldn't have prevented it, so I figured I would have to keep my back to him and Charity as much as possible during rehearsals. Nia got the part of Aunt Eller—which was an easy call since she could play that part as the black housekeeper "mammy" type instead of as Laurey's actual aunt.

When Guidry heard the news, he remarked, "Obviously Helen believes in type-casting—at least where you're concerned." Several other speech and drama kids, when the cast was announced, remarked to me that they couldn't have imagined anyone else playing Jud.

Despite my self-doubts about my singing and dancing abilities—and they were justified—I loved playing Jud Fry. I had never had so much fun with a part.

The character himself was scary already, but I played him scarier. It's impossible to play Jud Fry as a lovable dummy. He's one of the darkest characters in the American musical corpus— and, yeah, when I thought about it, I had to admit that he was a lot like me, personality-wise.

I wasn't over-the-top ranting-raving scary. I wasn't even particularly physical in my acting. But by then I knew how to use timing, how to use my facial expressions—which are hard to convey on stage, particularly in a big theatre like the State City High auditorium. But apparently I had taught myself to put my face across, in a venue of nearly seven hundred seats.

At one of the early rehearsals, in the course of running the scene where Jud first appears, I shot Aunt Eller a menacing look—I was being in character, I was acting—and Nia, playing her part, absolutely flinched away from me. I don't believe *she* was acting. You can tell when a person isn't acting. I actually spooked her. At the same moment, out in the seats where a lot of the rest of the cast was hanging around, I heard several girls give sharp little gasps—like they were scared of me too.

For the next several days—I don't know, it could have been my imagination—a lot of the girls in the cast would look a little apprehensive if I came near them, especially if I happened to smile at them. Which I did, from then on, as much as I could, because I was trying *not* to frighten them, but by then I feared I was in a no-win situation.

For all but the last week or so of rehearsals, that was the way it was. Axton was clearly afraid of me, too, even though he and I had always been friendly, and even though I made a point of taking it easy on him during the fight scene at the end of the show. He must have thought I might try to stab him for real or something. So I took him aside and worked with him on chore-ographing that scene so that on the one hand it would look real, and on the other, he could worry less about getting hurt.

You know that scene where Curly and Jud are talking in the shed, and Curly starts berating Jud for being so misanthropic? Once, after we had run that scene, Axton said to me, "You know that's not how I really think about you, right? You understand that, right?" I had to tell him yes, of course I understood that; we were acting, for Pete's sake. He looked genuinely relieved when I explained that to him.

I had to interact to some extent with Adina, and the dream scene was particularly painful for both of us because I had to carry her off the stage at the end. Every time that we rehearsed it—every time—she would cry "Eeew!" out loud when I set her down, backstage. Then she would actually brush herself off, as though to get rid of the kooties.

Oh, and that dance scene was a nightmare because, as I had predicted, I could not dance to save my ass. Dr. Pritchard modified the choreography a great deal, so that I wouldn't have to do any serious running or jumping, because even a slight leap was more than I could handle. The best I could do, during that scene, was to plant myself center-stage and look menacing. When I had to move I would lumber forward, like Frankenstein's monster only (I hoped) more awful. It did kind of work—at least, Dr. Pritchard told me it worked—but I was still acutely sensitive to the fact that Axton and Adina actually were dancing, while I couldn't even begin to.

As for the singing, I had only ever seen the movie version of *Oklahoma!*—the one with Shirley Jones and Gordon McRae—and I didn't realize that Jud's solo song, "Lonely Room," had been cut from it. I had thought that the only singing I would have to do was one comical verse of "Pore Jud Is Daid." The revelation that I would have to sing a big loud solo on an otherwise empty stage was a pretty nasty shock.

At the audition, Dr. Pritchard had only asked me to sing that one verse of "Pore Jud," and I was just barely able to remember the tune from having seen the movie, but when I found out there would be a lot more singing for me, I had to go see Dr. Pritchard and explain my predicament—which was, first of all, that I didn't know how to sing properly, and second, that I would have no idea of what "Lonely Room" sounded like, unless somebody were to sing it to me.

"You can't read music?" she asked.

"Not even close. I know Every Good Boy Deserves Fudge, but that's it."

Dr. Pritchard shook her head. "Then you'd better go talk to Mr. Y about it."

"Mr. Y" was Mr. Yabervoski, the choir director. I stopped by the chorus room after school that day, where he was about to start rehearsing the girls' swing choir, and told him what the problem was—feeling like a Class A dork, of course.

"How'd you come to never learn to read music?" he asked. He sounded as though he were asking—with genuine curiosity—how I had come to be a street-dweller. I felt the way I would have felt if I had been a street-dweller, and someone had asked that question.

Long story short, I waited an hour till Mr. Y had done with the swing choir; then he told me, "I guess the important thing for now is just to teach you how that song goes. We'll worry about reading music later." He sang "Lonely Room" through for me once, and had me repeat it to him. I couldn't remember the tune exactly the first time, so he sang it with me. Then he accompanied me on the piano while I tried to sing it myself. After we had worked together for forty-five minutes or so, I more or less had the tune in my head.

That didn't mean that I could *carry* the tune. Also, here's a funny thing: When I was in *Finian's Rainbow*, I had learned how to project my speaking voice, when I was acting, but my singing voice still didn't have any volume. So Mr. Y had to work with me on that, too, because "Lonely Room" is an aggressive song; it has to fill up the auditorium.

I still can't read music. All we had time to do was to get me singing well enough to carry off Jud's songs. I'm not going to claim it sounded pretty. Worst of all, "Lonely Room" is sung to minimal accompaniment; the pacing is tricky; the lyrics have *got* to be understood; I couldn't fake anything. I felt naked as could be, every night of rehearsal when I had to force myself, by singing, to make a bigger fool of myself than I was already.

About the only cast member with whom I had much to do was Guidry, and since he and I had very little interaction in the play—on stage at different times, almost entirely—we seldom had time to talk. I avoided even looking at Mark and Charity, unless I had to in the course of the play. And then there was Adina's "Eeew," every single night.

One evening, during the last week of rehearsals leading up to dress, I was sitting in the audience before we started working. One of the tenth-grade girls—Betsy Tolhurst, her name was, a plain-looking girl but really sweet and nice—came over and sat in the seat next to me. She was one of the girls who had been shrinking away from me for the past several weeks, but this time she sat right down and she said, "You know, I've been wanting to tell you: I love what you're doing with your part. You're so scary! A lot of us were talking about it yesterday. We all think you're the best actor in the show!"

No false modesty here: I knew I was doing a good job at the acting part, even if I was embarrassing myself with the singing and the dancing. But I hadn't imagined that it was being re-marked upon, aside from the fact that I was scaring everyone, or grossing Adina out, or both.

I thanked Betsy Tolhurst, and I must have smiled. She said, "Another thing I should tell you. Some of us were talking, and we all think it's so not fair that you don't have a girlfriend. It's so mean of Adina, the way she acts around you. She's a... a B. We all think you're so nice. I mean it."

"Oh, come on." I would have been the last one to know whether I was blushing, but it felt like I was blushing. "I'm not that nice. Not when you get to know me."

"Yes you are. You always say hi to us, and you're never snooty like some of the other seniors. Anyway we all really like you. Just thought I'd tell you." She got up and walked off.

I could have explained to Betsy that Adina was at least to some extent justified in acting hostile toward me—but I wasn't about to give her that story. If Betsy and the other sophomore girls wanted to go on thinking that Adina was a "B," I wasn't going to stop them.

*Oklahoma!* was a good production, if I say it myself. Sure, it was a high school show, with limited resources, but Dr. Pritchard and Mr. Y got us into shape and it seemed to me that everybody had a good time with it. Of its kind, it was first-rate. One defect in our production that I did consider rather glaring was the fact that Axton was so plainly effeminate. As he had gotten older he had developed the hissy manner and the girlish gestures, and Dr. Pritchard was—I don't know the word for it; too considerate? insufficiently brutal?—to train it out of him. She did try to tell him to stand tall and swagger, but at first he only swished his hips and flapped his hands all the more. Finally, she told him to act like he was expecting to take off and leap through the air in the next few seconds—and that helped slightly. It gave him a more confident and aggressive posture. But she apparently couldn't think of a diplomatic way of advising Axton to restrain his hands and wrists.

Still, Axton sang well. He and Adina had good rapport— partly because they had worked together before, and partly because they could be girls together.

§

If you don't have a few butterflies right before you go on, you're not an actor. Everybody has stage-fright—or if you don't, you're not going to perform well. As I had gotten older and more experienced, I had discovered that the butterflies didn't get any less—if anything they got more intense—but the more I had them, the more I liked having them. They were really kicking in for *Oklahoma!*

I don't know if it was (or is) common at other schools, but at State City High the actors—just the boys—generally went around shaking hands backstage before the curtain rose on first night (actually our first show was a *matinée*: right after school on

Wednesday, so it was first afternoon), and I took note of the various reactions I got. I shook hands with Mark: the first time we had ever done so. Guidry and I shook, and punched each other in the chest. Axton shook with me as though he were surprised that I would offer the gesture.

I was good. Damn good, the first performance and the next three. I was able to use my aura of menace to bluff my way through the dance scene. I got through the songs by more or less shouting them.

A funny thing about that first performance: You can't help catching sight of the audience while you're on stage, and in the opening act, at the very moment I came on, my eye fell on the first row of seats. There, front and center, was Coach Vance, with those bulging eyes of his that seemed to glow in the dark. That gave me extra motivation, knowing he was there.

In school the next day, I passed Coach Vance in the hall.

"Nice show, Palinkas." Vance held his thumb and middle finger a hair's-breadth apart. "You came *that* close to stealing it."

My parents came to the Friday night performance, and so did Joe and Rae Childress. They all came backstage after the show; Mom almost gave me a hug right in front of everybody—she stopped herself, I am pretty sure, because she didn't want to embarrass me, not because she didn't really want to give me a hug. She was all pink in the face.

"That was just wonderful, Andy," she said. Then she gave me a little hug anyway, and I returned it, gingerly. "I'm so proud of you," she added.

"So am I," Dad said. He clapped me on the shoulder.

Rae Childress said, "Very nice." She shook my hand in a formal, restrained way. Joe Childress also shook my hand, and he said in that soft voice of his, "Congratulations, Andrew Palinkas. Well done." I believe that was the first time he had ever spoken to me beyond a quick greeting.

I didn't see either set of parents congratulating Mark and Charity, although they must have done so. I was pleased enough with the reaction I had gotten out of them. Then the seven of us—the Palinkases and the Childresses—went out for pizza together: my parents and me in their car; Mark and Charity in her parents' car.

Which, now that I think about it, is a funny thing. At that age you're embarrassed by your parents; at least most kids are. The very fact of their existence is reason to resent them. Ordinarily, after a big event involving your schoolmates, you want to hang out with *them*, instead of with your folks. But for some reason this gathering was more flattering than otherwise—maybe because it involved more than one set of parents. It was almost an adult event. At any rate, as we drove to Parilli's Pizza Parlor I felt gratified; I had a sense that somehow I had finally *arrived*, finally amounted to something.

We got a long table at Parilli's. I deliberately sat at the other end of it from Mark and Charity, who were side-by-side. I sat opposite Dr. Childress, who looked completely out of place in a pizza joint, with his tweed jacket and ascot. I could not imagine him eating pizza. It was my fantasy that he had never eaten it in his life.

In the event, when the pizza arrived, he ate it the way any normal person would. I more than half expected him to request a knife and fork, but he didn't.

I glanced down the table and was immediately sorry I had done so. Mark and Charity were feeding each other pizza, giggling. Rae, who sat between them and her husband, gave me this arch, confidential smile and whispered, "They're so cute, aren't they?" I gave her a slow shrug, and bit my lips. She laughed. Then Dr. Childress looked at me, very serious.

"I'd be interested to know, Andrew Palinkas," he said, in that almost-British accent of his, "about the thought that went into deciding how you would interpret your character. Did you have a process, of some kind?"

Dr. Childress was talking to me as though he knew me. Maybe I was a subject of conversation at the Childress dinner table; how can I know?

"I guess I didn't have to think all that hard about it," I told him. "My main thought was to forget about making the audience feel one way or the other. So long as they felt *something*. Which meant that I couldn't play him as a melodramatic villain, right? Because if I did that, he'd be ridiculous. So I had to enter his world somehow—you know, pretend I was the same kind of crazy that he was—which wasn't that hard, because the character's not that different from me. So what I did, finally, is I basically played him as myself only more so."

Dr. Childress smiled, and looked wise, and nodded. "Like Zasu Pitts," he said, "a silent movie star from way back. Someone asked her how she did it and she said, 'I just act natural. Tell me anything easier than that!'" Dr. Childress chuckled without making any noise, and I smiled too although I didn't think it was all that funny. True, but not funny.

"Tell me, Andrew, are you thinking of pursuing this as a career? Acting?"

I had had that idea, here and there, but I had never thought hard about it. I had developed, recently, vague notions of becoming a lawyer. I knew that most politicians were lawyers, and being a politician was starting to have some appeal, because it would mean being famous, being noticed, being respected. Plus, it would be a way in which I could—with luck—demolish the Mitch Rosens of the world.

Realistically, though, politics would have been a mighty hard grind: not something I wanted badly enough to go after it.

I finally said, "I might as well be an actor. I'm no good for anything else."

"Any plans for next fall?"

This gives you an idea of how much has changed from one generation to another. As I understand it, today, no reasonably good student, in the February of his senior year of high school, will be in much doubt as to what colleges are his top picks. He might not already have committed, but he will be deep into the applications process and will have developed a short list. I hadn't even done that.

"I'll probably just go to State. Since I don't have much of an idea of what I'd be going to college for, it wouldn't make much sense to spend a lot of money going anywhere else."

"I expect the theatre department here at State will astonish you. It's vastly under-rated. We have some of the best teaching talent in the country here, not only in acting but in the technical aspects of production, sets, lighting, theatre history... I'm some-what involved, since the art department so often helps out with sets and so on."

Dr. Childress kept talking for another minute or so. Up to that time, it hadn't occurred to me how much work would go into a serious study of acting. I might believe, privately, that I was hot stuff, and on a high school level maybe I was, but it was starting to sink into my head that maybe I wasn't Paul Newman yet, that maybe I had a ways to go and some work to do.

"Andrew, I'd be interested to know," and I came back to attention as Dr. Childress addressed me, "do you have your own definition of bliss?"

My mind had been wandering for a few seconds, so I had no idea what he might have said that had led up to that question— if anything—but I heard the question and I took a moment to think about it. The first idea that popped into my head was that no, I didn't have my own definition of bliss, but perhaps I did have a definition of agony. The closest I had ever come to bliss, it then occurred to me, was when I had been engaged in some sort of fantasy, as a baseball manager, a brilliant soldier, an immensely popular President or King. Or when, in my daydreams, I had ended up first as the lover of Grace, and then in due course as her husband.

As that thought popped into my head, suddenly I was scared half to death that Grace's father would mention her name, or maybe he would wonder aloud why it was my younger brother, and not I, who was carrying on with his other daughter.

So I told Dr. Childress, "That just hasn't occurred to me. I don't know about bliss yet. I come pretty close to it on stage, because then I'm acting, you know. I'm not me. I'm being somebody else, and that's a lot more fun than reality."

"Yes, that's it, for some people, I think," said Dr. Childress. "To revise reality, to take an external reality and give it one's own interpretation. That's a personal bliss for many people. For people in the arts, at any rate. You're an actor and I'm a painter, and each of us takes either a real, concrete thing, or simply an idea, then internalizes it, then re-births it, so to speak, with our personal imprint upon it. And to do this well, I should say, makes a man immortal, in a way that simple biological reproduction cannot do."

That was a little much for me to respond to, but I do remember it, and I remember thinking I would have liked to tell him, "Okay, but you made Grace. And Grace had to have been a greater creation than any painting you could have produced," but I would never have dared to say that, aloud, and in any case I was so embarrassed—so embarrassed to have even thunk that hideously saccharine, mawkish thought—that I had to force myself not to physically writhe.

Dr. Childress went on, with what I thought was a wry, almost sardonic little smile: "And the consequences of producing a painting are considerably easier to deal with than the consequences of biological reproduction, I should say."

I have wondered, since then, what Dr. Childress might have been alluding to. What, after all, was the relationship between his daughters and him; between them and Rae; between mother and father as it affected those daughters? There has got to be a book-length story there.

He drew himself up a bit in his seat, and intoned, "He that hath wife and child, hath given hostages to fortune."

"That's not something I've ever thought much about either," I replied. "Having children. It's never been anything that interested me."

"Some would argue that it's a God-given duty. Particularly for a person of talent and ability, such as yourself. But that's merely an opinion, and I'm not even certain that it's my opinion. You're perfectly free to disagree with it."

"Well, Joe, maybe he's a ho-mo-*sex*-yew-al," Rae put in. "You never know."

I'll still can hear how Rae pronounced that word, in that big New York accent of hers, enunciating every syllable: "ho-mo-*sex*-yew-al." In another context, it might have been funny. As it was, she might as well have slapped me. I sat up straight in my chair and stared at her, with no idea of how to react. From the corner of my eye I could see her husband rolling his.

"Rae, for God's sake," he whispered.

"Well, if he is it's nothing to be ashamed of," said Rae. I continued to not know what to say.

"Oh, Rae," said Mom (she sounded even more timid than usual), "I don't think he is, and it's not appropriate to..."

Rae laughed. "Not in front of the children, you mean?" she asked. "Come on, Paivi, if Andy doesn't know what a homosexual is at his age, it's about time he knew."

"I know what a homosexual is," I said, in perhaps a firmer tone than would be considered polite for a teenager talking to a mature woman. "I don't happen to be one."

"Oh, well." Rae's eyes were still twinkling. "It occurred to me, because I'd have thought you'd have a girlfriend, too, you're so handsome and talented..."

What I could *not* stand was to be called handsome when I knew I wasn't. It made me cringe. It was almost worse than being called a homosexual.

"Girls don't find me attractive," I replied, and I looked right at Rae. I must have looked pretty grim, because her eyes shifted away from mine immediately.

"Oh, Andy." Mom sighed. "Anyway, Rae, there's plenty of time for Andy to find somebody. I think it's refreshing when teenagers don't pair up right away. I'm afraid children grow up too fast these days."

"Stuff and nonsense! Children grow up at the pace they ought to grow up, if only their parents will let them. Some parents try to infantilize their children at an age when the kids are trying to become human beings."

Secretly, I agreed with Mrs. Childress on this point, but I was too ticked off at her at the moment to lend her any support.

"For example," Rae went on, "we'd have a lot less trouble with teenagers 'having to get married'" (she made the air-quotes gesture) "if girls would go on the pill, or at least carry birth control with them—and if they didn't have to sneak around to do what we all know they're going to do anyway..."

It upset me to hear Rae talk like this, because I figured that maybe what she was implying really was true: that my peers, and kids even younger than I, were having sex outside of marriage and I wasn't, nor would I ever have it, because I wasn't attractive enough for any girl ever to want to have it with me.

"Oh, Rae, I don't think that's true," Mom said—again, tentatively, as though she were a little bit afraid to disagree with Rae. "I think most teenagers are pretty good about that sort of thing. I know sometimes it can happen, because some girls have such romantic ideas, and they think they'll be... well, loved and taken care of if they let a boy... well, and especially among people who don't have much education... but honestly, I don't think that ever happened where I went to school."

"Oh, Paivi, you're so cute! My God, to hear you talk, girls only ever do it because boys pressure them into giving up their precious virginity! I promise you that's not always the way it is."

Dr. Childress, at this point, was looking away from his wife as though Rae were deliberately farting—which, as far as my mother was concerned, she pretty nearly was.

Rae turned back to me.

"I thought you'd be the one to end up dating Charity," she said. "How do you feel about *that*?" She nodded toward Charity and Mark, who were still oblivious to everyone but each other.

"It's none of my business," I said.

"You know, Grace always adored you. She thought you were the sweetest boy. She told me so."

"In the abstract, I daresay I was," I replied, and Rae absolutely shrieked with laughter.

"Well, what else but in the abstract?" she demanded. "My gosh, I know you and Grace were friends, but you weren't thinking she might have been thinking of you *that* way, were you?"

"No, no, of course not," I said. "I mean a lot of girls think I'm nice—for somebody else."

§

"I sometimes wonder if Rae is quite right in the head," Mom said in the car later, when we were driving home. I was in the back seat. Mark was riding with the Childresses.

"That was something, wasn't it?" said Dad. He had hardly said a word to anyone the whole evening. "I wonder what old Joe will have to say to her, when they're alone."

"Probably nothing," said Mom. "I'm sure he's used to it. But, Andy, you and he seemed to be having quite the conversation."

"He was telling me about the drama department at State. I don't remember everything he said, but he was pretty enthusiastic about it. I might look into it for next year."

"I thought you wanted to be President," Mom said. I was pretty sure she was being jocular, so I forced myself to laugh.

"I guess if I'm going to be President I'd better learn how to be a better actor."

Mom didn't say any more.

We arrived in our driveway at almost the same time that the Childresses pulled into theirs. As my parents and I went into our house I could see Mark and Charity clinging to each other out there in the snow, kissing and kissing. I turned away.

The cast party, after the final performance on Saturday night, was held at the Axtons' house—only a block and a half away from ours. Mom had given me special dispensation—for once—to stay "as long as you want to. Just don't get in too late and don't make noise." Mark, who was two years younger, got the same permission, and as a result I don't think he ever had a curfew again, as long as he lived under my parents' roof. On this night, he would be with Charity, and I daresay my parents trusted her to see him home okay.

It was right after that party—like, a couple of days after—that the public displays of affection between Mark and Charity were toned down considerably. They still held hands, still walked with their arms around each other, snuggled on our sofa—but the blatant, ostentatious face-sucking stopped entirely, and did not resume again. In retrospect it's funny that even at that time—at my age, knowing as little as I knew about relationships between boys and girls—I knew why. And you know what else? I'll bet Dad didn't notice. Mom probably did—but I'll bet she closed her eyes to it, pretended she couldn't see what I saw.

The Axtons were pretty well off. They had a big house, lots of rooms. While I was at the party I was mostly talking with Axton, or Guidry, or Dr. Pritchard—or, finally, with a few of those tenth-grade girls. I was having a pretty good time, too. After the party had gotten well along, I remarked to myself that I had hardly seen Mark or Charity. I left by myself, around one o'clock, and was in bed and asleep before Mark got home. He was still asleep when I woke up in the morning.

The voracious kissing and all that: It can't be sustained, once sexual intercourse has taken place. Desire, and great affection, might well remain, but the urge to show it off in public disappears as soon as you find a way to do it in private. And it's funny—to me—that I sensed as much, at the time.

I didn't ask Mark what was going on. I never did know, after that, how and when and where they managed to do it. It wouldn't have been hard to find out if I had wanted to know. Mark probably would have told me. But the thought of it was depressing enough. The knowledge of it would have been worse.

My predominant feeling was rage. Not envy. Honest, I did not begrudge Mark having sex with Charity. And my rage wasn't directed at Mark. I figured if he liked a certain girl, and could get her, good luck to him. No, my rage was at *me*, for being such a repulsive dork that no girl would ever want to so much as kiss me, let alone go to bed with me.

# You're Doin' Fine, *Oklahoma!*
*By Mitch Rosen, Features Editor*

Despite many offers to take the show on tour, as well as requests for an extended engagement, the State City High Paint'n'Patches production of *Oklahoma!* folded after the traditional four performances this past weekend. This was an exceptionally ambitious project for a high school production, but the company—as well as the people behind the scenes—pulled it off perfectly.

For those of you who missed it, the plot is pretty simple. In Indian Territory (as Oklahoma was called, about 60 years ago, when the story takes place), a rootin'-tootin' cowhand named Curly (Jimmy Axton) falls for Laurey (Adina Owens), the prettiest girl in the settlement. She is also wooed by the evil Jud Fry (Andy Palinkas). In the comical sub-plot, Ado Annie (Charity Childress) has to make up her mind between another cowboy, Will (Gus Guidry) and the Persian Peddler Ali Hakim (Dave Albert). Overseeing the merriment are Laurey's guardian Aunt Eller (Antonia Garthwaite), the strict Judge Carnes (Rodney Partridge), and a chorus of "farmers and cowmen," farmers' daughters, and ranchers' gals.

The show featured a number of strong performances. Jimmy Axton has been the best singer in the school for as long as he has honored us with his presence, and he lived up to his hype, especially with the opening song, "Oh What a Beautiful Morning," and the rousing title song at the end. I would have liked it if he had played Curly a little rougher and tougher, but Jimmy isn't that kind of a guy and his acting was more than adequate. He also made up for any shortcomings in his acting in the "dream ballet" in the middle of the play.

Adina Owens was nimble and light on her feet. Her voice was faint at times (I sat toward the back on purpose, so I would be able to criticize singers for that!), but she played Laurey as a proud and feisty young lady, and Adina has a great future ahead of her as a stage actress—if she wants it.

Almost as big a future as Andy Palinkas. Everyone at State City High knows how scary "Gabby" can be in his everyday behavior—but that's nothing compared to his performance as Jud Fry. I don't think I've seen anything like it since *Psycho*, and I'll never be able to relax around Andy ever again! He's no dancer, and his singing leaves something to be desired, but that can be taught, and at least I could hear him. If Andy doesn't end up on Broadway or in Hollywood—or maybe both—then I'm a monkey's uncle.

Charity Childress sang her part very nicely—I had never heard her sing before and I was pleasantly surprised—but somehow I didn't think she managed to stop being Charity and start being Annie. That's probably because her own personality is so different from the character she was playing. Gus Guidry as her boyfriend was the opposite because he was basically playing Gus Guidry—and it was pretty good for an imitation!

And what can we say about Nia Garthwaite? Nia used her many facial expressions on stage just as she does every day at school, and she did a perfect "old lady" voice, both acting and singing. Special kudos to Dr. Pritchard for casting her in that part.

As usual, Dr. Pritchard gets congratulations overall for a show well done, as does Mr. Yabervoski for his excellent work with the singers. Great sets, great costumes, great chorus, great supporting roles, and if I say "great" any more I'll turn into Tony the Tiger. Congratulations to all—and I wish you a speedy recovery from all those broken legs!

# 21 CAREER COUNSELING

I still have that copy of the *Cat's Paw*, rescued from my parents' basement. The day it came out—the Tuesday following our last performance—when I walked into Scene Study class, Dr. Pritchard asked me, "Have you ever thought of making theatre your career?" I asked her how I would go about doing that, if I were in the mood to, and the upshot of it was that she spent the first ten minutes or so of that day's session telling all of us about the amount and type of study it would take, to make it as a professional actor.

"When you study drama in college," she said, "there'll be some acting classes like this one, but there'll also be more specialized classes, like movement, and voice, and you'll have to study the history of theatre, and learn some about sets, and designs, and costumes."

One of the girls asked her if the theatre department at State University was any good, and Dr. Pritchard replied that indeed it was. "If you're serious about a career in acting, you might want to go to a conservatory, in a town where there's real theatre going on, like New York or London. But the best of those are hard to get into, and they're not practical for most students.

"For most people who are thinking about acting as a career, it might make more sense to go to a university, major in drama, and get a teaching certificate along with it so that you'll have a career whether or not you make it as an actor."

This all sounded daunting to me—indeed, not that much easier than going to law school. Still, it seemed that a few people, at least, were thinking the same way on the matter—thinking that maybe I, Andy Palinkas, was cut out to be an actor, I mean. That night, over dinner, I once again mentioned to Mom and Dad that a career in acting might be the right choice for me.

I didn't say anything for sure: nothing in the way of, "I've decided I'm going to major in drama in college," let alone, "I'm going to forget about college and go out to New York or Los Angeles and get a job loading trucks till I'm discovered." None of that. Just something like, "I'm thinking I might like to major in drama in college." I don't recall that I got any reaction out of either of them immediately.

Not long after that, we had the auditions for the spring play. Dr. Pritchard usually had us do four shows a year: two regular straight plays, in fall and spring; some sort of experimental play; and a musical. The spring play was the one that she used to pay off her old debts: giving plum parts to the kids who weren't as talented and who had been good sports about taking the less prestigious parts in the other three shows. That spring, Dr. Pritchard had chosen *Rhinoceros*, by Eugène Ionesco. Surprisingly few people—and nowhere near enough boys—auditioned for the show. Spring fever kept a lot of them away, no doubt—notably Charity and Mark.

Those two spent a lot of time—when they were within adult purview—practicing accordion/clarinet duets. A lot of it was the klezmer-type music that they had been doing, and some of it was stuff that Mark composed himself. They were planning to do, in the summer, what the Crosstown Rivals had done the year before: entertaining in hospitals, schools, nursing homes.

Either I totally deserved it, or Dr. Pritchard didn't have much to choose from. I got the lead role in *Rhinoceros*: Bérenger. Guidry was cast opposite me as Jean. This wasn't so different from our respective roles in real life, I guess. Nia Garthwaite was cast as Daisy, and a few of the men's parts were tweaked to make them girls' parts, since we didn't have many boys.

The plot of *Rhinoceros* is pretty simple. It's set in a small town, apparently in the South of France (and you can bet I made sure, during rehearsals, that all French words and names were pronounced correctly), and in the course of the play, every person in the town metamorphoses into a rhinoceros. Except for my character, Bérenger. Most people believe that the play is an allegory about conformity, about how a whole bunch of people can be quickly and easily converted to a popular political cause, such as Communism or Nazism.

I have to take credit for making the production better than it would have been. I looked at the translation we were using and I thought it was pretty poor work. The English was stilted; it didn't sound conversational; it used words that aren't used in ordinary English speech—like "capitulate" instead of "surrender." So I asked Dr. Pritchard: if I could find the original French script, could I do my own translation, and we could use that? I also asked Madame Webster if I could do this as an extra-credit project for her class—not that I needed any extra credit there—and she was so tickled by the idea that she lent me her own French copy of *Rhinoceros*. It took me less than a week to do a much better translation.

The problem was, I wasn't a trained typist, so it would have taken me forever to type out a clean copy. We ended up using the original script, but Dr. Pritchard took my advice for the most part about making changes in a word or phrase here and there, to make the dialogue sound more colloquial.

In my opinion, *Rhinoceros* was my best work at State City High. I had been okay in *Finian's Rainbow*, as Senator Rawkins, and extraordinarily good in *Oklahoma!* as Jud—I'm not going to cry poor for the sake of politeness—but I was even better as Bérenger. We rehearsed it through April, and performed it the first weekend in May. Naturally it didn't get quite the turnout that we had had for *Oklahoma!*—but it was a good show and it got a lot of laughs. The art teacher, Mr. Parsons, devised some terrific rhinoceros costumes. Guidry almost stopped the show when he suffered his metamorphosis. I still remember it.

Guidry and I were such different actors. I have to say: Guidry was as good an actor as I was, especially in the comic roles. God, he was funny. He used his natural nervousness so well—that's the mark of a good actor, if he can take characteristics that might be considered handicaps, and use them to his advantage—and he was one of those actors who can come within a whisker of overacting, yet never be accused of it.

"Gus is so energetic, but you're even more so, even if you don't know it," Dr. Pritchard said to me at about that time. "You underplay. In most cases that would be a fault, but you... even when you're playing someone who's quiet and passive, like Bérenger, the energy just *radiates* off you. You could excite an audience by reading the phone book." This was news to me. I had known that I was no slouch of an actor, but this was the highest praise I had ever gotten for it.

§

Bérenger's final monologue is exceptionally tough to pull off. It's one of the biggest challenges for the actor that you can imagine. At the end of the play, he's the last person in town who hasn't given in to the idea of being a rhinoceros. At first, he wonders to himself how he might go about persuading these folks to turn away from their rhinocerocity (or their rhinocerosness, or whatever we might call it), and go back to being people. Then he has to accept the fact that there's no way he can do that.

In the final scene, Bérenger has a moment where he almost persuades himself that *he* is the misfit, that *he* is somehow defective, for not being able to turn into a rhinoceros like the rest of them. For a minute or so, he wishes he *could* be one of them. He castigates himself for his inability to be a rhinoceros:

"If you try to hang onto your individuality, it never ends well!"

Then he snaps out of it: "Well, tough. I'll take on the lot of them. I'll fight them all, the whole boiling of them!

"I will not surrender!"

Most actors perform Bérenger's last line, "I will not surrender!" as a loud, almost vainglorious declaration, shouted heroically to conclude the play. I did that, during the early rehearsals, but after a few tries I decided to deliver the line quite differently: as a man outraged, frightened, powerless—yet having finally found his personal dignity.

I said the line softly—emphatically, but softly—as a man might, if he were scared to death, sweating, damn near shitting his pants, and maybe trying to talk some courage into himself. Almost whispering, forcing the words out of himself, knowing that he might, after all, be making the wrong choice:

"I... will... *not*... surrender."

Staring out into the audience, utterly alone, knowing that he'll have to fight on alone, as the curtain falls.

Sorry, but I was good. More than fifty years later, I still look back and remind myself of how good I was in that part.

Five days after the close of that show—a Friday afternoon it was, shortly after he had come home from work—Dad said to me, casually, "Want to meet me downtown for lunch tomorrow? We haven't had a chance to hang out together for a while."

Dad would sometimes take me and Mark to lunch—often on a Sunday after we had played golf—but he seldom invited just me. Mark was more likely to get a solo invitation, since Mark had to be downtown every Saturday anyway for his accordion lesson (after he and Charity had spent a couple hours wearing their hair-shirts at the hospital). Be that as it may, Dad and I met up the following day at the Mainliner, which was a bar/restaurant that was got up to look like a mixture of a club car and a dining car of an old-fashioned railway train. It was across the street from the main part of the State University campus, so it was popular with faculty and older students.

As we sat down, Dad said, "I feel like having a beer. Want to join me?" In the past year or so, Dad had started allowing me and Mark the occasional can of beer at home. Mark got the privilege at the same time I did, of course. But I had never had a beer in a restaurant. It could be that Dad meant this to be a rite of passage. That was the way I took it.

It must have been about halfway through our meal when Dad said to me, "You know, Andy, your Mommy and I were talking, about what you said the other night about maybe majoring in drama when you go to college. I don't know how serious you were about it—maybe that was just one of several ideas you were considering—but I think your Mommy and I would be disappointed if you majored in drama at college."

Okay, that came as a complete surprise. I maybe had a sense that Mom and Dad had reservations about my possibly majoring in drama, but for some reason I was astonished to hear Dad explicitly advising me against it.

"Acting's fine as a fun thing, community theatre and so on, but you might live to be sorry one day, if you tried to make a career of it. And frankly, Mommy and I don't want you turning into one of that type of person. I remember what the drama students were like when I was in college: snooty, stuck-up, effeminate, phony..."

"What do you mean?"

"Oh, you know, they walk around campus with this haughty, affected manner..."

Here Dad mimicked a drama student presumably greeting one of his fellows, in a high, twittering, girlish voice. I couldn't help laughing. It *was* funny, the way Dad portrayed it, and indeed I had seen that type.

"I don't want you to turn into one of those. And I think your Mommy would be happier if you went into a profession where you were helping people—like a doctor, a lawyer, a teacher..."

There, for the first time in the conversation, I could feel my temper starting to build. Again with this "living for others" shit, I said to myself.

Why, why is it so important to other people that I live for others? If they think that helping other people is the most important thing in life, then let them devote their lives to it—or at least donate that portion of their lives that they currently spend trying to tell me how to live my life!

"It's entirely up to you," Dad said. "We don't mean to put any pressure on you. If majoring in drama is what you really want to do, you go right ahead. I'm just giving you something to think about."

Dad probably meant it—or believed that he meant it, anyway. If I had had the presence of mind, I could have told him that I would study drama with a view to teaching it, that most likely I would wind up with a job like Dr. Pritchard's. I'll bet that would have satisfied him and Mom both. No, scratch the "I'll bet." It undoubtedly would have.

That's the hell of it. I have to put most of the blame on myself. All of the blame, actually. It's all very well for me to complain about how my parents held me back, didn't encourage me, made me feel like I was less than Mark, that I was more an encumbrance to them than a source of pride. Did I think all that? You bet I did. But was I justified in thinking that? At one time, I was pretty sure I was. Today, not so much.

If I had been willing to fight for what I wanted, I could have done it. The fact that I didn't is entirely on me—and probably due to the fact that I didn't want it enough, whatever it was that I wanted.

"Just as a practical matter," Dad said, "it's incredibly hard to make a living as an actor. Only a very few people ever do it. Look, you're interested in public office. Why not work toward being a Governor or a Senator one day?"

I didn't point out the contradiction there. I must have been so rattled, at the moment, that I didn't even notice it, or I might have said, "And how many people get to be a Governor or a Senator, percentage-wise?" Besides, I had even less of an idea of what it would take to become Governor or Senator than to become a professional actor.

"Anyway it's something to think about," Dad said. "By the way, have you given any more thought to what kind of volunteer work you're going to be doing? Time's running out, you know." Dad gave me a pointed look with his one eye.

I had only had fantasies, before, of taking a serious balls-out stand on that issue, but I resolved, right then and there in that booth in the Mainliner, that I would do it: that I should, and would, resist to the limit. I don't know. Maybe if Dad had put it to me another way, at another time, I might have been more tractable, and I might have ended up emptying bedpans or doing whatever else I had to do to display my submission. But we can only speculate. I like to think, anyway, that my position would have stayed the same—and consequently, the outcome would probably have been the same.

Anyway, I told Dad, "My volunteer work will be that I'm going to fight against that requirement. If I have to, I'll find a lawyer and fight it in court, and if no lawyer will take the case I'll take it to court myself."

"You have to be twenty-one to do that, don't you? Sue or be sued. In this state."

"I'll do whatever I have to do, whatever it's in my power to do. I'm sorry if it disappoints you. But this is a principle, and I'm going to fight for it. If you want me to do something to help people, I guess this counts. At least I'll be fighting to keep other kids from having to do stuff they don't want to do."

"Andy, we all have to do things we don't want to do. It's part of life. I have to go to work every day to support you and Mark and Mommy, and sometimes I'd rather stay home."

"But it's something you chose. You got married and had kids knowing you'd have to support us. Nobody forced you. And when you work, you're paid for it."

"I pay taxes, too, though. Even if I'd rather not."

"Yes, and that's bad enough. But what if the City Council voted that you'd have to work a certain number of hours at some other job, for no pay? Would that be okay with you?"

Dad said "Hmmm," and thought for a moment.

I persisted: "Even if the City Council voted five-nothing to make you do the work, would that be right?"

"That's a point. But after all, young men get drafted into the army when there's a war going on. Or even when there isn't. We've had a draft in this country since before you were born."

"And there's been trouble about it, hasn't there?" I asked. "Riots, and all."

I almost added, "Anyway, you never had to go, because of your eye," but I knew that would be a cheap shot, so I didn't say it. I'm still angry at myself for just thinking it.

"You know, your great-grandfather served in the Union Army because a draftee hired him to take his place."

"Yes, but he offered to do it, and he got paid for it."

"I still think you should do this work," Dad said. "In the interests of general harmony. I know it would make your Mommy happy. And who knows? You might get something out of it. I don't hear Mark complaining."

"No, Mark wouldn't," I said, and we left it at that.


# 22 "I REFUSE!"

It wasn't long after that that I went into State City High's guidance office and picked up a State University catalogue to find out what, exactly, would be required of a drama major.

> **Degree:** Bachelor of Fine Arts in Drama
> **Required:** 124–128 semester hours, to include at least
> 36 hours at or above the 300 course level
> **Concentrations:**
> Acting

Design
Production
Education

The B.F.A. in Drama program emphasizes talent, study, and practice. Only students of proven talent, who continue to improve and perfect that talent through classroom study combined with participation in University and other productions will be granted a B.F.A. in Drama. Students will be formally reviewed, annually, to determine whether they are to be continued in the program...

Provisional admission is granted to the B.F.A. in Acting, Design, Production, or Education at the start of every fall semester. At the end of that semester, students will formally audition (for Acting) or be interviewed (for Design, Production, or Education) for formal admission to these programs, which is highly competitive.

In order to begin the process of developing appropriate professional understanding, B.F.A. Acting students must complete one production assignment each semester in the freshman year and a total of six more assignments during their sophomore, junior, and senior years. Four of the B.F.A. Acting students' production assignments must be in technical-related activities...

B.F.A. in Theatre Education students must maintain a 3.0 minimum GPA, complete 70 hours of pre-approved field experience in K—12 schools prior to student teaching, and complete a minimum of two stage management assignments in their program...

B.F.A. Acting, Design, and Production majors are required to complete an internship...

And then there were the core courses, which would be only the beginning of it. Historical Perspectives on Western Culture. Intro to Philosophy and Ethics. A math core. *Two* natural science cores, and I doubted if I could even pass a science course at the college level. Rhetoric (two courses: one speaking-intensive and one writing-intensive). Social and Behavioral Science. Then a bunch of department-specific cores. The only core that didn't strike terror in my heart was Foreign Language; I figured adding one more of those would be easy enough.

The courses in my major were even scarier. Voice. Movement. Stage combat. Set design. Set construction. Stage lighting. Costume. Publicity. Theatre History: Ancient Greek and contemporary traditions. Theatre History: Medieval Theatre. Theatre History: The Renaissance. An entire three-semester-hour course on Shakespeare (required). Theatre History: 18th and 19th Centuries. Theatre History: 20th Century. And on and on.

A music course was required. Three dance courses were required. Several other English classes were required. Actors had to complete several production assignments in scenery, costume, box office/publicity, running crew and other areas. If your focus was teaching, you had to take Educational Psychology, Teaching Techniques, Drama Teaching Methods...

Maybe worst of all, there was a Phys Ed requirement. I was starting to have doubts about majoring in drama. Now that it was getting closer to actually happening, the whole idea of going to college was worrisome to me.

There remained some question about whether I would even be allowed to graduate from high school. I couldn't quietly refuse to participate in community service, and try to work out some sort of a deal by which I might be granted an exemption. That would mean that the new rule would stand. All the other kids would be forced to comply—not just this year, but every year from now on, till the end of the world.

I concluded that I would have to take a public stand that would get noticed: a stand that could lead to the requirement being rescinded for all the kids, not only me. I could not let this just be about me. Even if only to let everyone know that somebody was resisting, I would have to resist publicly. If other kids wanted to join in, they could.

I thought about circulating a round-robin that students could sign, pledging that they would refuse to take part in this community service farce, but I decided against it. For one thing, I doubted I could persuade many kids to sign up. For another, I knew that almost all of the "respectable" kids would refuse to sign it, even if they secretly agreed with me, because what would people think of them if they signed? Besides, it might get them in trouble.

And if a few kids signed it? That was no guarantee that they wouldn't submit, after all, once the proper combination of carrot and stick had been applied.

So, instead, I spent the next several days drafting a letter— and wondering how I would produce and distribute it. Remember, nobody had personal printers or copiers in those days. If I wanted to provide copies to everyone in the school, how would I produce (roughly) a thousand of them? There was a Xerox machine in the public library that charged ten cents per page. For a document that might run four or five pages, a thousand copies, 5,000 pages, $500... And I barely had five dollars.

Maybe Dad had a Xerox machine at his office? Yeah, I was sure he would allow me to use it for my nefarious purpose.

How about if I stole some ditto-masters from the school office, and somehow snuck in and ran off copy after copy? First of all, I don't steal. Second, I might get caught. Third, I didn't know how to run the ditto machine. If I asked one of the secretaries to do a big dittoing job as a personal favor? Right.

The best I could do was to send the letter not just to the *Cat's Paw*, but to *The State City Examiner* and the State University paper, *The Daily Statesman*—and to *The Cedar Rapids Gazette*, which was the biggest paper in Eastern Iowa.

I REFUSE!

Talk of setting the young to compulsory
service of some sort--whether it's
charitable work, or simply hard physical labor to keep them out of trouble--
has been a pet recommendation of irri-
table older people for as far back as I
can remember, which I admit isn't very
far, but I bet our mothers and fathers
can remember hearing it when they were
teenagers, too.

Lately, the call for compulsory "voluntary" servitude has come from students
themselves: specifically, from a present and voting majority of the State
City High Student Senate. That body
recently approved a plan--which the
State City Board of Education has approved, and which is now in effect--to
include a certain amount of "community
service," along with the usual academic
benchmarks, as a requirement of graduation from high school.

I refuse to submit to this requirement.
If that means I will not be granted a
high school diploma by State City High,
so be it.

The backers of this requirement argued
that we all--all the students of State
City High--should feel the urge to
"give back" to our community. If we
don't feel that urge, we will be made
to "give back," nevertheless. When we
were debating this issue in the Student
Senate last November, both Student Senate President Mitch Rosen and Vice
President Adina Owens made the point
that community service was a discharge
of a social responsibility. I specifically remember Miss Owens asking, "What

311

are we on the Earth for, if not to
serve others?"

I don't know about you, Miss Owens, but
I'm here to make of my life what I
choose to make of it, and to work on
projects that are meaningful to me: not
to serve others because you tell me
that's what I'm here for.

We have been told that we have a choice
in this matter: We can choose our manner of service.  How could we object to
that?

Okay, supposing I said that in order to
teach you humility and empathy, to make
you know what it is like to go through
life with a disadvantage, I will make
it compulsory that one of your fingers
be amputated.  If you refuse, you will
be held down, and the job will be done
with a rusty bread-knife.  This will,
at least, make you feel grateful that
you still have nine fingers left, when
some people might have only five, or
none.

To give you a sense that you have a
choice, we will even let you decide
which of your fingers will be hacked
off.  You can't complain that an unfair
demand is being made of you.  After
all, this new rule was passed by the
Student Senate, whom you elected yourself.  Therefore, it's your doing, so
what right have you to complain?  (Besides, everybody has to do it.  What
right have you to claim special privilege?)

I have heard it argued that community
service has simply been made a part of
the curriculum, like math or English.

Not quite.  Math and English classes
impart skills and knowledge (alleg-
edly).  Compulsory servitude merely
teaches submission.  It gets us used to
being bullied, ordered about.  It gets
us used to the idea that we are the
property, and ought to be the property,
of people who know better than we do
and are morally superior to us.

Morally superior, my hind foot.  This
is about DOMINATION and CONTROL.  And
those who would dominate and control
others are not morally superior to me.
Rather, they are beneath my contempt.

I refuse to submit.  I can do no other.

--Andrew G. Palinkas

That was the first version. I ran it through a couple more drafts. Then, when Dad wasn't using his home office, I borrowed his typewriter. This was nothing unusual. Mark and I had to type stuff for school all the time. I went into Dad's study, looked around in his desk, and found some carbon paper. On those old electric typewriters, you could make up to three carbon copies at a time, without encumbering the typewriter carriage, although the second and third copies were somewhat fainter than the first.

I typed the essay four times, thus making sixteen copies, and signed my name to the bottom of each. On the Monday, I snuck fifteen copies into my bookbag—and hid one under my mattress since Mom had just changed the sheets and wouldn't be going there for a day or two. On the way to school, I mailed a copy to *The Cedar Rapids Gazette*. (I had left a nickel of my own money on Mom's desk in the kitchen, next to the stamps.

After school, I walked downtown, to the offices of *The State City Examiner*, and asked to see the editorial page editor. If it had been *The New York Times*, that might have been a bit of a job, but it wasn't hard to get into the presence of the Gods at a small-town paper like the *Examiner*. I walked straight into the news-room—one big room, like you used to see in movies—and asked to be pointed to the editorial page editor's desk. I can't remember too well what the guy looked like, except that he wasn't a whole lot older than I was. I bet he wasn't long out of college. I handed him my screed and asked him as politely as I knew how, "Would it be possible to run this tomorrow, or Wednesday at the very latest?" He looked amused. He speed-read what I had handed him, and whistled softly. Then he grinned.

"Well, well," he said. "This is quite something. I'm going to show this to the editorial board. We might run it as a letter, in which case it might have to be cut—but it's possible we could run it as is, as an op-ed. Thanks for bringing it by."

My next stop was at the *Statesman*, whose offices were in the basement of the Engineering Building on the State University campus. There, the editorial page editor wasn't in, but the managing editor was, so I gave my copy to her. I was big enough that I looked like a college student, so she glanced up at me surprised once she had read the opening lines.

"You're a high school student?"

I admitted as much, and she allowed as how local news involving high school students might not be the kind of news the *Statesman* would be likely to run, "But I'll show this thing around. You never know."

You never know.

At any rate I didn't know, for the time being, whether any newspaper would bite. On Tuesday morning I got to school early and posted copies of "I REFUSE!" on the drama club call-board, on the library bulletin board, on the boys' gym bulletin board. I taped a copy to the trophy case; one on the wall outside the cafeteria; one on the band room bulletin board; one on the choir room bulletin board. I gave a copy to Prick and asked him to post it on the auto-shop bulletin board for me. I gave a copy to little Betsy Tolhurst for the girls' shower room. She read it, and gasped a little, then giggled and said, "Count on me."

On that day, in every one of my classes, I got the teacher's permission to make an announcement—which was that I had placed an important communication around the school, and I urged everyone to read it. Some of the kids grinned and chuckled when I made the announcement, as much as to say, "Oh, there goes Andy, being Andy again." Most showed no reaction at all.

By lunchtime, it seemed, a few kids had read what I had written. Three or four of them came by my table at lunch to tell me, "That was different."

I walked around the school for a few minutes, after I had eaten, and saw that none of my copies had been taken down. But the few comments I had gotten at lunch were all the notice that came to my ear that day.

The *Examiner* was on our front porch when I got home; I brought it inside, and as usual I asked Mom if she wanted first crack at it. She asked, "What's the headline?" When I told her it was something about Viet Nam, she said she would wait. I went through the paper as casually, but as carefully, as I could. My piece wasn't in there, let alone any reference to it. Dad had the *Statesman* in his briefcase when he came home, but the *Statesman* hadn't run anything either.

At school the next day, I noticed that the papers I had tacked up on the bulletin boards were still there. I had expected Mr. Pope or one of his minions to remove them—but, no. A couple of them had "PALINKAS YOU SUCK" written across them in ball-point, apparently by the same hand. Nobody said a further word to me about them till lunchtime, when I sat down next to Guidry in the cafeteria. He nodded at me—barely.

"Evidently my little manifesto didn't change your mind any," I suggested.

"Hell, no." He had his full drawl on again. "Might as well call it the Ninety-Five Feces. Anj, Ah just don't understand you on this one. You're actin' like the Grinch who stole Christmas. Or more like, y'ever read a book called *Lentil?* By Robert McCloskey? You're Old Sneep, suckin' on your lemon."

"So, you're a real fighter for freedom," I said. "I guess as far as you're concerned, you're the property of the collective—and it sounds like you're proud to be. Well, that's fine for you, not for me. Look, you have the right to impose slavery on yourself, but you can't insist that everyone has to be a slave."

"When you use the word 'slavery' in this context," said Guidry, "you're trivializin' 300 years of what really was slavery. Ah thank that's despicable."

"Sorry you're so sensitive. This isn't the exact same kind of slavery, but it's gradual slavery. It might take a generation or two, but they're going to take away every last bit of freedom, till we're no better off than a Russian, or a German a few years ago."

"Who's 'they'?" Guidry countered. "It's 'we.' We the people. This is how democracy works. Me, Ah'm proud to be part of a democracy, and Ah'd be ashamed of myself if I'uz to try to weasel out of my duty."

"I don't see it as duty," I said. We went round and round over whether this was real moral obligation, or an imposed duty. The only reason, I believe, that it went on so long was that neither of us wanted to let the other one have the last word.

Finally, Guidry said, "Ah don't believe that if you see someone drownin' in the river, you don't have a duty to go pull him out. And Ah don't thank we either of us have any more to say about it," which allowed him, I suppose, to walk away from the table believing that he had somehow won.

By that time, I was so wound up that I didn't think to point out to him that this wasn't an argument about rescuing a drowning person. Even if I had had the presence of mind to do so, I would have done it to Guidry's back, because he was on his way to the rear of the cafeteria to turn in his tray.

I stepped outside for a few minutes after lunch. Arno Prick waved to me from the auditorium steps, where he was smoking cigarettes with some of his auto-shop friends. "Hey, Andy, that's great that you're fighting," he called. "That's a bag of bullshit, what they're doing to us. If I could think of some way to help you out, I would."

"Not much you can do," I said. I walked over to him. "Got an extra one of those?"

"I'm not gonna do it, either," Prick said, as he lit me up. "Volunteer, I mean. I might not graduate, anyway. I'm failing most of my classes. Might make a difference if I showed up."

It was true. Prick had been skipping school an awful lot, and more so as the year wore on. This was one of the few times I had seen him around, in recent weeks; he had even been skipping French, mostly.

"I'm probably gonna enlist in the Navy," said Prick. "It's a lot easier than the Army and you don't get shot at. Plus, I know about machines and stuff."

"Do you need a high school diploma for that?"

"I dunno. Maybe I should find out, huh? Anyway, man, you're the one making the sacrifice. You're the college guy; you should be going to... I dunno, Harvard or one of them places, but how are you gonna do that if they won't let you graduate from here?"

"I'll think of something," I told Prick, but I wasn't so sure that I would.

"You're the guy," said Prick. He slapped me on the shoulder. Some of his friends grinned at me too. I grinned back, and nodded at them, but the source of the praise—the auto-shop crowd—didn't make me feel good about receiving it. May God forgive me.

That afternoon, I came home, brought the *Examiner* in from the porch, sat down in Dad's customary chair in the living room, and checked the paper again. I looked first in the "Letters to the Editor" section, which was at the bottom of the editorial page. Not seeing it there, I almost missed the big boxed article immediately above the Letters. There it was:

# I REFUSE!

Not only was it on the editorial page: it had a substantial grey border around it. It was almost exactly as I had written it, with only a couple of light edits for tightness, which I had to admit were only to the good. I almost leaped out of that chair, there in our living room, but I forced myself to stay calm. I read it over twice, almost drooling at the excellence of my own words, literally tingling. Then I forced myself to scan the sports and the funnies before I folded the paper to the editorial page and placed it on the dining table.

"Looks like I'm in the paper," I said to Mom, who was in the kitchen. She scurried to the dining table, as I knew she would, asking me how I could have sent a letter to the *Examiner* without showing it to her. Then she sat down and read. She began shaking her head as soon as she had got to the first few words.

"Oh, Andy," she moaned. She kept shaking her head and tsk-ing as she read.

"Oh, Andy," she said again, and she stared out the window for a few seconds before tears started rolling.

With great tragedy in her face, she slowly got up from the dining table and went back into the kitchen. I made no attempt to follow or to speak to her. Only now do I remark on it, and

318

I'm astonished, at a remove of more than fifty years: I was beyond being hurt by her disapproval. It had taken a while but I had got there.

Mom didn't say, "Wait till your father gets home," and no doubt she would have been too aware of the *cliché* to have said that with a straight face, but I'm sure that was what she had in mind. That, I had to admit, I was pretty apprehensive about. I didn't think Dad would go crazy on me, or try to punish me, but Dad's approval, for some reason, was still worth something.

Dad surprised me. He was barely in the front door before Mom came up to him, all red-eyed, brandishing the paper, and hissed, "Look what our oldest son put in the *Examiner* today." Dad stood there reading it with his hat and raincoat still on, and his briefcase still in his hand.

Dad's expression changed hardly at all while he was reading. He looked a little astonished, I could tell, but no more than a little. When he got done he looked more bemused than anything. He gave one quiet little laugh and said, "That's our boy, all right."

"Is that all you've got to say?" Mom demanded.

"I don't know there's much more I could say. But, Andy, why didn't you clear this with us?"

"I can imagine what would have happened if I had."

"What will people think?" Mom shouted, apparently both to Dad and to me.

"They'll think you didn't raise me right," I replied.

Mom turned and stalked back into the kitchen. Dad looked at me, shaking his head.

"Andy, sometimes I don't understand you," he said, but he didn't sound angry, or even disappointed: just bewildered.

Not half an hour later the phone rang, and (thank God) Mom didn't think to ask who it was before she called from the kitchen, "Andy? Phone." When I entered the kitchen, Mom almost thrust the receiver at me, averting her face.

It turned out to be a reporter from KCRG-TV in Cedar Rapids, wanting to interview me at the school the next day.

In this case I was pretty certain that Mom would be listening, unless she were taking the opportunity to go into the other room and commiserate with Dad. I took the receiver behind the basement door and confined my responses to "Yeah," as much as possible. When the reporter asked when would be a good time for him to do the interview, for the next evening's six o'clock newscast, I said, "How about right before school, like eight or so? I'll be there."

Which was smart, because sure enough when I opened the basement door and stepped into the kitchen to hang up the phone, Mom asked "Who was that?" still not looking at me.

"Arno Prick," I said. "He wants to study with me for our French test tomorrow, so I'll get to school early." The reporter had had a young voice. As far as I could remember, Mom had never been introduced to Prick or spoken to him on the phone— she had heard me talk about him now and then, but I don't think he was ever in our house—so I was okay.

(Today, she could have used the phone's Caller ID to know who was on the other end, and she could have refused to let the media talk to me. For all I know, she might have kept me home from school for the rest of the week, if she'd thought I was going to be on TV, by calling the Sheriff and having him lock me up if necessary.)

Anyway, I got to school a bit before eight the next morning. Sure enough, a KCRG van was there, with a camera crew. The event itself was a bit of a letdown. I had spent quite a lot of the night before (and all the time as I walked to school) going over, in my head, what I was going to say. I was plenty nervous about it because nothing was coming to me that I hadn't said before. Being inexperienced, I didn't understand that that was what they wanted: a quick sound-bite that re-states your main point as concisely as possible. I had a speech prepared; I was ready to go on for ten minutes.

My part of the event lasted about five minutes; my interview in the school parking lot was maybe one minute. First the reporter—he was a guy aged thirty or so, in a dark suit and tie, which made me feel like a pipsqueak in my school clothes—asked me, "Why do you object to doing volunteer work?"

I was ready for that one. I said, "I don't object to doing volunteer work. I object to being forced to do volunteer work, in which case it isn't volunteer work. If I see someone I feel like helping, I'll help him. But just doing a certain number of hours of work to prove that I've hit some arbitrary standard of altruism—that's hypocrisy."

"But some people would say that teaching values like voluntarism is what school is all about," the reporter commented.

"First of all, public schools shouldn't be in the business of teaching values," I said. "Second, this isn't even about teaching values. This is teaching submission. This is teaching kids that their time and energy and other resources actually belong to the community; that they're not free people; that in effect they're the property of whatever government happens to be in power. On top of all that, the Board of Education has tricked the Student Senate into acting as their slave-drivers—making a few kids feel all high-and-mighty because they get to order the rest of us around—which is even more disgusting."

"Thank you, Andy," said the reporter.

"One more thing," I said into the mike. "High school kids all over Eastern Iowa should pay attention to this. You're next."

That was the end of the interview. The reporter asked if he could get some footage of me walking into the school and through the halls and stopping at my locker, all of which I did. There weren't many kids in the hall yet, but the reporter asked me to stop and chat with one of them—a tenth-grader whom I didn't know—so they could have some silent footage over which they could dub the reporter's voice. Then the reporter and the crew went down to Principal Poop's office.

I was pretty sure I had made an idiot of myself. For one thing, I was carrying a big honking zit on my chin that morning. At that age, you get those fucking cysts; there's not much you can do to prevent them. If you try to cover them up, they usually look worse. I had seen so little TV that I didn't realize that back then, the resolution wasn't good enough to pick up the zit, so in all probability I was fretting about nothing. I should have been worrying about my build. I wasn't seriously fat, but I was heavy, and I didn't know that TV has a way of making you look fatter than you are. Plus, I knew I was ugly.

My voice was probably too high. I was pretty sure it hadn't cracked in the middle of the interview, but I couldn't remember for certain. I hoped I had spoken clearly. I wondered if maybe I sounded like a nerd, using too many big words.

Maybe it was just as well that I didn't get to see myself on TV. I wanted to ask Prick if I could come over and watch it at his place, but he wasn't in school that day. I could have asked Guidry, but I was still about ready to smash his rudimentary nose out the back of his skull for the way he had acted the other day. I could have asked Charity, but that would have been an imposition. Chances were good that she would be enfolded with Mark and wouldn't want me around.

Besides, it was the six o'clock news. Most people in State City ate their dinners right around that time (including our family— we had to eat at six so that Mark could go across the street and watch *Batman* with Charity at 6:30). I didn't want to have to tell Mom and Dad why I was skipping dinner at our house, nor did I want to show up at anyone else's house during theirs, as though I were begging to be fed.

And in those days, there was no way to record video from your home TV, so if you missed a show, you missed it.

A lot of the students and faculty at State City High didn't miss it. Dr. Pritchard told me, the next morning, "You looked good. You sounded good—to me. Well, you're almost a professional-level speaker, after all. I have a feeling that to a lot of people you probably came across a little bit arrogant. Not saying that's how they should feel."

In gym class later that morning—we were outdoors, that day, doing archery, and I was ridiculously bad at archery because I was left-handed but right-eyed—Coach Vance came over to me, ostensibly to check my technique. As I was nocking my arrow he gave me one of his freezing white-eyed stares and said, "I saw that performance of yours on TV last night. What's wrong with you, Palinkas? These are the best years of your life. This is how you're spending them?"

Vance looked so furious that I thought for a second he might hit me; then I realized that at least he wouldn't dare to do that. I tried to smile.

"Gosh, Coach, I've never enjoyed high school that much. I sure hope these aren't the best years of my life. If it gets worse after this, I might shoot myself."

If it were possible, Coach Vance looked even more offended.

"Don't talk like that, Palinkas!" he snapped. "Don't *ever* talk like that. That's crazy. You've got your whole life in front of you! Don't you *ever* talk about killing yourself!" Like he thought I was truly going to do it.

Then he looked concerned, all of a sudden. He moved right close to me—he reeked of cigarettes—and said, in an undertone so only I could hear it, "Listen, do you mean that? Do you seriously think about... hurting yourself?"

"Not seriously," I said. I pulled my bowstring back. "I'm just saying I'm not liking this part of my life much." I released the

**323**

arrow, which missed the target by about eight feet. "I'm hoping I'll have more fun in adulthood."

"If you're not having fun now," said Coach Vance, "it's your own fault. We all make ourselves as happy as we decide to be. Didn't you know that?"

§

Not every family that had kids at State City High had watched the six o'clock news, and not every family that did, had watched KCRG, which was the ABC affiliate for Eastern Iowa. But this was the spring of 1966, when *Batman* was on ABC at 6:30 on Wednesday and Thursday nights, right after the news, so quite a few sets were tuned to KCRG, and a lot of my schoolmates caught me more or less by accident. At any rate, for the rest of that day—Friday—kids in the hall and in class were telling me, "Hey, you were on TV last night."

I got the impression that to most of them, it didn't matter what I had been on *for*. What was important to them was the coolness factor of having been on TV at all. That made me even more of a celebrity than before. A few of the kids had more or less understood why I had been on, and remembered what I had said. One kid, whose name I didn't even know, shrank back from me in the hallway in mock-horror, pointing his finger at me and crying, *"You're next!"* I forced myself to laugh, which I thought was a considerable step forward for me.

When I got home that afternoon—coming through the door with the folded and unread *Examiner* in my hand as usual—Mom came out of the kitchen and confronted me, there in the living room, hands on hips.

"Andrew Palinkas!" She was almost whispering, but her tone had the effect of a scream. "Rae Childress came over this morning and told me what she saw on TV last night. Why didn't you tell us that you were being interviewed? I bet that's why you went to school early yesterday, wasn't it? Don't you care about us? At all? Don't you care how you're making your family look?"

I didn't say anything.

"You are the most *selfish* person I've ever met," Mom went on. Then she stopped dead because, apparently, she couldn't think of anything worse than that. She turned smartly around and marched back into the kitchen.

After a few seconds she called back to me, "Why didn't you tell us, so we could see it? We would have arranged something, for God's sake. You couldn't even give us that much credit?"

Naturally, when I opened the *Examiner* a few minutes later I turned right to the editorial page, and sure enough there were four letters to the editor relating to the piece they had published on Wednesday. I had been pretty sure that one of them would come from Mitch Rosen, and I was right:

> Andy Palinkas is entitled to his opinion, as anybody is in a free country. I'm sorry that he takes such an attitude. I hope that readers of the Examiner won't judge all of State City's teenagers on the basis of a cynical essay by one of them. The overwhelming majority of us are idealistic, hard-working, "good kids" who are eager to serve our community and the world at large. Many of us have resolved to join the Peace Corps or VISTA after college, and only a small handful are resisting the new community service requirement. Most of us—I like to think almost all of us—regard it as a wonderful opportunity to show what we can do. Maybe by our good cheer and spirit of generosity, we can instill a little community spirit in Andy—by osmosis if nothing else.

Another one was from a man whose name I didn't recognize, and it was short:

> Andrew Palinkas is obviously intelligent and well-spoken. It's too bad he chooses not to use his talents to do good for

others. If he were my son, I would harness his intellectual energy with a strap across his behind.

A third was from a woman, whose name likewise didn't ring a bell.

> My heart goes out to the parents of Andrew Palinkas. The Bible tells us "How sharper than a serpent's tooth is a thankless child." I hope one day Andrew will outgrow his selfishness and apologize to his parents first, then to his classmates. And finally, maybe he will apologize to the community—by serving it.

A fourth was from a State University professor—Aldis Fox, from the History department—whom I had heard of. Mrs. Childress sometimes mentioned him, since he had been associated with various progressive political movements around town, and he got his name in the papers pretty frequently in connection with one or another of them.

> While I deplore Andrew Palinkas' reluctance to volunteer his time and talents, he's correct that neither he nor anybody should be forced to work for the community. If your sympathies are with the young men who are now being conscripted against their will for service in Vietnam—as mine certainly are—then your sympathies must be with Andrew Palinkas also.

So even the one guy who was agreeing with me technically, "deplored" my attitude.

When Dad got home, the first thing he said was, "Andy, I hear you're famous. You should have told us." I told Dad I hadn't been sure that KCRG was actually going to use the footage, which was true.

"Get a load of the letters to the editor," I said, and I handed Dad the *Examiner.*

"I have to admit, this Rosen boy sounds like an itch," Dad commented after he had read them. "Mitch the Itch. I know Fox, and he's a little bit of a horse's ass."

That evening, when we were alone in our room—Mark was getting ready to go out someplace with Charity—I said to Mark, "Didn't you find out last night that I'd been on TV?"

"Yeah, Charity and Rae said you'd been on, but I didn't see it. I didn't see the point of telling Mom and Dad. It's usually best not to tell them anything."

"Well, what did Charity and Rae say about it?" I asked.

"Charity thought it was funny, more than anything. Rae thought it was neat that you were on TV but she didn't say anything else. Or maybe they were just being polite."

That was that. I didn't hear any more debate, or comment, from anybody else after those Friday letters to the editor. Except for two things. One was, I was walking around downtown the next day, Saturday, and I passed Chuck Haviland on the street. By this time he was finishing up his freshman year at State University. As he passed, he didn't greet me: just laughed. Loudly.

The other thing was, in the school library, the next week, I passed by Mark and a few of his guy friends, whispering together. As I passed, they looked away from me, furtively, as though they had been talking about me. Mark pretended not to see me. I got out of sight, behind a carrel, and I heard Mark saying, "Hey, he's crazy. I can't do anything about it."

Then there was a third thing, after all. Mr. Pope called Mom on the phone on the Tuesday of that week and informed her officially that I wouldn't receive my diploma if I didn't do my community service. I wasn't there when she got the call, obviously, but I certainly did hear about it when I got home.

First, there was Mom, icily and portentously telling me, "Daddy and I want to talk with you when he gets home." I had no illusions as to what it would be about.

There we were, the three of us, sitting at the dining table, which hadn't yet been set for that evening's meal. Neither Mom nor Dad acted angry or threatening—give them that—but Mom was looking so earnest and emotionally moved, as though this were some kind of life-or-death decision that I was about to make. Dad was less emotional, but he was somber and pedantic, and when Dad did the somber and pedantic thing it meant he wasn't pleased.

No need to repeat the whole discussion. It was basically them telling me that I would be making a big mistake by not giving in, that there was such a thing as being too stubborn. Mom even conceded, "If you honestly believe you're right, I can't blame you for sticking to your guns, but..."

But nothing. I wasn't going to budge.

"Andy, I want to make this just as clear as I can," Dad said, and that made me feel apprehensive because usually when Dad used that turn of phrase it meant that he wasn't going to budge either. "Mommy and I don't agree with the position you've taken here. What's more important, we feel that you're doing permanent damage to yourself. To your whole life, if you don't get your high school diploma now. You might not appreciate, right now, how much it means, but if you persist in this course it's going to come back to haunt you in years to come, in ways that you can't even imagine today."

Dad paused. I was expecting to hear a long list of what the consequences would be, followed by a peroration to the effect that I would *have* to go through with the community service.

"But if this is absolutely the way you feel, if you insist that this is the way it's got to be, then maybe we can hire a lawyer who can find some way of getting around this rule so that you can graduate."

Mom whispered, "Steve, no," but Dad said, "I'm serious, Paivi. If Andy is so insistent on this..."

"Hold on," I said.

A thankless child I might have been—might still be—but if I ever felt grateful to one of my parents for anything, this would have been the time. It's not that I ever thought that my parents wouldn't have stuck by me. I knew that if it had been something really serious, like maybe me going to jail for something, Mom and Dad would have done whatever they had to do. But that they might stick by me for something like this, even to the point of hiring a lawyer: That was more than I had expected.

"Hold on," I said again. I was stammering. "Look... listen... That's great. I mean I really appreciate that. No kidding, that's nice of you to... to suggest that. But if you guys don't agree with what I'm doing, I'm not going to make you pay for it. It works both ways. The school doesn't have the right to demand any sacrifices from me—and that goes for me, too. If you don't approve, morally, of what I'm doing, then I have no right to ask you to spend your money to support it. See? Even if you offered it on your own, I wouldn't feel right about taking it."

Mom and Dad were both staring at me.

"What we could do," I said, "is we could call the ACLU or the ICLU, and see if they'll take the case for free..."

"That's exactly what we'll do," Dad said. "I'll call Bill Barclay right now" (Bill Barclay was our family lawyer) "and he can tell us how to proceed."

So Dad called up Mr. Barclay—at his home, at dinnertime—and started telling him the story with all kinds of mistakes and inaccuracies, with me standing at Dad's elbow, correcting him, till finally Mr. Barclay suggested that I be put on the line to talk to him directly. Once I'd told him the whole story and answered a few questions, Mr. Barclay offered to give Mr. Pope a call and let him know what we were contemplating. That, he said, ought to get the principal's attention.

# 23 SHOWDOWN

Thus it was that two days later, right after school, my parents and I sat in the guest chairs in the principal's office, across his desk from Mr. Pope. Next to his desk, facing us, in an extra chair, was a Mrs. Blanc, who was the President of the Board of Education. Mrs. Blanc was a thin woman, about my parents' age, with the biggest teeth I have ever seen on a human being, and greying blonde hair in an enormous beehive. No lawyers were present, as Mr. Pope had requested when he had called Dad to arrange the meeting.

After we had all been introduced—I doing my best to keep Deferential Earnestness in my expression, at first, trying to look like the goodest good boy in the whole U.S.A.—Mr. Pope started us out, asking me if I preferred Andy or Andrew.

"I usually call you Mr. Palinkas, but since your father's here I'll have to use your first name, for clarity," he said. He smiled, just a little. I noticed that he had a manila folder in front of him, on his desk, which I assumed was my dossier.

"Andrew, or Your Majesty," I said. Mom sighed, "Oh, Andy." Mr. Pope looked confused for an instant, then he saw that I was smiling, and he chuckled.

"Now, Andrew, what's the difficulty? I understand you don't want to do your community service."

So I had to go over the whole story yet again, which everybody in the room knew perfectly well. Mrs. Blanc just sat there staring. I couldn't tell if she was open-mouthed because she was horrified and incredulous, or because she was a mouth-breather, or because she couldn't shut her mouth on account of her teeth.

Mr. Pope leaned back in his swivel chair and began doing that steepling thing again. When I had finally gotten to the end of the story, he exhaled dramatically and tapped his fingertips together two or three times, then asked:

"Andrew, have you really thought out the consequences of all this?"

"Sometimes you just have to do what you think is right," I said. "Even if the consequences are... not very nice."

"You're only going to mess yourself up. This incident goes on your permanent record. If you don't graduate from State City High, I'm sure you could get a General Equivalency Diploma, but how do you think *that* would look on your record? And after an incident like this, how many of the top universities do you think will be interested in having you?"

I still hadn't applied to any. I didn't know what I wanted from college now that drama was apparently beyond my reach— and after that conversation with Dad, I hadn't given another thought to college at all. I assumed I would go—somewhere— because all respectable kids did. If you got a job instead, or went to a vocational school, it was because you were a loser, or of an inferior social caste—so it would have to be college for me, but I wasn't making any effort to plan for it.

"Sir, that's not the point," I said. "The point, and the plain fact, is that I'm not going to let a few snot-nosed ginks impose their values on me."

Mr. Pope looked startled, Mrs. Blanc's eyes widened considerably, and Mom gasped—but it sounded to me almost like a laugh that she was trying to fight back.

"Neither the Board of Education nor a handful of boot-lickers on the Student Senate are going to tell me what's good for me."

"But it's not being dictated to you," said Mr. Pope. "It's the democratic process. It was discussed and voted on. That's how things work in a democracy."

"Sir, a lynch mob is a democratic process. That's the trouble with democracy: It means that there are no rules that can't be changed by the opinion of the majority at the moment. None of us have any rights that can't be taken from us by a vote. We don't even have a right to our time outside of school, apparently, if the Student Senate can vote on how we have to spend it.

"Plus, this is a matter of principle. My convictions are not subject to a vote. Sorry."

(Only, some would say it wasn't my principles: It was my selfishness and general dickishness, which I was pretending were principles. Your mileage may vary.)

Mr. Pope was paying attention, even nodding slightly—not like he agreed with me, but like he was following what I was saying, at least.

"But by running for Student Senate President, and then getting elected to the Student Senate, weren't you tacitly agreeing to participate in a democratic system, and take the consequences?"

That wasn't a bad shot, and I had to think for a moment.

"You could say so. But you'll recall, my platform would have required me to leave people alone—that is, if I kept my campaign promise as I had intended to. If I had been President, when that... that directive came down from on high, I'd have told the Board of Ed that it wasn't the Student Senate's business, and if they wanted to give us a hard time they could do it themselves instead of pretending it was an opportunity for us."

I looked right at Mrs. Blanc. "If you want to talk about hypocrisy," I added, "that's the best example I can think of. That was shameful."

Mrs. Blanc's expression didn't change; maybe she was deliberately showing no reaction. Another thought popped into my mind.

"The real issue is," I said, "that this is a matter of improper jurisdiction. I was told, when I enrolled in this school, what the requirement for graduation was. I had to complete—what, 120 credits in three years, right? With a certain number of credits in certain subjects. And I've met all those requirements. And those requirements were—well, who sets them, Mr. Pope? Is it you, or the Board of Education, or the State of Iowa? I'm asking because I don't know."

"It's the Board of Education," Mr. Pope replied. "The State of Iowa has certain minimum requirements, and the local Board can simply follow those, or sometimes they'll add requirements of their own. Any changes they make have to be approved by the state government, and ordinarily the principal of the school is consulted—but our graduation requirements were set years ago, before I came here."

"Okay," I said. "They've been around a long time, these requirements, and everybody knows what they are. They don't get changed in the middle of a school year, do they? So that all of a sudden, you can't graduate if you don't take an extra math class: that wouldn't work, would it?"

"Well, no."

"Furthermore, does the Student Senate have any say, legally, in setting the graduation requirements? Much less, can the Student Senate change those requirements in the middle of the school year?"

"Of course they can't, but they didn't actually change the graduation requirements. They passed a resolution, a recommendation, that they presented to me, and I passed it along to the Board of Education. The Board added this requirement."

Again I turned to Mrs. Blanc. "You let the Student Senate dictate to you?"

"They didn't dictate," she replied. "They send us what we thought was a good idea, and we approved it."

"Yeah, after you'd effectively told them they'd better come up with a plan like this, or take the consequences."

"I don't know where you heard that," said Mrs. Blanc. "It was presented to your Student Senate as a suggestion, and they acted on it."

"They would act on it, wouldn't they?" I said. I wasn't even pretending that I wasn't sneering. "And you merely approved it. But that's not the point. The point is that you might think community service is a good idea. You might advise us to go out and do community service—but you can't change the rules in the middle of the year and hold my diploma for ransom. That's not legal, and if I have to take it to court I will."

"I don't think you can, Andrew," said Mr. Pope. "You're still a minor. Mr. Barclay said something about some organization like the ACLU suing on your behalf, but that will take some time, and in the meantime you want to graduate, don't you?"

"I want to graduate, the way I want to get anything unpleasant over with," I said. "But if I have to do community service, I won't graduate."

"You want to be a grocery bagger in Hy-Vee for the rest of your life?" Mr. Pope asked.

"Not especially, but I will, sooner than submit."

Mom, I could see, was ready to burst, wanting to say something in response to that, but she didn't. My parents hadn't spoken a word, either of them, since the initial introductions.

Mr. Pope stared at me for a few seconds, and shook his head, and at last he said, "All right, Andrew. I've come up with what I hope is a solution—if you're bound and determined to stick to your position. You might not like what I'm going to propose, but at least it'll take care of the problem, which to be perfectly frank with you is all that concerns me at the moment."

"By the way, Your Majesty," Mr. Pope leaned a bit forward in his chair and looked more friendly, "I admired your performance in *Rhinoceros*. I knew that play, but your interpretation of the character gave me some further insights into it. It's clear that you're a gifted actor."

I shrugged, and I tried not to smile, but I guess I did.

"You did some acting outside of school, last summer, you and a couple of your classmates," said Mr. Pope. "Improvisations, readings, that sort of thing, correct? Did you enjoy that?"

"Yes, sir," I said, and immediately I had an idea of where Mr. Pope was going with this. He would suggest that I put in my required hours on more of "that sort of thing": performing at hospitals and care centers and so on. And that would fulfill my supposed obligation.

But then I remembered that the resolution as passed by the Student Senate specifically excluded "Entertainment, such as music, theatre, or dance." Even if that exclusion were waived, I would be morally bound to refuse, it seemed to me, because if I agreed to it, I would be giving in. If I went and did my acting for community service credit, it would be to acknowledge that I was discharging a debt to the community—which I would not do.

If I refused—and I would have to refuse—I would look like an even bigger jerk for being so unreasonable, so mean and stingy that I wouldn't even do something I liked doing, for the sake of helping others and doing my duty to the community.

"Where were some of the places you performed?" Mr. Pope asked.

Grudgingly, I rattled off a few names of care centers, and various units of the University Hospitals. "There must have been at least a dozen places," I said. "Maybe more." I added the State University school for handicapped children, and a group home for emotionally disturbed adults.

"The rule on community service," said Mr. Pope, "is that in order for it to count, it has to take place during the school year, or during the preceding summer. And that it can't consist strictly of entertainment."

Mr. Pope paused, as if he were thinking, although I suppose he already knew what he was going to say.

"After all, you were performing at schools and group homes, and the clear purpose of your performances was... I'd call it educational outreach, or I might even call it therapy, rather than entertainment. What you did was... was of such an eclectic nature that I'd have to say it was partly instructional in its purpose.

"I won't actually bother to check the facts and figures—and of course you didn't keep score because how could you have known it was going to matter?—but I'm going to assume that what you did last summer amounted to more than the required hours in all."

Mr. Pope opened my dossier, and began writing at the bottom of a page.

"Therefore," he said, "I'm going to rule that you've already fulfilled the community service requirement, and that you're eligible to receive your diploma if you pass all your remaining courses. And that, I believe, renders this issue moot."

He was damn right I wouldn't like it. Something that I had thought of, to be nice to folks—oh, sure, it had been partly to show off, but also partly to be nice to folks—was now being treated as the discharge of an imaginary debt that I had refused to acknowledge.

But what could I do? Say, "No, I refuse to allow you to credit me"? That did occur to me, but even I could see that that would have been ridiculous.

I half-grinned, half-smirked at Mr. Pope.

"Very clever."

Mr. Pope looked offended.

"I didn't mean it to be clever."

Such a good boy was I—so eager not to be a bad boy at any rate—that I said, "No, sir, I'm kidding. If that's okay with you, it's okay with me."

"I suppose that will remove any difficulties regarding the graduation exercises," Mr. Pope added. "I'll pass the word along to your class graduation committee that you've fulfilled your community service obligation, and that should take care of it. I see you're in the top ten percent of your class, so you'll be sitting right up at the front. I'm glad we were able to work this out." We all stood. Mr. Pope leaned over his desk to shake hands with me, then he shook with my parents. Mrs. Blanc didn't offer her hand.

"To be even more frank with you, Andrew," Mr. Pope said, "I'm not sure this program is going to survive. The enforcement mechanism just isn't there; our secretaries are complaining about the extra paperwork. The intentions may have been good, but it wasn't well thought out. Not that that has ever stopped government from doing anything, as you know."

Mom, Dad, and I walked home together. As we left the school, Dad said, "That was as good an outcome as we could have hoped for, in the immediate term." Mom tsk'd. We didn't say much more, as we walked, and once we had gotten a good distance away from the school Mom started weeping silently.

"Honey, what's the matter?" Dad asked. "It all worked out."

"I'm so ashamed," Mom sobbed.

"Well, honey, we might not agree with our boy's set of values, but at least he's got principles. I don't know where he gets 'em from, but he's got 'em."

Mom blew her nose and stopped crying, anyway.

That evening, after dinner, Dad and I were sitting across the living room from each other, reading. Dad looked up from his book and casually mentioned that we had better start thinking about my plans for post-graduation.

"I guess we got sidetracked, with one thing and another. Have you even been applying to any colleges?"

"No," I admitted. "It looks like I'll just go to State, after all. They've pretty much got to take me, what with my grades, and I shouldn't spend your money on out-of-state tuition when I don't know what I'm going to do in college."

"It's technically your money, since we've put it in a trust for you," Dad said. "But you do what you think best. If you're going to go to State, though, of course you're always welcome to live here, you know that, but maybe it's time to start taking on some adult responsibilities, starting at the end of the summer—like paying Mommy some rent on your room."

I don't know where Dad got that one. Sometimes he would come up with these totally off-the-wall ideas that he would forget about if you gave him time—which is what I decided to do in this case. It was either that, or completely lose it, and blow up at him with something like, "Pay *rent*? What the *fuck* are you talking about? Pay rent for half of a tiny room that I've spent years in because somebody was too crazy to move us into a livable house? Pay rent for the privilege of living in *that room*? I'll live in the street first, and if you don't believe it, try me!"

I didn't think about it for long, let alone say anything, because Mom overheard Dad from the kitchen, and she called out, "Steve, don't be silly! Rent? For God's sake." Which was a nice surprise, and saved me the trouble of responding. But it did put the idea in my head that the whole point of going to college— well, okay, not the whole point, but probably the biggest point— was to get out of that house and start living on my own.

"Meanwhile, what are you going to do this summer?" Dad demanded. "I don't want you sitting around pitching dice. Why not do more of what you did last year? The acting and so on."

"I think Charity is going to be otherwise involved this summer," I said. "I don't know whether Guidry would be up for it."

Mom came into the living room. "Okay, but why not do some volunteer work, now that you don't have to?" she asked. "It's not like you're doing it because you have to. It would be... just the right thing to do."

I did the eye-roll and the exhale.

"If you insist," I said, "to please you—and *only* to please you—I'll do some type of volunteer work. You choose it. I'll do it, and you can know that you made me do it because of what other people might think. Or for the sheer pleasure of seeing me inconvenienced. If it will make you two feel so much better to see me doing something I don't want to do..."

"Oh, I give up," Mom bawled, and flounced out of the room. Dad looked down for a moment, shaking his head.

Real fast, before Dad could respond, I said, "Okay, I'm happy to work this summer. But it's got to be something profitable. I'll take a job, I'll start a business: something. Okay? You and Mom never wanted me to do any of that, before—I guess because there's something dirty about money in your mind, and a job is something lower-class kids do. But I agree with what you said before: I ought to take on adult responsibilities. Like a job."

Dad considered for a moment; then he said, "I don't see why not. But I have a feeling you'll get a song and dance from Mommy about it."

Here's a thought: Would I have refused to volunteer if Grace had been around—if Grace had been my girlfriend? Probably not, not if doing so would have put me at risk of her disapproval. But who can know? Grace might have agreed with my position—might even have fought at my side. But had she been the same age as I was, in the same class, and if she had been on the scene as my girlfriend, I probably wouldn't have done any of that crazy stuff in the first place—because I wouldn't have needed to.

Bear in mind: that was absurdly hypothetical, like *meta*-hypothetical. Having Grace as a girlfriend—even if we had been the same age—would have been utterly out of the question. The way I'm wired, psychologically—then and now—would have made it impossible for me to attract her. To say nothing of my physical appearance. I'm not talking exclusively or specifically about

Grace, either. Attracting any Nice Girlfriend, any ordinary girl, would have been beyond my capabilities.

Oh, sure, my friendly rival Mary Hurd liked me; so did little Betsy Tolhurst. But would they have done anything other than run away screaming—or hobble away screaming, in Mary's case—if I had made it clear that I saw them as girlfriend material? It's possible that I'm not fair to myself, but I can't help being certain I'd have alienated them somehow.

The more I think, the more certain I am that I was on a pre-destined and inescapable path to this outcome—and to just about every other outcome in my life. Not that there's some God up there in the heavens mapping out my life for me as though he were writing a play. No. My personality being hard-wired as it was, and is, no other outcome could have been possible.

So apparently I can't even take comfort in the idea that I made a courageous and principled stand on the issue of "voluntary" service. Maybe that's what it looked like. But some folks might say it's more likely that I did what I did because I was the kind of jerk who would do it—who couldn't help doing it.

# 24 GRADUATION

Over the next couple of weeks, the two big events upcoming were the prom, and graduation. I didn't have a date for the former, and my status for the latter had yet to be resolved, no matter what Principal Poop had said.

Mark was going to the prom as Charity's date. Oh, another thing: He and I were both licensed drivers now. Mark had had his driver's license conferred on him just a few days before, co-incident with his sixteenth birthday—and in time for the prom.

I certainly could have gone to the prom. At the speech and drama awards banquet, I had sat at a tableful of tenth- and eleventh-grade girls—they were agreeable company, too—and when one of them asked me whom I was taking to the prom, and I said I didn't have a date, three of the juniors (three!) simultaneously said, "I haven't got a date!" Which I took as a pretty broad hint, but I didn't act on it.

The fact that I didn't go to the prom was due strictly to my stupid cussedness. I didn't care to (as I perceived it) embarrass myself by going to the prom with someone I didn't have feelings for—although it was common practice for kids who weren't coupled to go to the prom with someone who was just a friend, so that both of them could go. If I had cared at all about this oh-so-significant moment in a teenager's life, that is what I would have done—but how would it have looked?

It's easy to admit, now, that none of my schoolmates would have cared if I had gone to the prom with someone I had asked at the last minute, while my younger brother—a tenth-grader—was there at the prom with his senior girlfriend. But *I* would have cared. I preferred to not go.

I can't escape the notion that another thing I preferred was this: to carry this grievance through the rest of my life. To forever be able to remind myself that I wasn't a cool enough kid to have gone to my own prom, because no girl I would have wanted to go with, would have wanted to go with me. How bizarre, to almost take delight in such reminiscences.

The Saturday before the prom, Dad took Mark downtown to Rosen's Men's Store to rent him a tux. Mark would precede me, thus, in ever having worn one. For some reason, that griped my ass worse than the fact that he had a girlfriend and I didn't. Or maybe I exaggerate when I say that. But it did bug me.

When they came home that afternoon, Dad said to me, "Andy, your reputation keeps on growing. Jake Rosen asked about you, when we were getting Mark all fitted out. He said, 'My son's told me all about your older boy. Says he's quite a guy.'"

"I'd be surprised if Rosen told his father that," I said. "At least, if he said I was quite a guy, I'm sure he didn't mean it in a nice way."

"Who knows? Maybe you *would* be surprised."

That next week—a couple of days before prom night—during a study period, Rosen came over to the carrel I was sitting at in the school library and plunked himself down next to me.

"Listen, Gabby, I'm glad we got that whole business worked out. About the volunteer work. You had your position and I had mine. And I respect you even if I don't agree with you. So, no hard feelings?" Rosen grinned and stuck his hand out.

I was about ninety-nine percent sure that Rosen was only approaching me because, being a politician through and through, he couldn't bear the idea of anybody harboring a grudge against him. I didn't think he really did respect me—but I could have been wrong. I don't know.

Either way, what I wanted to do was tell Rosen, "Look, you son of a bitch: You used us. You used every kid in this school, and years and generations of kids to come. You forced this extra work on us—to show off. That's all it was for: so that you could show off. You ought to rot in Hell."

I should have spit in his face for good measure.

But I'm a wimp, and a coward. I shook with him.

"So," said Rosen, "where are you going next fall; have you decided?"

"Just to State," I said. I had to remind myself to ask Rosen, "And you're going where?" to be minimally polite.

"University of Chi-caaa-go," Rosen said. He rolled his eyes skyward and rubbed his palms together in a kind of burlesque. I wondered whether he hadn't approached me mostly because he had wanted to tell one more person. "I got accepted by Cornell, and Stanford, and Princeton. Yale and Harvard didn't take me, but frankly I didn't expect them to. I decided that Chicago was probably the best, considering what I plan to do with my life. And what about you? Drama major?"

"I'm not sure," I said. "It's one possibility. I probably won't declare, first year."

"What are you up to this summer?"

"Not sure," I repeated. "Get a job, maybe. Or just await the sweet release of death."

Rosen guffawed and slapped me on the shoulder. The librarian shushed him, and Rosen put his fingertips to his mouth in mock-apology.

"Have you got any projects lined up?" I used library voice.

"Oh, man, I've got something great lined up," Rosen said, speaking softly too, but with tremendous enthusiasm. "It's something you probably would have had fun with too. Student Congress camp. It's at Purdue University. Five hundred and thirty-five kids from all over the country. You go there for three weeks; you stay in a dorm with a bunch of other kids who are interested in government; you do the whole mock United States Congress thing. It's supposed to be great preparation, if you're planning to go into politics."

"That does sound like fun," I said.

I meant it. I was pissed off at myself for not having found out about this camp. I realized, even then, that if I had not been so busy being self-absorbed, I might have heard about it, and—who knows?—it might even have been something my parents would have let me do. But even if I had applied for that program, I wouldn't have had the chops to get accepted. I hadn't done enough: not enough that would show up on my record. In the time it took to think about this, I went from annoyed to furious.

I was angrier at myself, in that moment, and more disappointed in myself, than I had ever been. It was an epiphany. Right there, I drew the comparison between where Rosen had taken himself, and where he would take himself, with his ambition— and where I had taken myself, and would take myself, with my own lack of it. Oh, it made me sick. Sick, and disgusted.

"What type of job are you looking for?" Rosen asked. "You know, if you'd like me to, I can put in a good word with my dad. He might be looking for help, since I won't be around so much this summer. How about it? I'll talk to him tonight, and I'll let you know if you can go see him."

I have no idea—I didn't then, and I never will—why Rosen made that gesture. Either it was a peace offering, or it was to heap coals of fire on my head, or it could well have been both. At any rate, I guess he might not have made it if I had let loose on him the way I had wanted to, instead of controlling myself.

Rosen reported back to me the next day that his dad would be happy to talk with me, the sooner the better.

I had met Jake Rosen a few times, informally, when Dad and I had gone into his store to buy winter coats or to replace a blazer that I had outgrown. In those days, every teenaged boy owned a blazer, for dances and what-not. I was wearing mine when I walked into Rosen's Men's Store, on the Saturday morning fol- lowing the junior-senior prom, for my interview.

Whenever I saw Mr. Rosen, he wore a plain blue or grey suit, or a blue blazer on weekends, and a white pin-collar shirt, usually with a club tie or a subdued foulard. Polished oxfords, a Rolex, and a wedding ring. He always had a big "pleased to meet you" smile; he was always hearty and welcoming. Head up, alert but relaxed. He had a strong handshake.

How I will remember Mr. Rosen, always, is seeing him lean- ing casually against one of the mahogany display counters at the front of the store, one hand over the other, ready to step forward and greet the next person who came through the door. That's how he was on that morning.

"Glad to see you again, Andrew—or Gabby," he said as we shook hands. His smile was less toothy than his son's, less effusive—but less overpowering, so I preferred it. "Mitch has told me a lot about you. He says you're one of the most interesting guys in the school."

"I suppose that's true," I said. I smiled back. "Whether or not that's something to be envied is anybody's guess." I was surprised, and impressed, that Mr. Rosen was too tactful to ask me what I was doing up so early on the morning after the prom.

I won't bore you with the details of the interview. Mr. Rosen wanted to know what I knew about clothing, which wasn't much. He showed me a suit, and asked me to pick out shirts and ties to go with it. Showed me another suit and had me do the same. Apparently I passed that test.

"Most men can't do that," he said. "You'd be surprised. Most men don't buy their own clothes, you know. You and your dad are unusual that way. It's more common for a man's wife or mother or girlfriend to buy his clothes, so men don't know how to dress themselves—and what's more, mostly the women don't know how to dress a man, either, because women don't understand that there are different rules for dressing a man than for dressing a woman. In terms of patterns, colors, all that."

Once Mr. Rosen got started on the subject of men's clothes, he was hard to stop. He began explaining some of those rules to me. He was infectiously enthusiastic about the subject, so I enjoyed listening. Then he asked me if I followed the Rivercats—the State University sports teams. I admitted that I didn't, not very closely.

I said, "I don't follow basketball, because I can't play it, and it's hard to stay interested in the football team, the way we've been playing the past couple of years."

Mr. Rosen laughed.

"That's true, but if you're going to work here you've got to learn to be a Rivercats fan. For one thing, the team and all the coaches get their blazers and slacks here. And those are customers you want to keep. For another, half the men who come in here are going to want to talk about the Rivercats."

"Makes sense. If I get the job, you can tell me how they're going to do this fall."

"Oh, they're going to stink the joint out again," said Mr. Rosen. "It's a no-brainer. For me, the only question is whether they'll be worse than last year. If you can memorize the starting lineups and fake the rest of it, you'll do fine."

Rosen's faced Lincoln Avenue, the main business street of State City, and the display window wasn't too crowded with merchandise. Through it, you could see almost the whole block.

"You couldn't ask for a better seat, if you're interested in the local drama," Mr. Rosen commented. "Which of course I am more than ever, now, being on the Council."

We talked for more than an hour. Mr. Rosen told me about his three daughters—two of them married, now, and the youngest of them finishing up her junior year at State.

"They're wonderful girls," he said. "And they kept me from being drafted, during the war, so I'll always be grateful to them." He laughed. "Seriously, a family is your best capital. Always remember that."

Mr. Rosen must have found me congenial, because at the end of that conversation he offered me a job: half-time all summer—then, if it worked out, I could continue during the school year, as many hours as I could handle so long as I kept up with my course work.

"School's the important thing," Mr. Rosen said. "Get your education; don't concern yourself too much with making money at first. There's plenty of time for that. If I had it to do over, I'd have gone to college too, instead of going right into business, but that was a rough time, you know, the Depression. We were so thankful that we had a business, and we were doing our damnedest to keep it afloat. And now, I'm thankful that it's better times for my kids. I'm tickled to death with what they've all made of themselves so far—and I bet your folks are proud of you, too."

I smiled. Not much I could say to that.

"We won't start you right after grad," Mr. Rosen said. "Take a week to relax and goof off. You'll have earned it. Then you can come in on the Saturday after. I'll have you work all day Saturday, then one to nine every Monday, and you can put in another few hours during the week whenever I need you."

Mom was the first one to hear my news, and all she said was, "That's fine, if that's what you want to do." Dad was slightly more enthusiastic. He even raised his wineglass to me at dinner that night: "To our oldest boy, the next owner of Rosen's!"

I laughed, and said that that wasn't my idea of what I wanted to do in life. I was pretty sure Dad was kidding, anyway, since he and Mom wanted me to go into a "helping" profession.

I had to take care of some unfinished business with regard to my graduation, too. A couple of days later, Guidry, who was on the Graduation Committee, stopped me in the hallway and told me that Adina Owens—who chaired that committee—was trying to get me barred from the ceremonies.

"At the last meeting," he said, "she was saying that the community service, the way it had been passed by the Student Senate, wasn't retroactive for this year, and Mr. Pope had given you special treatment by counting what we did last summer. I reckon she didn't take kindly to that. You know about that petition, right?"

I didn't know about any petition. Guidry looked peeved—probably more at the situation than at me—and exhaled sharply.

"There was a petition got up," he said. "In the last week or so. I guess I shouldn't be surprised you didn't know about it. Who'd have shown it to you? But a couple of girls—Adina's little bobos—were circulating a petition that they were going to send to you, asking you to stay away from the ceremonies. For not having fulfilled your duty to the community."

"Who were they?"

"I shouldn't be telling you this," Guidry said, but he gave me the names of two of our classmates, whom I knew to be acolytes of Adina's.

"The thing is, nobody would sign it. They asked me to sign it, and I wouldn't; I don't think hardly anybody else did. Anyway, it didn't get anywhere, obviously, if you never saw it. So at the committee meeting yesterday, Adina brought it up, like maybe we ought to flat-out ban you from the ceremonies, but there wasn't much enthusiasm for that, either, and it didn't go too far. But you should have heard her. She was... *exercised*, you might say." Guidry pitched his voice higher, trying to give an impression of Adina. "'Why should we make an exception for him as though he were better than the rest of us? He's not better than us; he's *worse!*'"

I didn't say anything; just raised my eyebrows and inclined my head. Guidry shrugged.

"I would have thought you'd have signed that petition."

"Hell no," said Guidry. "It's you who's got to live with your decision. It don't break my leg or pick my pocket if'n' you show up to graduate. And I guess that's the way all the other kids felt, too—all those other kids who wouldn't sign the petition." Guidry's voice dropped to the rasping whisper he used when he was trying to be dramatic. "You're. Just. Not. That. *Important.* 'Bout time you learned that."

Mr. Goddam Homely-But-Wise White-Hat Sonofabitch. It's a wonder my head didn't explode.

"You can tell Adina not to worry," I said. "I'm not going to show up. Wouldn't want to contaminate the proceedings."

"Tell her yourself."

I had to tell Adina, anyway, since she had to have a firm head-count in good time for the ceremony—but for once I decided to consult my parents about it, beforehand. I did so, that night.

I was expecting Mom and Dad to get pretty indignant at the idea of my not going through the graduation ceremony, but maybe they were burnt out from all that had gone before. At any rate, Mom didn't overreact. She looked mildly displeased, when I explained the situation over dinner, but no more than that.

"I don't want to sit there with a bunch of people who tried to prevent me from graduating till they'd imposed their will on me," I explained, "and furthermore I don't want anybody saying that I'm participating in a ceremony I don't have the right to be at. I'd just as soon have them mail me my diploma afterwards."

Dad said he could understand that. "But don't you want to show them that they haven't beaten you down?" he asked.

"At this point I don't care one way or the other," I said. "If you guys really want to see me graduate, I'll do it. For your sake. But frankly, I'd rather skip it."

"If it hadn't been for this community service thing, would you have felt differently about it?" Mom asked.

I thought about that for a moment. I replied, "Probably I still wouldn't have wanted to go through the ceremony. It doesn't mean that much to me except that high school is finally *over with*, thank God. But if it hadn't been for all this business, I wouldn't have thought about not doing it. And there wouldn't have been any reason for people to try to keep me out of it. So, yeah, I would have done it. But I wouldn't have wanted to."

Dad said, "Well, if you don't want to do it, don't do it."

Mom said, "But I do wish you wanted to." She was partly smiling and partly simpering. At least she wasn't crying.

I smiled back, trying to sweeten the pill if I could. I said, "I'm afraid 'wanting to' is not going to happen. But I'll certainly do it for your sake, if it matters a lot to you."

Mom said, "No, I understand. You feel that you weren't treated right, and it would be hard to sit there as though nothing had happened."

That was that. The next day, I approached Adina Owens at her locker and told her that I wouldn't be taking part.

I added, "That will probably please you, since I understand you've been doing your best to keep me out. Circulating a petition? And you didn't even have the guts to do it yourself; you had to have a couple of your stooges do it for you, didn't you?"

"I don't know what you're talking about."

"Come on," I said. I told Adina what I'd been told.

Adina said, "I didn't have anything at all to do with that. I didn't even know it was going on."

Which I was sure was a lie, but there's not much you can say when the other person flatly and coldly denies what you're accusing her of.

"You also brought it up to the graduation committee that you didn't want me to take part in the ceremony."

"I never said that! Never!"

"That's not what I heard. Something about how I think I'm better than everybody else when in fact I'm worse than everybody else?"

"I never said anything like that!"

"So supposing I change my mind right now and tell you I will be participating. That'll be okay with you?"

"It doesn't have to be okay with me." By this time Adina was inching away from me. "You do what you want. I have to get to class. Just let me know for sure by the end of today."

"I'll let you know now," I said. "Put your mind at rest. I won't be there."

I wasn't. Mark was. He went with the Childresses, to witness Charity's graduation. I borrowed Dad's car, that night, and drove myself over to Arno Prick's house. I had asked Prick, a couple days before, if it would be okay for me to come over and hang out on graduation night, since he wasn't graduating either.

Prick lived in a much tonier part of town than where we lived. Lawyers and physicians and so on lived in his neighborhood. Even so, Prick acted a little embarrassed, looked a little sheepish, when he greeted me at the front door. I'm sure this was my imagination, rather than fact, but it struck me at the time as though he didn't think it was quite right for him to be hosting me. Certainly not because of his house, which was a nice one, but because we belonged to completely different cliques. I was student government and speech and drama; he was auto shop. My social station would therefore have been reckoned considerably above his. I got the sense that he felt I was condescending most graciously, by accepting his poor hospitality. Maybe I'm projecting. Probably I am. I'm the type to do that.

We went down to the rec room in Prick's basement, where they had a pool table. We played eight-ball, speaking French the whole time. Prick's French had become a little rusty, but he was a decent pool player. He won each game. We each slowly drank a can of beer, as we played. Then another. Then I drove home. Two beers with Prick was my graduation evening, and I'm just as glad. It was relaxing; it was an evening with someone who didn't suck, who didn't think I sucked.

I wish I could recount that Prick and I had some kind of heavy philosophical conversation about what-all had happened—that might have made a better story—but we didn't. That wasn't the way our personalities worked, or we didn't have that type of friendship, or however else it might be explained. We just shot pool, and told dirty jokes in French: that was how we rolled.

Prick mentioned that he had enlisted in the Navy. He would get his equivalency diploma there, he told me. "*Un peu d'aventure, enfin,*" he added. ("A little adventure, at last.") He left town a week later.

The next evening—Saturday—Mark and Charity had plans to go to dinner and a movie, so my parents and I dined without him. Right before dessert, Dad handed me three envelopes. One, "from Mom and Dad," contained a hundred-dollar bill. One, "from Grandma and Grandpa Dahlgren," contained a hundred-dollar cheque. The third, "from Grandma and Grandpa Palinkas," contained a fifty-dollar bill.

I felt almost tipsy. I had expected a money present, but $250 was quite a lot in those days. I had no idea—at that moment—what I might spend it on.

"That'll get you a nice watch, or a new set of golf clubs," Dad suggested.

"Or maybe add it to your college fund," said Mom.

"He's earned the right to spend it on something fun, though," Dad said.

"I suppose so," said Mom. "But, Andy, do spend it on something worthwhile. Not on records, or more of those dice games."

It was then that I decided how I would spend it.

# 25 THE HAMLET

On Monday, early, I walked over to State City High to get my diploma. The students were all gone. It occurred to me, as I walked through the empty halls, that it felt almost as though I were in a movie where I was the only survivor of some pestilence or holocaust. Maybe I wouldn't have minded that.

The building wasn't entirely silent or deserted. The main office still had a few clerks and secretaries in it, wrapping up the year's final paperwork. Mr. Pope's secretary, Mrs. Rodgers, got my diploma out of a large cardboard packing box, next to her desk. It contained a dozen or so diplomas, for me and the other kids who hadn't made it to the ceremony.

"We missed you on Friday night," she said. She gave me a big friendly smile as she handed the document to me. It wasn't just a paper. It was bound like a book, in imitation red leather.

Mrs. Rodgers was about fifty, perfectly neat in her dark blue suit and white blouse. She had dark, short, curly hair. I don't believe she had ever spoken directly to me before.

"Congratulations," she added. "You livened things up, while you were here."

I wondered how much Mrs. Rodgers knew, about the late *contretemps*, but I wondered only for a moment. What was important was that I had the diploma in hand.

Still carrying it, I took the bus downtown to the State University campus, to register for summer courses as a "special non-degree student." I chose two: Advanced French Conversation, and Acting Workshop. I figured I might as well take stuff I wanted to take. Fall would be plenty of time for the core courses.

I then walked to the First National Bank and opened an account. I deposited my graduation money and had a half-dozen temporary cheques run off for immediate use. That done, I walked over to the north side of town, State City's oldest residential neighborhood.

Every day that the *Statesman* and *The State City Examiner* were published, you would find an ad in their "Rooms For Rent" sections, for a place called The Hamlet. Usually these ads would be written in a parody of Middle English, such as "Winter is icumen in, no sing cuccu / But it's nice and warm at The Hamlet, and we've got room for you." The phrasing would change with the season, but The Hamlet always ran an ad.

The Hamlet consisted of a parcel of maybe two acres, on which five houses stood: two brick buildings that had been there since the 1850s, and three wood-frames of more recent construction. The current owner, Henry Dobbs, had at first owned only the two brick buildings, which he connected with a long driveway that circled both of them. The City Assessor ruled that because of that driveway, the land would be liable to a higher tax rate. I don't know the exact details. But Henry Dobbs threatened to take the City to court over this tax issue. The City didn't want to spend a bunch of money on legal fees. Thus, they worked out a compromise: Dobbs would pay the extra tax, but in return, that driveway would be zoned as a street—which would enable Dobbs to build three more houses behind the two original brick buildings. The result: a whole bunch of cheap student rooms.

The Hamlet had a reputation. Arty, bohemian students typically rented rooms there. Even as sheltered as I was, I had heard rumors of wild parties and drug use at The Hamlet. The police had to visit, every now and then.

Henry Dobbs was about seventy-five; round, bald, pale, stooped-over. He wore denim overalls and a flannel shirt. He was a fixture at public meetings of the City Council, where he could be counted on to oppose practically any measure that was up for discussion. At least once he had had to be removed forcibly when he became obstreperous. On this occasion, he was sitting in a little wood-frame office that was attached to one of the brick houses. The door was open so I rapped on the jamb.

Mr. Dobbs looked up from the papers on his desk and said, "Hello, boy. What do you want?" He had a wheezy voice, and I couldn't tell whether his tone was jocular or hostile.

"I came to see about a room... sir."

"Is that a high school diploma you got in your hand? You bring that in here to impress me? Seeing as how you're a high school graduate you thought I'd rent you a room? Is that right?"

"No, sir, I just... I picked it up this morning. Sir. At the high school office. I missed the ceremonies."

Mr. Dobbs held his hand out; I started to take it, thinking he wanted to shake, but he drew his hand back and said, "No, boy, let me see the diploma." So I handed it over. He looked at it for a minute at least, nodding as he read.

"Andrew GA-bor PA-lin-kash. Why not Andras? That's the Hunky equivalent of Andrew. Your parents wanted to make you sound American? That right, boy?"

"We've been here since before the Civil War. Probably since when this house was built. Both sides."

"You graduated *magna cum laude*, huh? So you must have been a complete good little kiss-ass. What you coming here for? Your parents throw you out of the house?"

I explained that I had a job for the summer, at Rosen's, and money in the bank, and wanted to start college early—and I figured it was about time I started fending for myself. That seemed to please Mr. Dobbs.

"That Jew bastard will probably teach you all kinds of tricky ways to screw people. Always a good idea to work for a Jew at least once in your life, to find out how they operate. What fraternity are you pledging, PA-lin-kash?"

"I hadn't thought about pledging a fraternity. Sir. That's not something I know much about, I'm afraid."

"Good. If you'd told me you were pledging a fraternity I wouldn't have rented you a room. What's your major?"

"I haven't decided yet, but Drama, I hope."

"You a queer? They're all queers, aren't they? Drama majors. You a cocksucker, boy?"

"Not that I know of." I promise, I was not being cool under fire. I was coping, was all.

Mr. Dobbs walked me around his compound and showed me several units. Most were simply a bedroom, furnished with an antique bed, desk, and chair, with the bathroom down the hall and a communal kitchen on the ground floor. A few were larger, more completely furnished, with their own water closet and stove. I chose a basic unit, which cost forty dollars a month.

Back in his office, as I wrote the cheque for the first month's rent, Mr. Dobbs said, "You're in luck. June's the month I usually get my annual erection. I sell tickets to it. You can suck me off."

Mom about flipped when I got home that evening and reported on what I had been up to. She had known that I was going to register for summer courses, but she had no doubt assumed that I would live at home that summer, if not indefinitely.

"The Hamlet!" she exclaimed. "You just did that because you knew we wouldn't approve. That's why you didn't tell us till you'd done it. I suppose you've signed a lease and everything."

"It's month-to-month, not a lease," I said. "I'm pretty sure if it had been a lease, you and Dad would have had to co-sign. If I don't like it I can move back here." That was a sop, and I'm sure Mom saw through it.

"We'll pay you back," Mom wailed. "We'll give you back your forty dollars, if you'll stay here, or at least find a place that's more... respectable. What's wrong with staying here?"

I didn't trust myself to answer that one.

Dad was more concerned with my ability to live on my own. He asked if I had drawn up a budget—based on my pay from Rosen's, what I had in the bank, and what I might be able to take from my trust. I hadn't, but I agreed that I should do that. Aside from that, Dad pretty much accepted the situation.

I spent the following day packing up my stuff, and that night—a Tuesday night, the last I would spend in that house—as I lay in bed, I had the same reaction that I had had the night before we left Wisconsin: a panic attack, with an urge to call the whole thing off and tell my parents I was sorry—that I wanted to stay, after all. But that little crisis only lasted a minute or two:

not enough to keep me from falling asleep. Next morning, I couldn't wait to get out of there.

I didn't have a lot to move: my clothes; some books; my dice games; a set of sheets, blanket, and pillowcase; toiletries. Not much else. It all fit into the trunk of Dad's car—and Dad helped me to carry the stuff into the room, that Wednesday morning, before he drove the car to his office.

Mom had agreed to meet up with me later that day, downtown, to help me pick out a set of dishes and cooking pans. Her treat. I remember thinking it was funny—but gratifying for sure, don't get me wrong—that she was being such a good sport at last. That afternoon, I stopped by the offices of Northwestern Bell—this was back when the telephone company was a monopoly—and arranged for phone service.

At Mom's special request, I went back to the family homestead for dinner that night. But I'm afraid I couldn't disguise my itchiness to get out of there, to get back to my room at The Hamlet and set up my own establishment. Mom got pretty ticked at me, when I suggested that I wasn't hungry for dessert, and maybe Mark could run me back there.

Oh, I know. That was rude as hell. Inexcusable. I was immediately ashamed of myself. All I can say is that it was absolutely representative of how I was feeling—which I know perfectly well is no defense or excuse at all. But I wanted out of that house so bad, that evening. It was like I was trying to shake off a suit of cockleburs.

I did stay for dessert—not with good humor. I forced myself to stay about ten minutes more, besides, and Mom still did the "tsk" when I said I ought to be going back to my apartment if Mark didn't mind driving me.

Mark and I had not exchanged a word, over those several days, about the issue of my moving out. The only conversation that we had about it was that night, when he drove me over to

The Hamlet. I said, "From tonight on, you'll find it a lot easier to entertain Charity, I guess."

Mark laughed. "She's going to Barnard in the fall," he said, "and probably that'll be that. She'll meet plenty of other guys, wherever she goes—and I'm sure not going to wait around, and not see anybody else while she's gone."

"No, of course not."

"She'll turn into her mother one of these days, anyway."

That closed the subject, because I didn't want to mention Grace, and speculate on what Grace might have become, or would become.

"I hope Mom and Dad aren't too pissed off at me," I said. "But I had to do it."

"What, you mean moving out?" Mark asked. "Or the other thing? Dad's over that. I'm not so sure about Mom."

I let Mark see my room, which didn't take but a minute. When he left, it was still light outside, so I wandered about The Hamlet, checking out the grounds and the other buildings. I ran into people here and there—all of them apparently at least a couple of years older than I was—but I didn't introduce myself to any of them. It was nice being a total stranger, able to keep entirely to myself. I figured I might make some new friends eventually—but for the time being it was delightful, even thrilling, to be an island.

Then I went back to my room—my room and only my room, where nobody could disturb me or know what I was doing—and did what I'd never had the privacy to do before. It might be all sweet and romantic if I could recall that I was thinking of Grace when I did it—but in truth, I didn't have any fantasies, of Grace or of anyone at all, to help me along. I didn't need any.

## L'ENVOI

The Crosstown Rivals didn't reprise their act, that summer, but Mark and Charity played accordion and clarinet duets all over State City and in some of the surrounding towns—with full parental support—and sometimes actually got paid to play at parties and receptions. Mark and Charity's partnership didn't survive much beyond that summer, though. In September, Charity went off to Barnard. Mark told me later that when she said goodbye to him, "She was hanging all over me. Crying. Wanted me to promise to write to her—so I promised, but I've still got two years of high school to get through. Does she really expect me to, you know... ?"

Whatever Charity might have expected Mark to do, he didn't. Mark had a new girlfriend—one his own age—by October. He broke the news to Charity by letter, shortly before she was to come home for Thanksgiving. When I was at Palinkas Manor for Thanksgiving Day dinner, 1966, Mark told me that Charity had come over to the house that morning, to try to reason with him "... and I thought I'd have to throw her out. She kept going over and over the same ground for, it felt like two hours."

That afternoon, when we were finishing up the meal, the phone rang and it was for Mark: Charity again. Mark listened for no more than five or six seconds before he shouted into the phone, "Charity, I don't care for you anymore! Please just leave me alone!" He hung up, and returned to the dinner table, shaking his head. He muttered, "For God's sake."

Mom said, "Poor thing. I know you want to make a clean break, Mark, but still... I feel so bad for her."

Mark clenched his teeth and rolled his eyes a little, but no more was said.

Charity went back to Barnard. I never saw her again. I did hear of her now and then—but I didn't know, at the time, that I was hearing of her.

Charity has achieved a small career as a writer. She goes by her initials and her married name, C.C. Church, which is why I didn't make the connection till recently. Her by-line appears now and then in *The New York Times Magazine*. C.C. Church is sort of a minor-league Erma Bombeck, who writes self-consciously wry articles about the headaches of being a wife and mother—and, now, a grandmother.

Mark graduated two years after I did, and went off to Stanford. He then got a Ph.D. in engineering from M.I.T. Today he's a rocket scientist of some kind: yeah, literally. He works for NASA at the Ames Research Center in California. He's married to another engineer, and they have three perfect children who have lately been producing Mark's perfect grandchildren. He's quite highly regarded in his field, I believe, although I couldn't come anywhere near to telling you exactly what he does.

I used to see Mark every couple of years, when he would bring the family to State City to visit Mom and Dad. He and his wife stayed at my house in State City for a few days—yeah, I have my own house now, a big one all to myself, with a guest room to offer them—to help me go through Dad's stuff, after Dad died, before I sold our parents' house. We exchange emails now and then: at Christmas, on our birthdays.

That community service requirement? It got withdrawn, the summer after I graduated. The Iowa Civil Liberties Union got wind of it, and threatened to sue the State City Community School District on its own. Rather than go through the legal hassles, the Board of Education retreated. Years later, the requirement was re-introduced, and I understand it has infiltrated high schools all over the United States, formally or informally.

I dodged a bullet, on that Monday after graduation, by registering for summer classes at State University before I went and committed to my little room at The Hamlet. I found out, shortly thereafter, that unmarried freshmen and sophomores at State University were required to live either in their parents' home or in the dorms—which would have meant that I would have been required to move out of The Hamlet and into a dorm when the fall semester started. In other words, back to sharing a bedroom, no peace, no privacy, no space. Like home, only without the parents, but with enough noise and other annoyances to make up that deficit.

Luckily, when I had registered, I had put down my parents' address as my official residence, and that's the way it stayed for my first two years of college. I don't think my parents ever knew that I was evading a rule. I wouldn't have been the first. To give my parents credit, I have a feeling that they would have played along, and pretended that I was living at home for the University's purposes—if I had suggested to them that I had a right to get around an unreasonable rule.

I ended up going to State for the whole of my college career. I had to, because with all the confusion about my high school diploma, I hadn't applied anywhere else. State admitted me without any difficulties, on account of my high Accutest score and my having been in the top tenth of my high school class.

I worked at Rosen's part-time, all through those four years, and full-time during the holidays, even though I didn't need to, even though I had a college trust fund and could have gone through college without taking any job at all. Mr. Rosen and I got along great—I could not have designed a better boss—and I enjoyed the work. I came to love the environment of a men's store, where you interact with almost every family in town, in one way or another. You can keep your distance, while still getting to know a lot of people—and you hear a ton of gossip.

I didn't get drafted into Vietnam. During the early years of the draft they were taking mostly non-students and guys aged twenty-one to twenty-six. By the time I graduated from college, in the spring of 1970, the government had switched to a lottery system. I had one of the highest numbers in the country, and it didn't make much difference anyway, since we were finally, slowly, getting out of Vietnam, and the draft was being phased out. Even if I had been drafted, I'm sure I would have been rated 1-Y or 4-F, on account of my feet.

If I hadn't had my feet as an excuse, would I have gone? Probably. I'm arguably crazy, but I wouldn't have been crazy enough to have gone to prison—or to Canada. I would most likely have enlisted for some type of specialized service, so as to avoid combat duty. That's by the way.

Prick did go to Vietnam. He started out in the Navy, and was dumb enough to transfer to the Marines—which had traditionally been a small, *élite* corps but had been drastically expanded. The Marines did a lot of the fighting in Vietnam, and took a lot of the casualties. Including Prick—at Khe Sanh, in January of 1968. That's one guy I feel lousy about. Prick was kind, loyal, honest—never a mean thought in his head, never did harm to anyone—and that's what happened to him.

Gus Guidry went to State, as I did. He took ROTC, and transferred to the regular Army after he graduated. He retired as a full-bird Colonel. He lives down in Aiken, South Carolina, these days. We still exchange Christmas cards. I don't think we ever honestly liked each other after that last conversation in the hall before graduation, but we could never officially declare hostility—so we've stayed in touch, on that level, for all these years. He married, but for some reason he and his wife couldn't have children. It's just as well that that officious, self-dramatizing dickhead never reproduced.

I took acting classes, at State, and some business administration courses as well, since I figured it wouldn't hurt to know that stuff, working in a clothing store. But I didn't major in drama. The whole course for a drama major, as outlined in the catalogue, daunted me. I felt almost relieved, finally, that I had an excuse—my parents' disapproval—to keep me from taking that direction. Excellence in theatre would have required seriousness, dedication, study—and that quality I loathed: earnestness. It would have entailed doing a lot of stuff I didn't want to do.

I ended up with a Bachelor's degree in Business Administration. When I graduated, a new mall was in development on the south side of State City—well away from Downtown—and Mr. Rosen was planning to open a second store there. He offered me the management of it. Since I could think of nothing better to do with myself, post-college, I accepted.

At the same time, Mr. Rosen started talking about me as a possible candidate to take over his whole operation when he retired. Neither his daughters, nor his sons-in-law, nor his only son, Mitch, were interested in going into the business.

"I never thought Mitch would be," said Mr. Rosen. "He's always been cut out for a different kind of career." By that time, his son had graduated from the University of Chicago, and was planning to go to law school at Georgetown. (His campaign promise to join the Peace Corps after college had apparently been forgotten.)

A few years later—1974, it would have been—Mitch Rosen got his law degree and joined a "public interest" firm in Des

Moines. Mitch was quite the crusader, Mr. Rosen told me then, with considerable pride.

The younger Rosen was elected to the U.S. House of Representatives from Des Moines in 1978, aged only thirty. In 1982, the Democrats nominated him for Governor of Iowa. He stopped by Rosen's Men's Store during that campaign, for a photo op with his father—and with me, his earliest political adversary. I replied, "You can bet on it," when the reporters asked me if Mitch Rosen would get my vote—but if anyone actually had bet on it, they'd have been disappointed.

Rosen lost that election by a cat's whisker. In the last week of the campaign, a rumor spread that his wife—whom he'd met and married in law school—was waiting till the campaign was over to divorce him. That rumor may have cost him a few votes. At any rate, it was the first election he had ever lost. He had been slightly ahead in all the polls, right up to Election Day. That might explain why he got a little nutty in his concession speech, which he delivered just after midnight on November 3, 1982.

He referred to the Republican winner, Terry Branstad, as "Terry Braindead" and pretended it was a slip of the tongue. Then he made a falsely jocular remark to the effect of "the State House remains safely Christian"—which was funny, since Branstad was a Jew on his mother's side and had never made a secret of it. I had stayed up, watching the returns on TV, and I'll never forget that speech. The guy who gave it was not the unflappable Mitch Rosen I remembered from high school. He was clearly exhausted from the campaign, and he may have been drunk as well, after a long night of waiting for the final returns to come in. Or he might have simply been high on frustration.

Believe it or not, I felt sorry for him then—not because he had lost the election, but because he hadn't been able to cope with it. Old folks still remember that Election Night meltdown of his. That incident croaked his political career. His wife did, indeed, file for divorce a couple of weeks later, citing "irreconcilable differences," which could have meant anything. I never asked Mr. Rosen about the details, but I could tell he was pretty broken up about it. Almost as though he wondered whether he had failed his son, somehow.

Mitch Rosen then returned to practicing law. He became a pretty big-time insurance attorney in Des Moines. He made a pile of money. In the late 1990s, he got indicted in a fraud case. Something to do with Nigerian Internet scams, I understand, when that sort of fraud was just starting to become popular. The government wasn't able to pin it on him, though. His reputation was badly damaged—but at his trial, the judge ruled that the case hadn't been proven, and directed the jury to acquit him.

To be fair to Mitch Rosen, I have to say that I followed that case closely, and I concluded that the judge's decision had been correct. Rosen might have been guilty of extreme foolishness, naïveté, and imprudence, but there just wasn't enough evidence to prove him guilty of criminal behavior. I was amazed, though, at how stupid he had been. It's probably best that his mother had died, shortly before that case came to light.

Mitch Rosen kept on practicing law in Des Moines, following his acquittal. He's still doing it, and still rich.

That episode seemed to break old Jake Rosen's spirit. He had long since retired, by then, but I still saw him pretty often. His wife's death had taken the smile out of him, but his son's ordeal just plain finished him.

The last time I saw Mitch Rosen was at his father's funeral, in 2000, at the Sha'arai Shomayim Synagogue in State City. That, and Silda Rosen's funeral a few years before, were the only occasions on which I've ever worn a yarmulke.

When Mitch and I shook hands, at the reception afterwards, I told him, "Your dad was a hell of a man. I owe him more than I can tell you. Which means I owe you. It was your doing."

"Dad thought the world of you, too, Gabby," Rosen said. "Any time your name came up, he would tell me how much he admired you."

It had been right around the time of his son's gubernatorial defeat that I had slowly begun buying Mr. Rosen out. We didn't expand beyond those two stores, while Mr. Rosen was alive, but they ticked over pretty well through the 1980s and 90s, and into the 2000s. Mr. Rosen retired in 1986, at which time I became owner-president of Rosen, Inc. It occurred to me to change the store's name—to Gabby's, maybe—but I dismissed that idea at once. Rosen's was a name of long standing in State City: change it, lose business. Besides, changing the name would have been an awful insult to Mr. Rosen; I was ashamed of myself just for thinking of it. Later, I opened a third store: Rosen's Silhouettes, which specializes in bridal wear and men's formal wear.

For all that I had railed against forced participation in "community service," I learned that you have to get involved in it, at least minimally, if you want to be a successful businessman in a town like State City. So, nowadays, I participate as much as I have to, and as little as I can get away with. I'm a member in good standing of the Chamber of Commerce and of the Lincoln Avenue Business Improvement District. I even joined Rotary.

I gave up acting, entirely, after college. I didn't even do community theatre, for many years, although I got back into it when I was close to sixty. I still do a little acting, locally, but it's a mighty poor substitute for what I might have amounted to.

At times, it's painful. I can't help reminding myself that I should have been on the Big Screen, or on Broadway. The fact that I never tried to get there? That's my fault and nobody else's. You could say I killed that part of myself long ago. Just as surely as that Buddhist monk in Saigon, who set himself on fire. I did it more slowly, that's all, and maybe for a lot less of a reason: my own perversity.

I can't be called a failure. I have never been a financial burden to anyone. I have paid my way, all my adult life. I have plenty to retire on, with no danger of outliving my money.

On the other hand, I haven't done a lot of the things I was *supposed* to have done. I never got married. I haven't had a family of my own. I never came close to meeting any woman who wanted to marry me. I daresay I could have settled for someone who was willing to settle for me, for the sake of having a family, but it was my choice not to have one. The idea of inflicting life on someone—specifically, inflicting my genes on someone—well, I might be a bad person but I'm not evil enough to do that. Mom always said I didn't want children because I'm selfish. Maybe that's so.

I almost said, "I haven't done a lot of things that I wanted to do." But now that I consider it, I think that's a lie. Within the limits of my abilities, I did pretty much exactly what I wanted to do. Maybe I didn't do what I had *hoped* to do—but hopes are easily discouraged, then easily forgotten. Maybe I didn't do what I used to believe I *should* want to do—but, as I suppose I have demonstrated in this little memoir, "should" has never carried much weight with me. Maybe I didn't do what I had *dreamed* of doing—but dreams are often impossible fantasies. Maybe I didn't do what I *would* have done, if I had wanted badly enough to do that which I would have done.

One way or another—I'm convinced of this—most of us, for the most part, get what we want out of life, whether or not it's what we think we want. Our personalities are what they are, from the day we're in the world—and our personalities will propel us or limit us. We're hard-wired.

I don't believe in destiny, but I might believe in inevitability. That's a fine distinction, but an important one. The way I see it, destiny implies that there's some outside, independent entity—God, or The Gods, or The Fates, or some sentient "life force"—

that has mapped out a script, and sets each of us on an immutable course, according to that script.

Inevitability, on the other hand, doesn't require a God, or Fate. On the contrary. It almost argues against the existence of any such entity. Inevitability implies that we each of us act the way the wirings of our brains cause us to act—*force* us to act. Every time we "make a choice," we aren't acting on free will. We might think we're making a choice, but we're only doing what we can't stop ourselves from doing.

Thus, it follows that the outcomes of our actions, and of other people's actions and their consequences for us, are the inevitable results of *my* hard-wired brain interacting with *your* hard-wired brain, and the hard-wired brain of this other guy who's in the room with us, and that of the person who has just emailed me with her opinions, and that of the woman over there whose hard-wired brain caused her to adopt that yappy little dog whose bark might have startled us a moment ago.

But if that's the case, and none of us have free will, how can we ascribe good or evil, morality or immorality, to anything we say, do, or think?

If I believe in inevitability, then I can't blame myself for being such an awful person. If I'm awful, it's simply the way I'm wired, and I have no responsibility for it, right?

Only, as you gain experience and knowledge—and sometimes, perhaps, wisdom—you can gain self-awareness and self-control, can't you? Because of that, often, your regrets can be blamed on having lacked, earlier in life, the self-awareness and the self-control that you gained when it was already too late.

§

I had hardly anything to do with the Childress family once I had moved out of my parents' home. I would sometimes see Dr.

Childress on campus, or downtown, during my freshman year of college, and we would greet each other—but by the time I had started my sophomore year, he was no longer on the faculty of State University.

I have no idea how involved Grace or Charity were, in their parents' divorce—if they were involved at all. It caused a bit of a scandal here, in the spring of 1967. Truth to tell, once I had had a chance to reflect on it, this outcome didn't surprise me. All I ever knew about their marriage was what little I saw, plus Charity's article in the *Childress Chronicle*, and my parents' surmises. I didn't often visit my parents' house, once I had moved out of it, but I did notice, once when I was over there in the fall of 1967, that another family had moved into the house across the street. I also heard that Rae Childress had taken an adjunct position in the Sociology department at State U. I never took a class from her, and I don't know how long she taught there: maybe for a year or two, but probably not much more than that.

Joseph Childress went off to a new life at the Rhode Island School of Design—nearer his old stomping grounds—and took his graduate student girlfriend with him. It made sense. Dr. and Mrs. Childress hadn't seemed close, not at any time, on the few occasions when I'd seen them together—but at first blush, Joe Childress was someone I couldn't imagine having an extramarital affair, any more than I could imagine him knocking over a liquor store. When I thought it over, though, it seemed perfectly understandable that he would have had at least one affair. It made equally good sense to me that he and Rae would have stayed together for as long as their children were living with them—but once Charity had left for Barnard, they would have had no reason to force the marriage to drag on.

Grace must have been alive then, at least. If she hadn't been, news of her death would have gotten back to me when I was hearing about the divorce. For all I know, Grace might have spent some time in State City, during those years, without my having heard anything about it.

I have to wonder how that divorce would have affected the relationship between Grace and Charity, and their parents. Did either of them take sides? Was either of them particularly traumatized by it? There's probably a story there, but for now I can only guess at it.

I wonder about Grace, in particular. Did she not stay in very close touch with her family, after she went off to Leningrad? Was she happy enough to leave that house and never come back? Did she see her father, after that? What did he think about her, and her decisions, and what did she think about his?

So many questions. What was the dinner-table conversation like, at the Childress house, during that year when Grace and I knew each other? Did Grace end up with a career? Did she get married? When did she die, and what of, and where? Dare I try to find out? Would it be worth it?

Or would it be more fun to make up a story about her, write it, and then see how close to the truth I got?

Sure, when Internet search engines came along, in the 1990s, I tried to find Grace, but I couldn't. I looked up her father, and I found a minimalistic obituary for him—but it was no more than a notice that he had died. Nothing about his family. I couldn't find any information about Rae Childress after the early 1990s, which is when she left Iowa and—as I found out later—went to live with Charity. I found nothing on Charity, since I didn't learn her married name till Rae's obituary appeared. Maybe I'll contact her one day—but first I had to do my own bit of writing, here. I had to get my story down, before finding out whether Charity has anything to say on the subject.

That divorce—or something—had quite an effect on Rae Childress. By the early 1970s, her behavior was becoming erratic. She had moved into an apartment downtown, and some years after her divorce, I would regularly see her walking around the streets of State City in an extravagant wig and ridiculous amounts of makeup, muttering to herself, picking up cigarette butts that looked like they still had a few drags left on them, and depositing them in an old Pall Mall box she always carried.

Sixteen years after her initial run for City Council, she ran again, but by that time she was so out of it—her platform talked about turning State City into another Venice, with canals replacing streets—that she literally got fewer votes than I had gotten in my race for President of State City High's Student Senate.

Whenever our paths crossed, downtown, Rae would return my greetings, clearly aware that she knew me but not quite able to remember where she knew me from.

"You're Charity's old boyfriend, aren't you?" she asked me once. "Or was it Grace that you dated?" She chuckled. "I remember now. You broke Grace's heart."

The aging process hit her hard. In her sixties, she could have been taken for eighty. She lived on for quite a while, but in the early 1990s—she would have been in her seventies then—I stopped seeing her on the street. I didn't see a death notice, at the time, so I assumed she had been institutionalized.

Her obituary appeared in *The State City Examiner* three years ago. I'm guessing Charity wrote it.

## Ra'el Milstein Childress

Ra'el "Rae" Milstein Childress, long-time State City resident and community activist, died July 12 at the Bethel Care Center in Hartford, Conn. She was 94.

Ra'el Ethel Milstein was born March 29, 1920, in New York City. She grew up on Manhattan's Lower East Side as a "Red Diaper Baby," by her own description, and was a lifetime fighter for social justice. She earned a bachelor's degree from City College of New York and a Master's in

Sociology from New York University. In 1942 she married Joseph Childress.

The Childresses came to State City in 1961. While her husband taught at State University, Rae immersed herself in local politics. She was instrumental in promoting State City's urban renewal plan, and twice ran for City Council. State Citians will remember her for her quick and erudite wit, her colorful dresses and big hats, and her "get out of my way or fall in behind" attitude—as well as her wonderful baking, which her lucky friends were able to sample at her innumerable literary tea parties and political meet-ups. She moved to Connecticut in 1992 to be near her family.

Rae always said that her goals in life were to be an extraordinary mother and to leave a grand legacy through her deeds. She is in fact survived by her deeds, and by a daughter, Charity "C.C." Church (Doug) of West Haven, Conn., three grandchildren, and three great-grandchildren. She was preceded in death by her former husband, Joseph Childress, and her daughter Grace.

So, that is how I know that Grace is dead. Knowing that, is what caused this memoir to get written. I no longer have to think about how embarrassed I would be to show it to her. I don't have to think of the horror (even if it had been amused horror) with which Grace probably would have read it. Even though Grace knew a small part of the story—she lived it—I always have wished I could have told her more of it, the rest of it, from my point of view. Of course I knew I could never have had the nerve to do it.

I still don't have any idea of what Grace's life looked like, after she left State City, or how long it lasted.

I wanted to find that out, but I knew I wouldn't be easy in my mind till I wrote this—and I knew it wouldn't be what I wanted to write, if I knew too much. Rae Childress's obituary provided the catalyst: knowing that Grace was dead. Since I know to a certainty that Grace is far beyond reading this memoir, I can say what I like.

Grace. Oh, Grace. You might have laughed, if you had read this. But you wouldn't only have laughed. I can also imagine telling you this whole story face-to-face. Giving you my side of what you experienced. I can see you sitting next to me: considering what I was telling you; looking back at me with that so-serious expression of yours, while I was revealing all this private stuff. You might have said something like, "I never thought of it that way, Andy. It's fascinating to hear about all this from your perspective. You always tell me something new. It's why I so enjoy talking with you."

I know: In the running for your heart, I was such a long shot as to have been virtually a non-starter. But ever since we said goodbye for the last time—fifty-three years ago, now—I have been unable to dismiss the idea that there could have been some other outcome. If only I had had a bit more self-awareness and self-control, back then. If only I had known how to be patient and cagey. If only I had been wired differently.

I might have played it smarter. I might have given you all the time and space you wanted, and courted you ever so subtly, perhaps for years: so subtly that you would never even have guessed that I was courting you at all, till that glorious day when you fell—willingly, eagerly—into my arms.

Almost certainly not, right? But if I could lay aside all my other regrets, still that one will stay with me to my death.

I loved you so.

Made in the USA
San Bernardino, CA
19 January 2020

63387186R00236